STAR COPS

CHRIS BOUCHER

Chris Boucher broke into high-profile television writing with three sets of scripts for *Doctor Who* in the mid-1970s: *The Face of Evil*, *The Robots of Death* and *Image of the Fendahl*, each of which featured the character of Leela, his own creation. He was recommended by *Doctor Who* script editor Robert Holmes for the vacant script editor's position on the then-embryonic BBC science fiction series *Blake's 7*, a role which Boucher occupied for the show's duration of four series. Having moved on to work on more mainstream BBC drama such as *Shoestring*, *Bergerac* and *Juliet Bravo*, he returned to science fiction with the creation of *Star Cops* - a troubled production eventually broadcast on BBC2 in 1987, now widely recognised as one of the BBC's most ambitious and well-written forays into science fiction. More recently he has returned to his roots, writing four *Doctor Who* novels - *Last Man Running*, *Corpse Marker*, *Psi-ence Fiction* and *Match of the Day* - for BBC Books.

First professionally published in the UK in 2013 by
What Noise Productions,
Third Floor,
207 Regent Street,
London,
W1B 3HH

www.whatnoise.co.uk
Text © Chris Boucher 2013.

This novel is a work of fiction and the characters and events in it exist only in its pages and in the author's imagination.

'Head Music' is an imprint of What Noise Productions.
Design and layout by David Darlington & Daniel Latimer.
Proofread by Robert Dick.
Edited by David Darlington.

Printed and bound in the UK by Biddles,
part of the MPG Printgroup, Bodmin and King's Lynn.

The moral right of the author has been asserted.
A CIP catalogue record for this book is available from the British Library.

ISBN 978-0-9575239-0-6

All rights reserved. No part of this book may be reproduced or transmitted by any person or entity, including internet search engines or retailers, in any form or by any means, electronic or mechanical, including photocopying, recording, scanning or by any information storage and retrieval system without the prior written permission of the publisher. This book is sold subject to the condition that it shall not, by way of trade or otherwise, be lent, resold, hired out, or otherwise circulated without the publisher's prior consent in any form of binding or cover other than that in which it is published and without a similar condition including this condition being imposed on the subsequent purchaser.

STAR COPS

CHRIS BOUCHER

HEADMUSIC

An Instinct for Murder

Crime Scene

There was a chilly breeze blowing. It chopped the surface of the reservoir into small, brisk waves, but the man did not seem to notice. He walked across the green-slimed shingle and into the water with none of the shivering hesitations of the average swimmer. He did not pause to tug at his shorts or adjust his goggles or check that his hair was completely covered by his swimming cap. He simply walked out until he was waist deep, and then launched himself forward into a smooth and unhurried crawl.

Somewhere overhead, in geosynchronous orbit approximately twenty-two and a half thousand miles out from the Earth's surface, a construction engineer paused briefly at the access hatch of his living quarters to check the tell-tales on his suit. Satisfied that all the readouts were in the green, he cracked the airlock seal and with a practised push launched himself forward into space.

Like the swimmer, the engineer's action was smooth and unhurried. Like the swimmer, the engineer had perhaps five minutes of life left to him.

In the middle of the reservoir, when his wrist-counter told him he had completed four hundred metres, the swimmer switched from crawl to backstroke. He was slightly more vulnerable now, though nothing he did could save him from the killers rising towards him from the green shadowed depths of the murky water. Even if he had been able to see the tell tale lines of needle-thin bubbles and to realize what they meant, escape was already an impossibility.

The engineer had used his jet pack sparingly, so that his float across the gap between the main complex and the construction area was no more than a controlled drift. He reached the spiderwork of new girders without a suit-damaging collision, and carefully adjusted his direction and slowed his relative velocity. Like the swimmer, the beauty of his surroundings no longer startled him. Lost in routine, he hardly noticed the high whites and deep blues of the Earth as he steadied himself against a cross-member on the latest section of the station to be completed. The quality control inspection he was about to start was standard, but it was necessary, and he was a conscientious man. Completely absorbed in looking for faults and fractures, he was an easy kill.

The attack, when it came, was too sudden for the swimmer to understand what was happening. It came from below the water, which gave his shocked senses nothing reasonable to work on. For a stunned moment when the hands grabbed him, he was surprised – but not afraid. Then, as the two frogmen dragged him below the surface with splashing and bubbles echoing in his ears, fear came abruptly. He lashed and struggled. Suffocating panic held him in the darkness. He tried to scream, and only sucked sour water into his choking throat.

The engineer was just as disoriented. The first jarring contact was unthinkable. There was no logic to it. He should have been alone but then abruptly he was lurched into from behind as though he was on a busy street in his home town. Absurdly, his first impulse was to apologies to the two spacesuited figures who crowded in on him. Nothing in the situation was familiar enough to trigger his survival instincts, and he watched in a sort of daze, wondering at the bizarre deliberateness with which the two reached towards him.

Still he could not work out what they were trying to do. He made several attempts to speak to them, but his suit radio produced only static. Carefully, the two silent figures forced him against a stanchion and pinned his arms between them. His surprise gave way to anger, then. He bellowed at them, but the sound remained stubbornly trapped in his own small bubble of air. One of the figures reached across to his backpack, and for several moments worked on it with an adjuster. Desperately, he craned his neck trying to see what was happening. Then the air began to vent from his suit.

Like the swimmer, the engineer panicked. Like the swimmer, he struggled and screamed. Like the swimmer, no one heard him.

At the muddy margin of the reservoir, the swimmer floated face down in the shallow water, his corpse rocked gently by the small, wind-chopped waves. Far out from him, the dead engineer floated face towards the Earth.

His spacesuited corpse drifted very slightly, almost a rocking motion, as though it too was lapped by small waves.

Chapter 1

"He didn't drown there, presumably."

Detective Chief Superintendent Nathan Spring sipped his coffee and waited for Brian Lincoln's inevitable misreading of the comment. Something was wrong about this one, he thought. Or rather something wasn't right. Yes, that was what it was. Something wasn't right about this one.

On the big communications screen, Detective Inspector Lincoln shrugged his slightly drooping shoulders wearily. "*There's a breeze. He'll likely have drifted.*"

"What do *you* think?" Again Nathan knew what the older man's answer would be, knew that the answer would irritate him, and wondered in passing why he had asked the question at all.

Lincoln looked down at the corpse where it lay in the water and scratched his beard thoughtfully, then he shrugged again. "*We'll see what the machines have got to say.*"

Nathan slammed down his coffee cup and thumbed the one-to-one circuit. Lincoln lifted his hand and looked at the communicator strapped to the inside of his wrist. A small close-up of his tired, baggy face appeared as an insert in the top corner of the big screen, and beside it was displayed the image of Nathan he would now be seeing. "Damn the bloody machines Brian," the image raged, "what have *you* got to say?"

Lincoln's expression remained unchanged, but he blinked slowly, as if he was trying to focus his eyes. "*There's not much to go on, is there?*" he said. "*Not yet awhile.*"

Nathan's anger subsided when he saw the nervous spasm it had prompted in the older man, and he felt guilty as he always did after he had lost his temper. He leaned back in his chair. "Not until the machines have run the probabilities, right Brian?" he said and smiled wryly. The smile, he knew, was a saving grace – perhaps his only one. At its most sardonic, it was charming and open, and made him look much younger than his forty-one years. He used it with shameless calculation, and it worked even with people who knew him.

Lincoln beamed back at him from the screen. "*Why keep a dog and bark yourself?*" he said cheerfully.

Nathan said, "It isn't just barking we've given up, though, is it?"

"*If you say so, sir.*"

"I do say so." Nathan rose from his workstation, and went into the kitchen to pour himself more coffee. "And rather too often these days. I'm beginning to bore *myself*."

Lincoln waited for him to come back into the scanning range of the communications screen before speaking. "*Can we go ahead with disposal?*"

"Removal logged at twelve oh two," Nathan said, and time-coded the main visual record.

On the big screen, Lincoln moved forward and gestured to the paramedics. Two of them, in full protective suits and masks, waded into the water to gather up the corpse. On the bank, a third unrolled a body bag, while a fourth checked a small case of instruments. Lincoln watched for a moment, then moved back out of shot and addressed the wrist screen.

"*There was a time when this man's police force had more coppers than forensic medics,*" he said. "*Some days I have trouble remembering those buggers work for us and not the other way round.*"

"That's because they don't work for us, Brian, they work for the computer. And mostly they're cheaper than we are."

"*They may be cheaper than you are, sir, but I doubt whether they're cheaper than me.*" Lincoln smiled as he said this.

It seemed to Nathan like a genuine smile. From most others in the department it would have been an ingratiating expression that would have done little to disguise the hostility. His comparatively rapid rise to Chief Superintendent had made him a few enemies, and fewer friends. But if Brian Lincoln shared the general resentment, he hid it well enough and Nathan was grateful for that. It almost compensated for his Inspector's stubborn refusal to think for himself. Almost, but not quite. "You get what you pay for, Inspector."

When Nathan didn't smile, it was difficult to pick the jokes. Lincoln had never made the mistake of trying. "*So what do you think, sir?*" he asked carefully.

"I think I want this one investigated, Brian. Whatever the machines say, Brian." As Nathan said this, a data window flashed on in the bottom right-hand corner of the main screen, and the preliminary readouts from the paramedics' instruments began to scroll up.

There was nothing in these immediate data to support his instinct that this was a wrong 'un, and he was conscious that right now the central computer would be marking the case down, *way* down, in the priority action listing.

He keyed a replay window and looked again at the undisturbed bank next to the body. Prior to the police team, no one had walked there recently, certainly not within the time frame of the death. It seemed unlikely that this was where he would find an anomaly, a logical inconsistency that might interrupt the computer's inexorable progress. He was still hesitating about whether to risk an overspend and call up enhancement and spectroscopic analysis when Lincoln interrupted his thoughts.

"*Is there anything else you want me to do here before I start back?*"

Nathan made up his mind abruptly. "Take a scanner round the reservoir," he said.

Lincoln lowered his wrist, and moved into the main frame. He gestured vaguely across the water. "*Where to? Anywhere special?*"

"I want a record of the bank. Ten metres or so from the water's edge."

"*Yes, but where?*"

"All of it, Brian."

"*That'll take bloody hours. Look at the size of this place.*"

"You'd better get started then."

Lincoln was back on the one-to-one screen. He wasn't smiling any longer. "*I'm off shift in fifty minutes, sir.*"

"I'll authorize the overtime. You were the one who was complaining about not being paid enough. And keep your eyes open. Maybe you'll find it before you've done the full circuit."

"*What am I looking for?*"

"If I knew that, I'd know where to send you."

Lincoln grimaced, a small doubtful scowl. "*Sir, don't you think that's a bit...?*" His voice trailed off, but the doubtful expression remained.

"A bit what?" Nathan prompted – though once again, he knew what the other man was going to say.

"*A bit extravagant, maybe?*" Lincoln offered. "*I mean, that would be a pretty detailed approach for a triple-A rating, and this hasn't even been allocated a file yet.*"

"At least they'll know I'm serious."

"*If it doesn't get rated, Accounts'll have your balls.*"

"It's been tried before," Nathan said, and wondered whether giving the bean-counters another shot might not be such a good idea.

"*Practice makes perfect,*" Lincoln murmured, echoing his thought. "*And suppose we do all that –*" he went on.

"*You* do all that," Nathan corrected.

"*I do all that,*" Lincoln agreed mournfully, "*and we still come up empty?*"

"What's not there can be more important than what is, Brian, you know that."

"*Like balls, sir?*"

Nathan smiled. "Just get on with it, Inspector," he said, and broke the connection.

The median age for people earning their living off-Earth was currently thirty-four, and in this respect flight engineer David Theroux was statistically unremarkable. There were, however, three other fairly obvious characteristics that did set him apart from his colleagues on the European space station *Charles De Gaulle*. He was American; he was black; and he was a cop, though not necessarily in that order.

Today, as he propelled himself through the rigid connecting tube and floated towards the Communications Centre where he was already overdue for his second-eight shift, it was his problems as an Inspector in the International Space Police Force that were at the front of his mind.

Originally he had taken the job because he had nothing better to do with his off-duty hours and because for a part-time appointment the pay was generous. He realized almost immediately, though, that it was a mistake; police work was not for him, but by then it was too late to cry off. Theroux had been brought up to believe that if you take the job you do the job. Whatever the job is. Not only that, but you do it right; by the book, if there is one. There were days, however – and this was definitely such a day – when he wished that games had been more to his taste. At least chess and weightless volleyball did not usually involve looking at corpses. God, he hated looking at corpses. And, just recently, he seemed to have been doing a lot of looking at corpses.

"Godbenighted routine bureaucratic bullshit," he muttered, regretting that free-fall made kicking the furniture difficult. "Why doesn't it rubber stamp its own fucking decisions, and leave me the fuck out of it?"

As required by the manual, he had just been to the sickbay and viewed the mortal remains of Gunter Stein, the unfortunate engineering supervisor who had died a routine death while on an outside structural inspection. He had recorded, also required by the manual, his personal confirmation of the computer's forensic analysis and conclusion that death was as the result of suit failure. He confirmed – or, more accurately, he did not deny – the probability that an initial malfunction of the waste gas elimination system had already rendered Stein unconscious and unable to call for help when the main and fatal failure had occurred. Since the manual did not require it, Theroux had not recorded his feeling that the computer analysis was a bunch of crap.

"*You have got some special balls,*" snarled the Commander, leaning in so that his face loomed forward on Nathan's screen in what he fondly imagined was a thoroughly intimidating way.

Nathan smiled back at him. "Thank you, sir. I appreciate that." It was difficult, he thought, to be intimidating when you took that much trouble to hide your age with makeup, hair-transplants and face-tucks.

"*It's not a compliment.*"

"I realize that. I meant I appreciate the point." As Nathan expected, in huge close-up the Commander's unnaturally tanned and taut face now began to flush with fury, and his scalp tightened sweatily so that the carefully worked hair looked oddly tufty all of a sudden. A part of Nathan felt sorry for him – and anyway, winding up his superior was becoming too easy to be entertaining these days. "I meant I understand, sir."

"*You have absolutely no evidence,*" the Commander spluttered. "*Nothing! Worse than that, worse than that, what evidence you do have points in entirely the opposite direction!*"

"Is this the 'absolutely no evidence' I have," Nathan said, conscious that it was a cheap shot, "or is this some other evidence?"

"*Not up to your usual standard, Nathan.*" The Commander smiled thinly. He had his temper back under control, and it had happened very quickly. "*But then, neither is the impulse to waste valuable resources investigating an accidental death.*"

Nathan shook his head, aware that he was over-emphasizing a lie. "It wasn't an impulse."

"*If I were you, I'd settle for that,*" the Commander said. "*The alternative would seem to be deliberate stupidity.*"

"Can you be deliberately stupid? Stupidity is something you can't help, surely. Sir." It was the fractional pause before that final 'sir' that made

Star Cops

it offensive.

The Commander rose above the insult. "*Be very careful, Nathan,*" he said. "*I've allowed you to go your own way far more than anyone else. But now you're a long way out, with a long way to fall.*"

"I don't understand."

"*Yes, you do.*"

Nathan knew he had missed something. The man had something else on his mind. With a deliberately dismissive edge to his voice he said, "Whatever. This is all beside the point, isn't it? I'm quite convinced the death wasn't accidental," and watched the Commander's face closely.

The response was irritatingly bland and confident. "*The computer disagrees with you. And I agree with the computer.*"

"Which leaves us with the question of what the hell it is you pay me for," Nathan said. "Or does the computer have an answer for that as well?"

"*Doesn't it occur to you that second-guessing a machine projection with a probability which is as close to certain as…*", he breathed deeply as though searching for some appropriate analogy.

"…as anything the Accounts Committee could hope for, yes, sir, you don't have to spell it out for me."

"*If that were true, Nathan, we wouldn't be having this conversation, would we?*"

"The computer reached a premature conclusion."

The Commander smirked. "*It rushed things because it was anxious to prove that it's cleverer than you, presumably.*"

"There isn't enough evidence for the conclusion it's drawn," Nathan said, and thought *there is, actually, and that shouldn't be a problem, so why is it a problem?*

"*To err is human,*" the Commander snorted, "*but it's quicker with a machine.*"

For some reason that still wasn't evident, the man seemed to be enjoying himself. Nathan decided to try a deliberate flash of anger. "I'm serious! The fucking thing's not clairvoyant!"

"*And you are?*"

"I ask questions. It's called police work. Or it was before the rubber stamp brigade took over."

"*I'll tell you what else the computer isn't, Chief Superintendent. It isn't arrogant. It isn't ambitious. And it certainly isn't insolent and insubordinate!*"

"It isn't right, either," Nathan said calmly.

This time the Commander paused before responding, and it seemed almost as though he was reminding himself of something – like an unhappy kid remembering that Christmas wasn't too far away. Eventually, he said, "*I've had Lincoln recalled to base.*"

Nathan glanced at the time-code in the corner of the screen. "He can't have finished the scan. Not unless he sprinted round that reservoir."

"*I don't know. Lincoln's never struck me as the sprinting type. But I don't know, I didn't ask.*"

"You didn't ask."

"*It wasn't relevant.*"

Nathan nodded, real anger this time draining colour and expression from his face. "You simply countermanded the order. My direct order to one of my subordinates?"

"*I simply withdrew the authorization, Nathan. An authorization which you hadn't bothered to obtain in the first place.*"

"You know as well as I do that evidence can disappear in the time it takes to get authorization."

"*The Great Pyramid could disappear in the time it would take to get authorization for that particular investigation. Now the subject is closed. And so is the case.*"

"Is that all, Commander?" Nathan reached for the screen override.

"*Not quite,*" said the Commander.

Nathan made a point of not withdrawing his hand from the control, and said, "Only I have some free time coming, and I'd like to take it now."

"*A meeting, Chief Superintendent Spring. My office. Tomorrow.*"

"What's wrong with a screen conference?"

"*It isn't a conference.*" The Commander smiled. Christmas looked to be getting closer all the time. "*It's just you and me, Nathan.*"

"Can't we deal with it now?"

"*No.*"

"The circuit is secure, sir. Digit encryption was reset yesterday."

"*My office. Shall we say oh-eight-thirty?*"

"In the morning?" Nathan couldn't keep the discomfiture out of his voice. The bastard would be suggesting American-style breakfast meetings next, he thought.

"*I suggest we talk over breakfast,*" the Commander said. He was positively beaming as he broke the connection.

Star Cops

"It was the expression on his face."

"Stein's face?" Simon Butler looked up from the main communications and traffic control screen and smiled. He seemed to find his friend's police work endlessly amusing.

"Someone else die while I was down in med-lab?" snapped Theroux. "What else have we been talking about here?"

Butler yawned. "Sorry, my mind wandered for a moment. Orbital trajectories, flight vectors… that sort of thing." He pushed a hand through his unruly, non-regulation curls, and scratched his scalp vigorously. "Irritating the way my work can interfere with your hobbies, I realize."

Theroux reached across the cramped cylindrical cabin, touched a screen and rechecked the various countdown displays. Everything was running according to schedule. "All on the money, and in the green routine," he intoned and then said, "Unless I'm missing something?"

"Like what, for instance?"

"Like if I'm boring you, for instance. You only have to say so, Simon."

"Boring, you? Boring, police work?" He threw up his hands in mock horror. "Heaven forefend. And perish the thought."

"Fine." Theroux nodded. "You only had to say."

Butler looked pained. "You're not going to sulk, are you?" he said. "I hate it when you sulk."

Theroux shook his head. "Not sulking," he said sulkily. "Let's talk about something else." He unclipped a self-chill squeezey-pack from the refreshments rack, broke the seal and took a suck of fruit concentrate before it had cooled properly. "Anything exciting happen while I was away having fun?"

Butler sighed. "At least Stein *had* a face," he said. "Your next case could be a full decompression. Now there is an appetizing thought." He smiled broadly. "In space, no-one can hear you squelch."

Theroux was not to be placated. "It's okay, we don't have to talk about it. Really we don't."

"Oh fine," Butler shrugged, "if that's how you feel…"

After a moment's silence Theroux said, "The thing of it was, the expression on the guy's face was not… natural."

"Define natural."

"What do you want me to say? Relaxed. Normal."

Butler yawned copiously. "I know that sooner or later, death is as inevitable as sunrise, David old thing, but I don't imagine that means one greets it like the dawn." He nodded in the direction of the rack. "Flip one of those coffees over will you."

Theroux pulled a coffee tub and passed it across, making sure he did not release it until Butler had it in his hand. "Stop testing me," he said.

Butler said, "Your devotion to rules – any and all rules – is just a bit obsessive. You do know that, don't you?"

"So I'm a zero-tolerance cop."

"As opposed to an anal-retentive mummy's boy?"

Theroux gestured a casual two fingers at him. It was an English insult he found more satisfying than simply flipping the bird – it was more exotic, somehow. "Stein was scared shitless," he said. "And mad as hell. Both at the same time."

Butler raised one eyebrow and smirked. It was his favourite wry Englishman pose. "You do surprise me," he said.

Theroux shook his head. "He was supposed to be dead before he knew he was dying. Why did he look angry and frightened, can you tell me that?"

"Maybe it was his natural expression. At rest I mean."

"Listen, whatever else this guy was, at rest he was not."

Butler's smirk widened into a grin. "Shouldn't let superstitious primitives like you look at corpses, really. It unsettles you. You'll be rattling bones and waving chicken feathers about the place before you can say…" he paused for a moment, as called for by the rules of the trivia game they had devised to pass the slow shifts, then said, "'*We have the motive, which is money, and the body, which is dead*'. I'll give you five points for the film and five for the actor."

Theroux glowered. "For Chrissakes Simon, someone died."

"Is that a counter quote? Are you bidding?"

"Don't you think maybe it's important?"

Butler stopped grinning and nodded solemnly. "Yes, I suppose it is," he said. "Ten points for the film and ten points for the actor. Fifteen? That's my final bid."

Theroux ignored him, and switched his back-up monitor screen from scanning radar to the station personnel file. A soft electronic bleep registered the change. "You know how many guys we've lost recently?" he asked.

Butler said, "You know how many points you've lost recently?"

There was another bleep: the warnings were set to get louder and more frequent the longer the screen was off-line. It bleeped again, and again Theroux found himself depressed by the computer's unwaveringly routine systems. "Shut the fuck up," he muttered.

Butler sniffed theatrically. "Smells like a diversion to me," he said. "The bid is fifteen. You don't know it do you? Twenty. Twenty points apiece. The bid is twenty. Better speak. I'm going to wipe you out." He was smirking now. "And you know what a bad winner I am."

"*In The Heat Of The Night*. Rod Steiger," Theroux said.

Butler was crestfallen. "Oh. Shit. You were bluffing."

"Simon," Theroux said flatly, "I just want you to shut the fuck up so I can think."

Butler sighed. "The dark-skinned races are so moody, aren't they? Great sense of rhythm, no sense of proportion."

But Theroux was not really listening, so there was no chance that he would react. He was looking at the list of fatalities for the last three tours of duty. "Too damn many," he murmured.

"I'm sorry?" Butler looked politely interested, another of his stock, typical Englishman poses.

"Four deaths in nine months."

"All suit failures?"

Theroux nodded. "Yeah." He flicked the screen back to the real-time scanning display and killed the increasingly shrill alarm.

"All krauts?"

"What?"

"Were they all Germans?"

"No, they weren't all Germans. What's their nationality got to do with anything?"

Butler shrugged. "Possible explanation that's all."

"Possible explanation? What possible explanation?" Theroux couldn't see a promising link, let alone a possible explanation. "What the hell are you talking about?"

"It occurred to me," Butler said, "that God might have it in for our Teutonic cousins."

Theroux tried not to sound disappointed and disapproving at what was just one more of Butler's bad taste jokes. "That's pretty sick isn't it?" he said, sounding disappointed and disapproving. "Even for you."

"I hope so," Butler smiled. "They're such humourless buggers, don't you think? Krauts?"

Theroux snorted, unable – as ever – to stay mad at his friend. "Do you believe half of what you say, Simon?" he asked.

Butler beamed. "About that, yes. Which makes me more reliable than the average."

Theroux shook his head. "You think?"

"Well, not more reliable than the average Star Cop of course."

"We agreed you wouldn't call me that, you smartass sonofabitch."

"And much less reliable than a computer."

An odd thought struck Theroux. "You think?" he said thoughtfully.

"You're repeating yourself," Butler said.

It was a bothering thought, contained in an obvious question. "How does a computer understand what a guy's face means?" he asked.

"It doesn't," Butler volunteered. "That's the great strength of the computer. What can't smile can't lie." And then he smiled, as if to emphasize the point.

Chapter 2

The full-frame vision screens, which replaced three walls of the Commander's office cubicle, were new and were playing calm vistas of idyllic English countryside viewed from treetop level. Since they were sitting on the thirty-fourth floor of Europol's inner-city headquarters Nathan found this slightly disorientating. He was not sure whether the effect was deliberate so he put aside his irritation at being called in for a face-to-face and offered a show of polite interest instead. "Very pleasant, sir. But don't you find them a bit distracting?"

The Commander shook his head. "It's a feedback system. Cost a bloody fortune to set up. It's tuned to my particular brainwave patterns."

Nathan said, "I can't think why that should have been expensive," and then smiled.

On the wall-screens, a small cloud drifted across the sun as the Commander smiled back thinly. "You can never resist it, can you?"

"I'm sorry – I just meant the technology isn't really new."

"You're not sorry. And that's *not what you meant!*"

The clouds were now thickening and getting darker by the moment. "The feedback system does what, exactly?" Nathan asked, watching the gathering storm with genuine interest.

The Commander glanced round at the screens, flexing his neck stiffly as he turned his head. Then he closed his eyes and took a couple of deep, slow breaths. "It responds to my moods," he said, as the sun came out over broad-leaf woods, and meadows filled with wild flowers.

"You're feeling bucolic, sir?"

"Relaxed, Nathan. I'm feeling relaxed," said the Commander, opening his eyes again. "It's supposed to be good for your health."

"The countryside."

"Being in touch with your responses. Controlling your…"

"Temper?"

"Mood swings!" snapped the Commander as the sun hazed over again. Nathan nodded. "Fascinating." He felt better. Clearly the screens were not a further product of the Interrogation Section. Or if they were, then it was another fine mess they'd gotten everyone into. "So what was it you wanted to discuss, sir?" he asked.

The sun came out with a sudden bright intensity, and the cubicle was momentarily vivid with warm light. "How's your case load at the moment? Anything you can't leave?" asked the Commander.

"Actually there are a couple of things I want to stay on top of," said Nathan. "I decided against taking the break."

"You should take your leaves when they're due. Nobody's indispensable."

Nathan smiled. "That's usually a good reason for staying put," he said.

"However, it wasn't your leave I was thinking about," said the Commander.

Nathan waited, then after a brief silence he asked – more or less politely – "Well, what then?"

"It's your application," said the Commander.

"I'm sorry?" For a moment, Nathan found himself wrong-footed.

"The Commander's job with the ISPF. Surely you haven't forgotten?"

"Oh, that."

"You *had* forgotten," said the Commander with obvious relish.

"It wasn't worth remembering," said Nathan.

"You're not normally so negative, Nathan." The Commander and the sun were both beaming now.

"I was going through the motions. It was a formality, sir, nothing more."

"In that case, the news will be all the more welcome," said the Commander, and paused momentarily for full dramatic effect. "You've been short-listed for the job. Congratulations."

Nathan remained expressionless. His self-control was good, but his autonomic responses let him down again, and colour drained from his face. The Commander's weather had settled on the perfectly summery as he enjoyed his moment of triumph. Nathan said, "I'll withdraw the application immediately."

The Commander shook his head. His hair remained perfect, his smile still unnaturally smooth. "Not a very good idea," he said. "In fact, a very bad idea."

"I don't want the job. I never wanted the job, you know that."

"Do I?" The Commander looked vaguely doubtful.

"I didn't want to apply," said Nathan.

"Just testing the water, eh?"

"You should know, sir. You suggested it."

"*I* did? Are you sure?"

"You were quite insistent, as I recall." Even as he said this, it struck Nathan, with a small shock that was almost physical, just how comprehensively he had been outmanoeuvred.

"I don't remember that," said the Commander, smiling serene sunshine from every direction on all the screens. "Good idea, though. Put down a marker. Remind us all that you're not content to stay in your present rut. It's not enough to be ambitious, is it? You have to be *seen* to be ambitious. That's why withdrawing at this stage… not a good career move. No. Not a good career move at all."

"Whereas Commander of the International Space Police Force would be," Nathan said, unable to keep the sarcasm out of his voice.

"A Commander at your age? I'd say so, yes."

"The ISPF is a token. That's all it is."

"That's all any police force is, Nathan. A token. A token of people's desire to be civilized."

Concerned not to underestimate the Commander's low cunning any more, Nathan bit back his instinctive reaction, and determined to be reasonable. "It doesn't *do* anything," he said. "It's a political public relations exercise."

"You couldn't be more wrong, you know," said the Commander, sounding some way short of sincere.

Nathan said, "It's just there to take the blame if anything goes irredeemably pear-shaped."

The Commander nodded sagely. "That's all any –"

"And don't tell me that's all any police force is there for," Nathan snapped, his temper finally getting the better of him. "It may amuse you to pretend to be stupid sir, but don't bother to pretend that I'm stupid as well. A force of twenty or so part-timers? They're a *joke*!"

"You're exaggerating," said the Commander.

"They were nicknamed the Star Cops, for God's sake," Nathan said, beginning to recover his self-control.

"That was a cheap journalistic jibe," said the Commander with an almost straight face.

Nathan smiled. "It stuck though, didn't it?" he said.

"They need someone like you, Nathan. Someone to shake up the organisation."

"Someone who's never left Earth in his life, you mean."

"Spacemen are ten-a-penny," said the Commander. "What they need is a good copper."

Nathan shook his head and said, "It's like that old joke about not being drunk if you can lie on the floor without falling off. Well, up there, you can't."

"*Out* there," said the Commander. "I'm told the expression is 'out there' rather than 'up there'."

"The expression is 'no, thank you', sir."

"You're the only Brit who's been short-listed. It would look very bad if you withdrew your name before the final adjudication."

"I didn't realize this was Telesport Supernational. Do I have to wear a sponsor's logo?"

"No. But you do have to attend the final round of interviews and tests. Assuming, of course, that you wish to continue in your present career. Do I make myself clear, Detective Chief Superintendent Spring?" said the Commander, knowing quite well that he did. He stood up and flexed his neck again. "Shall we make our way to the canteen? I find I'm really quite peckish now."

"*This is the Space Station Coral Sea, a development of the First National Pan-Pacific Basin Consortium,*" the perfectly proportioned receptionist said, smiling her perfect smile from Theroux's communication screen. "*How may I help you?*"

"Connect me with Inspector Pal Kenzy."

"My feeling is," murmured Simon Butler in the background, "if you're going to connect with a colleague, connect with a pretty one."

On screen, the receptionist looked sincerely apologetic. "*Inspector Pal Kenzy is unavailable at present. Do you have an alternative?*"

Theroux had spent his rest period trying to decide what to do about his misgivings over the death of Gunter Stein. Discussing them with Kenzy seemed marginally better than the only alternative, which was to do nothing. He wasn't exactly sure what he expected from her, but what he didn't expect was not to get her at all. "Shit," he said, then, "Put out a general call for Inspector Kenzy. Make it priority."

"*I will need authorization.*"

Theroux keyed in his police authority code.

"*I will need authorization,*" repeated the receptionist.

"Oh no. I don't believe this!"

"*I will need authorization,*" repeated the receptionist. "*I will need authorization.*"

"Not now." He keyed a bypass code and said, "*Coral Sea*, you have a malfunction on the reception program; please reroute and reboot."

"*I will need authorization, I will need authorization, I will need authorization, I will need authorization,*" continued the receptionist imperturbably.

"Christ I hate computer personals," said Theroux.

"*I will need authorization, I will need authorization, I will need authorization —*"

"Their conversation is a bit limited," Butler said.

"*I will need authorization, I will neeeeeeeeeeee.*" On Theroux's screen, the receptionist froze and then faded, to be replaced by the FNPPBC's corporate montage of product images, accompanied by orchestral variations on their theme jingles.

"But when they fuck up like that," Butler continued, "I must confess to a certain sneaking affection for them. They seem almost human, then. Don't you think so?"

"No."

"You're just pissed off because it got between you and the object of your lust."

"Are you serious?"

"In thrall to your glands, all you tinted types. That's why we do our best to keep you away from the white women."

Theroux shook his head. "That's not why," he said.

"No?"

"No. You're afraid they'll find out we got bigger dicks than you white boys."

"With most of the women I've known, David old love, that would not be regarded as an advantage. I understand Kenzy is a colonial of course, so her attitude might be…" He paused delicately. "…more robust?"

"I wouldn't know. This is strictly business."

"Of course it is."

"She's an experienced police officer."

"I had heard that."

"I mean she's got a lot of service in."

Butler remained deadpan. "Did Freud die in vain, I ask myself?" he said.

"You're a real scumball, Simon."

"It's a thankless task, but I do my best. All right then – if it's not sex, what is it?"

"Police business," said Theroux.

Butler chortled. "Police business. I'm impressed. No, really, David, I am."

Stung, Theroux said, "I still don't like the way Stein's suit failed."

Butler controlled his amusement with some small difficulty. "I don't imagine Stein was exactly thrilled," he said, "but these things happen. It's the law of averages."

"I don't trust laws I didn't get to vote for." As Theroux said this, his communications screen cleared of corporate babble, and a woman, with enough imperfections to establish her humanity, glared out at him.

Pal Kenzy was in her thirties, slim and sharp-featured with white-blonde hair, cropped short for free-fall living. This, together with her very pale skin, would have made her look like an albino, were it not for her startling deep blue eyes.

"*This better be important, Theroux,*" she said. "*I had to fold three queens to come to a screen.*" Kenzy's Australian accent tended to be noticeable only when she was irritated – as now.

Slightly taken aback by her reaction, Theroux said, "Death rate from suit failure," rather more abruptly than he intended. He had only spoken to her a few times before, but she made a big impression on him, and – as Butler had shrewdly observed – his admiration was not entirely professional. It made him clumsy.

"*What about it?*" she said.

"What are your figures like at the moment?"

"*This is a joke, right? You interrupted the first winning streak I've had in months to check actuarial tables?*"

"Some of us are on a losing streak," snapped Theroux, embarrassment increasing his anger. "Are your figures up or down?"

"*Down,*" said Kenzy, puzzled by his vehemence. "*Have been for a while.*"

"What does your computer make of that?"

"*Nothing,*" she said. "*Death rate for all the orbit stations plus Moonbase is constant. Why, does yours say something different?"*

"Nope," said Theroux.

"*So what the fuck is the problem?"*

"We had another death," he said.

Kenzy looked at him for a moment. "*A friend, was it?"* she asked.

Theroux shook his head. "Not really."

"*Then why all the angst?"*

"It bothers me."

"*Come on Theroux. You win some, you lose some. Christ."*

"It's a little more permanent than folding three queens," said Theroux.

Kenzy shrugged. "*Same principle."*

Glancing away from the screen, Theroux thought he saw Butler watching him and smiling. On the screen, Kenzy said, "*Am I boring you?"* and he looked back at her.

"I get this really weird feeling we're being jerked around," he said.

"*Put in for some groundside time,"* said Kenzy, not unsympathetically. "*Could be a touch of cabin fever."*

"Thanks."

"*Listen, it happens to the best. Who died, and made you Superspacejock of the solar system?"*

Theroux nodded and smiled, in what he hoped looked like a reasonably sane way. "I'll bear it in mind. Nice talking to you, Kenzy," he said, and reached for the screen switch.

"*Hey, have you heard anything about the Commander's job yet?"* Kenzy asked quickly, before he could break the connection.

"I could care less," said Theroux.

"Frankly, my dear, I don't give a damn," murmured Butler in the background – in a passable imitation of Clark Gable. He grinned when Theroux scowled at him.

From the screen, Kenzy said, "*So you don't know who's on the short-list then?"*

"Are you?" Theroux asked, joking.

"*I didn't get an interview,"* she said.

Again, Theroux was taken by surprise. "You mean you did apply?"

If she noticed the surprise, Kenzy gave no sign of it. "*Damn right,"* she said, "*I don't do Star Cops duties for love, I do 'em for money. And that job's worth a lot of it."*

"It doesn't pay that well," Theroux said.

Kenzy's smile did not reach her eyes. "*Neither do most elected offices, but how many poor politicians do you know?*"

Before Theroux could decide on an answer, the flat tones of the Earth-12.00 shuttle pilot came through on the general overrides. "*Eurostat, Eurostat, Euroshuttle Seven copy?*"

"Euroshuttle Seven, Euroshuttle Seven, Eurostat copy. Go ahead," Butler responded automatically. He was the only human professional-class flight traffic controller on the orbit stations and had responsibility for all flights in the European sector, as well as co-coordinating non-routine traffic movements between the others.

"*They still haven't replaced you with a nice respectable computer, then? Like on the grown-up stations?*" said the shuttle pilot.

"Gotta go," Theroux said to Kenzy. "I'm on back-up traffic control, and we've got one inbound."

Butler said, "Dealing with morons is best handled by a human being, they felt," – continuing the ritual exchange of insults which had become as much a part of the routine as the confirmation of approach vectors.

"*Oh, so they are replacing you, then,*" said the pilot.

"*If you do hear anything,*" said Kenzy, "*let me know. Maybe we can pull some strings.*"

Theroux said, "To do what, for Chrissakes?"

"Euroshuttle Seven, this is Eurostat *Charles De Gaulle*, we have you inbound on green two with fourteen minutes flight time remaining, your estimated docking is twelve seventeen," Butler chanted.

"*Roger Eurostat.*"

"*Wake up, Theroux,*" said Kenzy. "*Suit failures could be the least of your problems if they give us some idiot with slogans where his brain should be.*" She broke the connection.

"You'll miss me when I'm gone," Butler said.

"*You think so?*" said the pilot.

"Oh yes," said Butler, then added, "More to the point, you'll probably miss the docking bay…" He glanced towards Theroux and smiled, but got no reaction.

As per standard operating procedure, Theroux had switched his screen to the approaching shuttle and was watching the spacecraft. It was clearly visible now, though in truth he was hardly aware of it – and of the readouts scrolling across the bottom of the screen, only their green colour was registering with him. A sudden anxiety had unfocused his thoughts and cramped his concentration. Up to this point, it had not even occurred to him that a newly appointed Commander could be one more problem in what was already a miserable, shitty fucking job.

Chapter 3

"*I thought the Commander said to drop it.*" Lincoln was peering closely from the small tollbooth screen, trying to get a better look at Nathan's face.

Nathan glanced out through the booth's perspex dome towards the distant reservoir. He told himself that tollbooths were more secure, but the truth was that the new generation mobilinks made him uncomfortable, and he avoided carrying one. There were times, though, when his aversion to being constantly available for the 'unbreakably close person-to-person contact' promised by the manufacturers was definitely inconvenient. He said, "We had a meeting."

"*Are you sure?*" Lincoln pressed. "*Only he seemed pretty definite.*"

Nathan turned back to the scratched, slightly hazy callscreen. "Only he seemed pretty definite, *sir*," he said mildly.

Lincoln's saggy expression did not change. "*Sorry. Sir,*" he said, without rancour. "*I just wondered what had changed, is all.*"

Nathan smiled. "Yours not to reason why, Inspector. Yours but to go and talk to the dead man's business partner."

"*Anything particular you want me to ask him?*"

"You're investigating a murder by drowning. I expect you'll think of something."

"*It uh... it's been confirmed as murder then has it, sir?*" Lincoln asked, trying not to make too much of the question, but still making it sound a bit like an accusation.

"*I'm* confirming it," Nathan said. "Consider it confirmed. It's a murder. Right?"

"*Right,*" said Lincoln. "*We... uh... we still don't have a budget number, presumably?*"

"Stop thinking like an accountant, Brian. That's my job. Your job is to think like a copper."

"*Perhaps I could question him over a screen link. There'd be no need to book that.*"

"For Christ's sake, Brian!" Nathan's anger was only partly because of his Inspector's dogged refusal to buck the system; mostly it was because he knew Lincoln was right. Right from his point of view, anyway. And that made losing his temper with the man even more pointless. He forced another smile. "You've got to do this one face to face."

"*If you say so, sir. What about the widow?*"

"I'll talk to her," Nathan said.

"*Another face to face?*"

"You can't tell they're sweating if you can't smell they're sweating, Brian."

"*Do widows sweat, sir?*"

"Depends what they've been doing. Report to me direct as soon as you've seen the partner, okay?" Before Lincoln could acknowledge the order, Nathan touched the end link panel on the callscreen.

He withdrew his ID from the reader and, pocketing the card, he stepped out of the booth and crossed the road towards the reservoir.

"You have not verified the details of that call," his own voice said from the pocket of his jacket. Nathan ignored it, and turned onto a grass track that led through some birch scrub in the direction of the reservoir.

"You have not verified the details of that call," his voice repeated.

"I heard you the first time," said Nathan.

"You took no action," his voice said.

Resignedly Nathan took out his ID, and thumbed the edge to activate: recall payment. Without bothering to look at the call details the holographic lens was magnifying, he waited a few seconds then thumbed: confirm input. "Happy now?" he asked.

"Do you require an answer to that question?" his voice asked.

"No," he said.

"Do you require an answer to that question?" his voice asked again.

Nathan reached into his pocket and withdrew a plain black box about the size of a cigarette packet. "Can you hear me now, Box?" he said to it.

"Yes," the box replied, in a weirdly undistorted copy of his own voice.

"Then I do not require an answer to my earlier question: happy now? Is that clear?" Nathan said, then added quickly, "I mean is that understood?"

"It is both clear and understood," said Box. "The requirement to check all transaction details so that only correct payments are authorized –"

"Shut up, Box," said Nathan, putting it away and wondering – not for the first time – whether the bloody thing wasn't actually more trouble than it was worth.

He walked on briskly for maybe a mile without seeing anybody at all. If a man preferred his own company, he thought, this was certainly the place to come – which was when he remembered he was supposed to be meeting Lee that evening. "Box," he said.

But Box had not been closed down long enough to clear itself. "-is a statutory one," it said, finishing what Nathan had blocked. "You have now complied with the law. Do you require details of the relevant sections and paragraphs of the Order?"

"No. Book a table at the Lotus Garden for tonight please. Contact Lee and arrange a time for me to meet her there."

"She prefers you to do these things in person," said Box.

Nathan said, "Don't identify yourself. Tell her you're in a hurry. Be abrupt. Chances are, she won't notice the difference."

Nathan pocketed Box as it said, "Very well. Processing is under way."

When Nathan reached the reservoir, the sun was shining and there was only the very lightest of breezes. He sat down on a low grass bank, which gave him a clear view across the broad expanse of glinting water.

Although this was still officially designated as a Category Three Storage Facility, the reservoir no longer fed the main supply grid, and had been left to itself. Vegetation had been allowed to begin colonizing the banks. Trees which would normally have been cut back and rooted out, to avoid leaf debris silting up the water, were already growing taller than simple scrub. Reedmace, rosebay, willowherb and ragwort grew between the slope on which Nathan sat and the water's edge. Behind him, silver birch trees – first colonizers for new woodland and one of the few genuinely native trees – moved in the soft wind, their vivid trunks drifting below vastly intricate cascades of tiny shivering leaves. The place was growing beautiful.

Nathan flapped a midge away from his face and looked at his watch. He shifted uncomfortably. The grassy bank was not as restful as it looked. He stood up and brushed the seat of his trousers, trying to feel if it was damp. The grass had seemed dry when he sat down, but now his backside felt distinctly chilly. He was regretting the impulse that had brought him here. It was not one of his more rational notions. "This was a stupid idea," he said aloud, and looked at his watch. Okay then, with a two and a half minute margin either way, the pathology unit had set – *this* – as the time the victim lost consciousness.

He stared at the lake, trying to picture it happening; trying to see how it could have happened. He shaded his eyes, and scanned the banks slowly trying to see… what? He didn't really have any idea.

He completed the survey. Nothing.

He was starting to feel more than a little foolish. Nobody lurking about? Nobody revisiting the scene of the crime? Shit. That was the trouble with murderers, he thought and said, "You can't rely on the buggers to play the game."

He turned round to start back the way he had come, and found the old man standing behind him with a stick raised above his head.

"Christ!" said Nathan.

"Afternoon," said the old man, and threw the stick down the bank. A black and white terrier burst out of a clump of bushes and raced after it with silent ferocity.

"You frightened the life out of me," Nathan said and smiled his best smile.

The old man smiled back. "You took me a bit by surprise," he said.

The dog overran the stick, and fell in a rolling heap as it tried to stop.

"Enthusiastic," said Nathan, watching the animal scramble to its feet and rush at the stick.

"Not the brightest I've ever had, but he's got a lot of heart," the old man said. "Never gives up."

"I had a Russell when I was a kid," Nathan said, altering history and taking a friend's pet for his own. "People don't realize what's involved, do they? Looking after a dog."

"That they don't," said the old man, as the dog headed back with the wrong stick, this one much larger than the one that had been thrown.

"They've got their little routines," Nathan said. He could still remember the tyranny of that small dog's habits. "Eat, sleep, crap, walk. Set times for all of them." When his father had offered to get him one of his own, Nathan had declined in favour of a rabbit. It had turned out to be just as demanding – and boring, as well.

"We're all creatures of habit," the old man was saying, "one way or another."

Nathan nodded. The dog was struggling to get the stick past some brambles. "You walk him here every day, do you?" he asked.

"Rain or shine," said the old man, "regular as clockwork. Not as quiet round here as it used to be, mind. Lot more people."

* * *

"Even if we 'ad the people, which we do not…" The general manager of the *Charles De Gaulle*, Françoise Lancine, was looking at Theroux as though he was several *canapés* short of the full *hors d'oeuvres*. "…budgets are tight."

Theroux said, "You mean it's cheaper to replace the corpses, is that what you're telling me?"

They were facing one another across a small desk – large by station standards – in the full unit work-module which was designated as an office, and which came with the job of general manager.

"What I am telling you," Lancine said, "is what you already are aware of. It is not practical to insist always on two people being out there together. We can not afford to return to the buddy system for EVAs."

She was a handsome woman, in that elegant European way which Theroux always found too tight-assed to be really sexy. Her auburn hair was cropped no shorter than absolutely necessary, brushed carefully and pulled back into a small bob to show off her narrow, fine-boned face to advantage. A minimum of make-up was perfectly applied to highlight the bone structure and the clear brown eyes. Not a trace of fat anywhere on the long-legged, light breasted figure. She had to be good-looking, of course. Good-looking and tough. No way, no day, she'd get charge of one of Europe's top scientific and civil engineering projects, else. And all that stylish control not moved by weightlessness, by knowing she was held in position at her desk by Velcro patches on her slippers, knees, elbows and tush. Or maybe ambition generated its own gravity. She was certainly ambitious. Simon called her 'the climbing frog', which was one of his less slanderous insults. Aloud, Theroux said, "The deaths have all been guys working alone."

"Naturally, this is 'ow most of us work."

Theroux was tempted to ask when she next planned to go on an EVA, but confined himself to saying, "Not most of us."

"Most of us for whom suit-failure is a routine risk."

"A risk we can eliminate by changing the routine."

Brushing a well-manicured finger lightly above her ear, unconsciously checking that no hair was out of place, Lancine said, "No. We can not. The next death –"

"The *next* death?" interrupted Theroux. "You say the *next* death?"

"It is statistically inevitable, is it not? And it could 'appen to anyone, in a work team, alone… it could 'appen in the dark, or in full view of the world."

"Very poetic," said Theroux. "And total crap."

Lancine frowned. "It could be suit-failure, solar flare, meteor strike."

"Could choke on an olive pit, but five'll get you ten a suit system fucks up and there's no witnesses when it does."

"So he didn't actually see anything? This old man and his half-witted dog?"

Lee wasn't laughing at him, but she wasn't taking him entirely seriously either.

Nathan said, "Precisely because he was delayed by a total stranger asking for directions."

"Well, yes. But then again, if he hadn't been a total stranger, he wouldn't have needed directions. Would he?"

She looked up from poking a chopstick dubiously into one of the bowls ranged in front of her, grinned, and then leaned back, tilting her head slightly to stop her hair falling across her face.

Despite the current fashion for the off-Earther's crop, Lee Jones wore her thick, brown hair shoulder length. Her figure, too, was softer and slightly fuller than was fashionable. Her face was round and gentle, pretty rather than beautiful, and her grin was slightly mocking, but never malicious.

As he sat across the table from her in the Lotus Garden, it struck Nathan suddenly that she was extraordinary, and he was a fool to hesitate. "I don't know why I bother to tell you my theories," he said.

"Who else do you trust, love," Lee said. "If you don't count that creepy Box, there's no-one to talk to apart from me."

"Are you suggesting I'm paranoid?" Nathan leaned forward, and glowered theatrically.

"I wouldn't presume, Chief Superintendent."

"Good," Nathan said, and twitched so that the food dropped off his chopsticks. "I am not paranoid. I've just got a lot of enemies, that's all." He glanced round, as if trying to see past the video panels which screened off each of the tables in the restaurant.

"Be funnier if it wasn't true," she said.

"I'm not paranoid," said Nathan laughing. "Am I?"

"No. But you have got enemies."

"Who gives a shit about them?"

"You do, love," Lee said and looked into his face.

"I can live with it," he said, and thought, *as long as I've got you I can live with it*, but couldn't bring himself to say that out loud. He reached for more food, taking elaborate care as he scooped rice and flaked fish into his dish.

Lee said, "Oh no, here comes that bloody panda again."

"What's wrong with pandas?"

Lee nodded at the video panels. "Haven't you noticed the wallzac is the same damn thing over and over again."

"That's what wallzac is."

"It's what wallzac is in cheap dives like this."

"You get the best food in cheap dives like this," Nathan said.

"So you keep telling me. As justifications for thrift go, it has the virtue of…" she paused. "Actually, I'm not sure what virtue it does have, really."

"Paranoid *and* cheap," said Nathan. "I can see why you find me irresistible."

Lee waved a chopstick at the panel. "Every half hour or so, that panda arrives, trots about. Eats some bamboo shoots…"

"I like it," Nathan said.

"Well don't get too attached to it, because it's edited out pretty abruptly. It does something unappetizing, I imagine."

"You don't want to talk about my murder, then."

"I'm not sure what makes you so certain it was murder."

"I'm not certain," Nathan said without emphasis.

This time Lee looked at him with genuine surprise. "Then for God's sake, why are you making trouble?"

Nathan shrugged, and shook his head vaguely. If he was honest, there was no compelling reason.

"You haven't got enough problems already?" Lee asked.

He shrugged again. "Man's a problem-solving animal," he said.

"You're bored?" There was a small irritation in Lee's voice.

He shovelled rice and fish into his mouth with the chopsticks, and chewed for a moment to give himself time. Even then, the only answer he could come up with sounded defensive. "Not exactly."

"Not remotely, I hope," Lee said. "You do realize that I turned down the promotion today?"

"That was today was it?"

"Isn't that why we're having this…" She gestured at the bowls on the table.

"Outstanding Chinese meal?" Nathan suggested.

She grinned. "Yes."

"No."

"Oh. Something else, then?"

Nathan shook his head. Why upset her? He had no intention of getting the damn job, anyway. He said, "I knew how much you liked this place, so I thought…" and smiled.

Lee recognized the smile. "This drowning case isn't worse than you're telling me, is it?" she challenged.

"How do you mean?"

"It isn't a career-breaker?"

"It's nothing like that," Nathan said, and shrugged and shook his head yet again. He was conscious that he suddenly seemed to be developing a bunch of unconvincing spasms and twitches. "It's not important. It's just that I've got a feeling about it."

"Feelings are good," said Lee and grinned.

Nathan went on, "The decision was too quick. The machine was too sure, that's all."

"It is just a machine."

"Exactly. It's got no instinct for the job. I have. It's called a detective's nose." He turned his profile to her. "I have a particularly fine nose, wouldn't you say?"

Lee was frowning slightly. "You're beginning to sound as if you think of the regional crime computer as a rival."

"No." Nathan knew what was coming, and he badly didn't want to get into it.

"You're not in competition, Nathan."

"I'm not sure the boss would agree with you."

Lee said, "Your dad –"

Nathan cut her off angrily, "I don't want a rehash of the crap the marriage contract counsellor gave us."

"I wasn't going to."

"I've had the blood test and the psych evaluation. I was passed fit on both," he continued, though his temper had peaked and he was already feeling stupid. "It's no guarantee, I know, but as it goes I'm pretty nearly normal. Ish."

"I was just going to say –"

"I know what you were just going to say, Lee. I don't want to hear it, okay?"

"Your father did not think more of the machines than he did of you."

"Fine."

"Sooner or later you'll have to come to terms with the fact that he loved you, but he wasn't very good at showing it."

"Right."

Lee looked him in the eye. "It's not an uncommon trait," she said.

Nathan said, "I don't believe a buyer for Corner Store International is really qualified to judge what my old man was or was not good at." He kept his voice flat and cold, and he regretted the words even as he spoke them, but he couldn't help adding, "Especially ones who never met the cold-arsed bastard."

"Senior buyers for Corner Store are blessed with superhuman skills. Especially ones who turn down promotion to Chief European Buyer to devote themselves to having the children of the sons of cold-arsed computer salesmen."

"Pity taking a hint isn't among your super-human skills," Nathan said – but he was smiling now.

"It is," she said, "but this meal only entitles you to the economy package."

"Why don't you hate me?" he asked.

"I like to be different," she said.

"In that case, the least you can do is believe in my murder theory."

"If it's a theory it doesn't require faith," Lee said. "It requires testing."

"That's what Lincoln and I are in the process of doing. Smart arse."

"I thought you liked my arse," she murmured, and under the table she pushed her shoeless foot between his legs.

Nathan jumped slightly. Behind him a waiter said, "Everything to your satisfaction, sir?"

He blushed. "Yes. It's fine, thank you." Under the table, Lee rubbed his groin with her foot and grinned.

"Madam?" asked the waiter.

"I'm bored with the wallzac," Lee said, as Nathan tried to move away from her foot. "Do you have anything different you could play?"

"I will check, madam."

When he was sure the waiter had gone, Nathan grabbed Lee's foot and tugged so that she almost slipped off her seat. "Don't do that," he said.

"You know I don't like it."

"It felt as though you liked it," she said.

"You know what I mean."

"Yes. I'm sorry," she said and tried to pull her foot away.

Nathan gripped her ankle. "You don't sound sorry," he said.

"I am. Honestly."

He smiled, put a finger lightly on the sole of her foot, and brushed it up and down.

"No, don't," said Lee, going rigid. "*Don't*. I shall scream." She giggled.

Nathan tickled a little harder, and she was instantly reduced to helpless laughter. Just before she reached the screaming stage, he let go of her foot and said, "I remember my old man talking about the early chess computers. You know what he said?"

"Bastard," Lee gasped.

"No, that's not what he said."

"You know I don't like that."

"It sounded as though you liked it."

"Bastard."

Nathan said, "What he said was that anyone could beat them if they only grasped the simple notion that the machines could never resist a deliberate sacrifice."

"Very gnomic," Lee said. "Has this got something to do with your murder theory?"

"It's why I don't trust machines."

"No it's not."

"It's a reason for not trusting machines."

"Well, possibly, but it's one of many, surely? Most of them are more or less neurotic," said Lee. She watched Nathan switch her off without taking his eyes from her face, and with almost no alteration in his expression or the tone of his voice.

"The machines have become evidence," he said.

Lee had never quite got used to Nathan's habit of keeping the conversation going while in fact he was thinking aloud. "You lost me," she said.

"They calculate the probabilities before we actually do anything," he said. "That makes them part of the evidence." For a moment he was lost in thought, then his attention focused on her again.

"If you ever do that when we're fucking," she said, "I'll never forgive you."

"No problem," said Nathan. "I promise never to eat Chinese food when we're fucking."

On the screens, the wallzac changed to white cranes and paddy fields. The waiter returned and bowed from the waist. "Is to madam's preference?"

"Thank you," Lee said. After he had gone, she watched the video loop not quite holding true and making the stereo effects quiver slightly. "Are you going to tell me?" she asked brightly.

Nathan was cautious. "Tell you what?"

"Don't bullshit me, Nathan."

"I'm not."

"All right." She sighed and said, "So what's the plan then?"

"Haven't got one, really. The next step is to see the widow."

Lee said, "I meant our plan."

"Oh shit. Yeah. Sorry. Well… we're not in that much of a rush, are we?"

"Is that what this is about? Have you changed your mind?"

"No, of course not."

"You still can, love," she said calmly. "If you've decided the homemaking bit is not for you. You only have to say."

"For Christ's sake!" Nathan blustered. "I haven't changed my mind."

Lee nodded solemnly. "Because if we are going to have a family, then there isn't that much time to waste," she said.

Nathan tossed down his chopsticks. "Have you finished eating?" he asked, and made as if to slide under the table.

"Not funny," Lee said.

"You don't like this place, so we probably won't be coming back here anyway." Nathan smiled, knowing that didn't make the joke any better and seeing puzzled hurt in Lee's face.

"What is wrong with you tonight?" she asked.

But he still couldn't bring himself to tell her. He knew that if he didn't talk to her about the Star Cops job, then he didn't have to think about it. Not yet. He didn't need to face the bind he might find himself in. Not yet. And there was something else, too. Something shameful. Something he definitely wasn't ready to think about yet. But it was there in his head. Something that job might offer, which nothing much else could. A way out…

Crime Scene

The red plain stretched to the horizon, bleak and inhospitable despite its rosy hue. The sky was a matching pale pink, and the colour co-ordination intensified the alien hostility of the place. Though the ground looked smooth and featureless at a distance, close up it was a desert of stones and small boulders scattered across the coarse sands and oxides of iron that made up the soil. Here and there, the surface was broken by gullies and cut by sudden deep fissures. Theory suggested that these were carved out by the water that had long since vanished into the fierce climatic imbalance which overwhelmed the planet.

In these surroundings the members of the Base One Ground Team: Mars Geological Survey looked sadly insignificant, and a lot more vulnerable than the work logos on their spacesuits suggested. The six shambling figures, each one trying to maintain visual contact with the person on their right, were strung out in a long uneven line as they struggled through the difficult terrain.

They were using satellite navigation to pinpoint positions so they could plant small seismic charges in a carefully predetermined grid pattern. It was gruelling work, and their suits – though lighter than those needed for the high vacuum – hampered every movement.

At the extreme left-hand end of the line, Tolly Jardine had stopped to place his fifteenth and last charge of the day. It was standard operating procedure to describe what he was doing to the next person on the short-range loop. "Placing it now," he said as he leaned his hip against the stock of the charge gun and pushed the barrel into a patch of sand. "Ready to fire." Although it was primed, there was absolutely no danger of the charge exploding when he shot it down into the subsoil. The seismic cartridges were guaranteed safe. They could only be set off by a microwave trigger which would be placed and keyed by the team leader when the grid was complete and the rest of the team had withdrawn. During the course of the Mars survey not one seismic charge had ever gone off prematurely. But still when the time came to release the CO_2 and punch the cartridge home there was always a moment's tension. "Firing," said Tolly, and he felt the gun's solid recoil against his hip pad.

"*Okay, lets move on, Tolly.*" Even over the crude headset in the suit helmet, Stella Dearman's voice sounded tired. "*I've still got my last to place. Assuming I can reach the damn position.*"

"Hold it a minute," said Tolly. Below a small boulder, near where he had placed the charge, surface sand was collapsing into what appeared to be a small hole. "We seem to have some surface instability here." As he watched, the sand at the edges continued to fold down, making the hole larger and larger.

Stella's voice was suddenly loud. "*Don't just stand there, you stupid bastard. Get the hell out! The whole area could be loose.*"

The hole was now the size of a space helmet and seemed to have stabilized. The interior was in deep shadow, black and impenetrable. "There's a hole opened up," said Tolly. He bent to peer into it.

Stella reacted to the movement. "*What are you doing?*" her voice demanded.

"I think there's something in it," Tolly said.

"*If it turns out to be you, you're on your own. I'm not digging you out. I'm a surveyor, not a Saint Bernard. Jesus, Tolly!*"

Tolly put his hand into the hole. "I'm reaching into the hole," he said, automatically reverting to talking through his actions.

From her distant viewpoint, Stella watched him remain crouched, unmoving and silent, for what seemed like several minutes. She was about to hit the man-down panic alarm when his voice said, "*My God, Stella. You're not going to believe what I've found.*"

Star Cops

Chapter 4

"*You haven't got the first fucking idea what you're looking for, have you?*" Butler's voice drawled over the communicator stuck behind Theroux's left ear. "*Well, have you?*"

Theroux pulled the last of the backpacks from the freight lock and pushed it gently towards the others. Then he signalled to the Russian technician that he was ready to seal his end of the transfer tube. The Russian smiled and nodded goodbye as he tugged himself back into the cargo shuttle.

Holding the brace bar with one hand, Theroux pushed the circular hatch closed with the other and checked the telltales for leaks. Then he floated back through the inner lock and repeated the procedure – except that this time, he dogged the hatch shut using two solid-looking sliding levers. For all practical purposes, these levers were clearly unnecessary; air pressure would have held the hatch closed against the vacuum under all survivable conditions. But it had been realized early on in the development of the orbit stations that people seemed more comfortable and better able to cope with stress if obvious examples of physical security were designed into the systems wherever possible. Experienced personnel tended to scoff at such devices, known as wacsobs – white knuckle security blankets – but everyone seemed to use them nonetheless, and Theroux was no exception.

"*Control to cargo bay one, control to cargo bay one,*" murmured Butler's voice in his ear. "*Flight engineer Theroux, do you copy?*" The procedural formality was ironic and mildly irritable.

As he tugged himself round from the hatch, Theroux touched his throat mic and said, "I'm busy here, okay? This is hard work." Weightlessness did not make basic physical tasks easier, it just made them different. You used unusual muscle groups and your hand-eye co-ordination was never exactly normal. And it all got tougher if you strayed from the routines designed into particular sections and modules. Suit Transfer and Storage was cramped, and 'cramped' threatened chaos and gridlock in whole new ways. The last thing Theroux needed right now was more of Butler's crap.

"*Lift that barge, tote that bale,*" Butler murmured. "*It's what you black folks was put off the Earth to do.*"

"Go fuck yourself, Simon."

"*Temper.*"

"I'm trying to do my job." Theroux struggled to get the newly serviced backpacks into a manageable group.

Butler persisted. "*It's not your job. You volunteered, remember?*" He sounded peevish. "*And I repeat, you don't know what you're looking for.*"

"No," Theroux said, "I don't." He pushed the drifting cluster of jostling backpacks towards the storage racks preformed into three sides at one end of the module. "Satisfied now?"

Butler's voice took on a more businesslike tone. "*I'm not, actually. You should leave playing boy detective until there's less in the way of traffic knocking about. And I use the phrase advisedly.*"

"Boy detective?"

"*Knocking about.*"

Theroux prepared to check each backpack prior to clipping it into place in the racks. "You've never complained before," he said, as he took the first one, and began by making sure the transparent dustcover was unbreached.

"*My dear old thing, I will stretch myself to cover for any reasonable pastime. Sex, gambling, imbibing unhealthy quantities of brain-liquidizer.*"

Without removing the cover, Theroux checked that all the service inspection tags were in place. So far, so routine.

"*But I draw the line,*" Butler's voice continued, "*at playing second banana in your comedy cop routine.*"

Theroux finished the visual examination and considered what else he could do to satisfy himself that the unit was sound. The truth was, of course, that short of suiting-up and using it outside there wasn't anything much. He began to wonder what the hell he really thought he was doing. Was this honestly a search for evidence, however vague and unfocused? Or was it just that he was feeling guilty... about what, for Chrissakes? What was he trying to prove? He wasn't responsible for the deaths. It wasn't his fault. And nobody else gave a shit.

"*You're wasting your time,*" Butler's voice said.

Theroux clipped the backpack into place and began the same routine on the next. Through his earphone, he listened to Butler deal with the departing cargo shuttle while continuing to bitch at him. "*Thank you Red Star, disengagement is confirmed.*"

Since communication with the shuttle was on a different channel Theroux could not hear the pilot's responses. Strictly speaking he should not have been able to hear the controller's end of the transaction either, but speaking strictly according to RT procedures was not something to which Butler paid much attention. "*And what's more important you're wasting my time,*" his voice complained, then, "*Roger that, comrade, you have clearance for minimum thrust,*" before continuing seamlessly, "*I've got your number, Peace Officer Theroux.*"

That was something he could do, Theroux thought. Numbers. If he made a note of the numbers, the unit numbers and the rack numbers as he clipped them up, should any of this batch fail, he could at least trace them back here to storage. Maybe there would be something about the way they were racked, or the order they were used in, or something…

"*It's all just an excuse to play with yourself while I do the real work.*"

He began to dictate the numbers into his wristfile. While he was at it he noted the serial numbers of the separate parts which made up the units, and even the inspection tag numbers. That was the trouble with data; it expanded to fill the time available to collect it. And there was no way to be sure what you might find useful.

"*How much longer are you going to be, David?*"

Theroux switched on his throat mic and said, "An hour maybe."

"*An hour? Christ I'm off shift in less than that. Minimum thrust is confirmed. Thank you comrades. Keep the faith.*"

Theroux pushed another backpack into place. "Comrades?" he said. "You know how much they hate to be called comrade."

"*I thought 'keep the faith' was a nice touch too.*"

"Pissed with me, so you take it out on the Russians, huh?"

Theroux heard the smile in Butler's voice when he answered, "*Not especially. I was merely reminding them what old-fashioned capitalism is really about.*"

"I'll buy it," said Theroux.

"*I was thinking more of the customer's right to be gratuitously abusive.*"

"Mustn't be nice to the backpack service man."

"*I should say not.*" Butler's voice took on a studied, wry drawl. "*We don't want the Russian workers getting above themselves, now, do we? Look what happened last time. And I mean, it's not as if their stuff is exactly ultra-*

reliable these days is it?"

"That's the sixty-four thousand dollar question, Simon," Theroux said flicking off his throat mic and returning to his laborious recording of backpack numbers.

The woman who released the locks and admitted Nathan to the lobby was plain and dumpy, and dressed with what looked like an almost self-conscious lack of style. She was clearly a little shaken to find him at her door.

"I'm sorry to bother you, Ms. Carmodie," Nathan said, proffering his ID as a matter of politeness though the house security system had already verified his identity. "I realize this must be a difficult time."

To his surprise, the woman took the wallet and examined the plate and the badge. Nathan noticed that her hands were slim and long-fingered and her grey eyes were bright and intelligent. The plump figure and the plainness should not have made these details unexpected but they did.

"I didn't realize you people still made house calls," she said and looked into his face as though comparing it to the picture. She closed the wallet and handed it back. "You must forgive me. I never expected to see one of those close up. The picture doesn't do you justice." She was over her initial discomfiture. "How can I help you, Chief Superintendent?"

"I'm investigating your husband's drowning."

"Obviously." She said it without edge; calmly. There was confidence now. "Shall we go and find somewhere to sit?"

She led the way, waddling slightly as though her hip joints were stiff. As he followed her through the immaculate and tasteful hallway, it occurred to Nathan that her appearance made it easy to underestimate this woman, and that she might well be encouraging that. He stopped at an unexceptional watercolour, probably hung only because it matched the rest of the decor, and said, "This is nice."

The woman stopped and turned back. Her hip joints were not stiff.

"My husband chose it," she said. "He had very good taste." She moved back into what Nathan now felt sure was an act – though whether or not it was a *conscious* act, he couldn't yet decide.

"Perhaps you'd like to see his office," she continued. "He was particularly proud of his office."

The room into which she showed Nathan was a reconstruction of a Victorian study, or what Nathan imagined a Victorian study would probably have looked like. The woman sat down behind the heavy, highly polished desk and gestured him to take the chair opposite her.

Nathan looked round appreciatively. "It's remarkable," he said.

"Yes." For no obvious reason, she moved the writing set from one side of the desk to the other. "I can't say I like it much – but then, it isn't really a woman's room." She shifted the lamp into the middle of the desk.

Nathan said, "They're beautiful reproductions."

"Oh, they're not reproductions. Everything in this room is genuine. My husband was very meticulous. Obsessive, even. I was only allowed…" She paused, and then with a slight smile corrected herself, "Even I… was only allowed in here on special occasions. Normally he kept it locked."

"Probably a sensible precaution," Nathan said. "Given the value of everything,"

She shrugged a small shrug of agreement. "I suppose so."

Her resentment towards her husband was clear, but Nathan knew she could have reached that stage of grief by now. He said, "I'm told he swam at the same time every day."

"Yes."

"Was there a reason?"

"He liked to keep fit."

"I meant for the time."

"Oh. No, I don't think so. It was just a routine."

"Did he have routines for other things?"

"Yes."

Nathan thought, this is like pulling teeth, and wondered if she was doing it deliberately. He said, "For example?"

"Chief Superintendent, there wasn't anything my husband did not have a routine for. Except dying, perhaps… As I said he was a very meticulous man." She stood up, and crossed to the sideboard. "I think I'll have a drink. Would you like a drink?"

"Thank you."

"Scotch? Sherry?"

"I'd prefer coffee, if it's possible."

"Of course."

When she had left the room, Nathan got up and took Box from his pocket. "Box," he said to activate the machine, then, "take an inventory of the contents of this room."

He made two three hundred and sixty degree turns so that Box could scan everything.

"File complete," Box said in its exact simulation of his voice.

Nathan looked round the room. Something in the way the woman had played with the desk arrangement bothered him. *'Even I was only allowed in…'*

"Box. The contents of this room are all authentic mid-Victorian antiques."

"The file is amended accordingly," said Box.

"Check the insurance database and tell me the value."

"Is there a cross-reference?"

"The owner's name is Carmodie."

"Checking."

Nathan went back and sat down. Box said, "Do you wish the figure for the actual or the insured contents of the room?"

"What's the difference?"

"Items on the database are not on the recently completed inventory."

"What's missing?"

"A clock, a small oil painting, two china dogs, a paperweight."

Behind him, the door began to open. Quickly, Nathan said "Thank you Box," and closed down the machine.

The woman backed in, carrying a tray of coffee. "Talking to yourself, Chief Superintendent?" she said.

"It's a bad habit, I'm afraid," Nathan said, and smiled his most disarming smile.

"Not really," said the woman, without responding to the smile. "It's just a sign of loneliness that's all."

She took the hot coffee pot from the tray, and put it on the unprotected highly polished desk top.

When Nathan got home, Lincoln's report was waiting on his workstation screen-hold. He skimmed it as he got changed; he was already running late for the ISPF recruitment board.

The interview with the dead man's business partner had produced a great deal of information, most of which was of no interest at all. One unremarked detail did strike him, though. He punched up Lincoln's workscreen, and caught him just as he was logging-off to leave for home. "What put you onto this unregistered loan, Brian?"

Relaxed as ever, Lincoln showed no sign of irritation at being delayed.

"He volunteered it. Along with his life story, business career and inside leg measurement. I think I made him nervous."

"That's why it's better face to face."

"He wasn't expecting to see me, certainly."

"Why cash? Was it just to avoid the bank computers?"

"You want to review that section?"

Nathan frowned, "I'm running late, but – yeah, all right."

Lincoln checked the timecode on the interview tape. When he keyed the playback window, it automatically showed a freeze-frame of a small, well-fed man in his sixties. With ID and context established, the image mixed to a close-up of the face and the interrogation resumed. The man looked worried. *"I always said his obsession with fitness would be the death of him."*

"Obsessive about it, was he?" the unseen Lincoln prompted.

"Oh God, yes. He was obsessive about every damn thing. Neatness, punctuality, routine. Christ, there were times when I thought he was more like a machine than a human being. I mean, it made for a good business partner. He did more than his share of the work, but even so…"

"Can you think of any reason why he might have wanted to kill himself?"

The man was obviously taken aback. *"Kill himself?"*

"It wasn't suicide, Brian," Nathan said.

On the main screen Lincoln nodded, *"This is the bit coming up."*

In the screen window, the little man shook his head and went on: *"He wouldn't have killed himself."*

"He wasn't short of money, say?" Lincoln suggested.

"Why, what makes you think he might have been short of money?" The little man looked momentarily defensive, and slightly shifty.

Lincoln's voice hardened. *"I'm asking you."*

"I loaned his wife some money."

There was a pause, before Lincoln said politely, *"I don't think there's any record of that, is there?"*

"It was a private transaction."

"No bank transaction is private from a police computer investigation, sir."

"This was cash. I got it through some contacts which I shan't tell you about so there's no point in asking."

"Why would she want cash?"

The man had recovered his composure and was more confident now. *"It isn't illegal, you know. Not quite. Not yet."*

"Most of its uses are, though, wouldn't you say?"

"Yes. And I suspect that what she had in mind probably was, too. I think she was going to buy something on the black market. Something for him. Something really special, you know? She mentioned an anniversary surprise. But it didn't happen. After he drowned, she returned the money to me."

Nathan said, "Okay thanks, that's all I wanted."

Lincoln stopped the playback. *"It seems the husband collected antiques,"* he said.

"That was good interrogation, Brian. Well done."

"He reckoned that's what she was getting him, but either she couldn't get it, or it wasn't what he wanted. So is that it? Can I close the file now?"

Nathan was in too much of a hurry to waste time on irritation. "No, Inspector. We'll talk tomorrow."

Lincoln smiled. *"Somebody getting married?"*

"Sorry?"

"Your neck scarf's crooked."

"Oh, the wedding suit?" Nathan looked down at himself. "Job interview," he said and broke the connection.

It was typical of the whole shoestring operation, Nathan thought, that the electronic conference room was a public facility hired by the hour. And it didn't help that the control system was programmed so that the real-time holograms of the board members were just a little larger than life-size. The difference was hardly noticeable, but it was enough to be intimidating if you were not aware of the interview technique involved. If you were, and any experienced interrogator ought to be, then the effect was absurd at best. Under the circumstances, the absence of an American and a Russian on the board seemed entirely appropriate. The set-up was too amateur and the threat too professional for either power to wish the ISPF well. All in all, the arrangements served only to confirm Nathan's original attitude to the Star Cops job.

"Why do you want the job?" asked the token industrialist, Nashu Yakasone, from his office in Tokyo. Of the five people facing Nathan across the table he looked the most real. There was no shimmer on the pool of light in which he sat, and all background visual had been screened out. He could almost have been in the room.

Nathan looked him in the eye and said, "As it stands, I don't want the job. I'm a professional policeman. I should hate to waste my time on an under-funded, over-extended public relations exercise."

Lars Hendvorrsen, tipped – at least by his tireless press agent – for high office in the Europarliament, snorted with theatrical amusement. "*Typical,*" he said. "*He hasn't got the job yet, already he pitches for a bigger budget.*"

Françoise Lancine, General Manager of the ESA's *Charles De Gaulle* said, "*Is it your intention to bargain with us, Chief Superintendent?*"

"I'm a thief-taker, ma'am, not a bargainer."

"*A thief-taker?*"

"Detective."

"*Ah. I understand.*"

"*The successful candidate would be off-Earth for three years. How would you regard such a tour of duty?*" asked Neela Shah, the elegant Indian space physicist and acting Liaison Co-ordinator.

"With unbounded enthusiasm," Nathan said dryly, and then allowed himself to smile at her. She was a pretty woman. She smiled back. Nathan found himself regretting that what faced him was just a hologram; generated in Venice, if the view from the window behind her was real.

"*Yes,*" she said, "*it's one of the drawbacks of our development programmes. It's healthier to have a realistic attitude to the problems.*"

"*Unfortunately,*" Hendvorrsen butted in, "*a realistic attitude is something the development programmes conspicuously lack, as our esteemed Liaison Co-ordinator should be well aware, don't you agree, Chief Superintendent?*"

Deadpan, Nathan said, "I always try to be agreeable, sir."

"*Representative Hendvorrsen's contribution to the debate has always owed more to political ambition than to realism,*" said Shah coolly.

"*Unlike you, Ms. Shah, I was elected to my office,*" Hendvorrsen said, limbering up for the sort of row his career thrived on.

"*But not to this board,*" she snapped back. "*You shouted your way onto this.*"

As if to confirm what she said, Hendvorrsen increased the volume another notch. "*The voice of the people should not be heard in the places where their money is spent,*" he declaimed. "*Is that your opinion?*"

Nathan relaxed a little. If these people were more prepared to bitch at one another than they were to interview him, then maybe he was off the hook.

"*It is my opinion,*" said the only police professional on the board, "*that we should get back to the business we are here for.*" Marie Mueller glanced at the papers in front of her, and went on, "*Chief Superintendent; you have been a police officer for fifteen years?*"

"Yes, ma'am."

"*You have reached your present rank faster than you would have done in my force. What do you put this down to?*"

"Caution?"

"*You are cautious?*"

"No, ma'am. You are."

Mueller frowned. "*Your Commander gives you an excellent report. You are it seems an outstanding officer.*" She looked at him and waited. Nathan stared back at her. The uncomfortable silence was another routine technique which was wasted on him. "*Do you have any comment?*" she asked eventually.

Nathan shrugged. "He'd be unlikely to give me a bad report under the circumstances."

"*Tell me Chief Superintendent –*" Hendvorrsen began.

"*I had not finished with the candidate,*" Mueller said, and went on before Hendvorrsen could protest. "*Can you suggest why, if you are so valuable to your superior, why does he recommend you so warmly for this job?*"

"Perhaps he wants to get rid of me," said Nathan.

"*Why would you think that?*" asked Mueller with a small, triumphant smile.

"*Obviously,*" said Françoise Lancine, "*because no sensible executive wants people below them who are trop… uh… too clever. Can we get on, please? There are many calls on my time, and on the power I am using for this link.*"

"*I have not finished with the candidate,*" said Hendvorrsen, and paused for objections. When there were none, he said, "*How do you feel about the waste of resources the whole endeavour represents?*"

"The Star Cops?" Nathan asked, deliberately using the disparaging nickname.

"*Space exploration,*" said Hendvorrsen, who had a point to make.

"I suppose it is expensive," said Nathan, "if all we're going to be is tourists. But then again, where do you send the man who's been everywhere?"

"*A joke? You think of it as a joke?*" asked Lancine.

Nathan shook his head. "Where else is there for us to go?"

"*Good answer,*" Hendvorrsen said. "*It is The Last Great Adventure.*

The problem at the moment is that it is administered by fools, charlatans and rogues."

"My professional concern is only with the rogues, sir. The fools and charlatans I leave to your profession."

"*Good answer,*" said Lancine, making no attempt to hide her amusement.

"*You regard a police force as necessary out there?*" asked Yakasone.

"I regard it as inevitable, sir. Where there's living, there's policemen."

Neela Shah moved to close the proceedings. "*Do you have any questions for us?*" she asked.

Nathan smiled again and said, "What exactly *is* a Liaison Co-ordinator?"

"*It's Eurobabble for chairperson,*" she said. "*And, in that capacity, I must ask if you have any preference about which station you wish to visit for your acclimatization trials?*"

"Do you have one within commuting distance of say... Venice?" Nathan asked. When she smiled and lowered her eyes momentarily, he felt guilty, as though he'd actually been unfaithful to Lee.

"*The German candidate,*" said Mueller, "*has indicated the European station would be a logical choice.*"

So there was a German candidate, Nathan thought. That explained her attitude. "I wouldn't presume to quarrel with German logic, ma'am," he said.

"*I am arranging a fact-finding mission there myself,*" said Hendvorrsen. Nathan noticed Françoise Lancine react to this news, but she said nothing. "*I may seek you out,*" continued Hendvorrsen, "*so you can give me your assessments of the station's inefficiencies.*"

"Without prejudging the issue, *naturellement*," Lancine said dryly.

Shah said briskly, "*I will make the necessary arrangements, Chief Superintendent. In the meantime, I suggest you pay serious attention to the astronaut training. It's intended to fit you for a hostile environment.*"

"*Out here, you get very few chances to learn from your mistakes,*" Lancine said.

"I'll try to remember that."

"*Thank you, Chief Superintendent Spring. I'm sure I speak for the other board members when I say it's been a pleasure to meet you,*" said Shah and smiled. "*Ladies and gentlemen, the last candidate is waiting in Barcelona, if you would be kind enough to reset.*" As her hologram faded, Nathan was almost disappointed that her smile was not the last thing to disappear.

When they had all gone, he leaned back in his chair and sighed. "Some days," he said aloud to the empty room, "try as you will, nothing goes wrong."

Crime Scene

As the last of the cargo was being lifted by lunar tug to rendezvous with the freighter *Dædalus*, the loading manifest was still unchecked by the pilot. He had remained in quarters on Moonbase with his co-pilot – who was now naked, and had just taken his erection in one broad palmed, stubby fingered hand and eased it into place. He groaned softly as she began to push herself onto it, wriggling her hips very slightly from side to side. When he felt the slippery warmth begin he dug his fingers into her small round buttocks and lifted them so that he could thrust forwards.

"Slowly," she gasped.

"This is slowly," he grunted, thrusting in again so that she arched her back slightly, and wrapped her legs behind his as she raised her hips to meet him. Sex in one-sixth G is not easy but, as Mike and Lara had reason to know, the difficulties are as nothing compared to weightless fucking. It was understandable then that they should be making the most of their stay on Moonbase. For anyone who knew them, it was obvious that they would be having altogether too much fun to waste time on screenwork.

Operationally, all that was actually needed was for a pilot or co-pilot to initial the computer's freight listing and bill of lading. In practice, though, most cargo-jockeys ran an eye over what they were carrying and where it was stowed in the pods. Flying inter-orbit freighters like the *Dædalus*, flimsy and light-framed because they never made surface landings or lift-offs, it might just pay you to know how easily and cheaply you could jettison the more volatile items if the ship ran into a solar radiation front or a particle storm. It seldom happened – but survival, like luck, favours the prepared.

Mike and his co-pilot Lara were fucking when they should have been preparing. They were in love, which made them horny, careless and ideal murder victims. When they finally boosted the *Dædalus* out of lunar orbit, both pilot and co-pilot were already dead – though it would be several weeks into their flight to Mars before they or anyone else would realize that.

Chapter 5

"Why in the hell is this place so popular all of a sudden?" Theroux asked. "What have we got that the other orbit stations haven't?" He could have added: *apart from you as general manager*, but he didn't.

Lancine shrugged, and said as if answering the unspoken thought, "It was not my idea, believe me."

Theroux saw no particular reason why he should. "No publicity's bad publicity, huh?" he said.

"The only sort of publicity that accompanies Lars 'endvorrsen is bad. He is as you say a son of urh…"

"Sonofabitch?"

She nodded vigorously and said, "A scum-sucking son of a bitch, yes. And a problem we do not need at this time."

Theroux smiled. "A problem you do not need at this time," he said mildly. "I don't see that it has too much to do with me."

"Well, yes, but you are the law, are you not?"

"Yes and no. Mostly no."

"So you will be concerned by the visit."

"Now wait just a cotton-pickin' minute here. You're not trying to shuck this politician off on to me, are you?"

"You are the resident peace officer."

"Fine. If he disturbs the resident peace I'll bust his ass, otherwise he's yours, Madame Lancine."

"Please do call me Françoise."

"Françoise."

"As a favour to me, Daveed. I would not ask but you 'ave the Star Cop candidates, any 'ow."

"I do?"

"Surely there is no question about that."

Theroux took a long pull on the drink she'd had waiting for him when he got to her office. It was good coffee, at just the right temperature. Even the squeeze-pack it came in was tasteful, elegant almost. The woman had class. Pity she was such a devious bitch.

"I'd say there was a question about that," he said.

"What question?"

"Did you seriously imagine that if you threatened me with this Hendvorrsen guy, I'd accept responsibility for the others without thinking?"

"I do not understand."

"Yes you do."

"You are refusing to 'elp with any of these people, Inspector Theroux?"

"*Au contraire, Madame la directrice*. I'll help any way I can. But they're *your* visitors to *your* station." He released himself from the chair. "You could have put them off if you'd wanted."

"It was not in my power."

"It was not in your interest."

"You overestimate my authority."

"I know what authority station managers have. And the privileges that go with it." He put the stylish squeeze-pack into the top-of-the-range disposal unit. "Thanks for the coffee, Françoise," he said, and then, not bothering with the walking strip, propelled himself with lazy expertise towards the door. It was a minor breach of etiquette that gave him a lot more pleasure than was strictly rational.

Nathan – twenty-five micro-sensors stuck onto and into various parts of his person – plodded doggedly on, his pace dictated by the medical computer which controlled the exercise machine. He had been speeding up and slowing down at regular intervals for the best part of an hour, and he was getting bored.

"How much longer have I got to do this?" he asked, and was rewarded with a red light on the control panel.

"*This is a silent routine,*" said the computer. "*Accurate diagnosis depends on absolute adherence to instructions.*"

"I need a break," said Nathan.

"*There is no indication of distress,*" said the computer.

"I didn't say I was distressed, I said I needed a break."

"*There is no indicated requirement for physical relief of any kind.*"

"I have to talk to someone."

"*This is a silent routine,*" the computer repeated.

"Why am I arguing about this?" snapped Nathan, and palmed the abort and reset panel. As the belt stopped and he stepped off, he was irritated to see that ten minutes of the tests were being reset by the machine.

"Ten minutes? We can't have lost ten minutes." The machine remained silent. "Explain test reruns."

"*The subject's non-routine break was not included in the test hypothesis,*" said the computer. "*Findings are therefore invalidated. Investigation has been re-framed.*" The control board flashed up the green lights. "*Subject will indicate readiness by resuming position on the exercise belt.*"

"Bloody machine logic," muttered Nathan, as he crossed to the communications console and notified Lincoln's pager that he wanted him on full screen. "I haven't got time to waste on this."

When Lincoln came up on the screen a few moments later, he found Nathan lost in thought. "*You wanted a word?*" he asked, after waiting a decent interval.

Nathan looked at the screen. "How does a computer cope with the totally unexpected, Brian?"

Lincoln scratched his beard for a moment then said, "*I suppose, philosophically speaking, it can't. If it's unexpected, then it can't have been programmed for. And if it isn't programmed for...*"

"It's fucked," said Nathan. "And the converse?"

"*The converse of fucked?*"

Nathan shook his head, too absorbed to acknowledge the joke. "How does it deal with the totally expected?"

"*With a smile and a song?*"

"Where was Carmodie when he drowned?"

"*In the lake.*"

"Stop pissing about, Brian."

"*Sorry. I thought it was a trick question.*"

"I haven't got time for trick questions."

Lincoln smiled. "*I heard you were off into the wide blue yonder. I envy you.*"

"I wish I shared the general enthusiasm."

"*The Last Great Adventure?*"

Nathan grunted. "There's a little too much stress on 'last' for my taste."

"*Be glad to go in your place...*"

"You might get overexcited."

"*Me?*"

Nathan smiled for the first time since arriving at the Cambridge Centre for Space Medicine. "Over-enthusiastic, then. I don't intend to

Star Cops

take any risks with this situation, Brian."

"*Seems reasonable,*" said Lincoln, with the slightly doubtful expression of someone for whom it does not seem reasonable.

"You might just get carried away and get me the damn job."

Lincoln said, "*You mean, you don't want it?*" He looked genuinely surprised. "*I heard it was promotion to commander.*"

"Whereabouts in the lake was Carmodie when he drowned?" asked Nathan.

"*How can you not want promotion to commander?*"

"I prefer Sherlock Holmes to Dan Dare. Has Forensic done the calculations yet?"

Lincoln looked lost for a moment.

"For Christ's sake, Brian," Nathan said irritably, "I'm standing here with diagnostic probes in places where I didn't know I had places. Concentrate, will you. If I have a fucking short-circuit and fry something useful, you'll pay with something equally tender, believe me. Exactly whereabouts in the lake was Carmodie when he drowned?"

Lincoln opened a window in the top corner of the screen and played the forensic computer's reconstruction in it. The machine had taken the moment when the man had lost consciousness, the timing of which was accurate to within five minutes, and used wind speed, water circulation, drag coefficients, body weight – a whole series of variables – to calculate back from where he was found to where he was drowned.

"*They're pressing for a budget number on this stuff,*" said Lincoln.

"Don't worry about it," Nathan said, his mood improving rapidly as he watched the concluding computer animation.

Behind him a medical supervisor bustled into the test area. "Is there a problem Chief Superintendent?" she asked.

Nathan turned from the screen. "No. No problem."

"Only if we are to prescribe flight medication, the computer has five more hours of tests to run."

"Five hours?"

"That's assuming it doesn't have to cope with any further unscheduled hold-ups."

"Look, isn't there some way to speed this up?" said Nathan. "I need to get back to work."

The supervisor looked dubious. "There is a single test which could provide all the data. I don't recommend it though. It's our equivalent of one of those whatyacallit… heroic surgical procedures?"

"*We're all heroes in Crime Division,*" said Lincoln from the screen at Nathan's back.

The woman peered round Nathan and smiled. She had, it seemed, a soft spot for men with beards. "In these circumstances," she said, "'heroic' never refers to the patient. Take my word for it."

"How long is this test?" asked Nathan.

"You could be on your way in an hour. Possibly."

"Can you set it up for me?"

"If you're sure." The medical supervisor left, still smiling, and Nathan turned back to the screen.

"*Could have been a mistake,*" said Lincoln. "*I didn't like the sound of that.*"

"Make sure this forensic data stays live and online, Brian."

Lincoln shrugged. "*If you say so. I don't see that it helps us much.*"

"It proves murder," said Nathan. "And that it was professional. Two mechanics, at a guess, using scuba gear and probably lifted in and out by chopper."

"*Any offers as to names and social security codes?*" Lincoln asked cheerfully.

"Maybe whoever paid for the hit can tell us that, but I doubt it."

"*And you know who that is, of course,*" smiled Lincoln.

"Yes?" enquired Nathan.

Lincoln shook his head. "*I meant, you, specifically, know who that is,*" he said.

"Oh," said Nathan. "In that case. Yes."

For once Butler's sense of the ridiculous seemed inadequate for the situation, and he did not so much as raise a quizzical eyebrow as he said, "Three ambitious cops and an egomaniacal politician?"

"What other sort is there?" Theroux said.

"Cop or politician?" asked Butler – then, without waiting for the obvious reaction, went on, "It would be a recipe for disaster even if they had experience and we had spare cabin space and life-support," at the same time as checking a target on the long-range radar, confirming the departure of a freighter from lunar orbit en route for the Mars colony and logging the sighting.

On the local scan, Theroux cued computer enhancement of the

Star Cops

Earth-Moon shuttle only to find that what he was locked onto was just an aggregation of the drifting junk which cluttered most of the standard orbits. It was a growing problem despite lucrative contracts handed out to private salvage companies. "Godfuckit," he muttered, "what do those garbage sweeping bastards do for their money?"

"Our money," said Butler. "And whatever it is wouldn't seem to feature sweeping, though one assumes they must scoop up the occasional 'o' ring or the odd explosive bolt, if only for appearances."

"You see any sign of it?"

"Perhaps someone should run the numbers. Check the projections."

"You volunteering?"

Butler said, "I thought you might want to. Checking seems to be your thing these days." He smirked a little. "Bring your Star Cop training to bear. Impress your new boss when he visits us."

"Simon. You're a shithead," said Theroux, cueing a wider search across the jumble of radar targets, and again failing to find the Earth-Moon shuttle. "Have you logged E-M transit?" he asked.

"Lift-off was down twenty," Butler said without looking at his screen prompts, "picked up five on initial boost, transit commencement predicted in fourteen."

"Thanks for warning me."

Butler shrugged. "I didn't realize you still couldn't tell shit from shuttle," he said.

"Without the computer, nobody can," Theroux said. "Not even you."

"Don't take any bets on that, David old love," Butler said, and Theroux realized that his friend was probably one of the few people who could tell at a glance what the radars were showing. Jumble wasn't jumble if you knew what wasn't jumble, he thought, but he was fucked if he was going to tell the smug bastard that.

"And don't take any bets on the climbing frog's school fete and open day being anything other than a fiasco," Butler went on. "A dangerous fiasco, to boot."

"Fiasco I'll go with, but dangerous?" Theroux reached for the half-eaten chocolate bar that was in his console clip. "They'll have basic training for Chrissakes." He fumbled the chocolate, and it drifted away from his hand. "Fuckit," he said flatly, trapping the free-falling bar between finger and thumb. He glanced guiltily across at Butler, but he seemed to be totally absorbed in the screens. He thought he had gotten away with it when Butler said, with such delicate amusement that it was hard to be sure it was there, "No substitute for experience," adding without change of tone, "and you owe the loose-box a dollar."

"How did that count?" Theroux said.

"Floating free," said Butler. "Whatever it was."

"Whatever it was?"

"You always say 'fuckit' like that when you let something go." Butler took a savorysoupasnackpack from his equipment pouch and twisted the flow-tube. "You know what I miss most?" he said, while he waited for the contents to thicken and warm through.

"Eating with a knife and fork," said Theroux.

Butler sighed. "Do you ever get the feeling we've been out here too long?"

Nathan stepped down into the snug, windowless metal and plastic compartment, and sat in the contoured seat. "*Place your arms in the armrests with the palms of your hands facing downwards.*" The control computer had been given a soft female voice, presumably because this was felt to be calming. "*Place your feet in the footrests and relax. The seat will now adjust to fit you exactly. This is for your own safety. Please do not attempt to move around while adjustment is in progress.*"

"*And afterwards, you won't be able to,*" said the voice of the medical supervisor cheerfully over the inboard communication circuit. "*There was nothing to indicate any history of claustrophobia,*" she went on, "*so I trust this won't be a problem for you.*"

Padded bracing closed over Nathan's arms and legs, and the seat inflated slightly around his back, his shoulders, his neck and the back of his head. The sensation was not unpleasant, but he found that he was indeed unable to move at all. "Be a hell of a time to find out," he said.

"*That's what we're all here for, Chief Superintendent. To find out what makes you tick, and adjust the clockwork as necessary.*"

"Where exactly is the 'here' that we're all for? I don't see much sign of you. I seem to be the only one who is actually... *here*."

"*Didn't the computer say?*" The medical supervisor sounded surprised.

"Policemen and liars need good memories," Nathan said, remembering the smile on her face when he asked for this test. "I don't usually need the same information twice."

"*Sorry. Our fault entirely. The computer's on N-A-C. Non-Alarming*

Star Cops

Calming mode?"

"It isn't working," said Nathan irritably.

"*I can see that from your readouts. What you're in is a multi-directional centrifuge.*"

The muted whine of the apparatus powering up did nothing to help Nathan's sudden nausea, as he realized just what his impatience was about to cost him.

"*Spins, rolls, pitches, turns: all controlled to a seven-G peak,*" said the medical supervisor – or maybe it was the computer reset to an Alarming Non-Calming mode, Nathan's capacity to distinguish such niceties already deserting him. "*There's no need to panic,*" the voice continued, "*we haven't lost a patient yet.*"

"I hope this contraption has easy-clean surfaces," said Nathan.

"*That's the spirit. A sense of humour'll get you through anything.*"

"I wasn't joking," Nathan said. Then the first acceleration hit him – and though there was nothing moving in the totally enclosed compartment, he shut his eyes anyway, and began to take deep gulping breaths as he tried not to throw up; he turned his mind to the Carmodie case and concentrated on checking his solution again; he hoped against hope that this might stop him from vomiting. It didn't.

The woman was sitting behind her husband's desk when they served the arrest warrant.

"Mrs. Lisa Carmodie," Brian Lincoln said, though Nathan found himself thinking bizarrely that she ought really to be addressed as Widow Carmodie, "You are arrested and detained for the murder of John Leon Carmodie."

The plump, dowdy woman looked puzzled, confused, disbelieving. It was a careful performance spoiled only by the eyes which were cool and watchful.

"You are not obliged to answer police questions," Lincoln continued, "but any refusal will be recorded together with any and all answers and the complete record of interviews, commencing now" – he indicated the linked vision recorders they had set at each side of the room – "will be made available to the examining authority. Do you understand?"

"No."

"You do not understand what I have said?" asked Lincoln, formally. "Do you wish me to repeat what I have said? Do you wish an interpreter to be activated?"

"I understand the words," said the Widow Carmodie, "but I don't understand what's happening." She looked at Nathan with those sharp grey eyes, and said in a nervous, pleading voice, "Can you explain what's happening, Chief Superintendent Spring?"

Nathan thought: *I expect you're all wondering why I've called you here to the library, well one of you is a murderer...* and then realized, as he waited for Lincoln to complete the caution, that the space-flight medication they had given him was having definite side effects.

Lincoln said, "Duty advisers are on database file PIC-CD-DA 1thru7 if you need help to which you do not have immediate access. Do you understand what I have said?"

"Yes I understand."

Nathan said, "Ms. Carmodie, we have established that your husband could not have drifted to where he was found from where he actually drowned. So he must have been placed where he was found."

"You mean he drowned somewhere else and someone took him to that lake?"

"No, that's not what I mean."

She folded her hands on the desk in front of her and looked earnest, interested and not very bright. "I don't understand," she said.

Nathan thought: No, and if you keep your nerve and stick to that approach, you might just get away with it, because what I've got's distinctly skinny. He said, "Your husband drowned in the middle of the lake. He could not have simply drifted to where he was found in the time available."

"Can you tell that?" she asked.

Nathan decided it was time to remove the barrier which the desk put between them. He moved to look at the contents of a bookcase on the wall to one side of the desk.

The woman turned her attention to Lincoln and redirected the rest of the question at him. "Can they really tell whereabouts in the water someone drowned?"

Nathan said, "I have a witness who can place your husband in the middle of the lake at the time of his death."

Her shock was genuine as she said, "Someone saw him die?" and turned towards Nathan. He could see her feet braced tight against the desk so that there would be no unconscious fidgeting to betray her. She really is remarkable, he thought.

Star Cops

"Someone saw him almost every day, at almost the same time."

"Almost?" she asked, and Nathan knew that in the end, she was not quite clever enough to hide her cleverness.

"He had always reached the same point in his swim."

"Did they see him that day?"

"Your husband had routines for everything, I think you said."

"They didn't see him that day, did they?" she repeated.

"A very meticulous man, you called him? Obsessive even."

"I didn't say he was obsessive," she said.

"That's right, you didn't," Nathan said and smiled. "You have a good memory."

"You borrowed money from your husband's partner," Lincoln said. "Why?"

"I paid it back."

"That's not what I asked."

"I didn't use it."

"You got it in cash. Why did you want cash?"

Nathan thought: *because contract killers don't give credit.*

"I don't think that's funny. I don't think you should make jokes about things like that," the Widow Carmodie said sharply.

Nathan looked at Lincoln's expression, and it occurred to him that he must have spoken the thought aloud. "I seem to be having some sort of reaction to the stuff they gave me in Cambridge," he said. "I'm sorry about this."

"Are you all right, sir?" Lincoln said as if he had not heard.

Did I say that or not? thought Nathan.

"Did you say what?"

Nathan shook his head and gestured for Lincoln to continue with the interrogation.

Lincoln shrugged, and turned back to the woman. "When you got the cash what did you do with it?"

"Do with it?"

"It was a lot of money. What did you do with it? Did you carry it around with you? Did you hide it? What?"

"I carried it with me."

"At all times?"

"Yes."

"And your husband never noticed?"

"Why should he?"

"It's bulky. Did you carry it under your clothes?"

"Under my clothes?"

"In a belt? A money belt?"

"Oh. Yes. Yes I kept it in a money belt."

"Yet your husband never saw it, or felt it?"

"My husband never looked at me," she said. "As for feeling it…" Her face remained expressionless as she let the sentence die.

"Tell me why you wanted the money," asked Lincoln again. "Tell me what it was for."

The woman stared, as if trying to make up her mind whether to confide in him or not. This could have been an important moment in the interrogation. This could have been the moment when she was ready to give up a little of what she had been trying to hold back. Pass this moment successfully, and you could take her all the way to the truth. That was clearly what Lincoln saw. But Nathan knew she was playing games. He knew too that he had some problems of perception.

"You borrowed cash," he said slowly, and waited to see if they looked at him; they did; so he went on but still quite slowly, "to pay for your husband to be killed." Though obviously for different reasons, Lincoln and the Widow Carmodie both looked surprised by the manner of the interruption. "Once he was dead," Nathan went on, "you sold some of his antiques and paid back the money you had borrowed."

"That's what all this is about?" Mrs. Carmodie said. "That's what makes you think I murdered him?"

Nathan looked round the room as though cataloguing the missing items. "A clock, a small oil painting, two china dogs, a paperweight." Lincoln and the Widow Carmodie were waiting for him to speak. Nathan concentrated and said slowly and distinctly, "A clock, a small oil painting, two china dogs, a paperweight."

"I honestly have no idea what it is you're talking about," said Mrs. Carmodie. "I did not kill my husband."

"You bought it done," said Nathan, "it's the same thing." And then, because there was no longer any way he could tell thought from speech, he went to her and held out his hand. Warily, she placed her hand in his, and after a moment he pulled her gently up out of the chair so that she stood facing him. He did not let go of her hand. "I would have noticed," he said and thought. "You're too remarkable to hide from me."

She stared at him. This time she *was* deciding whether to confide in him or not.

"I realize I should have worked this out for myself," Lincoln said, bringing a fresh pot of coffee from Nathan's kitchen, "but was there a reason why they shoved Carmodie's body into the shallows? I mean, you wouldn't expect mistakes for the sort of money she paid, would you? Or would you?"

"It wasn't a mistake. They were trying to fool us, which means they were trying to fool our computer. It was supposed to look like an accident. As far as the computer is concerned, accidents can be expected in a dangerous environment like water, unless there's something to indicate otherwise. Once Carmodie's death had been classified as a routine drowning, that would have been it. No investigation, no problem. But for that to happen there had to be a body. They put it in the shallows because they couldn't risk letting it sink. That would have been a disappearance. Chances are we'd have investigated a disappearance."

"No?" Lincoln shrugged. "Okay," he said, "but I still think there had to be a reason."

Nathan was on his fourth cup of coffee when he finally got the medical supervisor on screen. "There appear to be some contra-indications to this shit you've given me," he said.

"*Yes Chief Superintendent Spring?*" she said. "*What can I do for you?*"

Lincoln said, "Shall I?"

Nathan nodded.

"There appear to be some contra-indications to this stuff you've given him," he said.

"*Oh shit!*" she said. "*I knew we shouldn't have tried to rush things. Sit tight, I'll run the data and get back to you.*"

"One thing you can tell me about that interrogation," said Lincoln as they waited. "Why did you keep calling her Widow Carmodie? What was the strategy there?"

Crime Scene

They had been on the outward leg for several weeks now, and there was still no sign of anything worthwhile. Marty, ever cautious, wanted to call it off and head back for Moonbase. He reckoned to pick up a routine trash run, which would at least cover the next payment on the ship and some of the losses they were clocking up on this trip. The thing of it was, he said, the longer they went on the bigger the score would have to be to make any sort of profit for them. They were bound to reach a point sooner or later – sooner in his view – when it would be very unlikely that they could make a profit, no matter what it was they found. Assuming they found anything which, again in his view, was very unlikely.

Lauter felt that for a young man – youngish anyway, certainly a good bit younger than her – Marty lacked enterprise. He was a percentage player. Had been as long as she'd known him. But no-one made a fortune playing the percentages, and if they didn't take a few chances they weren't ever going to make enough to get out of the salvage business. Years of graft, and what did they have to show for it? A second-hand cargo shuttle they still owed money on. Well, she was tired of it. Or maybe she was just tired. But whichever it was, this could be the biggest score of their lives, their best chance at the brass ring, and she had made up her mind that they were going for it. Marty would have to live with it this time. She was the pilot, she was the senior partner, and if the information she'd been given was right…

"If the information was right, this could be the biggest score any independent has ever made," she said for the umpteenth time.

"It's still a bloody big 'if'," Marty said, "and it's not getting any smaller."

"It's got to be worth trying for," she insisted. "We could be rich and famous."

"I hate to piss on your boosters, Lauter, but if what that drunken journo told you really was kosher –"

Lauter interrupted angrily, "She wasn't a drunken journo."

"She was legless every time I saw her."

"She couldn't get used to moon-G that was all."

"Okay," Marty said patiently, "okay. But drunk or just a gravitational underachiever, if the information was genuine, how come none of the big boys are looking?"

If there was one thing she hated about him, and right now there was more than one thing she hated about him, she hated it when he was patient. "They don't know about it!" she snapped.

"Which means it either doesn't exist, or the whole thing is as bent as a three-dollar note."

"Marty, dear heart," she said through gritted teeth, "bent is not our problem. Cash is our problem."

"You could be something of a crook if I let you," he said. "Isn't that right?"

"We are going on," she said. "I don't care what you say. We are going on."

"I know," he said, without any sign of surprise or resentment.

Lauter began a period of dignified sulking, but got bored with it after a little while and said, "You are a miserable bugger, Marty."

"One of us has to be," he replied gloomily.

"It's a good thing you've got a nice bum or I'd have found myself a new partner years ago."

"If you'd been with anyone but me," Marty said, "you'd have gone broke years ago."

"Feels like I did," she said.

It would take more long weeks to get any sort of confirmation that there might be something to what the journalist had told Lauter that night on Moonbase, after the Guild of Independent Space-Salvage Hauliers annual booze-up and shagathon. It would take much longer for them to find out that 'bent as a three-dollar note' did not begin to describe the situation.

Chapter 6

He had expected to be heavy and clumsy, but it came as a shock to find how vulnerable it made him feel. He had tunnel vision, a sort of numbness and partial paralysis of the limbs, and an itch in his crotch which there would be no possibility of scratching for several hours. They had assured him that in the weightless vacuum of space it would be less cumbersome, and the fierce hostility of that environment would make it as comforting as his mother's womb, but on present evidence it seemed to Nathan unlikely that he would ever be at ease in a spacesuit.

"Damn, blast and double fuck it!" he shouted into the muffled acoustic of his helmet, as the spanner slipped and he dropped it yet again.

He watched it fall away through the water, but before it reached the bottom of the training tank one of the scuba divers rolled down in a lazy glide and caught it with a flourish, like a kid diving for tourist coins.

The voice of the principal instructor crackled in Nathan's ear. "*I don't think language like that helps anybody, does it, sir?*"

"It helps me!" Nathan snapped back.

"*You mean if you stayed calm, you'd drop the spanner more often?*" the voice enquired politely.

Nathan turned and peered towards the observation port where the instructor was standing. With difficulty he flexed his armoured fist and gave him the finger.

From beyond the glass, the instructor waved back. "*Very good, Mr. Spring,*" said the voice in Nathan's ear. "*I told you those gloves were fully articulated once you got used to them. Before you know it, you'll be able to wave with your whole hand.*"

The scuba diver did a victory roll as he returned the spanner. Nathan signalled his thanks and said, smiling, "And you can get fucked as well," as he took a firm grip on the tool and turned back to the mock-up station module he was supposed to be repairing. He finished tightening the faulty joint and moved on. If this was the nearest thing to weightlessness available on the Earth's surface, then he'd better get as much from it as he could. He

Star Cops

didn't want to get the Star Cops job, but he didn't want to get dead either. He lumbered towards the gantry where the next task awaited him. "Oh, look at this," he muttered.

"*You will see that two of the PVAs are burnt out,*" intoned the instructor. "*You'll need to remove them and get replacements from the equipment bay.*"

"I'm a copper, not the Wichita Lineman," Nathan muttered, as he searched his equipment belt for the appropriate tool.

"*Without functioning photovoltaics there wouldn't be much to sing about out there,*" said the instructor and promptly filled Nathan's helmet with a loud and tuneless rendition of the old song, which was currently enjoying a revival as a corporate advertising jingle. "*I'm not distracting you, am I?*" he asked, after singing the verse and three choruses.

"I assume it's a test of my concentration," commented Nathan, concentrating fiercely on not dropping the small cutter he was using to free the array of power cells.

"*No, I just like to sing,*" responded the instructor cheerfully. "*Bear in mind that the thermic tip on that scalpel will cut through anything.*"

"Yes."

"*It's probably not a good idea to rest your free hand on what you're cutting.*"

Nathan reacted immediately, jerking his hand back, losing concentration, and letting go of the scalpel, which switched itself off and fell away.

"*Oh dear, oh dear.*" The instructor's voice was smug. "*I can see you making a real contribution to the space litter problem, sir.*"

Furious with himself, Nathan lunged out and snatched at the drifting scalpel. He missed. A scuba diver was already moving to collect it. Without thinking, Nathan reached out his arm with his hand open and launched himself from the gantry.

"*Not a good idea, Mr. Spring!*". The instructor's voice was neither smug nor amused now.

Nathan ignored him. He was falling out and down, but there was little sensation of movement. He reached for the scalpel, and when he thought he was close enough, he grabbed. Feeling no contact, he was slightly surprised to see it spin. He tried again but now he watched his hand, moving it more slowly and using only vision to guide him, as though he was operating a remote control device. He stopped the scalpel spinning and caught it easily this time and, with moments to spare, he adjusted his fall so that he hit the bottom of the tank feet first. He waved the scalpel at the scuba diver, who swam round him checking for damage to the suit. In his helmet the voice of the instructor was coolly matter-of-fact. *"Out there, there is no bottom to the tank, sir. Whatever the direction you push off in, that is the direction you'll fall in. Forever."*

"I knew that," said Nathan.

"Then behave as though you did. We train survivors here not fucking jugglers!"

"I don't think language like that helps anybody, does it?" said Nathan.

Theroux was sleeping soundly when the wake-up whispered to him. He came to abruptly, unzipped the bag and pushed himself out of the frame. He was tense and unrefreshed, but he knew from experience that this would pass once he got focused and moving.

The ergonomics specialists agreed that sleeping in zero-G was best done upright in what amounted to a large papoose-carrier attached to the wall. In an environment where 'up' was arbitrary, with everyone simply agreeing which direction it should be, there could be no possible difficulties with the upright sleep frames. They were efficient, safe and relaxing. Except that at the instant of falling asleep, and for the few seconds it took to wake up, they were anything but relaxing. The problem was panic, as the sleeper's brain demanded the submission to gravity which lying down had represented during a short and stressful evolution. Horizontal orientation of the frames was pointless since 'horizontal' was as fundamentally meaningless in zero-G as 'up' or 'down'; but for those who tried it, like other equally meaningless wacsobs, it did seem to help. For most people, though, there were simpler explanations for their brief exhaustions, and there was much talk of biorhythms, mineral depletion and vitamin loss. As they acclimatized, everyone slept better. But the falling asleep and the waking never seemed to improve.

Theroux heated a coffee pack and looked blearily at the other six zombies who were working the second-eight shift. Clutching coffee and the products of industrial food processing, they were attaching themselves to the seats of the cramped mess module. None of them was a cheerful breakfaster – least of all Simon Butler who seemed this day-start to have settled only for the 'unlimited choice of premium beverages' option.

"Not hungry?" asked Theroux, as he settled next to him.

"Egg'n'baconmacburger? What's that got to do with being hungry?" snapped Butler.

Star Cops

"There's other stuff on the menu."

"An egg'n'baconmacburger by any other name. I still can't work out how your countrymen got the catering franchise on the European station."

Theroux shrugged. "It's called competitive tendering," he said. Then, as the coffee hit and he began to feel better, he added, "It's the good old reliable, capitalist way. I thought you were all in favour of that."

"I bet the Japanese don't have to put up with that stuff."

"Egg'n'whalemacburger, they tell me. You want some more coffee?"

"It's tea, and no, I don't. Thank you."

Theroux looked at his friend solemnly, and then smiled. "They reallocated your cabin too, huh?" he said, taking a bite of the breakfastburger bun and chewing stoically.

"Is that a guess," asked Butler, "or did you have something to do with it?"

Theroux swallowed the piece of bun and shook his head vigorously. "Uh-uh. Ain't no way I'd get involved in any of that. Cabin allocation? Men have died and worms have eaten them, but not for love. But for cabin allocation? You bet your ass."

Butler did not smile. "I'm not sure they can treat someone of my grade in this fashion," he said, his languid Englishman pose slipping towards pompous petulance. "Proper cabin facilities are a specified part of my contract. There were no riders about giving them up for politicians and cops."

"I bet your union's hopping mad," Theroux said, as he opened the remains of his bun and peered at the contents. "How can this shit be nutritionally optimal if you can't eat it?" he asked of no-one in particular.

Butler ignored him and went on, "That bloody Lancine woman has gone too far this time."

"If it's any consolation," Theroux said, "I'm sharing with two of the cops."

"No. It isn't any consolation."

Theroux gave up on his examination of the breakfastburger. "With my luck, they'll snore. Or barf everywhere. God, I hate chasing vomit globules around the place. Still, it beats eating this crap, I guess." He shoved the breakfastburger into the disposal bag. "Have you ever noticed how really disgusting sick smells as an aerosol?"

He grinned at Butler who finally remembered that whining lacked style and said, "I suppose if one of them was a rampant sausage jockey –"

"I'm sorry?"

"If one of your bunkmates turned out to be a fudgepacker, it might be some sort of consolation."

"An introduction, is that what we're talking here?" Theroux asked, with an open-faced innocence which was only just overdone.

Butler smiled thinly. "Perhaps industrial action is the answer," he mused. "If I withdraw my labour, the bastards couldn't get here at all which would make stealing my cabin somewhat problematical for them. And Shakespeare doesn't count, by the way. In case you were looking to turn a small profit from my discomfiture?"

Theroux looked blank. Butler said, "Men have died, and worms have eaten them?"

Theroux grinned. "Oh that. I was just showing off."

"Shall we go to work?"

"You were impressed, I can tell."

Theroux and Butler detached themselves from the mess table. Around them, the other workers were dumping the remains of their breakfasts into the disposals and preparing to make a move to their various workstations. As they filed out, everyone used the cramped heel-and-toe step which kept at least one of their Velcro soled slippers in contact at all times with the walking strip on the floor. Nobody floated.

It was a convention, in most of the orbit stations, that regular personnel never floated in the presence of others when it was possible to walk. This had started as a professionals' game, a demonstration of skill, but quite soon it became a routine which was used to separate the clumsy groundsider from regular off-Earthers. Once this had happened, it was only a matter of time before the routine became a ritual, a question of good manners and proper etiquette. To be an off-Earther was not yet to be a member of a new social class, but the professional group which earned its living in space was working on it.

"At least," said Theroux, as he and Butler waited their turn to file out, "they gave us fair warning."

"Well woop-de-doo," Butler murmured sourly.

"Politicians have been known to creep up on targets like this. 'Specially creeps like Hendvorrsen."

Butler scowled. "Nobody creeps up on the climbing frog," he said. "She's one of Nature's planners." Then he suddenly smiled a small, self-contained smile. "But we still can't rule out the possibility of it all going pear-shaped for her, can we? I mean, there's nothing to beat a few groundsider tourists to fuck up the best planned operations."

On the completion of his course, Nathan was issued with a Certificate of Space Flight Competence. This CSFC did not mean he was competent to undertake a space flight, but it was required if he was to get legal insurance cover to leave Earth.

The training had been intensive but brief, and at the end of it he was aware of how little he could remember of what he had been told. Suit pressure adjustments, warning telltales, emergency systems, elapsed time equalizations, RT procedures, self-medication requirements and dosages: the list was long, clearly essential and deeply boring.

"How much of this stuff am I actually supposed to remember?" he had asked at one stage.

"All of it!" the instructor had shouted, and then added, "If you didn't need to know it, we wouldn't be telling it to you now would we, sir?" with that ponderous irony which Nathan thought never to hear again once he'd graduated from the police college.

Initially it struck him as odd that these high frontier trainers were so old-fashioned. He found himself wondering whether the criminals out there were just as traditional, and what that might mean for the ISPF and its methods.

When he thought about it, the idea of crime in space began to intrigue him, and he would have found the exploration of such case histories as there were mildly interesting if it was not for one serious drawback.

And he was sitting in a major element of that drawback right now.

The midday shuttle to the European Space Station *Charles De Gaulle* was close to lift-off from the Kourou spaceport in French Guyana.

The countdown was in its final stages:

T minus sixty seconds and counting.

In contrast to the tropical humidity outside, it was cool and fresh in the passenger cabin, but that was all there was to recommend it as far as Nathan was concerned. He would have been more than happy to forgo the benefits of air-conditioning for the rest of his life if he could have got back onto the ground right now.

T minus fifty-five and counting.

Of course, that would not be too much of a sacrifice, since, as far as he could see, the rest of his life was going to be a fairly short period of time.

Time was what he lacked now.

Time was eroding, second by second.

His life was being counted out, second by second.

And he could see it happening in front of him, and he was helpless to stop it or control it, or very soon to control himself...

T minus forty-five and counting.

It was customary for the final countdown to show on the liquid crystal display above each seat. Most passengers preferred to know how the count was progressing, but for those who did not, the individual information and communications consoles had control panels set in the arms of the seats. Each infocomcon had an array of displays available: entertainment, news, down-line computer links, interactive voice/vision channels.

T minus thirty-five and counting.

It was possible for a passenger to talk to friends, family, psychotherapist, priest: or the meter-a-medic, dial-a-divine public paycall equivalents.

T minus twenty-five and counting.

They could take care of business, or relax to soothing sounds and images.

T minus twenty and counting.

And yet, with all these options open to them, most people sat silently watching the countdown tick away.

T minus fifteen and counting.

How many of them were fighting panic – as Nathan himself was – and how many were actually interested, it was difficult to judge.

T minus ten and counting.

Nathan had the feeling

nine

that it would only take one person to lose it

eight

and begin to yell and

seven

the whole damn

six

passenger compartment

five

would become

four

a seething mass

three
of
two
scrambling
one
bodies
ignition sequence
he just hoped it wasn't him
lift-off
who broke first.

The thrust hit, slamming Nathan back into the shock-absorber padding of the acceleration seat. He closed his eyes and thought of England as his stomach sank and his weight rose. The noise of the engines was surprisingly low but the vibration – '*You will experience some vibration in the initial phase of the flight, this is quite normal*' – pushed up towards a teeth-shattering intensity which nothing could possibly...

"Is there anything I can get for you, Chief Superintendent?"

He opened his eyes, and looked up at the flight attendant who was standing in the aisle, feet gracefully braced, one hand lightly holding the grasp rail on the side of the seat. The vibration had stopped. Everything had stopped. It was quite eerily quiet. The flight attendant smiled her professional smile. "Is there anything I can get you?" she repeated.

Nathan tried to smile back, but had the feeling that what twisted his face was more grimace than grin. "Are we out of parachute range?" he asked.

"I'm afraid so, sir. Would you care to visit the flight deck perhaps?"

The thought of having to move from his seat sent a wave of nausea through Nathan, leaving his face damp and chilly. He swallowed his smile, breathed deeply, swallowed again and said, "Somebody breaking the law up there?" as he forced the smile back into place.

"One of your colleagues expressed an interest in seeing it."

Irritation overcame his motion sickness. "My German colleague, I imagine."

"Yes, that's right," said the flight attendant.

"And presumably Representative Hendvorrsen is on the flight deck already?"

"Yes, he is."

"Must be getting pretty crowded up there."

"Your Spanish colleague... Superintendent Sanchez? ...he is planning to join them."

"Got to be against the rules surely," asked Nathan hopefully. "Flight safety regulations or something?"

"It's entirely at the captain's discretion."

"Then thank the captain for me, but I think I'll just stay here and die."

"If you change your mind, just let me know," said the flight attendant, and moved on down the aisle. Nathan noticed that the heel-and-toe walk which kept her feet anchored to the walking strip gave her bottom an appealing extra wiggle. At least, it would have been appealing if he had been feeling a little better. He had read somewhere that seasoned space-workers never floated if they could walk. He wondered vaguely if that was why.

"Eurostat, Eurostat, this is Euroshuttle five inbound on green two, twelve minutes flight time remaining, estimated docking twelve zero one GMT confirm please."

Butler glanced across at Theroux and raised his eyebrows slightly. "We're very formal today. Who's flying, do you know? It's not that piss-artist Johnson is it?"

Theroux shrugged. "Didn't sound like him."

"Do you copy, Eurostat?" persisted the shuttle pilot.

"No, that's not Johnson," said Theroux.

"You can do the honours," Butler said.

"Me?"

"They're your coppers."

"You sure this doesn't make me a strike-breaker?"

Theroux switched on his throat mic. "Euroshuttle five Euroshuttle five this is Eurostat, confirm green two, ETD twelve zero one GMT. Very formal today guys, and almost on time too. Who've you got running the railway now, Mussolini? Hey, you haven't put in for another salary review, have you?"

"Eurostat, Eurostat, this is Euroshuttle Five, listening out."

Theroux flicked off the mic and frowned. "Was it something I said?" he asked looking at Butler who suddenly said, "When is Hendvorrsen supposed to be due?"

Before Theroux could answer, the shuttle pilot came on again. *"Eurostat, this is Euroshuttle five."*

"Copy Euroshuttle five," Theroux said.

"*Sorry about that. Representative Lars Hendvorrsen and a couple of brown-noses were on the flight deck.*"

"Shit!" said Theroux over the open mic.

"*That was pretty much my reaction.*" The pilot's voice was amused. "*We didn't get any notice either.*"

"I knew it," muttered Butler in the background. "That sneaky bastard!"

"He isn't due for another two days," Theroux said.

"*How does ten minutes grab you?*" asked the pilot.

Butler cut across the transmission. "It doesn't do a lot for us," he said gleefully, "but it's going to be a joyful surprise for our esteemed station manager."

Theroux closed his mic. "You gonna let her know, or am I?"

Butler was smiling broadly. "Why don't we wait ten minutes or so, and let her find out for herself?"

While Nathan waited for the shuttle to complete its approach manoeuvres, he experimented with weightlessness by floating a coin in front of him and poking it around. He immediately formulated another theory about why experienced people avoided floating: looking at it did not help your feelings of queasiness at all. He also revised his attitude to crime in space. It couldn't happen. No-one could function well enough in this miserable environment to care about wealth or power or love in its many and destructive forms. You needed motives for crimes. Out here, who could possibly sustain a motive? 'Where there's living, there's policemen' was what he had always maintained. Well, clearly, this was the exception that proved the rule. Except that it wouldn't be. And he knew it wouldn't be. What he didn't know was that crimes set in motion long before he left Earth were developing even now, and that the first was going to happen very soon and very close.

Chapter 7

"Theoretically, anyone who 'as been issued with a CSFC is competent to undertake a spacewalk. But theory and practice are not the same thing." Françoise Lancine glared across her desk at Lars Hendvorrsen. She could not decide what mistake it was that he was trying to force her to make. He had arrived two days early without any warning and now he was insisting that while he was here he wanted to inspect the progress of the new construction.

"I have taken all the necessary courses in Extra Vehicular Activity," he insisted. "My instructors congratulated me on my instinctive understanding of the procedures."

"I'm sure they did," Lancine said, not quite managing to keep the scorn out of her voice. "For obvious reasons, they very seldom tell VIPs they are a menace to themselves and everyone around them."

Hendvorrsen looked bored. "You may trust my judgement on this," he said. "I know when I am being told the truth."

"Then you will know that I am saying the truth when I tell you that EVAs are not for amateurs."

"What are you trying to hide, Ms. Lancine?"

"What is it that you expect to find, Mr. 'Endvorrsen?"

"I expect to find the answer to where a great deal of public money, taxpayers' hard-earned money, has been wasted."

"I will tell you where it 'as not been wasted!" snapped Lancine. "It 'as not been wasted on safety procedures for our workers."

"The people will be as shocked as I am to hear you admit that," Hendvorrsen almost whispered, as he contrived to sound suitably shocked.

"I am sure they will," Lancine sneered, "but the point is that if I cannot guarantee the safety of experienced workers, 'ow can I guarantee *your* safety?"

"Am I to regard that as a threat?"

"I am not in the business of making threats."

* * *

"This is the police office, gentlemen." Theroux folded back the stiff plastic door curtain, and showed the three candidates the quarter-module which was the ISPF's allocation on the station.

The German pulled himself inside. He was obviously determined to be positive and thrusting, and demonstrate all those other important leadership qualities which selection boards liked. He floated across to the equipment console and pulled himself down to look at the terminals. He was followed closely by the Spaniard who had clearly been on the same management courses and did not intend to be outshone. Both seemed quite comfortable with zero-G. In fact, they both seemed to be enjoying the sensation of floating.

The Englishman stayed outside the door. He looked to be the youngest of the three and definitely the sickest, and he was, Theroux noticed, making clumsy efforts to resist weightlessness. His feet were braced on the walking strip, and he was holding the grasp rail as though his life depended on it. If anyone was going to barf in the cabin, it was going to be this guy.

"Do all the stations provide these offices?" Hans Dieter asked, in his almost-too-flawless English.

"It is part of the agreement which set up the force," Geraldo Sanchez said, before Theroux could answer. "I'm surprised you did not know this, Hans."

Dieter smiled good-naturedly. "There's a lot I don't know, Geraldo. So I look, and I ask."

It struck Theroux that you could probably like the guy if you worked at it, and he said, "As you can see, there's not a whole lot of privacy in here."

"Not a whole lot of room, either," commented the Englishman.

Nathan was beginning to get claustrophobic as well as nauseous. He peered into the cramped and dimly lit room. It was tubular in cross-section, like the architecture of practically every piece of space hardware he had come across so far. The Last Great Adventure be buggered, he thought, this was One Hundred And One Things To Do With Tubing.

The black American who was showing them round said, "That's a general problem out here, sir. Making large structures is relatively easy, but the delivery and maintenance of life-support within them; that costs."

"The low light level is to conserve power," Sanchez said.

"I knew that," said Nathan.

Theroux said, "Actually, that's only partly true."

"What other explanation do you suggest?" asked Sanchez.

"One of the light units is on the fritz." He pointed to the dead light strip. "Maintenance haven't gotten around to replacing it yet."

"This office does seem to contain everything that's needed, though, wouldn't you say so, Mr. Spring?" asked Dieter, who had been careful from the moment they had been introduced to observe the proprieties which went with Nathan's superior rank.

"Apart from the lighting, you mean," Nathan answered, adding, "And please call me Nathan."

Dieter looked pleased. "Thank you, I will; Nathan."

Nathan caught Theroux's slightly puzzled look. "The etiquette of rank," he said. "I'm a chief super. Hans is a superintendent."

"I am also a superintendent," Sanchez chipped in.

As far as Nathan was concerned, the American couldn't be much of an investigator if he needed to be given simple background information which professional curiosity should have prompted him to find out for himself.

Realizing that he probably should have known that, Theroux said, "Must make you front runner then, sir."

"I see no reason why our respective ranks should be a deciding factor," murmured Sanchez.

"And running doesn't feature high on my agenda," the Englishman said as he attempted to turn towards the main bulkhead door, lost his footing and floated upwards from the floor. "As you can probably tell."

"Some people take to it naturally I think, and some do not," Sanchez commented, pulling himself to the door and holding out a hand to Nathan, who ignored it as he struggled to get his feet back on the Velcro strip.

"The trick is to be able to fly and chew gum at the same time," said Theroux.

"I thought the trick was to be able not to fly and chew gum at the same time," Nathan gasped – and Theroux thought he understood now what the effort was for. The guy was trying to fit in. "Takes time," he said.

Nathan smiled as he got his breath back and said, "I don't intend to be here that long."

The smile was open and youthful and Theroux found himself grinning back. "Listen," he said, "there's no fine for flying but it costs you a dollar if you let anything but yourself float loose."

"Anything at all?"

Star Cops

"Anything at all."

"Christ," said Nathan, who had had trouble changing into the station-issue coveralls, and at one stage had all his clothes and personal effects orbiting the changing cubicle, "the job could end up costing you money."

"We give new people forty-eight hours to get used to things. They usually stop feeling sick by then, too."

"After that, we pay?" asked Dieter.

Theroux nodded. "Dollar an item. Can't afford disorder in this sort of environment."

"Not at those prices, certainly," said Nathan.

Dieter turned his attention back to the computer terminal and communications equipment. "Can we get direct communication with Earth from here?" he asked.

Again, Sanchez answered before Theroux had a chance to open his mouth. "All communication is routed through the station traffic control centre," he said.

"You've certainly done your homework, sir," said Theroux. "P'raps you'd better show me around."

Sanchez was the only one who did not smile. "I believe in being prepared," he said. "It is an essential of good police work."

"It is an advantage to know more than anyone else, that is certainly true," Dieter acknowledged, still grinning.

"Wasted if you let them know it, though," murmured Nathan and Theroux saw that he was no longer smiling.

"Shall we take a look at the traffic centre?" Theroux suggested and stepped past Nathan into the linking passage.

Dieter and Sanchez propelled themselves to the door – and then got in a small tangle as they were forced to abort the manoeuvre, because Nathan had moved awkwardly and was now blocking their exit. He was even more hesitant and ungainly than before, though it did seem to Theroux that his co-ordination suddenly improved once the confident progress of other two had been balked.

Theroux wondered for a moment whether it was a smile he had seen on the Englishman's face as it happened, but the expression had been so fleeting that he could not be certain. "Everyone on the station has at least two specialties," he continued as the floaters sorted themselves out. "I work as back-up in traffic and communications."

"I take it police work is not your other speciality," Nathan said.

Theroux could not decide whether this was criticism or just an observation. He said, "I'm a flight engineer by profession."

Nathan nodded but his face remained expressionless, so Theroux was none the wiser.

Sanchez and Dieter meantime had got themselves untangled, and the Spaniard was eager once again to demonstrate his superior preparation. "His speciality could not be police work, how could it? None of the ISPF personnel are police professionals."

"I hate to disagree with all that background research, Geraldo," Nathan said mildly, "but anyone who gets paid to do something is a professional. We can argue about how well they do it, if you like…"

Theroux made up his mind that it had been a criticism. No question about it. He also decided that it would be better if Nathan Spring did not get the commander's job. No question about that, either.

Nathan was trailing some distance behind the others by the time they reached the large module which housed the main communications and radars for the station. Moving in zero-G, particularly in the restricted way he had chosen for himself, called on muscles he did not normally use – so, on top of everything else, he was beginning to ache.

The way things were going, he thought, the medical and psych tests he would have to take when he got back to Earth would probably rule him out for the job without the need for anything else to be considered. Theroux was waiting by the entrance hatch when he reached it.

"Are you okay, sir?"

"No. And stop calling me 'sir', for Christ's sake. I have no standing here and I'm not that much older than you. Though God knows I feel a hundred and forty just at the moment."

"What would you prefer I called you?"

"Nathan'll do."

Theroux looked dubious. "And what happens if you get the job?"

"Don't worry about it," Nathan said.

The entrance hatch was part of an emergency bulkhead designed to isolate the module in the event of an accident and life support failure. Each main section of the station and all of the major modules had these bulkhead hatches, which were not wacsobs, but genuine safety features. They were also extremely difficult to get through unless you floated, since there was a rim almost a metre high all round the circular access port.

Star Cops

Theroux stepped aside and watched as Nathan approached the hatch. To 'walk' through, it was necessary to lift the lead leg, reach through blind, and touch it down on the other side at the same time as the trailing foot was released from the link-tube walking strip. It was a sort of hop and even the experienced could come unstuck, with undignified and painful results. Nathan looked at the entrance for a moment, then reached forward with his hands and, letting both his feet drift up from the walking strip, carefully floated through. Once down on the other side, he looked back at Theroux and shrugged. "No sense in being a damn fool about these things," he said.

As he waited for Theroux to step through, Nathan looked about him. Again a tube, though larger than any of the others that he had been in, and again dimly-lit, but this time only to make it easier to see the various screens presumably. And there were certainly plenty of those: banks of radars; a couple of standard-looking communications screens; a couple of larger mixer-screens, one of which was in use and was switching through inputs from the other sources; some picture units showing feeds from cameras which looked to be mounted at strategic points on the outside of the station; small multi-screen readouts which must come via the life-support computer from monitoring points throughout the station. This place, it seemed, was the eyes, the ears, the mouth, in fact, cliché or not, it was the nerve centre of the station.

A stocky, youngish man with a round, pale face and thinning butter-yellow hair was operating one of the mixer-screen control consoles. The speed and dexterity with which he worked suggested great expertise, unless he was just playing random silly buggers to impress ignorant visitors from Earth. Butler looked up from what he was doing to watch Theroux shepherd the three policemen closer to the screens. "More tourists?" he enquired sourly.

"This is the traffic control and communications module," Theroux explained, sounding to himself more and more like a groundsider tourist guide, and not a very good one at that. "You might call it the nerve centre of the station."

"Only if you had a masterful grasp of the English language and a towering imagination," said Butler, to no-one in particular.

"We are professional policemen," Sanchez responded politely. "Imagination is not something encouraged by our work."

"I had heard that about professional policemen," Butler commented.

"You misunderstand my colleague," Nathan said, irritated by the man's superciliousness. "If you define imagination as the exaggeration of experience, no copper can afford it if he wants to stay sane."

"And if he doesn't want to stay sane?"

"He gets into pointless discussions with total strangers."

"I'm sorry," Theroux said quickly, "my fault. Gentlemen, this is Simon Butler. What he doesn't know about station communications and traffic control just ain't worth knowing. And the same could probably be said for the man himself. Simon these are Superintendents Sanchez and Dieter, and this is Chief Superintendent Spring. You two are fellow countrymen." When neither man showed any sign of responding to this last part of his introduction Theroux said, "Or am I mistaken?"

Dieter smiled. "I think you will find that no two Englishmen are ever 'fellow countrymen'. They are very German like that."

"My God," exclaimed Butler, "what a philosophical group of professional policemen you are. Positively sensitive. You must contract out the rubber hose work these days, I imagine?"

Dieter continued to smile cheerfully. "You don't like the police, Herr Butler. Why is that, I wonder?"

Butler said, "I have a guilty conscience," and turned back to his workscreen.

Theroux felt it was probably time to get on with the conducted tour. Simon was obviously still pissed about all the visitors, and was cranking up his 'eccentric Englishman' routine to full sonofabitch level. "As I told you, I spend most of my duty shifts in here," he said, "at this control console."

"This is where the crime is to be found, perhaps?" asked Dieter in what could have been a ponderous attempt at a joke.

Nathan thought, *And they say the Germans have no sense of humour* – but then felt oddly disloyal to Dieter, who was likeable enough in a pushy sort of way. Certainly preferable to his own 'fellow countryman', as the idiot American called him. He turned to watch Butler checking vehicle movements in his own and neighbouring control sectors, and was almost impressed when the man said, "We do our best to be entertaining," without interrupting his routine, adding, "especially as we seem to have developed into a weightless theme park for bored groundsiders, just recently."

"Yes?" said Nathan. "Well you can have my ticket to ride, and welcome to it, friend."

"The romance of space not for you?" asked Butler, still not pausing in his work.

"He's sick to his stomach," Theroux said.

Butler said, "Get your medication checked. There's no need to suffer. Mild discomfort maybe, nothing more."

"He's allergic to it," said Theroux, and looked at Nathan. "Why else would you go through that? No sense in being a damn fool about these things," he quoted.

It occurred to Nathan that maybe the American wasn't a total idiot after all.

"It's a pity," said Butler, "that the same problem doesn't afflict our visiting politician."

"Lars Hendvorrsen?" asked Dieter, looking puzzled.

"A once warm and wonderful human being," said Butler, "emotionally crippled, no doubt, by a lifetime of thrashing himself with wet birch twigs."

"You don't like him?" said Dieter.

"I don't have to like him. He's got nothing to do with getting me a job."

"And he's commandeered Simon's cabin," Theroux said, and smiled so that there could be no doubt in anyone's mind that what they were hearing was just a fit of childish pique.

Butler stopped what he was doing and rounded on Theroux angrily. "That's got absolutely nothing to do with it! The man's a pompous prick!"

"You've met him," Nathan said in a tone that could just have made it a question.

"The self-important oaf was in here telling me, telling *me* mind you, how to do my job."

"He has a lot of energy," Sanchez said, "and an instinctive understanding of the procedures."

"The man has the brains of a mushroom," said Butler.

"I cannot agree," said Dieter.

Butler sneered, "Why doesn't that surprise me?"

"I find his grasp of the problems facing the ISPF quite exciting," Dieter went on imperturbably. "What do you think, Nathan?"

"I think nausea and disorientation are quite enough excitement for the moment."

Butler turned back to his mixer-screen, and as he resumed his checking routine, he said, "European Parliamentary Representative Lars Hendvorrsen, self-made squillionaire, self-appointed guardian of the public purse and all-around nice guy, surpasses them effortlessly."

"You may have noticed that my colleague does not respond well to criticism," Theroux said, vainly hoping to interrupt the tirade.

"My feeling is," Butler continued, "they made a mistake with his heart transplant and gave him an armpit."

"The screen which Simon is using," Theroux said, trying to get back to the official tour at least, "takes feeds from any of the other sources via the control console. This allows him to pull in any information he needs without having to switch his attention between separate monitors."

"Did you know he plans to go floatabout?" Butler asked.

Theroux was genuinely shocked. "Jesus," he said.

"Man claims to be fully cleared for EVAs."

"We are all cleared for Extra Vehicular Activity," said Dieter.

Butler ignored him pointedly and went on, "Insists on going outside. Calls it 'The Last Great Adventure'."

"Dumb reason for putting on a spacesuit," commented Theroux.

Nathan was puzzled by the reaction. "How dangerous is it?" he asked.

He had addressed the question to Theroux, but it was Butler who answered. "It's difficult to say for certain these days, but we could be sitting in a major branch of Fuck-ups'R'Us."

"Oh, come on," Theroux protested, "not even our losing streak could be that bad."

"Speaking personally, I wouldn't want to bet my life on it," said Butler. "Though, if I'm honest, I've got no fundamental objection to betting Hendvorrsen's."

"Is there a particular problem at the moment?" asked Dieter.

"Obviously there is," said Sanchez. "What is the problem you have?"

Butler sighed. "The backpacks. They're the working bits of a spacesuit. They provide the air, control the temperature, waste elimination, mobility jets."

"Yes, we know that," Sanchez cut in, impatiently.

Butler turned from his screen to look at him, before turning back and continuing with his lecture. "If you think of the spacesuit as keeping you in and the vacuum out, the backpack does everything else." He paused again, and this time glanced round at Theroux enquiringly. "How was that?" he asked. "Will I make a tour guide, do you think?"

"What about the backpacks?" asked Nathan, with weary impatience.

Theroux said, "We've been getting failures."

"And?"

"And people die."

"That tends to happen out here," said Butler wryly, "when equipment fails. In case you hadn't noticed, it's an unforgiving environment."

"So what is it you're saying?" Nathan asked.

Theroux shrugged. "I'm not saying anything."

"Are you saying it's deliberate?" Nathan persisted.

"I don't know what it is."

"He thinks it's a mystery, don't you, Sherlock?" Butler said. "But it's no mystery. I keep telling him it's no mystery. Backpacks need regular servicing. There's a Russian conglomerate that has the monopoly of the work."

"State run concern?" asked Dieter.

"Just like the old days."

Sanchez was nodding. "It must be a big business," he said, "and must be getting bigger all the time. Only their state sector could handle it."

"Wrong again, Geraldo," Butler mocked.

Again? thought Nathan, wondering suddenly whether Theroux's comment that the police office lacked privacy was an understatement.

"That's exactly what they can't do," Butler continued. "They're having trouble coping. Efficiency is not a word that you can render into Cyrillic script. End of mystery."

"You don't think so," Nathan said to Theroux.

"I think there's more to it. There's something wrong with the way our computer's responding to what's happening," Theroux said, and shrugged. "It's just a feeling I have."

"Any evidence to back it up?"

"Not yet, no."

"Are you looking?"

"Yeah."

Nathan shook his head. "Something of a waste of resources. I thought the organisation was short of funds."

"Seems like there's enough in the budget to pay a commander's salary," Theroux said coolly.

"Be money well spent, by the sound of it," said Nathan.

Sanchez had finished examining the screens and could find nothing else to interest him. "What's next on the itinerary?" he asked.

"Repair bays and engineering section," Theroux said.

"Shall we go?" said Sanchez, pushing himself towards the hatch.

Nathan yawned. "What's the rush?"

"I want to see everything. Representative Hendvorrsen asked for my views."

Dieter said, "He asked each of us for a report, or had you forgotten Nathan?"

"It's not part of the brief, Hans. And even if it was, I don't think I'm up to making reasoned judgements just at the moment." He was about to add that he had decided to call it a day and go and try to get some sleep.

Sanchez said, "Maybe you should go back to the sleeping quarters and rest."

Irritated, Nathan said, "I paid for the ten cent tour. I wouldn't want to miss any of it. Besides, there are probably bonus points for vomiting in the engineering section."

"Better there than in the sleeping quarters," Theroux said, as he waited for Nathan to make his laboured way to the hatch.

The newscaster, a strikingly beautiful black Australian, had an Earth-wide following and a slow news day. She smiled brightly into camera and said, *"And finally, little green men from Mars are making a comeback, it seems. Some highly placed government sources are showing a marked reluctance to deny the rumours that something astounding has been discovered by the Mars Survey. No information is available about what this discovery might be. All anyone will say is, if it's true it could, quote, change forever the way man sees himself, unquote. And women too, presumably, but leaving that aside, is this just another of those instant myths which are suddenly on everyone's lips, and which are just as suddenly forgotten? This reporter is inclined to think there may be more to it. Stay tuned; this story could run and run. This is Worldwide News; my name is Susan Caxton."*

"Christ on a bicycle," Nathan muttered, cutting the table screen and concentrating on the coffee, which was passable even if you did have to drink it through a straw. "Talk about clutching at straws."

He was alone in the mess module. It was mid-shift, people were working or sleeping. Hans and Dieter were diligently writing up their reports for Hendvorrsen, who did not seem to sleep at all – or work, either, unless you counted antagonizing everyone he met as 'work'.

Nathan felt as though this was the first time he had been alone since he left his apartment on Earth. When he thought about it, he realized that apart from changing into station coveralls on arrival and evacuating his bowels, it *was* the first time he had been alone. Off-Earth living was communal; oppressively so, he was beginning to find.

"Feeling better today?" Theroux asked from behind him.

"Good morning, David," Nathan said, without turning round. "What's on offer for our amusement this time?"

Theroux got himself a coffee pack and brought it over. "I get the feeling you don't take any of this very seriously," he said, as he settled into the seat on the other side of the table.

"On the contrary, I never felt more serious in my life."

"Still no better, huh?"

Nathan shrugged. "It comes and goes."

"Well, I have a rare treat for you, which may just help to take your mind off how you feel."

"Nothing to do with little green men from Mars is it?"

"Excuse me?"

"Keeping groundsiders distracted takes imagination," Nathan said, "so what have you got for us?"

"The Last Great Adventure. The all-singing all-dancing Lars Hendvorrsen float-by. With full supporting cast including Geraldo 'Where Hendvorrsen's arse is, can my nose be far behind?' Sanchez, and Hans 'Ditto' Dieter."

Nathan did not smile. "They're both good coppers. And one of them will probably be your next boss."

"Not you?"

"Do I look as though I can function out here?"

"Your Admiral Nelson did okay, and he suffered from seasickness, I was told."

Nathan rubbed his face, and said, "Yes, that's what I was told too. And I don't believe a bloody word of it." And then what Theroux had said registered. "Full supporting cast? They're going outside with him?"

Theroux shrugged. "I tried to talk them out of it," he said. Then, mimicking Dieter's voice, he added, "We are *all* cleared for Extra Vehicular Activity."

"No-one's suggesting I join them, are they?" Nathan made no attempt to disguise how little appeal the idea had.

"Hell, no. I thought you might like to watch, is all."

* * *

They were kitted up, their spacesuit checks complete, and the six of them were waiting at the airlock, when Françoise Lancine suddenly called for another RT drill.

She wanted each of them in turn to make a panic squawk direct to base control.

It was base control, Theroux explained to Nathan, who was responsible for recognizing if something was going wrong while they were outside, and it was he who called up the appropriate emergency procedures.

Butler had been designated base control for Hendvorrsen's party because by general consent he was the best available. He was also the most expensive. The EVA was not scheduled during his routine shift and the extra payment he demanded for the job included an element of what he described to Theroux as 'punitive damages'. That may have been why Lancine had demanded the extra drill. Or it could simply have been that she was nervous.

In the traffic control module, Butler left no-one in any doubt what he thought of the idea. "Stupid bitch!" he bitched as he checked the warning circuit lights. Then in the neutral, matter-of-fact tones of the professional controller he reported back to her, "Base control, all circuits confirm positive."

"*Emergency tests will commence on my mark.*" Lancine's voice was small and flat, the distortion of her radio accentuated by the suit helmet, her own enclosed world.

For no particular reason Theroux found himself remembering a long-dead friend from his student days: *We all live in small worlds, knowing nothing – wanting to know nothing – about other people in other small worlds. Some people's worlds shrink to the point where they are its only inhabitants and mostly they die. But that's not the point I'm making. The point I'm making is that the worlds are separate and enclosed. It's not unnatural then that the rich should occupy such an enclosed and separate world but it is unfortunate; they own and control the best of everything, the most of everything, and ownership and control remains locked up in their small world. This is unjust since no matter what others deserve or even need, the rich retain it all, whether they deserve it or not...* Christ he could hear his voice, see his face almost, a sweet natured revolutionary, is it my fault he's dead? What the fuck was his name...?

"Listen, Françoise," Butler interrupted before Lancine could give the signal, "there's no point in doing this by numbers. They have to do it

Star Cops

randomly, paying no attention to each other."

"Some will overlap."

"You mean they won't panic in an orderly fashion?"

"I mean you will 'ave more than one at a time to deal with."

"Isn't that why you're paying me the big bucks?"

"Can we get on with it?" There was no sign of nervousness in Hendvorrsen's voice, only impatience. "I am not impressed by these delaying tactics."

Nathan looked at Theroux and raised his eyebrows slightly. Theroux shrugged and shook his head.

"Impressing you is not my concern, Mr. 'Endvorrsen, and kindly remember the training you are so proud of and do not interrupt communication with base control!"

"Or as the technical jargon has it: shut the fuck up, you stupid prick," said Butler smiling. Then flicking on the mic he intoned, "Base control standing by. Have you made a decision Françoise?"

"Very well, base control. We will do it your way. In your own time gentlemen."

"There's nothing like a good panic," Butler said, as the alarms began triggering on the monitor, "to waste time and energy."

None of the alarms could be killed until Butler had identified the spacesuit and its wearer, and confirmed to the computer that this was an equipment test. Each alarm allowed twenty seconds: miss the time limit on any of them, or get some detail wrong, and the computer would take over. While it worked out what to do, the machine would put every safety system in the station on standby. With some needing manual override, it would take a minimum of two hours to reset them.

"This is base control, safety check is complete all suit alarms confirmed functioning."

"*Very well base control. Commencing airlock procedures.*"

Butler sat back and sighed. He had dealt with all the alarms without missing a detail or a beat, and he had made it look easy. "The bloody system will be on a hair trigger now of course," he complained loudly.

"Question," said Nathan, who found as always that his admiration for talent was unaffected by his feeling, in this case his dislike, for the talented.

"Yes? The sickly looking student at the back?" Butler pointed at him.

"Asshole," muttered Theroux. "Can you believe this guy is actually funny sometimes?"

"Isn't a hair trigger system a good idea under the circumstances?" asked Nathan.

"Only if you want every safety door in the place slamming shut the first time someone farts within fifty feet of a detector."

"Sounds good to me," said Vanhalsen, the duty traffic controller, from his position at the main mixer-screen console, "I've been around when you broke wind, Butler. I'd say it was a life-support hazard, definitely."

"I love witty Dutchmen," said Butler. "They are such a novelty aren't they?"

"*Base control? We are ready to leave the airlock.*"

"Base control standing by. Let's be careful out there." Butler glanced at Theroux. "Five is bid for the title, nothing more, just the title."

Theroux shook his head.

"It wasn't a movie," Butler said. "That's all I'm giving you."

"Concentrate for Chrissakes, Simon."

Lancine was the first out of the airlock. She was closely followed by Hendvorrsen, who was impatient, suspicious about the delays. Sanchez and Dieter were next and the two engineers, detailed to guide the visitors through the construction area, brought up the rear.

Nathan watched fascinated as the group of figures, tiny and toy-like on the video monitor, drifted from the lock and moved very slowly up the side of the station. It seemed to him that it would have made sense to link them together in some physical way, light rope maybe.

Theroux quickly disabused him of that idea. "This is the ultimate action-reaction environment. Link 'em together and you'd see Newton's Cradle meet Chaos Theory." Seeing Nathan's blank look, he explained, "They'd all end up pulling every which way. It'd make for a very unstable chain."

The station's exterior cameras were positioned to give wide fields of view. Being safety features they were low-bid, no frills, fixed-focus models designed to meet SAA regulations as cheaply as possible.

There was no way of telling from the pictures which figure was which, but Nathan could see that the leader was moving too slowly for the next in line, and listening to the RT exchanges confirmed that Hendvorrsen was still not happy with the progress the group was making.

"Please keep your place in the line, Monsieur 'Endvorrsen."

Butler said, "He's really got the climbing frog hopping hasn't he."

"We do not 'urry zees sings."

"Funny how her accent gets more marked when she's agitated." Butler was almost gloating now.

"Happens to most people," Nathan said, "when they're frightened or angry."

"Yes well you'd be the one to know about frightened and angry people I suppose," Butler murmured just loud enough to be heard.

"*Out here the quick and the dead are one and the same.*" That was a new voice. Must be one of the engineers, Nathan thought. Why are Sanchez and Dieter so quiet I wonder?

Hendvorrsen sounded to be breathing harder than before. "*We have only a certain amount of life support, do we not? Time is limited.*"

"This is base control," Butler announced. "You have thirty-four minutes remaining on the outward, maximum."

"*Thank you base control.*" Lancine sounded less than grateful.

"Sanchez and Dieter aren't saying much," Nathan commented.

"It's their first time outside," Butler said dismissively, as though the explanation should be obvious to anyone.

"It can be sort of overwhelming," Theroux explained.

"Is that why you can't look directly out of this place?"

"Man wants windows," chortled Butler.

"The idea is not that stupid," Vanhalsen said looking up from his work.

Butler said, "If you're a groundsider, possibly not."

"It was a false economy, in my view," Vanhalsen continued. "Or rather, perhaps, in my lack of a view."

"Just cost, then," said Nathan.

Theroux nodded. "If you want more than depressing little slits to peer out of; and you want them safe."

"And curtain material's an outrageous price these days," said Butler.

On the screen, the figures were beginning to drift out of line a little as they inched their way towards the edge of the picture.

Butler flicked on his mic. "This is base control; you are approaching the limit of our vision. Monitoring will continue by suit telemetry for one hour. Do you copy?"

"*We copy, base control.*"

"You will have thirty minutes to the outward maximum on my mark. Please acknowledge individually. Four, three, two, one, *mark.*"

There were six acknowledgements then Hendvorrsen began to complain again. "Can we get on with this, please? Thirty minutes is barely time to see what I want to see."

Nathan said, "Doesn't seem to have overwhelmed Hendvorrsen."

"He hasn't had a clear sight of Earth yet. We'll see how chatty he is when he reaches the construction zone and gets an uninterrupted look at it," said Butler.

"My impression," said Vanhalsen, "is that an uninterrupted look at the construction zone is what that bastard has in mind."

"This is base control. You have two minutes to maximum. I repeat, in two minutes, you must begin the return trip to the airlock. This is your two minute warning. Time to pack up the picnic baskets and start for home. Acknowledge please."

"*Lancine acknowledge.*"

"*Dieter acknowledge.*"

"*Sanchez copy two minutes.*"

"*Brownly, roger that.*"

"*Goff, aye.*"

Butler waited a moment, and then said, "Hendvorrsen, do you copy two minute warning, acknowledge please." Off-mic he muttered, "Come on, you stupid prick, I thought you were supposed to be fully checked out on this."

"What's wrong?" Theroux asked quietly.

"Nothing. Everything's normal. Suit readouts are optimal. Nothing's wrong."

"Jesus not again," muttered Theroux.

"Hendvorrsen, Hendvorrsen, this is base control, do you copy?" Butler kept his voice professionally calm and casual, but Nathan could see the sudden tension in every physical gesture.

"Maybe it's the radio," offered Vanhalsen.

"Françoise, do you have vision of Hendvorrsen?" Butler asked.

"*Oui... non. 'E was there...*"

"Can you see him or not?"

"*What is wrong?*"

"*I can see him.*"

"Who's that, Brownly?"

"*Yes.*"

"Is he moving, can you see?"

"*Not that I can see.*"

"Shit," Butler mouthed in silent fury, then glancing across at Theroux said, "Code blue, David."

As Theroux hit the alarm switch, Butler instructed the outside party calmly, "I think Hendvorrsen may have a problem with his radio. Brownly and Goff make your way to him, instruct him to return to base and assist as necessary. Sanchez and Dieter will start back to the airlock immediately, with Lancine in attendance."

Theroux keyed the internal station communications. "Blue alert, blue alert, resuscitation team to main EVA lock and stand by."

"This is base control, please acknowledge and confirm," said Butler, his professional coolness never faltering for a moment. Listening to the confirmations that his orders were being carried out, he said to Theroux, "I'll give you long odds he's dead."

"No bet," said Theroux.

They stared at the video screens, waiting for the first of the figures to come back into vision. The electronic klaxons continued hooting all around them.

Crime Scene

Though it was not the furthest from Moonbase itself, Outpost Nine was one of the most isolated of all the lunar installations. State-of-the-art computer surveillance protected its perimeters. Visitors were seriously discouraged. Routine supplies were left in a loading bay, which remained sealed off from the rest of the complex throughout the delivery.

The only thing outsiders knew for certain about Outpost Nine was that there were eight scientists working there. What they were working on was classified at the highest level and subject to the standard 'neither confirm nor deny' official response to questions. The project director Dr. Michael Chandri, noted only for being the eldest son of a multi-billionaire industrialist, also had a very simple way of dealing with the casually inquisitive. He ignored them. For months at a time he kept himself and his team cut off from all outside contacts, leaving routine communications to be dealt with by computer.

In these circumstances, anybody arriving unannounced at the Outpost Nine perimeter should have had a wasted journey. But the unremarkable-looking stranger calling himself Dafyd Talor was admitted immediately and taken straight to Michael Chandri. The two men had never met before, nor would they ever meet again, but their conversation would result in murder on a massive and horrifying scale.

Chapter 8

For the three ISPF candidates the journey back from Earth orbit was properly sombre. In Nathan's case this was not particularly a mark of respect for the corpse in the shuttle's cargo bay. The mortal remains of Lars Hendvorrsen – on their way to forensic tests, a full post-mortem and then, as befitted a rich and influential politician, burial in an authentic cemetery plot – hardly figured in his thoughts at all.

What concerned Nathan was the disappointing discovery that he was no more comfortable on the return shuttle than he had been on the one which had taken him out to the *Charles De Gaulle*. The motion was just as debilitating. He felt just as lousy. It seemed that he had made no progress whatsoever towards acclimatization. Of course his failure to get his space-legs was of no real importance. He still didn't want the damn job. He especially didn't want the damn job now he had firsthand off-Earth experience. But it was a failure of sorts, and failure made him uncomfortable. He disliked the feeling of being unable to cope. He disliked the feeling of inadequacy. Most of all he disliked the feeling of unrelenting nausea...

Dieter and Sanchez on the other hand did appear to have been genuinely affected by their close encounter with what some wag in the tabloids had already headlined 'The Lars Great Adventure'. They were both markedly subdued, and since Dieter was occupying the acceleration seat next to his, Nathan was grateful for that. He would have been disinclined to cheer the German up even if he had been in a fit state to do so, which he wasn't.

Apart from the routine courtesies, Dieter had not spoken at all during the early part of the flight, so it was another disappointment for Nathan when he suddenly turned to him and asked, "Do you know the purpose of philosophy, Nathan?"

Nathan's impulse was to say *I don't give a flying fuck, just let me die in peace*, but it was difficult to be deliberately offensive to someone like Dieter, so instead he said, "To investigate the nature of being? Something along those lines."

"The purpose of philosophy is to explain death."

"It's a point of view."

"When you are young you think everything is to do with sex. But it is not. It is to do with death."

"I'm not sure what that says about your sex life, Hans," commented Nathan and then, horrified by the thought that in his present mood he might just confide what it did say about his sex life, forced a smile and added quickly, "and I don't want to know."

Dieter looked at him. "Doesn't it frighten you?"

"Sex or death?"

"It is such an easy thing," Dieter continued.

"Must be death," said Nathan.

"To die," Dieter went on. "And the more alive you are..." His voice trailed away.

Nathan said, "The more alive you are, the less you think about death, surely."

Dieter shook his head and frowned. "I am used to it," he said. "Men in our position get used to death, do we not? I am not appalled by it any more. Violent death is our stock-in-trade."

"One of them," said Nathan.

"And yet..." Dieter needed to explain, it seemed – but whether to himself or to Nathan was not clear. "I was cut off in that spacesuit," he said. "I was so close when he died, but I was completely cut off in that suit." He shook his head again. "It seemed as though there were people all around me, but I could not tell who they were or what they were feeling. Or even if they were alive..."

Nathan was puzzled. He sounded like a man working up an alibi, offering a pre-emptive excuse: get your justification in first, before somebody asks an awkward question – but the tone was wrong. "What did you really think of Hendvorrsen?" he asked.

"I admired him," said Dieter thoughtfully. "His methods were crude. His manners were coarse. He was a political demagogue whose personal ambition outstripped everything else."

"You did say you admired him?"

Dieter nodded. "He was a positive man. He had drive and enthusiasm. He took risks. He was very..."

"Very alive?" suggested Nathan.

"Powerfully alive, yes."

From the other side of the central aisle, Sanchez leaned back in his seat and called across to Nathan. "*Worldwide News* has an update on the story."

Nathan switched on the seat screen. Susan Caxton was the news reader again. She seemed to be Worldwide's Space correspondent, Nathan thought, glancing back through the text of the beginning of the report. Satisfied that he had not missed anything important, he cued the real time broadcast and a press office montage of Lars Hendvorrsen's best moments and moves filled the screen behind Caxton, who was just hitting her stride.

"*To ongoing controversy over costs, the tragic death of this popular politician is bound to add questions about the safety and administration of the European space program, and maybe space exploitation in general. The trade-and-aid pact with the Russians will probably be an immediate casualty, but as of now the whole future of the ESA in particular could be said to be hanging on a knife-edge.*"

Nathan scowled. "*Balancing* on a knife-edge," he muttered. "At least get the fucking clichés right."

"*Meantime,*" Caxton went on, "*for the Star Cops, much-criticized lawmen of the new frontier, help is at hand. Career detective Nathan Spring, a forty-one year old Englishman, is to take over the investigation of the Lars Hendvorrsen tragedy.*"

"You are joking?" Nathan demanded of the screen as the Hendvorrsen sequence was replaced with an equally large still of himself.

"*Chief Superintendent Spring has total backing to do whatever it takes to get results, and informed sources have told this reporter they interpret that as meaning he is going to, quote, kick arse, unquote. Could be that's exactly what's needed.*"

Nathan stared at his image, only half-seeing it as he tried to make sense of the news story. He shut his eyes. He was surprised and angry enough to want to laugh. He tried to breathe more slowly. Unremarked, the Worldwide news bulletin rolled on to the next item.

Beside him Dieter said gravely, "Congratulations, Nathan. If there is anything I can do to be of assistance, please call on me."

Nathan opened his eyes. "I don't understand this," he said.

"It seems our respective ranks have been a deciding factor after all," said Sanchez who was now out of his seat and crouching in the aisle beside Nathan. "I mean, you are most uncomfortable in space, is that not so?"

"Yes, Geraldo, that is definitely so," said Nathan.

Dieter said, "Nathan has an outstanding record as a brilliant detective."

"Not out here. Out here, he does not have a record."

"Out here no-one has a record," said Dieter.

"Exactly as I have said."

Nathan held up his hand. "Gentlemen," he said, "would you mind not talking about me behind my back in front of my face. I'm nauseous, not deaf, half-witted or dead. Though someone I know seems to be working on that."

The Commander settled himself behind his desk. The office moodwall showed only a slowly developing abstract pattern. It did not even flicker when he smiled warmly at Nathan and said, "It was a completely unauthorized statement. You didn't think I'd allow them to talk to the press before I'd had a chance to talk to you?"

Nathan did not smile back. "You didn't issue a denial."

"It wasn't a false report, Nathan. Premature, yes. But not false."

Nathan badly wanted to shout at the smug bastard, but he was aware they'd had this argument once already and he had lost it.

"What happened to the wall?" he asked.

"Nothing," said the Commander. "It's on manual override that's all."

"Your brain pattern was too much for it I suppose."

The Commander ignored the comment, put on a serious expression and said, "This Hendvorrsen business is a mess."

"Or did someone point out that what you've got there is a wall-size lie detector?"

"Can we talk about the Hendvorrsen case?" said the Commander.

Nathan said, "You'll have to have it taken out, you realize. As long as you've got it switched off people are going to assume you're hiding something. Like the truth. You bastard."

The Commander looked disdainful. "Don't you think you're being a touch childish about all this?" he asked.

Childish? The bastard fucks with my life, Nathan thought, and then he calls me childish for objecting. Angrily, he got up out of his seat, but he was still suffering from shuttle-lag, and the sudden movement made his head swim. He slammed his hands down on the desk and leaned on them hard. The gesture was more aggressive than he had intended.

"Who nominated me for the poisoned chalice?" he demanded, keeping his voice low to try and compensate for his actions, but succeeding only in making the whole effect more threatening. "It was you was it?"

"Sit down, Chief Superintendent!" snapped the Commander, leaning forward to glare into Nathan's face. "I said: sit down!"

Nathan sat down, furious with himself for giving the other man the advantage of seeing how he felt.

"You were there," said the Commander, comfortably in control now, "you were the obvious person to head up the investigation."

"And Dieter and Sanchez?"

"You had seniority."

"Presumably I have a choice," Nathan said.

"Absolutely," said the Commander. "I can't remember: did I mention there was an opening in Computer Management? It's not exactly fast-track, but there are people who find it interesting."

"How long have I got?"

The Commander leaned back in his chair and steepled his fingers in front of his mouth. "We're under the hammer on this one," he said.

We? thought Nathan, and said, "Who's the pressure coming from?"

"How long a list do you want?" said the Commander.

In the Lotus Garden, the panda was still trotting round the same wallzac loop, but Lee did not seem to have noticed. They were eating the same dishes that Nathan always ordered, but she had not bothered to complain this time. She was trying not to be hurt, at least not to look and sound hurt, and she was not succeeding. She had obviously been putting off saying it and the effort had made her quiet, the meal tense. Nathan was waiting for her to say it, and trying to stop the silence from becoming unbreakable in the meantime. The effort had made him prattle.

"So," he said, "the ESA want a result. Preferably one which says it wasn't an accident and it wasn't their fault. The Russians want a result which says it wasn't an accident and it wasn't their fault. The media want a result but they don't care what it is so long as it's gaudy and can be explained in a thirty second news bite. Everyone involved would like it to be murder. The computer says it isn't."

"That shouldn't be a problem," Lee said without looking up from her food. "It didn't stop you going after that poor Carmodie woman did it? In fact it was the reason you went after her as far as I remember."

"That poor Carmodie woman?"

"What would you call her?"

Chris Boucher

"How does murderous bitch strike you?"

"Crudely."

"She had her husband killed."

"Why? Did you ever wonder that?" Lee asked.

"No," snapped Nathan, irritated because he hadn't been able to put a solid motive to the crime and it bothered him. "That's for the psych people to worry about. And I didn't go after *her*. I went after an answer."

Lee said, "Any answer, so long as it was different from the one the regional crime computer came up with."

Nathan was hurt. "That's not fair," he said.

Lee put her chopsticks carefully down onto the table, pushed her hair back from her face and said, "It's an unfair world." Then she looked him straight in the eyes and asked, "How is it I was the only one who didn't know?"

Nathan knew better than to try the glib joke. And anyway, he was glad that she had finally got it said. "I didn't know myself."

"I didn't even know you'd applied for the job."

"There was no point in telling you," Nathan said and immediately regretted the phrasing.

"Thanks," she said.

"Look I didn't want the Star Cop job. I had no intention of taking the Star Cop job. I still haven't."

"Don't treat me like a fool, Nathan."

"I'm not," he protested.

"I see," she said. "You were on that space station by accident, were you? You sent in your box tops and your membership application for the Junior Space Cadets and it got all fucked up by the computer, is that it?"

"Okay, okay," said Nathan.

"Or was it just that there was trouble out there and so, shazzam, suddenly Captain Fantastic is on the space station and on the case."

"Chief Superintendent Fantastic, if you want to be strictly accurate," Nathan said.

"Oh, by all means," said Lee, "I want to be strictly accurate. Is it strictly accurate to say that you've been short-listed for the Star Cop job? This Star Cop job you don't want. This Star Cop job you have no intention of taking?"

"I applied for the damn job as a formality. I didn't do it because I wanted it. I did it because I was expected to do it."

Lee nodded. "That's rather the way you agreed to a marriage contract with me isn't it," she said. "If we're being strictly accurate."

"The bastard!"

Theroux transferred the memo from the communications screen to the notepad in his wrist unit.

"Two word clues don't count," Butler said, as he hopped through the bulkhead hatch and hustled towards his workstation. "Give me the year, the star, the director, and a reasonable bid, and we're in business."

"You're late," said Theroux.

"Our well-beloved general manager wanted to go over the details one more time," Butler said. "She's hoping to find someone to blame before someone finds her to blame. Oh the wailings and moanings, the rending of garments and gnashing of teeth." He beamed suddenly and chortled, "I love it, I love it, I love it!"

"Yeah, well, it could be that she's not the only one who's running for cover. Take a look." Theroux cut his communications console output onto Butler's mixer screen.

The message which flashed up read: *David Theroux return Earthside soonest. Report Detective Chief Superintendent Spring, Europol 7. Timecode as set.*

Butler was even more amused. "Looks like that newscast was right. It's bum-kicking time and you're up, David old love."

"Why me?" Theroux demanded. "Why are you getting off so goddam lightly? You were base control."

Butler stopped grinning. "You're not suggesting it was my fault, I hope?"

"I'm not suggesting anything. As it happens, I don't think it was anybody's fault." Theroux rubbed his eyes, and wondered why the fuck he was lying to Butler. "I can't answer for this Spring guy, though." That much was true anyway. Jesus he was tired. He didn't seem to have slept since the two engineers, Brownly and Goff, had tugged Hendvorrsen back to the airlock and through to the waiting resuscitation team. Way too late for the poor bastard. Another one who had died angry and frightened, by the look on his face. More angry than frightened, maybe, but then the guy made a profession of 'angry'. This time it could be that it was his natural expression, at rest, as Butler had said about that other poor bastard, Stein. But even so. Somebody was to blame. And it sure as shit wasn't him. Not this time it wasn't. Not then either. It wasn't his fault that Gary died. *Gary*, that was his name. Gary Benson. And the others. Where the hell were they now? What happened wasn't his fault. Was it?

"That Spring looks like a hard man to me," Butler said, interrupting his thoughts. "He's the type who'll knock all your teeth out then kick you in the stomach for mumbling. Ten, the bid is ten."

"Not now, Simon."

"Yes now," insisted Butler. "You have been preventing me from recouping my losses. I think it's a deliberate strategy. The bid is ten going once, going twice."

"*The Big Sleep.*"

"Wrong," Butler crowed. "It's *The Long Goodbye.*"

"It's *The Big Sleep.*"

Butler shook his head. "It's *The Long Goodbye*," he said. "And it's altogether more appropriate, given your present circumstances, don't you think?"

"Fuck you," Theroux said flatly.

A standard spacesuit lay in its separate pieces on the polished wood floor. Nathan was carefully checking through the component parts of the backpack, the main operating units of which had been set out in a rough semblance of their functioning order. He was following the sequence using a step-by-step, interactive maintenance guide displayed on the screen of his communications unit.

At least, Theroux assumed that's what it was, though it looked to be a good deal more responsive than most of the interactive training packages he had ever come across. It seemed to be responding to every tiny move the man made, displaying prompts and offering on-screen evaluations not just of the machinery, but of his actions in relation to it. It was like a teacher stopping a pupil from skipping over essential parts of a lesson. And like a teacher, it did not seem keen on interruptions.

"I'll be with you in a moment," Spring had said to him when he stepped out of the elevator into the apartment which doubled as the man's home and the detective office designated *Europol 7*. "Only if I leave this now, I shall have to start again, and I haven't got the time to waste."

"No problem," he'd said and then had stood watching as the fool played forensic analyst with a piece of hardware even specialist engineers only understood bits of. The bits they were trained to understand.

"Make yourself comfortable," Nathan said without looking up from what he was doing. "Help yourself to anything you need. Coffee? Take a bath if you like."

"Does my personal hygiene give offence?" Theroux asked with wry politeness.

Nathan glanced up to see that the man was half smiling, and the hostility he had shown when he came in was more marked now. "A bath was one of the things I missed most out there on the station. Thought you might feel the same way."

"Not really. I'll take the coffee, though."

Nathan nodded towards the kitchen. "Through there," he said. "Get me one while you're at it, will you?"

"Yazzer, boss," muttered Theroux as he walked away.

Nathan put down the catalytic coupler he had been examining and watched Theroux disappear into the kitchen. What was the man so tense about? He looked as though he hadn't slept for days. Hostile, exhausted and... what else?

"That is an essential link between waste gas analysis and the emergency purging system," Box said.

"I know that," Nathan replied. "And my instruction was screenwrite, not oral."

"Your action indicated that you had overlooked the screenwrite."

"The action was misinterpreted. Just follow my instruction, please." Please was the command word which was supposed to reinforce current operating instructions. As often happened though the complexity of Box's systems produced a response which was slightly different from the expected one.

"Your instruction," Box said, "was to familiarize you with the basic construction and working of the Mark 14 standard –"

"Box," Nathan interrupted, using the word which activated the device and so was the command override, "screenwrite."

The rest of what Box had to say printed up on the communications screen in slightly larger than normal script.

In the kitchen, Theroux had listened to the exchange with mounting consternation. *Shit*, he thought, *the guy is talking to himself and he's throwing his voice while he does it. It's a paranoid schizophrenic vent act.* He ground the coffee – at least the guy went in for the real stuff – and waited while it perked, wondering what the hell he was supposed to do now.

By the time Theroux brought the coffee through to the living room, Nathan had finished the backpack tutorial and was reviewing how little he had learned. Exasperated he pushed the suit away and got to his feet.

"I worry about my memory," he said. "Policemen and liars need good memories."

"You've got a problem?" asked Theroux.

Nathan smiled, "I don't seem to retain as much as I used to."

"Could be you need professional help," Theroux suggested.

"Professional help?"

"Maybe it's organic."

Nathan took his coffee and went back to looking at the spacesuit, poking the pieces dubiously with his foot. "Well, if it is," he said, "the last person to know will be me. Bit like dying."

"Excuse me?" said Theroux.

"Assuming death is the end of it, the only person who'll never know you're dead is you."

Theroux tensed visibly. "Me?"

Nathan wondered in passing whether the American was on something. "Anybody," he said, adding, "Sorry, I got into a rather morbid conversation with Hans Dieter on the flight back." He sipped his coffee. "It's taken a while to shake off the shuttle-lag. I expect you've got the same problem."

Theroux shook his head and said, "The medication works for me."

Nathan put down the coffee mug and began to reassemble the spacesuit. "Any connection between these deaths of yours, apart from the extreme environment?" he asked.

Theroux said, "The computer couldn't find one." *These deaths of mine?* he thought. Even if this guy did turn out to be crazy it didn't follow that he wasn't capable of putting a frame round anyone who'd sit still for the picture.

Nathan said, "Except that they were suit failures."

"You can get all this from the ESA computer, you know," Theroux said.

Nathan was disappointed. The American had given him no particular cause to expect better than that, and yet somehow he had. "I don't want it from the computer," he snapped. "I want it from you. Inspector. What about the other stations?"

Theroux scowled. "They have failures," he said, coldly.

"As many?"

"Some do, some don't. Year on year, the statistic doesn't change. Overall, the percentage of suits that fail is constant."

Nathan said, "That's how the computer sees it. What about the people?"

"What *about* the people?"

Nathan stood up and brandished the half-assembled suit. "Christ, man, if my life depends on this thing, I find it hard to be philosophical about its failure rate, however constant that might be."

"Do you require a prompt for the next step?" Nathan's voice asked from just behind Theroux.

"Jeezzus!" Theroux gasped, and turned too quickly for the medication to prevent his head from spinning.

"If I need a prompt, I'll ask for one," Nathan said.

"Very well," said Box, and Theroux focused his eyes and located the device where it rested on the desk workstation.

"It's a remote self-selecting machine interface and system controller with some personalized algorithms thrown in," said Nathan. "I call it Box. It's a sort of customized personal assistant."

"I thought you were talking to yourself," said Theroux, staring at the less than impressive-looking box.

"According to the man who gave it to me it's not unlike that, apparently. I'm not convinced, myself."

"What does it use for a carrier beam?" Theroux asked.

"Whatever's appropriate," Nathan said, irritated that Box would now be a source of curiosity to the American. "You were telling me about the reaction to the suit failures?"

Theroux moved to examine Box more closely. "It's controlling the interactive instruction manual, is that it?" he asked.

"It's tailoring one to my needs, yes."

"That's an impressive piece of kit."

"So is this," said Nathan, putting the spacesuit back on the floor and taking the next element for reassembly. "Tell me how the users feel when it doesn't work properly."

Theroux turned to look at Nathan. How did a cop get to own something like that? "They get tense," he said.

"And?"

"And there was some pressure brought. The Russians undertook to improve their quality control standards."

"And?"

Theroux shrugged. "And you can't make any system perfect."

Nathan said, "In fact, the failure rate was unchanged, if not very slightly worse," and thought, *This is no detective, what the hell sort of questions has he been asking?* "What was the feeling then?"

Theroux said, "That the purchasing people were probably on the take."

"Corrupt officials accepting substandard equipment," Nathan said pedantically, sounding a bit like a court transcript – which was not the effect he wanted, and which did nothing for their mutual confidence.

"Any port in a shit-storm," said Theroux flatly.

"What's that supposed to mean exactly?"

"People look for plots."

Frowning, Nathan glanced up at Theroux. "But no-one complained," he said.

Theroux's smile did not get as far as his eyes. "Who would you suggest they complain to?"

"You?"

"That's a joke, right?"

Nathan stared at the screen, trying to decide why he could not get a hose coupling to fit. "That is what the police are normally for," he said.

Theroux said, "But we're not normal police, are we?"

"You're better paid for one thing," Nathan said.

On the screen, the explanation of where he was going wrong was displayed in shamingly graphic detail. He connected the hose coupling, then said, "I didn't ask for a prompt, Box."

Theroux finally could stand it no longer. He peered theatrically at the laid out spacesuit. "What exactly are you looking for here?" he demanded. "Some sort of clue? Should I play boy detective too, or do I just watch? Shit, I want to give value for money here, boss."

Nathan sighed and got to his feet. "David," he said, "I don't know what your problem is, but there are three things we should get straight between us. First I'm not your boss."

"That's just a formality. Question of time."

"Second, I'm not looking for clues here, I'm uprating my training. If there's a chance I might die in one of these things, I'd like some idea of how. It's less easy to scare me if I understand what's happening. Not impossible, but less easy. Ignorance isn't bliss, unless you enjoy being afraid of the dark."

"And the third thing?"

"The third thing is you make terrible coffee," Nathan said, and smiled his most disarming smile. "Box, end session."

The communications screen went blank. As Nathan took the coffee mugs back to the kitchen, he said, "That must be why you resigned from the American space programme, I suppose. Career prospects blighted by poor coffee making?"

"Who says I resigned?"

It was a clumsy evasion, and Nathan wondered if the American was naive enough to suppose that he did not already know his background. "So what is an American doing on a European station?" he asked conversationally.

"Just trying to make a living."

Nathan spooned fresh beans into the grinder and set it. "Where there's living, there's policemen," he said, quickly transferring the coarse ground coffee into the percolator. "That's one of nature's rules."

Theroux watched him carefully measuring the precise proportions of coffee and water. "You seem fond of slogans," he said, remembering Kenzy's scathing comment about slogans and brains.

Nathan paused in what he was doing, as if considering this idea for the first time. "I suppose I am," he said, "but they're aphorisms, aren't they? If you want to be strictly accurate about it." He smiled again. "The wit and wisdom of the bumper sticker, my father used to call it."

Despite his weary wariness, Theroux found himself smiling back. The guy did have charm, he thought, no question. The smile was a killer; he'd noticed that before. Probably made him even more of a threat – what can't smile, can't lie…

Nathan was relieved to see him smile. It had begun to look as though they weren't going to be able to work together after all. This might not be the best detective he had ever come across, but he was going to need someone with experience out there if he was going to limit the damage the investigation was going to do. Too many damn people sweating on a result. Even Lee. He had calmed her down, convinced her that he had no choice – but for how long?

"How long do you want me to stick around?" Theroux asked.

Nathan said, "How long have you been a Star Cop?"

"Two years?"

"Solved many cases in that time?"

"We don't really do that. It's not what we're for."

"What are you for? You never really explained that."

"You tell me," Theroux said sourly, thinking, *Looks like we carry the can for careerist sons-of-bitches like Hendvorrsen, and you.*

Nathan said, "It's not a trick question."

Theroux shrugged. "We keep space safe for democracy. I don't know, what the fuck does a peace officer do when things are peaceful?" He shrugged again. "We validate the legal procedures."

"You rubber stamp computer decisions."

"Yeah, if you want to put it like that."

Nathan watched the freshly brewed coffee dribbling into the jug. "When did you start to doubt those decisions?" he asked.

"I didn't. I was just uncomfortable with a run of suit failures. Christ, you make it sound like I had some sort of a religious conversion."

"Questioning the infallibility of the one true God?" Nathan said wryly then, changing the subject abruptly, asked, "The Russian spacesuit test figures. Have you seen them?"

Theroux was only momentarily thrown. "I've seen the figures their PR outfit published," he said.

"As it happens, they're not much different from the unpublished averages," Nathan said.

Theroux was genuinely surprised. "They let you see their classified stuff?" he asked.

Ignoring the question, Nathan poured two mugs of coffee and went back into the living area, leaving Theroux with no choice but to follow.

"If the figures are accurate," Nathan was saying, "then suit failure should be zero, near as makes no odds."

Theroux sipped his coffee. It *was* better. Why the hell *was* that? "But it's not," he said. "Two percent of the suits develop faults, pretty much the same as always. And people are killed."

Nathan smiled a small, thoughtful smile. "Supposing for the sake of argument," he said, "the Russians have put in a lot of extra effort. Supposing their numbers are right. It'd be ironic if all they'd achieved was to let someone fake an accident anywhere they chose without alarming the computers."

Theroux looked doubtful. "Why would someone want to do that?"

"Motive should be the easy part," said Nathan, "but it never seems to be." His smile broadened. "Still, if it's difficult for us, it's bloody impossible

Star Cops

for a computer."

"Besides which," said Theroux, "why should the unpublished stuff the Russians showed you be any more reliable than the published stuff they showed everybody else?"

"They didn't exactly show it to me."

"You hacked in? You know that's illegal."

"It's a moot point."

"Moot my ass. Where I come from that's called Grand Theft: Data. Mandatory one-to-five."

"My machine is self-selecting: it could be seen as a system malfunction."

"Only if you straightened the judge."

"Box?" said Nathan. On the corner of the workstation, Box flickered indicator lights.

"Did you book the restaurant?"

"The Taj Mahal, for three, twenty hundred hours."

"Lee?"

"Lee Jones will meet you there."

"Thank you, Box." The indicator lights flickered off again in response to the 'thank you close down' code.

"As I said that's an impressive piece of kit."

"Yes," said Nathan. "You do like Indian food, I suppose?"

The principal design difference between the Lotus Garden and the Taj Mahal was the wallzac. As might be expected from the name, the screens in the Taj Mahal were showing video loops of the famously beautiful mausoleum which stood in Agra, Uttar Pradesh –

" – until Sikh militants destroyed it in retaliation for the bombing of the Golden Temple at Amritsar. The Taj Mahal was built in the seventeenth century by the Mogul emperor Shah Jahan as a memorial to his favourite wife, Mumtaz Mahal."

"Thank you, Box," said Nathan, and returned it to his pocket. "I hope you're taking notes, there will be a quiz at the end of the meal."

"You could become sort of dependant on Box, don't you think?" asked Theroux smiling.

"Creepy bloody thing," said Lee. "Do you know, at a pinch, I think it could supply all his needs. In the way of companionship, I mean. Well, almost all his needs." She smiled at Nathan and, to Theroux's surprise, he blushed a little.

To break the moment of slightly awkward silence that followed, Theroux said, "It's been a while since I had a chance to eat with a knife and fork."

"Is that what you miss out there?" asked Nathan. "Food laid out flat, with random lumps?"

"After a while," Theroux said with a sigh, "you forget what you do miss. Trees; beautiful women; cruet sets that don't have to be strapped to the table."

"Of course if you want to be really authentic, you're only supposed to use bread to eat this meal," Lee said.

Theroux grinned. "I'm ready to sacrifice a little authenticity for a lot of convenience," he said.

Lee looked round that part of the restaurant which was not obscured by the table's wallzac screens. "Do you know, this is the first time Nathan's ever brought me here? I love Indian food too."

"I'm not real familiar with it," Theroux said. "My culinary adventures sort of stopped at Chinese."

"You should have said. There's a place called the Lotus Garden we use. Nathan insists that dives serve the best food. We eat there a lot. Don't we?" She glanced at Nathan, but he was staring towards the doorway and frowning. She followed the direction of his look and saw that Brian Lincoln had just come in and was talking to the waiter who was pointing towards their table.

Rising, Nathan said, "I'd better see what he wants. Excuse me for a moment, will you?"

"So this Lotus Garden is what you might call your special place, is it?" said Theroux politely, as Nathan walked unhurriedly away to where Lincoln was waiting.

Lee chuckled softly. "Oh my lord, you're a romantic. I thought they were extinct even among Americans. Our special place? I don't think that would even occur to Nathan. We'll suggest it to him when he comes back. Maybe it'll improve his mood…"

On the other side of the restaurant, Nathan's mood was not being improved. "We've already released her," Lincoln was saying, "I thought you should know, but I couldn't exactly call you about it. Not on the office circuit, anyway."

"Why wasn't I consulted?" demanded Nathan, though he already knew the answer.

"You're on attachment to the ISPF. It's not your case anymore."

"There wouldn't be a fucking Carmodie case if it wasn't for me."

"That's true. But the point is, it doesn't look as though she did it after all."

"Of course she did it."

"The psych department report says they can't be certain about her."

"Psych department reports," Nathan said with exaggerated patience, "always say they can't be certain about anything, Brian, you know that. That's why we don't rely on them."

"The Commander took personal charge, and he decided that the balance of evidence –"

Nathan interrupted him. "Since when does that prat know anything about evidence?"

"Yeah, well there was some new evidence that's only just been made available. It does seem to clear her."

Lee watched Nathan coming back to the table. His face was expressionless and pale. "I get the feeling it wasn't good news," she said.

As he sat down Nathan said, "The bastard is trying to discredit me."

"This would be the Commander-bastard I imagine?" asked Lee, and Theroux saw Nathan relax and then smile at her. These people are close, he thought, closer than maybe even they realize.

"Nice of Brian to tip you off," she went on. "So what's the plot this time?"

Before he could answer, Nathan's muffled voice began to call from his jacket pocket.

"Nathan? Nathan?"

He gave a small apologetic shrug and put Box on the table. "Yes, Box?"

Cleared to continue by the 'yes' command, Box said, "A news item of the category you specified is broadcasting on *Worldwide News*. Susan Caxton is the news reader."

"It is a space story, more or less," said Nathan. "Box, put the *Worldwide News* feed onto this wallzac screen."

From other tables in the restaurant there were mutterings of surprise and irritation as Box overrode the main video output, and replaced bland images of tourist India with huge and equally artificial pictures of Lars Hendvorrsen. Sitar music was abruptly interrupted and Susan Caxton, at her most dramatic, spieled from every screen speaker:

"*The Russians give no details apart from the name – Svetlana Tereshcova.*

We understand, however, that Ms. Tereshcova is a senior engineer and mother of two. Once identified as the technician responsible for servicing the spacesuit Lars Hendvorrsen was wearing when he died, Ms. Tereshcova was immediately arrested and charged with murder-by-negligence. This carries a possible death sentence when space-related, and we have it from a reliable source that if found guilty Ms. Tereshcova will be executed. This is Worldwide News; more after this break…"

"Box, reset wallzac."

Without a flicker, the screens returned to normal, leaving some people unsure whether what they had seen was real or imaginary.

Nathan said, "I was afraid they might be panicked into some sort of stunt."

A waiter arrived with the first dishes of food and many and humble apologies for the circuit fault in the wallzac which had never happened before and which he absolutely guaranteed would never happen again.

"How does it affect your investigation?" asked Lee, when he had gone.

"Makes it pretty much irrelevant," said Theroux. "If they find her guilty, then everyone's off the hook, right?"

"Wrong," said Nathan. "Until our investigation is finished, nobody is off the hook."

Lee frowned. "Will the Russians wait for you?"

"Hell, no, they won't wait for us," Theroux said firmly. "If they were planning to wait, why bother with the press release? Looks like Boris's Backpack Repair Shop have got the 'business as usual' signs up."

Once again, Nathan's opinion of the American's intelligence went up.

"That poor woman," Lee said.

Nathan nodded. "They arrest one who's probably innocent, and we release one who's undoubtedly guilty."

"Excuse me?" asked Theroux.

"They released that poor Carmodie woman?" said Lee.

"It's only temporary," Nathan said.

Lee's disapproval was obvious. "This from the man who says he's not out to get her," she remarked.

Nathan smiled coldly. "She'll keep," he said. "Lets hope the same can be said for Svetlana Tereshcova."

Chapter 9

He had said goodbye to Lee at the airport. She had insisted on seeing them off on the first leg of the journey to the orbit station, the flight to Kourou.

It had been a strange parting. Lee had behaved as though he was leaving her for good; not that he was never coming back, but that he was never coming back to her.

"Take care of yourself," she had said. "Just because you're a Star Cop, it doesn't mean they're not out to get you."

"I'm not a Star Cop," he had told her.

"Slip of the tongue."

"I am a fully trained spaceman though, with several days experience."

"Imagine. And I knew you when you got sick in express lifts and giddy on ladders."

"I shan't be gone long," he had said.

"No."

"When I get back, we'll sort everything out."

"It's a long way to get back from," she had said.

He had put his arms round her. "This doesn't change anything."

She had said, "No. I realize that now."

He had kissed her. She had kissed him back – but, like their lovemaking the previous night, it didn't bring them closer. "I promise it doesn't," he had repeated.

"Don't make promises, Nathan. Find some other way to reassure yourself."

"You're being enigmatic, Lee. You know that always makes me nervous."

"Take care of yourself, love," she had said. "Try to remember not to look down."

As he and Theroux were going through airport security, he had glanced back but she had already gone. He had thought about her throughout the flight to Kourou. He should have been thinking about the case.

Waiting for lift-off had been no better than before, even though Theroux had tried to distract him with determined and confident conversation.

"But if all you've got against this Carmodie dame is the cash, and it turns out that she gave back the same notes she borrowed – the same numbers and everything – where does that leave you?"

"Wondering why anyone would know the numbers."

"People take numbers when they can't think of anything else to check…" Theroux had said, his voice faltering briefly, as though he might have been remembering something.

Nathan had intended to ask him about that, but the final countdown had been a distraction, and afterwards the inevitable nausea had made it irrelevant. And now here he was, back in the cramped police office of the *Charles De Gaulle*. His personal life, his career, the survival of a woman he had never met; all depended on his finding the reason for Lars Hendvorrsen's death, and finding it quickly.

"Back so soon?" said the voice behind him, the tone amused but not unfriendly. Nathan turned and nodded a greeting to Simon Butler, who was standing in the doorway smiling.

"You have to begin at the beginning," Nathan said.

"Very profound," said Butler. "Not always easy to spot where that is surely?"

"When you've got nothing else, you go to where it happened."

Butler grinned. "If you're planning to look for footprints, you're going to have a thin time."

"You'd be surprised the traces people leave."

"Not out there." Butler made a vague gesture towards the outer wall of the station.

"I wasn't planning to go outside," said Nathan.

"David told me you weren't a fool. Didn't you?" he said, moving aside to let Theroux past him and into the office.

"Snooping, Simon?" asked Theroux.

"Nothing is secret from your friendly neighbourhood traffic controller, David," he said cheerfully.

"Yeah but eavesdropping in doorways is sort of tacky wouldn't you say?"

Still grinning, Butler said, "You may be right," and moved off down the link tube, walking with that confident and well-practised ease which

Nathan doubted he would ever master, no matter how much weightless time he logged.

When Butler was finally out of earshot, Theroux said, with an air of barely suppressed excitement, "I've been doing some checking."

Nathan took out Box, and clamped it to the side of the equipment console. "Yes?" he said.

"I thought over what you told me. About how I should have investigated the rumours of corruption? I guess you were right. So that's what I've been doing."

"Better late than never."

Theroux ignored the jibe. He was too pleased with himself and his discovery to be put down by what he had come to think of as Nathan's habitual sarcasm. "I've been looking at the personnel records of the main off-Earth purchasing agencies," he went on, "and correlating individual wealth with equipment contracts, that sort of thing?"

Nathan nodded. "And you found Miller," he said, matter-of-factly. Theroux's disappointment showed, though he did his best to hide it. It was almost a pity to spoil his moment of triumph. At least he was thinking now, but it was too little too late…

Theroux said, "You know about him?"

"I found Miller too."

"He's been robbing his department blind."

"He would have been if he was real, but he's not. He's part of the security set-up."

"Fuck! You mean he's a system check." If kicking the furniture had made any sense in a weightless environment, Theroux would have done it.

Nathan said, "Their computer always generates at least two theoretical villains and sets them running around in the system somewhere. If the audit and security people don't spot them within a time limit, the machine registers a loophole and triggers the alarms."

Theroux said, "I know how it works."

"You should have been expecting something of the sort then," Nathan said. "And they've added an extra fail-safe. While they're redesigning to plug the loophole, every last employee gets a triple A check just to be on the safe side."

"A self-refining system. Pretty much foolproof, huh?" It struck Theroux that Box must have found all this shit out, and if the guy knew it all already he could have saved him some time.

"It's beatable," Nathan was saying, "they're all beatable. Probably have to be a one-off, though. Regular bribes to look the other way? I don't think so."

"If you knew it all already, you could have saved me some time," Theroux said.

"I'm not a mind-reader. You didn't tell me that's what you were doing." He looked towards Box. "Box, I want you to run a triple A personnel check for this and every other off-Earth station." Then he looked again at Theroux. "I got the feeling there were some different numbers you were going to check."

"What different numbers?"

Nathan took a wild guess. "Suit components?" he suggested.

Theroux was startled. "How did you know that?"

Nathan smiled. "It's called a detective's nose," he said and almost believed it himself.

Box said, "A full database check? All personnel?"

"Yes please, Box," Nathan confirmed. "And I want to know where everyone was at the time of each of the suit-related deaths in the last eighteen months."

"The computer did that already," Theroux said. "It's a totally routine procedure."

"Totally routine procedures always have weaknesses," said Nathan. "In this case the computer did what it always does and it treated each death individually."

"Death strikes me as pretty much of an individual sort of thing," Theroux said.

"The computer," said Nathan, "asked where everyone was when the death occurred, at the location where the death occurred."

"Yeah."

"It didn't ask where everyone at every other location was."

"These are isolated places. You don't just walk from one to the other."

Nathan nodded. "The suits aren't reliable enough, for one thing," he said and Theroux half-smiled as though he wasn't sure whether it was intended to be a joke. "There are plenty of orbit vehicles around," Nathan went on, "are you going to tell me they're never used unofficially?"

Theroux had to admit to himself that it was a possibility. "They're easily spotted, though."

"How easily?"

Star Cops

I didn't realize you still couldn't tell shit from shuttle, he remembered for no obvious reason. "Traffic controllers vary," he said. "A competent operator shouldn't have any problem."

"Good. Box, put the investigation readouts on all Star Cop consoles and make sure the officers are aware of them."

"Audible and visual prompts?" asked Box.

"Thank you, Box."

"Is that a good idea?" said Theroux.

"Maybe," Nathan said, "they'll come up with some ideas about how this should be handled."

"You can bet on it. None of the offices are any more private than this one. These stations breed rumours like sewers breed rats. What you're doing will get to be common knowledge, real quick." Theroux peered at the screen where the first details of Box's investigation were already scrolling up. "It's going to look like everyone's being investigated. They're going to think they're all under suspicion."

"Well there's not much I can do about that," said Nathan irritably. "Strictly speaking, they *are* all under suspicion, aren't they?"

When Theroux entered the communications module, Butler was staring at a console screen. The output had not been switched onto the main mixer, but Theroux knew what it was. "That's confidential," he said.

"What the hell does your man imagine he's doing?" Butler demanded, still watching the small screen intently.

"You're not supposed to be looking at it, Simon."

"If he wanted it secret, he should have coded it properly. Jesus Christ, look at that. You do realize the bloody man's got my background and employment record scrolling up here for anyone to see."

"It's not *anyone* that's eyeballing a confidential transmission. And you must know that stuff already, right?"

"It's the principle of the thing."

"Yeah right. The principle of the thing? You couldn't even spell the word."

"T-H-I-N-G," said Butler, finally looking up and grinning at Theroux. "So what is he up to?"

Theroux said, "It's just a data check to see how good our security systems are."

Butler hunched himself down slightly, and narrowed his eyes. "You always have a very smooth explanation," he said in a passable imitation of Peter Lorre.

"Points?" asked Theroux.

"Five; you're not nearly reluctant enough."

"It's *The Maltese Falcon* and the next line is," Theroux essayed his more haphazard Humphrey Bogart, "'What do you want me to do, learn to stutter?'"

"That's the worst Donald Duck I've ever heard," said Butler. "You should stick to your Pluto impressions, they're much more convincing. Where is Mickey Mouse by the way? Retired to his quarters to think deep thoughts and throw up?"

"Who's covering for me in here?" asked Theroux.

"I am," said Butler. "Don't I always?"

"Operating solo as ever?"

"You meet a nicer class of person that way."

Theroux sat down at the back-up console and flicked through the internal communicator circuits. "Pluto to Mickey Mouse," he muttered. "Come in, Mickey Mouse."

Nathan was alone in the suit storage section of Cargo Bay One. As he moved slowly along the line of spacesuits, he was making no attempt to combat the nausea-inducing weightlessness. Quite the contrary. Using the storage racks as springboards, he was twisting, rolling, bouncing off the walls and doing somersaults. At one point he pedalled his legs in a furious cycling motion to see what gyroscopic effects he could produce. There were none that he could detect. Had any of the regular personnel seen him they might have been forgiven for thinking that Nathan was just another zero-G tourist letting himself go the way most of them did. But that would have been a mistake. He was not playing, and he had the sick-bag to prove it.

"*How are you doing?*" Theroux's voice suddenly boomed in his ear.

"Deaf!" Nathan snapped. "How the hell do I turn this down?"

With neat precision he halted an 'upward' swoop he had been practising, coming to rest against the 'top' of the cargo module, where he steadied himself delicately. He hung there for a moment trying to relax and stop all movement, but he found that complete stillness was impossible to achieve. He could not eliminate the small twitches and involuntary muscle-flexings which seemed to jog and nudge him.

"*Sorry.*" The volume of the voice in his ear had dropped sharply. "*That better?*"

"I'll let you know when my head stops ringing," he said, pushing himself off the wall and flying slowly back to the racks and the spacesuits he was supposed to be checking.

"*Numbers tally?*"

"So far," said Nathan, who had only looked at the service inspection tag numbers on a couple of randomly selected suits to satisfy himself that Theroux did accurate work.

"*How far have you got?*"

After that he just glanced at the occasional serial number as part of his self-imposed training regime. "Halfway, give or take." Once he had completed each bout of stomach-churning aerobatics, checking a hard-to-see number against Theroux's interminable list seemed like a reasonable test of co-ordination and concentration.

"*Feeling nauseous?*"

"No David, I always go this attractive green colour when I'm having fun."

"*I did offer to do it.*"

"Checking your own work is a fast way to make the same mistake twice," Nathan said and thought, *and in this case it would be a complete waste of time.* There's only one suit that would have been tampered with, and that's back on Earth with Forensics who didn't seem in any hurry to supply the appropriate list of inspection tag numbers. "Any response from Forensics?" he asked.

"*Yeah. They want to know why we want to know.*"

"'Because I fucking say so, you bureaucratic groundsider prat'?" said Butler admiringly, as he slid uninvited into the seat next to Nathan and across the table from Theroux. If he realized he was interrupting their conversation, it clearly did not bother him. "That message," he went on, "may just have saved your reputation out here. These security checks you've been running are not exactly popular, in case no-one's mentioned it. I particularly liked the use of 'groundsider'. That was subtle, extraordinarily subtle for a policeman, if I may say so."

"You think that's subtle," said Nathan, "you should see the way I get rid of people I don't want sitting next to me when I'm talking business."

"You're not supposed to talk business in the mess. Bad form. I don't expect David to understand, being a colonial, and a tinted colonial at that, but you're English. It should come instinctively to you."

"Excuse us, will you," said Nathan politely.

"Leaving already?"

"No."

Butler looked hurt. "You want me to leave?" He looked at Theroux. "You realize you could get blackballed for this," he said.

"Goodbye, Simon," said Theroux amiably.

Butler got up. "I'm tempted not to tell you why I sat in the first place," he said.

"Have you ever considered joining the job?" asked Nathan.

"The job?"

"Police work," Nathan said and smiled. "You'd probably be very good at it. You have all the natural attributes of a top flight detective."

"Is that right?"

Nathan nodded and still smiling said, "You're nosy, thick-skinned, and won't take 'bugger off' for an answer." Then he allowed the smile to fade from his face.

Butler took a mini-CD from his pocket, and floated it towards Nathan. "Your list of serial numbers came through," he said. "They're on track twenty-nine." Nathan made a clumsy grab, and bobbled the catch elaborately.

As the tiny, shiny disc flashed away, Theroux reached out and snatched it down. "That's a dollar you owe the fund, Simon," he said.

Back in the office, when they compared the list of serial numbers from Hendvorrsen's suit with the list of numbers Theroux had originally taken, they found that one of the inspection tags was different by three digits. It was not a vital component. It had not been involved in the failure which killed Hendvorrsen. Box estimated an acceptable probability of human error in recording the number.

Theroux too found this explanation acceptable. "I could've taken the number down wrong. I must've done."

"Three digits," Nathan said thoughtfully.

Theroux shrugged. "If that's the only mistake I made in a full rack check, it wasn't a bad effort."

"Maybe it was the only mistake someone else made."

"In what, for Chrissakes?"

"A duplicate spacesuit? Rigged to fail."

"Oh come on, Nathan. You want to kill a guy out here, it's not that complicated. You can find a hundred ways to get dead."

"The motive might dictate the method."

"I thought motive was the easy part."

"In theory there's only one question: who stands to gain?"

"So?"

"So, you have to define 'gain'."

"Hendvorrsen died of asphyxia when the waste gas elimination on his suit went down. Chances are he was dead before he knew he was dying. Who stood to gain from that?"

"Box," said Nathan.

"Is Box cued only to your voice print?" Theroux asked as Box's indicators flickered on.

"Unless I instruct it otherwise."

"Voice prints can be faked: you thought of that?"

"Anybody wants the thing that badly can have it."

"You have an instruction?" asked Box, as the preset time limit was reached.

"Yes, Box I want to know if any of the off-Earth personnel has a connection with corporations involved in spacesuit technology, or sensitive strategic materials. Look also for links with extreme right wing political groups and anyone in the off-Earth purchasing agencies. Same Star Cop notification procedure as before. Thank you, Box."

Theroux looked baffled. Nathan waited for the inevitable questions, hoping that he could come up with some plausible explanation.

"Sensitive strategic materials?"

"The confrontation commodities," said Nathan. "There's money to be made from tension and little wars, even little cold ones."

"Right wing groups?"

"Crusaders for capitalism. Some Russians are still socialists at heart. Apart from the usual mafia."

Then Theroux saw what he was getting at. "You think someone's trying to get the suit servicing contract away from the Russians?" he asked, not trying to keep the disbelief from his face and voice.

"It's a possibility," said Nathan. Lee had thought it was a possibility.

It could be very profitable, if the right palms were greased in the purchasing departments.

You know it never really occurred to me before, but is that how you buy for Corner Store?

Nah. It's against company policy. Besides, when they find out you're sleeping with a policeman, you stop getting the worthwhile propositions.

And still Theroux did not ask the obvious question: why was this investigation being pushed out onto screens with little or no security, screens that people had been primed to sneak a look at?

When the most dangerous of them came looking for him, Nathan was alone in the Engineering Equipment Store.

It had been difficult to find places to practice his weightless techniques unobserved. He had managed two solo visits to Cargo Bay One; and he had played up the nausea to get time alone in the sleeping quarters. In other solitary moments when he had to be more circumspect – in the mess for example – he limited himself to practising hand-eye exercise; floating and retrieving small objects, or batting coins and food packs from hand to hand like an apprentice juggler who had yet to master the upward arc.

He was not really sure why it was important to him that no-one else should be aware that he was trying to improve his physical control and co-ordination. He knew it was partly embarrassment; he had never grown out of a childish shyness which had made him dislike being seen doing anything at which he was less than totally competent. There had to be more involved here, though, because as his skills improved, he instinctively strived to conceal them. This in itself forced him to progress further. It was a paradox he quite enjoyed – that he had to keep improving, in order to hide his continuing improvement. He half convinced himself that it was just another exercise, another way to develop the professionalism called for by the job. He knew he could not be as good as the people around him, but maybe he could make up for that by being better than they expected. You could improve the impact of a skill by making it an unexpected skill. It was always an advantage to have people underestimate you. But as he practised a controlled drift between the storage cages of construction materials, he was not sure what it was about this situation that made him feel that he needed such an advantage.

"That stuff you've been putting out about us is *shit!*"

Brownly shouted the last word as he stepped out from between the stacks. He was a tall, thin Irishman, and he was shaking with rage as he confronted Nathan. His naturally pale face, made almost translucent by

Star Cops

months on the station, was flushed with angry blood, the colour clashing strangely with his close-cropped, red hair.

"What stuff is that?" Nathan asked, jerking himself down to the walking strip, trying to look as though he had been struggling for equilibrium.

"You know very well what stuff is that," Goff said behind him.

Nathan spun round. It was a manoeuvre he could now manage easily, but he nonetheless allowed himself to lose contact with the floor strip, making it necessary to clutch at an equipment cage to steady himself.

"You are trying to make us the scapegoats," Goff went on, "for the death of that...fool."

The squat, dark-featured Swiss was an odd pairing with the gangling Irishman. They might have made a comic duo if their intentions had been less obviously aggressive. As it was, their grotesque contrast only served to emphasize the threat.

Nathan anchored himself again, standing so that he could look at each of the men without needing to turn round. His back was against the cage in case it came to a fight, though he hoped the move did not look defensive – that might be all the cue they needed.

The two men had good reason to be hostile. As Box refined and narrowed the definitions of what would constitute a suspect in the Lars Hendvorrsen killing, the names Brownly and Goff kept on showing up. The two of them were present at the crime scene; it was they who retrieved the body; they had technical backgrounds and a lot more EVA experience than anyone else out there that day; and now, most damning of all, there were share portfolios which had been carefully concealed through nominees and dummy companies. Here were incriminating links with corporations who might make substantial profits from a change in the status quo. A strong circumstantial case had been building against Brownly and Goff. It was happening in full view of anyone curious enough to put a small effort into eavesdropping, and that was probably most of the off-Earth community.

"I don't know where you're getting your information from," Nathan said, "but it's not very reliable, trust me."

Brownly sneered, "Trust you?" Then, unable to contain himself, he shouted, "Our fuckin' heads don't zip up at the back, yeh bastard yeh!" and began to move down the walkway towards Nathan.

"Take it easy, Liam," said Goff, also moving in Nathan's direction.

"Listen to your friend, Liam," Nathan said, watching Brownly's advance and wondering how effective a kick to the balls would be in this situation.

"Shut your mouth!" Brownly shouted.

Nathan put his left hand behind him and grasped the mesh of the cage.

Goff said, "If you attack this man he will only use it to make things look worse for us."

Brownly stopped. "How could they look worse?" he demanded. "He's got us in the frame, Oggy. You're too Swiss to understand." He took a step closer. "You haven't seen how the English branch of Europlod gets the job done." He reached forward to grasp at the front of Nathan's coveralls.

Still holding onto the cage with his left hand, Nathan grabbed Brownly's wrist with his right. "I wouldn't," he said flatly. "Assaulting a police officer is an offence."

"You're an offence," Brownly snarled and pushing forward, his feet braced as leverage, he jabbed a punch with his free hand.

Although the chance of a fight had occurred to him, the punch came as a shock to Nathan. He was used to the aftermath of violence, but the habit of aggression was not part of his life. Automatically, he ducked down and the punch took him high on the forehead. There was no pain but a sudden flash of outraged fury blazed through him. He straightened, and using his hold on the cage to keep himself anchored and his grasp on the man's wrist to give the leverage, he kicked up hard between Brownly's legs. It had no effect except to detach Brownly from the floor strip, twist him free of Nathan's grip, and push him backwards in an untidy somersault.

With the fierce clarity of his adrenaline rush, Nathan watched him tumble away and thought that if you wanted to damage a man, kicks and punches were not how you did it. You needed a whole different technique out here.

That was when the still spinning Brownly pulled a spring-loaded switchblade.

He bounced off the curved module wall and as he came lunging back he thrust the knife out in front of him. Nathan saw a small green flash from the tip of the blade.

With no gravity to slow him down, Goff's squat build was not a handicap. He leapt to intercept Brownly, expertly avoiding the blade and deflecting his flight. "Not here!" Nathan heard him say. "Not now!" – and Brownly's knife vanished, as quickly as it had appeared.

Nathan relaxed a little. Goff planted himself firmly in front of Brownly, who made no more attempts to attack. The Swiss was the controlled and calculating type. If he made a move there would be nothing impulsive about it and it would be the more dangerous for that. But whatever he was here for, violence was not part of it. Not yet.

"What exactly is it that you gentlemen want?" Nathan asked, trying to keep his face and voice expressionless.

"A warning," said Goff.

"I've already given you one," said Nathan.

"You're going to die, Spring," Brownly said softly. "You are dead meat."

"You're determined to get yourself arrested aren't you, Brownly?"

"Try me."

Nathan smiled coldly. "Shouldn't that be 'You'll never take me alive, copper'?"

"It would be wise of you to think of us seriously," Goff said. "There are many ways to die, once you have left the Earth behind."

"So I've been told," said Nathan.

"You should listen," Brownly commented. "Some of them are really unpleasant."

Nathan, his voice flat and slightly bored, said, "I've seen flick-knives before," and held out his hand, "and they're illegal, especially with laser-tipped blades – even out here. If you surrender it voluntarily, it may not be necessary to proffer charges." Brownly stared at him, blank with surprise. Nathan moved towards him. "Or have I got to take it from you?"

"Give it to him," said Goff, grabbing his arm. "Stop behaving like a fool and give it to him."

Reluctantly Brownly took out the switchblade, and propelled it in Nathan's direction. Nathan made a show of his difficulty in catching it, and for the first time Goff smiled. It was a wry, knowing smile. "We will not allow you to use us to make your reputation," he said, as he pushed Brownly in the direction of the access hatch.

"That's it?" Nathan called after them. "That's all you came to tell me?"

When they had hopped through the hatch, Brownly turned to look back at him. "You'd be amazed," he said, "at the unexpected dangers there are. Take storerooms, for example. Very dangerous places, storerooms." He pushed the hatch closed.

For a moment Nathan did not react, then, as he saw the hatch seals operating, claustrophobia clutched at the back of his eyes. Hurriedly he lifted his feet from the floor and he was about to launch himself towards the hatch when the lights went out. At the same time, the atmosphere scrubber purred to a stop. With the system closed down, he knew the unused oxygen would automatically be cycled out of this section of the module. He would suffocate. How soon? Soon. Too soon. He tried to picture the hatch and its position in relation to where he was floating. He shoved off hard in that direction. Too hard. Fear robbed him of technique and he rolled, flapping his arms and legs in an ineffectual effort to get control. He was instantly dizzy. His breath was short. Was that his panic, or was the air already getting thin? He was in no position to tell. He was in no position to care. Frantically disoriented he groped around the first surface he came up against. There was no sign of the hatch. Where was it? For Christ's sake, *where was it?* He knew there was an emergency override switch. It was in the centre of the hatch cover. It was for just this situation. Everything into reverse. Lights, atmosphere purge, way out. Wait, wait, think, it was lit, the override had its own light source, its own small light source, he should be able to see it, he must be able to see it, *why couldn't he see it?* He peered despairingly into the darkness, and in a moment's sudden lucidity he realized that his eyes were tightly closed.

The small bright glow was below and to his left. He reached down and pressed the switch. An electronic bell registered the emergency.

Lancine was furious. Her face was set in a rigid mask of iron-willed self-control, but this did nothing to disguise her feelings from Nathan as he made his laboriously awkward way into her office. Even if he had not been expecting her anger, he would have recognized the behaviour of the elegant general manager. She was reacting almost exactly as he did himself. He wondered in passing what else they had in common. Her much derided ambition perhaps?

He heel-and-toed it slowly across the carpet to the chair she indicted and pulled himself down onto its Velcro pads.

"Do you wish coffee?" It was no more than a curt reminder that she was civilized and in charge.

"Thank you, no," Nathan said.

"Then I will come straight to the point. I wish to know what 'appened."

Nathan shrugged slightly. "I did file an accident report," he said.

Lancine said, "I do not expect a groundsider policeman wiz your limited experience to understand 'ow we work out 'ere. 'Ow we all depend

Star Cops

on each other."

"I take it I wasn't your first choice for Star Cop Commander?" Nathan asked politely.

"You showed no wish for the job, nor any aptitude for the life. You still do not."

"I can't argue with that," said Nathan, and flashed his most charming smile.

Lancine was not to be mollified. Stone-faced, she said, "You did, 'owever, argue with Auguste Goff and Liam Brownly, did you not?"

"Oggy, Liam and I had a lively discussion. These things happen."

"Not in an environment like this. Where we live so close together, we cannot 'ave arguments."

"You can't have crimes either, but you do."

She gave him a long look of cool appraisal. He stared back and wondered suddenly if she liked to make love. Skinny women had never appealed to him much but the thought of Françoise Lancine on her back, all that cool control abandoned in a thrusting rush of hungry sensation… He put the images from his mind. Nothing like a brush with death to make you horny, he thought. My God, walking around with a hard-on was ungainly enough. Floating around with one would be positively grotesque.

"You 'ave evidence?" Lancine asked. When he stayed silent, she let her anger show for the first time. "I am entitled to know what progress you 'ave made."

"No," said Nathan mildly. "You're not."

"You are refusing? In that case, you leave me no choice but to 'ave you recalled to Earth immediately. I shall recommend that you be replaced by a more reliable officer."

Nathan nodded, and stood up carefully. "Thank you for warning me," he said. "I appreciate your candour."

She did not get up as he made his way to the door. "This is not a personal matter, you understand," she said. "I am responsible for this station. For the personnel of this station. Your behaviour is not in the best interests of their safety. You 'ave conducted your enquiries unintelligently and wizout discretion."

Nathan paused in the doorway. Conscious that the gesture was not unlike Brownly's parting shot in the storeroom, he turned and said, "You overlook one thing. I'm on attachment to the ISPF. The Star Cops may be crap, but they're independent crap, so I'm afraid you can't get me recalled.

You see, I'm a police officer on a lawful enquiry, and no jumped-up office manager has the authority to interfere with that." He smiled. "This is not a personal matter, you understand."

Nathan found Theroux sitting in the mess. Butler had stopped to chat on his way through to start his shift, but it was clearly not the relaxed conversation that they had previously taken for granted. Theroux looked distinctly ill-at-ease. To Nathan, his difficulty was obvious, easily recognized by anyone who had ever joined the job. As ISPF liaison, Theroux had been stood down from his other duties. Effectively, he was now a full-time policeman. This set him apart, and while neither he nor those around him might understand it yet, there was a distance between them which would be there for as long as he was a copper.

Nathan nodded to Butler, and noted that, for once, the irritating bastard did not offer any smartarse backchat. Gossip about the run-in with Brownly and Goff had circulated quickly. The other people in the mess stopped talking and looked at him. They did not try to hide their hostility. "I've changed my mind," he said, just loud enough for everyone to hear. "I'll need to do an EVA after all. And fairly soon. Set that up for me, please, David."

"You're not serious," said Theroux. "You want to go outside? What in the hell for?"

"I'd think again if I were you," Butler said quietly and more-or-less politely, "it's no place for tourists. The Hendvorrsen thing should've convinced you of that if nothing else."

"The Hendvorrsen thing isn't a problem any more," said Nathan, not lowering his voice. "I know what happened to him. I know how it happened. I shall need to go outside to check a couple of things though."

"I don't think the jumped-up office manager is going to be terrifically chuffed with that idea," said Butler.

Once again, Nathan registered the man's use of the exact quote and wondered whether Butler had mistakenly given away the presence of the bug he had in Lancine's office, or whether he just didn't care. "Do you have any other amazing talents, Mr. Butler?" he asked more quietly. "Apart from the superhuman hearing you keep demonstrating?"

"Modesty forbids," Butler said, and then added, grinning broadly, "It's a bugger, isn't it?"

Theroux, conscious that everyone in the mess, which was at its busiest now with the change of shifts, was still watching and listening, lowered his voice almost to a whisper. "Listen, Nathan, Brownly's always been flaky. He's done a double tour this time, so chances are he's got cabin fever. And he and Goff are close, you know what I mean?"

"What are you trying to tell me, David?" Nathan asked more quietly.

"He's trying to tell you," Butler cut in, "that if you'd had that little scuffle, outside you'd have been dead meat."

Nathan considered this. "You're telling me it is possible to kill somebody outside without being detected."

"Depends on the detective, I imagine," Butler murmured.

"What I'm telling you," said Theroux, "is that Brownly might just be past caring."

Butler raised his voice. "And our careers," he said, looking round the mess, his smile encompassing everyone present, "couldn't stand another high profile fatality. Not even one with no mystery involved."

"There's no mystery about Hendvorrsen's death," said Nathan, equally loudly, and also looking round to include the audience. "He was murdered. Right there. Right in front of our eyes."

Chapter 10

Nathan slipped easily into the shower bag, and then spent a couple of minutes struggling to seal the neck band. As washing systems went it was not particularly efficient, relying as it did on fine mist sprays of premixed soap and water solution which were sucked and blown around inside the bag. Despite a slightly obsessive concern with personal hygiene, however, it was not the contraption's cleansing capacity that concerned him this time. He was hoping that by energetic twisting and scrubbing he could thoroughly soak himself and neutralize any short-range, skin scale microbugs that might have been attached to him. It was unlikely that Butler could afford anything that state-of-the-art, or would go to that much trouble even if he could, but there was no telling about people's hobbies, and it wouldn't hurt to be thorough. He had already damp-towelled his face and head so vigorously that Theroux wondered aloud whether it was displacement activity brought on by stress at the thought of going outside. Nathan had offered him no explanation but instead had sent him to get two pairs of fresh coveralls, with explicit instructions not to say who they were for. That had *really* got him worried.

By the time Nathan had finished the shower and blown himself dry, Theroux was back. Nathan made an appropriately ungainly scramble of getting out of the bag, retrieved his discarded coveralls and pulled a note from the pocket. He handed the note across without comment. It read: Have we got the equipment for a bug sweep?

"A bu-?" Theroux began but was cut off by a fiercely withering look from Nathan, who was unfolding the first of the clean coveralls and looking for signs that they had been opened already and refolded. Frowning, Theroux watched him, then said, "Who we?"

"Cops we."

"It's a part-time force, for Chrissakes. What equipment we do have is shared, military surplus, or outdated stock."

"That's a 'no'?"

"That's a 'fuck, no'."

Star Cops

"Stick in a requisition for the best that Europol have in their technical stores. In the meantime, we'll have to make do with Box. Lets hope we're not looking for this year's model."

Nathan put on the fresh coveralls and, carrying the pair he had changed out of, headed for the sleeping quarters, leaving a worried and sceptical Theroux to follow.

In the cramped cubicle, Nathan instructed Box using its seldom-needed touch pad, and with slow and careful sweeps scanned the coveralls he had been wearing. As Theroux watched, his scepticism mounted, and it was about to get the better of his patience when Box's screen indicator flashed the discovery of a thread transmitter in one of the seams which held the garment's crotch zip in place.

"Typical," muttered Nathan, drawing the tiny nylon fibre from its hiding place.

"Sonofabitch," exclaimed Theroux.

Nathan checked the rest of the garment and, satisfied that this was the only bug, checked the same place on the new coveralls he was wearing. He was mildly surprised to find there was a bug there too.

He floated Box at Theroux and indicated that he should check his own crotch. The result was the same. It began to seem more than possible that all the standard issue coveralls had short-range transmitters concealed in the zip seams. Was it all standard issue everywhere? That would make it a major conspiracy. Who would do that and why? Who *could* do that? Nathan saw by his face that similar questions were probably just occurring to Theroux.

Silently they destroyed the bugs, including the one which showed up in the second unused pair of coveralls, and Nathan made a cursory scan of the quarters without turning up any more. Only when this had been done did Theroux say, "What the fuck are they for?"

Nathan shook his head. Butler obviously knew enough to tune into them when he wanted to snoop on meetings and conversations. The question was, did he stumble across them, or did he know about them from the beginning? Part of the conspiracy or a lucky busybody? "Maybe we should ask your friend Butler," he said.

"Simon?" Theroux laughed, his amusement at the notion quite genuine. "Gimme a break. You're not suggesting he's behind these things?"

"I don't know, David. But I do know he's been listening into my conversations."

"You sure about that?"

"Fairly sure." And if he's been listening into *my* conversations... Nathan thought.

"Shit," said Theroux, no longer amused. "And if he's been listening into your conversations, five'll get you ten he's been listening into everyone's."

Obscurely sorry for the American, Nathan said, "Not necessarily. It depends on what he wanted to know."

Theroux turned towards the doorway. "And why he wanted to know it," he said grimly.

"Where d'you think you're going?" asked Nathan.

"I think I'm going to tackle him. Maybe about chest high. Hit him in the numbers, like they used to say."

"No, you're not." It was a flat command, and it stopped Theroux in his tracks. "There's no point," Nathan went on. "You wouldn't learn anything you didn't know already; and he would."

Theroux turned slowly. He was still angry, and knowing Nathan was right did nothing to help. "You don't think he'll notice maybe, that his bug went off the air?" he asked trying to sound sarcastic, though his heart was not really in it.

Nathan returned Box to the equipment belt attached to his sleeping frame. "Sooner or later," he said. "You want to make it sooner, and tell him why?"

"Smart-ass," Theroux muttered.

"Knowledge is power," Nathan said, "and the fewer people that have it, the more powerful it is."

"Very deep," said Theroux, "What's it from: *Dictatorship for Fun and Profit*?"

"Something like that," said Nathan. "The good guys should bear it in mind, though, don't you think?" He smiled his most charming smile. "Assuming they want to survive. So, shall we go and select a suit for me? Preferably one that'll keep on functioning while I'm out there?"

Even after the water tank training and all the extra studying, fitting on the spacesuit and checking the seals and systems still felt like a brand new experience to Nathan. The suit was clumsy and confining, and despite the lack of gravity seemed almost heavy. It was like being enveloped in a leather duvet. So much for the rubbish the instructors had given him about weightlessness making the difference. Already he had a touch of claustrophobia, and they hadn't got to the helmet yet.

Theroux fastened the equipment pouch to the left hip and wondered what it was that Nathan was so keen to take outside with him. He tapped the pouch. "Camera?"

"Sandwiches," Nathan said.

The backpack was selected from the racks at random, and as Nathan watched Theroux strip the wrapping from it, he said, "A new pack, gentlemen. Check the seals are unbroken, remove the deck, discard the jokers, cut the cards and shuffle."

"You're a gambler?" Theroux asked, mostly just for something to say.

"It seems so."

Nathan was conscious suddenly of just how big a risk he might be taking, and it must have shown on his face because Theroux said, "Look I know you've made a big production out of this solo stunt."

Nathan interrupted hurriedly, "I don't think so."

Theroux raised an eyebrow. It was a wry expression he had perfected as a kid after seeing one of the old-time movie stars do it, but he hadn't used it much since. "Right," he said, matching the voice to the face. "Canine Megaballs launched their last concert tour with less hoopla and pre-publicity. If there's anyone off-Earth who doesn't know you're going outside about now, they cannot have been paying attention is all."

"A slight exaggeration."

"Point is, you're not ready, Nathan."

"It's now or never," Nathan said.

Theroux sighed. "There's no shame in delaying it for a while."

"Yes, there is."

Theroux slotted the backpack into place and began connecting the umbilicals. "He is very young and very proud," he muttered in a bad Mexican accent.

Nathan said, "The graveyards are full of kids who were very young and very proud."

"You know that quote?"

"I know *The Magnificent Seven*."

"You're full of surprises man."

"What's so surprising about that? Did you think you were the only person who ever saw an old movie?"

With the backpack in place, Nathan found that the suit was not much more cumbersome than before, so the instructors were partially right anyway. He picked up the helmet. It was too bulky and too small, both at the same time. He rotated it slowly, as he had been taught, and checked the locking seal for any sign of damage or deterioration.

"At least change your mind about going solo," Theroux said. "I mean why risk going solo, for Chrissakes?"

Nathan said, "For those of you who still need the details of the plot explained to them: there's no-one I trust to go out there with me."

"Crap! I told you I'd go with you."

"Then there would be no-one I trust back here. I'm relying on you to keep tabs on Brownly and Goff and make sure they don't follow me out."

"No problem."

Nathan bent his head. "Exactly," he said, and prepared to ease the helmet on, prior to seating it onto its neck rings. "No problems."

Theroux locked the helmet into place and checked the telltales as Nathan switched to the spacesuit's self-contained breathing system. "I said no problem," he said, though Nathan could no longer hear him. "I didn't say no problems."

"Spring to base control, Spring to base control, do you copy?"

There were no obvious signs of panic in Nathan's voice as it came over the RT. Butler did not respond, but sat listening to it with the slightest of smiles giving his face an oddly satiated look, as though he had just had a large meal, or sex.

"Base control can you hear me okay? I'm waiting to go into the airlock. Base control?"

Still Butler delayed answering.

"Base control? Shit. David? David… He…Can't…Hear…Me."

Butler's smile got more pronounced. "Neither can he, you arrogant prick," he muttered.

Theroux came over on one of the internal circuits. *"Are you there, Simon?"*

Finally Butler keyed the suit link and said, "Base control to Spring, hold your position please," then switched to Theroux's circuit and asked, "Is there a problem, David?"

Theroux's irritation was plain to hear. *"Are you getting voice from Nathan's suit?"*

Butler switched back to Nathan. "Base control to Spring, voice check please."

Star Cops

"*Spring to base control, do you copy?*"

"Base control to Spring, I copy, thank you. If you are happy with your checks I have a green board and you are cleared to enter the airlock."

"*Very well base control.*"

"No problem with the RT that I can find, David," Butler reported. "May have got excited and missed the circuit key. He's got some way to go before he gets his space-walker's merit badge after all."

"*Have you given him airlock clearance?*"

"Are we in that much of a rush?"

"*He's on the move. Get your rear in gear, Simon, and make sure nothing happens to him, right?*"

Claustrophobia within claustrophobia. Cramped inside the suit inside the cramped airlock. Featureless, grey metal shell, water jacketed thick, smothering radiation soaking solar surges pushing at the suit, water layered trickling cold pressing at him drowning him in –

He closed his eyes for a moment and tried to breathe slow, deep breaths.

In through the nose, out through the mouth.

In through the nose, out through the mouth.

In through the nose.

Out through the mouth.

In.

Out.

Slow. Relax. Control. Smells of plastic touched the air and the sound of his own breathing, magnified by the helmet, sounded louder than normal and yet somehow faraway.

He opened his eyes. The airlock pressure gauge showed the atmosphere evacuation cycle was complete. He sucked spit into his dry mouth, swallowed and said into the helmet mic, "Spring to base control. Ready to open outer lock hatch, base control."

"*For a minute there I thought you'd gone to sleep. All that heavy breathing? Either that or you'd found a way to play with yourself in a spacesuit.*"

He was probably only trying to keep things upbeat, but even distorted and distanced by the suit radio, Butler's manner grated on Nathan: what was it about the man that made him so irritating? It wasn't just his bugging activities – assuming they *were* his – there was something more, something basically indecent about him. "Have I got clearance to open the hatch, base control?" Nathan snapped.

"*Whenever you feel ready you can go ahead. But don't rush it, you've got plenty of time.*" Now Butler's professional voice was smooth, full of calming reassurance.

"Thank you, base control." Nathan grasped the release wheel, and began to turn it slowly.

They were scheduled for exercise, so where the hell were they? Theroux peered round the gym section as if there was somewhere in the tiny space where they might be hiding. Treadmill, press-up harness, pull straps: the technology of body maintenance had changed little since the pioneer days probably because advances in medication could now keep bone and muscle wastage under control without the need for punishing bouts of exercise. Regular short sessions were still prescribed, however, and there was a roster so that all the station personnel could get their turn with the equipment. It was one of those routines that most people followed most of the time. It was reckoned to be good for cabin fever and, if nothing else, it made returning Earthside a bit less exhausting and generally irksome.

Theroux checked his wrist-log again. Yeah, this was the time when Brownly and Goff were supposed to be working out all right. Shit. Keep tabs on them, the man said? Christ, he couldn't even find them. For all he knew, they might be outside right now. They might be out there, waiting for Nathan. He flipped over and kicked himself off towards the access hatch. This was no time for bullshit professional games, he thought.

When the seals were fully retracted, Nathan pushed at the airlock hatch so that it moved out onto its runners and slid smoothly aside. Although this was not as large as the cargo 'lock that the Hendvorrsen party had used, the opening was big enough for two people to move through comfortably. To Nathan it still looked cramped and narrow. Outside all he could see was blackness. And yet, bright sunlight was spilling into the airlock from somewhere. Darkness and light. Both needle sharp. The bloody place was bizarre, unnatural, no place for a man to be. Any man. Men. A small step for man… why wouldn't Armstrong get it wrong? He pushed himself forward to the edge of the hatchway, and gingerly reached out and clipped his safety line to the first anchor point he could find. That done, he gave the line a small tug and slowly drifted out into space.

* * *

Star Cops

They weren't in their quarters; they weren't in the mess; there were only so many places you could be on a station the size of the *Charles De Gaulle*... so where the fuck were they? Theroux was getting desperate. He hadn't quite believed that Brownly and Goff were crazy enough to try to kill Nathan – not while Butler was watching, him and half the station for all they knew. Now he wasn't sure. They couldn't hope to get away with it, could they?

Only someone *had* been getting away with it. Them? It must be them. "Simon? You awake, Simon?" he all but yelled into the communicator.

It was unreal. He floated, staring. It was bigger than he expected. And brighter than he expected, much brighter. And it was beautiful beyond imagining. "Christ," he said softly.

"*Are you all right, Spring?*" Butler's voice managed to convey a degree of urgency and concern without being alarming. "*Spring? This is base control, do you copy?*"

"I never saw the Earth before," Nathan answered after a moment.

"*Ah. Yes, of course. It's quite a view, isn't it?*" Nathan continued to stare in silence, resenting the sound of Butler's continuing chatter. "*Everyone should see it once. Trouble is, there's not much left to see after you have.*" Nathan sighed. It was wholly involuntary, a genuine reaction.

"*Nathan?*" Theroux's voice was suddenly on the base control circuit, flouting procedure and making no obvious effort to avoid alarming him. "*Are your suit system readings optimal?*"

Nathan pulled his eyes away from the Earth, and focused on the heads-up display reflected inside his helmet. "Yes, they are. What's going on, David?"

"*Enough with the sight-seeing. Do a three-sixty and tell me what you see.*"

Nathan took a firm grip of the anchor point and turned slowly round, being careful to avoid tangling himself in the safety line. Procedure dictated that he should have unclipped before doing this sort of manoeuvre but he wasn't ready to float free quite yet.

As he rotated he peered about him and was surprised to find how much the helmet narrowed the effective field of vision. When the Earth filled his eyes it had been deceptive. What he could see was severely limited. He had no peripheral vision at all. "What am I looking for?"

"*Not what; who.*"

"You stupid shit!" Butler raged. "What are you trying to do, panic him?"

Theroux's gaze flicked from screen to screen, checking the station video feeds, then Nathan's suit telemetry, then back to what the fixed video cameras were showing. "You were letting him daydream, Simon," he snapped. "He can't daydream out there, for fuck's sake!"

"Base control decides what he can and can't do, and I am base control," Butler said more coolly. "Now you will behave like a professional, David or you can get the hell out of here. Right now." He overrode the board Theroux was using and deactivated it. Flicking on his own mic he said calmly, "Base control to Spring. Sorry about that interruption. Your second-in-command had an attack of the silly buggers."

"*Any particular silly buggers?*"

"He felt you needed livening up, that's all."

"*Don't bullshit me, base control. I'm tense enough as it is.*"

Theroux glared across at Butler, who pointedly refused to meet his eye. "Let me talk to him?"

"No."

"I need to talk to him."

"No."

"*Talk to me, base control. Who am I looking for, and why?*"

Theroux said, "Okay you tell him. Tell him I can't find Brownly and Goff." Butler turned abruptly from his board and stared at Theroux, who said, "They could be outside with him." Butler frowned. "Tell him," Theroux insisted.

Butler hesitated, seeming to think about it. He turned back to his board and scanned the monitors, then he said, "Listen Spring, we want you alert because you're on your own out there."

"What?" demanded Theroux.

"*What? Say again.*"

"Did you hear what I said?" Theroux almost shouted.

Butler gestured him to be silent and went on, "There is no-one near you at present, but don't worry about it. You have a green board and all the time in the world to get back inside in the unlikely event that it became necessary to abort the EVA."

"*Very well, base control. I'm going to take a couple of minutes to orientate myself now, then I'm going to try and retrace the last moves that the Hendvorrsen group made.*"

"Not all of them, I trust," Butler said.

"*Thank you, base control.*" Nathan's voice did not acknowledge the joke.

Butler now turned back to look at Theroux. "They're not out there, David," he said. "There's nobody out there. Where have you looked for them?"

"Everywhere."

Butler thought for a moment. "Did you check the Engineering Equipment Store?"

"Yeah, I checked it."

"Thoroughly?"

Theroux shrugged. "I looked in there."

"If they were hiding, that would be a good place."

"Why the fuck would they be hiding?"

Butler smiled. "If they knew you were looking for them," he said, "why the fuck *wouldn't* they be hiding?"

It was time to let go. Nathan unclipped the safety line and reeled in the slack. He had put this off as long as he could, but now there was no more time. At least the claustrophobia was under control, and minute by minute he was becoming less immediately conscious of the restrictions of the suit. He was never going to be comfortable in it. There was none of the advertised womb-like security. But he was getting less uncomfortable.

He held onto the anchor point a moment longer, and peered at the curved side of the first of the station's modules looming over him. Like the Earth, it too was bigger than he had anticipated. It was oddly comforting. You could make a mistake on a thing this size and not be punished for it. And any mistakes he made out here would be real ones. Death was too close to risk a show of ineptitude, no matter who was watching.

With one hand he pushed himself away slightly, and with the other he gave a simultaneous tug on the thin metal bar, released his grip, and took off in a perfectly controlled drift across the surface of the station. In his ear, Butler's voice said, "*Very impressive. But don't rush things. Remember the rule: slow out; fast back. You have forty to the outward maximum. On my mark. Do you copy?*"

"Copy," Nathan said, glancing up at the reflected chronometer display and squeezing the time-elapsed to zero plus forty minutes.

"*Mark.*"

He cued it, and the display began to deduct the time he had left before he must turn back. The logic was that however long it took you to get wherever you got, it must take you the same time or less to reverse the trip. Thus it was standard operating procedure to make a slow outward leg and give yourself a margin for error on the return.

Nathan had calculated that this should not be a problem for him. The Hendvorrsen party, needing the larger airlock so that they could stay together, had approached the construction zone from the other side of the station. The smaller lock he was using was closer. He could get to where the incident occurred with plenty of margin to get back, no matter how fast he moved now.

Not that there was any reliable way for him to tell what his speed was. Watching the grey metal surface of the station fall soundlessly past his face, he lacked the physical sensation of movement. The only noise he could hear was his own breathing and that had no perceptible connection with what seemed to be happening in front of him. He lifted his eyes and looked ahead. The curve of the module was dropping away from his line of flight. Some distance beyond it, across a terrifyingly wide expanse of space, he could see the construction zone which Hendvorrsen and the others had been inspecting when things had gone wrong. If his nerve held, he need do nothing at all and his present flight path would take him exactly where he needed to go. Unless his jet pack malfunctioned, and with no way to slow up he smashed himself into the framework of girders, or cannoned off them spinning and unconscious, or missed them altogether so that he fell straight into infinity... He should test the jet pack. But then he'd lose the line of flight, might lose control completely...

"*Base control to Spring.*" Butler's voice interrupted the spiralling panic. "*Be advised that at your present velocity you will leave the limit of my vision in three, I repeat three, minutes. Monitoring will then be by suit telemetry. Do you copy?*"

Brownly and Goff were not in the Engineering Equipment Store. Theroux moved down the central aisle and peered round the storage bins. It was a stupid notion. He felt like some fool being set up for a practical joke or dragged into a boring kid's game. Then he saw it. The toe of a standard issue slipper was poking out from behind a double-stowed bin at the far end, where someone was hiding in the shadows. A foot shot?? Come on. What was this, some corny fucking melodrama for Chrissakes?

"What is this, some corny fucking melodrama, for Chrissakes?" he said aloud. "Come out of there. I can see you, man."

When nothing happened, he moved towards the hiding place. As he closed on the lurking presence it crossed his mind that if it was Brownly and the guy had flipped out totally, he could be in deeply serious shit here. This could be peace officer's hide-and-go-seek he was playing: homicidal rules.

He stopped just short of grabbing for the figure and shouted at it angrily, "Come the fuck out of there! I'm tired of your bullshit games, friend. Come out of there now, or I'll bust your ass and you'll be Earthside from fucking here on."

Still there was no response. Maybe no-one was there. Maybe it was a trick of the light. Maybe it was just a slipper some moron had fixed there as a joke. Warily he moved closer. No, there *was* somebody there. He leaned forward and peered round into the darkened recess. A face peered back at him. It was Goff. With a grunt of shock, Theroux jerked away. "Shit, Goff. That's not funny," he said.

There was still no sound from Goff. Theroux waited a moment, then keeping as much distance as he could between himself and the gap, he looked again behind the storage bins.

Goff had not moved or changed his expression. It seemed to Theroux that the man's intense stare was turned inwards as though he was trying to focus on himself, a self that had faded and then was lost to emptiness. Fanciful thought. From the twisted angle of Goff's head, it looked like his neck had been broken. He wouldn't have had time to focus on much of anything before he died.

Odds on, the body was upright because it was easier to cram it into the narrow space that way. It was for sure that Goff hadn't squeezed in there himself and then twisted his own neck until the spinal column ruptured. Not much room for doubt that he'd been murdered. Not much room at all.

Nathan was relieved to find the jet pack worked and the tiny braking jets were properly balanced so that his approach was slowed without any directional deviation. He was not ashamed of the way he managed to come to a full stop just on the fringes of the jumble of thin girders and partially assembled modules; he was almost sorry not to be on camera. "Base control, this is Spring. I'm at the main construction area now. I have about twenty minutes for a look round, yes?"

"*Look: don't touch. That suit you're wearing is not puncture-proof so do not, repeat do not, go any further into the construction zone.*"

Any further? Nathan wondered. Can he tell just from suit telemetry exactly where I am? He's good, but is he that good? Unless it's a radar plot. Yes it's probably a radar plot. Chances are he can see more of what's going on right here where I am now than I can.

"Very well, base control," Nathan said, and, using the finest calibration available on the jet pack, he set himself rotating slowly. As he turned, he craned his neck within the suit helmet, straining to see just how much of the area could realistically be inspected from a stationary position.

Again he was struck by how restricted seeing was: not impaired, not even by the photo chromic sun filters laminated into the face cover, but narrowed to a sort of tunnel-vision. You could see more or less everything, but only by scanning each area in smallish sections. Even so, it would be difficult to conceal anything out here, and when Hendvorrsen died, there were five other people floating around and watching. And there was Butler as base control, the self-proclaimed best in the business, which on present evidence he probably was. It seemed unlikely that anything could get past that lot unseen, kill Hendvorrsen before he was able to hit the suit's panic button, and still leave no obvious trace. Had he reasoned it wrong? Was it simply the freak accident which Box calculated was acceptable as a probability? Maybe he was out here for nothing... He tweaked the jet controls and stopped his rotation so that he was facing the half-completed extensions to the station. The light was vivid on the spars and crossbeams making them stand out starkly against the background blackness of space. The open shells of the unfinished modules sliced through the brightness, cutting solid shadows deep within their curves. Despite Butler's instructions, he was curious to look more closely into one of those dark places. As far as he could see, there was plenty of room to move through the spider work of girders, if he was careful.

He nudged forward on the barest touch of a jet and stopped himself with his hands against a tubular reinforcing strut. From here it should be possible simply to pull himself through the gaps and thread his way in the direction of his chosen module. He looked towards the largest. That seemed like a sensible choice, given his difficulties with claustrophobia. And it was not too far in. He should be able to make it there and back here to the jump-off point for the return to the airlock with time to spare.

Taking elaborate precautions to touch the structure only with his hands, he started the controlled drift into the construction.

"*Base control to Spring. What are you doing?*"

"There's something I want to look at more closely. It's not that far," Nathan murmured without slowing his progress.

"*No!*"

"I'm not taking any unnecessary risks." Nathan was breathing harder now.

"*All risks are unnecessary!*"

Butler sounded slightly rattled. Sweat prickled at the back of Nathan's neck. Am I missing something? he wondered suddenly. Can he see something that I can't see? Where? He glanced round quickly, taking in the suit's readouts as he did so. There wasn't anything. "I'm almost there," he said. "I can't see anything wrong." Ahead, he could see just a main crossbeam and strut to be negotiated, and he would be at the open edge of the module.

Butler's voice took on an almost strident edge. "*This is base control. I am giving you a direct order, Spring. Get back out of the construction zone!*"

The professional *sangfroid* seemed to have deserted the man completely. What the hell was wrong with him? Nathan slid between the woven alloy crossbeam and the smooth tubular strut, and pushed himself gently across the remaining space to the lip formed by the line of outer panels which had been welded into position.

The way the module was being assembled meant that, at this stage, it looked as though a huge wedge had been carved out down part of its length. In cross-section, perhaps a quarter of the outer circumference was missing here, but its alignment still cut off the interior from all but the faintest of reflected light.

Nathan floated above the opening and stared downwards into the total blackness inside. As the suit's sun filters adjusted, his eyes began to play tricks. He thought he saw a movement in the glimmering darkness. He killed the heads-up display, thinking it might be a multiple reflection on his face cover. It made no difference. He stared harder, trying to resolve the wavering shape that suddenly appeared. It expanded as he watched, and for a moment he thought it must be puffing itself up. What on Earth would do that? Not on Earth, though. Then he realized. It wasn't getting bigger, it was getting closer. It was rising out of the black towards him. He stared and stared, not able to look or move away. Not able to move at all.

Whatever it was, it was coming straight at him. Whatever it was.

When he finally saw it clearly, he tried to duck back and kick himself off from the panels. Recklessly uncaring of the close dangers of the girders, he struggled to pull away. But it was too late to escape the spacesuited figure which lunged out of the darkness and grabbed at him.

Chapter 11

They set off the hazard alarms, because it was the fast way to get the attention of all personnel to warn them that one of their number was deranged and running amok. It was not a textbook use of the *Charles De Gaulle*'s safety systems, but there was nothing in the book to cover this situation. Once the alarms were triggered, the computer immediately sealed and isolated the main sections of the station. It was a logical damage limitation procedure in almost every accident scenario, and in this case it had the advantage of limiting Brownly's movements and minimizing the damage he might do to life support. Of course, it did have the disadvantage of maybe trapping someone in a severely confined space with what they had just been warned was a homicidal maniac.

Inevitably, the result was chaos.

Men and women who had come to terms with the calculated dangers of working off-Earth were stripped of logic and abruptly lost in the unreasoning terror of the bogeyman. Brownly the Ripper lurked in every dark place, and all over the station people hit the nearest panic button and yelled for priority assistance.

The traffic and communications centre was swamped with alarms. Not even Butler could be expected to cope instantly with everything that was coming in. Theroux tried and failed to get through to him from the general manager's office, where Lancine was already regretting putting the station on emergency alert.

Wim Bentinck tried and failed to get through to him from the suit storage bay, where he had barricaded Claire Folger in a locker, convinced that she was Brownly.

In the madness of those early minutes, not even the man who really knew where Brownly was hidden could get through.

Although he had been prepared for it, the assault panicked Nathan, and for a few precious seconds he had thrashed and yelled and punched frantically at his spacesuit's emergency alarm.

The attacker, still only half out of the module, clung onto him grimly, holding him against the panels. He seemed to be trying to smother Nathan's struggles and keep him from tearing free and jetting away. It was a bizarre fighting style, and this as much as anything helped Nathan get control of himself and remember that there was another man somewhere out of sight. Another man waiting to come at him on the blind side.

He tried to twist round so that he could get a glimpse of the second man, but the one who was holding him was braced somehow and his grip was gradually becoming more powerful. Was that possible? With sudden, cold clarity, Nathan knew that the grip was not more powerful; he was weakening. He knew too that his suit emergency alarm had failed. Butler was silent and there was no sign of the computer override. There would be no help coming. No-one knew what was happening to him. No-one would know what had happened to him. He was alone.

He leaned in and tried to see who it was that was holding him, but the sun filters had not cleared enough and they made it impossible to distinguish the face. For a moment, he felt oddly uninvolved and the thought occurred to him that spacesuits were the ideal disguise; everyone looked the same.

Leaning in had been stupid. The embrace was tighter now, more restrictive. A movement back among the girders tugged at the corner of his vision. He turned his head quickly, as far as the helmet would let him, but there was nothing to see. Whatever it was had gone. Not whatever it was – *who*ever. Reality rushed back at him. Time was running out. These people intended to kill him. They wanted him dead. This wasn't a practice exercise. This was happening *now*.

If he could just get a hand to the equipment pouch on his left hip… but his right arm was blocked, and there was not enough flexibility to raise his left high enough to reach the fastening. He tried to get more room to move, but he could not get a purchase on the side of the module. He struggled, pushing with his ponderous legs, which paddled and scrambled in a slow-motion nightmare. The only effect was to exhaust him. He was breathing hard now, and despite the suit's cooling system, he was bathed in sweat.

He had lost it.

They were going to win.

These bastards were going to beat him after all.

And second prize was to die looking stupid and confident and wrong.

I do not expect a groundsider policeman wiz your limited experience to understand 'ow we work out 'ere.

Spacemen are ten-a-penny. What they need is...

You 'ave conducted your enquiries unintelligently and wizout discretion ...a good copper.

Who else do you trust love. If you don't count that creepy Box there's no-one to talk to...

He's trying to tell you that if you'd had that little scuffle outside you'd have been... apart from me. Point is, you're not ready Nathan ...DEAD MEAT.

He caught a movement again. Glancing sideways, he saw him this time. The second man, coming fast. Using his jets? Jets among the girders? A risk. Stupid risk. Time running out for them, too? He bent the fingers of his right hand back in the thick gauntlet, feeling for his own jet pack control. He knew it was useless, though. He knew he could not release the small joystick from its wrist mount without using his other hand. The jet pack was as inaccessible as the equipment pouch. Christ, there was nothing he could do. He was tired now – breathless, sweating, and tired to death.

And then, with a muffled slam, the second man cannoned into him. The shuddering blow was shocking. Everything seemed to jar in the heavy-breathing, suit-enclosed, silence.

It was a mistake. The man had been hurrying, travelling close to the limits of control, and he was fractionally late with his braking jets. Worse, he was not coming straight, so his momentum was angular and for a moment his accomplice inside the module had to slacken his grip.

Nathan found himself loose. Not free, but with enough room to cross his left arm between his suit and the module panels. Faster than he realized he could do it, he released the jet pack control. As soon as the joystick slotted into his right hand, he thumbed maximum forward thrust. Keeping the jets open and using all the power the pack would develop, he pulled the directional guidance up and, when he saw that he was beginning to rise, drove it down again hard.

He watched himself tilt slowly forward over the edge and into the light-less pool of the module's empty interior. The man who had been holding him rolled backwards, still clutching on and trying to pinion him. The second man made a lurching grab at his backpack and was dragged with them into the dark.

Chris Boucher

The three of them somersaulted eccentrically as they fumbled and struggled. In the blackness, there was no sensation of this head-over-heels motion, no sensation of any movement at all except relative to each other. All space and time was finally reduced to a faintly seen, hardly felt, almost silent, scrabble to kill.

Nathan let go of the thrust control and twisted the joystick, so that it sprang back into its wrist mount, leaving his right hand free again. Using his other hand to push the frontal attacker away, he reached down to his left hip and released the fastening on the equipment pouch.

The man lunged back and clamped both arms round him, holding him tightly and preventing him from getting his hand into the pouch.

At the same time, Nathan knew, the man behind him would be working to open the access panel on his backpack. That had to have been their plan all along. And they were not about to give up on their plan. Not even if the victim understood what was happening and put up a fight. How long a fight? They must hit the other side of the module eventually. Would that shake them loose again? Was there time?

Pale flickers of reflected gleams fleetingly glimpsed in the face cover of the man who held him. The man behind had working lights. These two had come prepared to kill in any conditions. Nothing left to chance with an unfortunate accident to arrange. Another unfortunate accident. Well, not this time.

Well, not *this* bloody time!

The outrage which blazed when he had been attacked in the engineering store flashed through Nathan once again, and with it came furious energy. He forced his hand into the equipment pouch and felt for the spring-loaded switchblade it contained. Brownly's knife remained where he had clipped it, and as he pulled it clear he pressed the catch and the blade snapped open. Without pausing to think, he slashed the laser tip upwards across the chest of his first attacker's spacesuit. The green pinpoint of light made a shallow incision, opening only the outermost layers. Water from the cooling system exploded, ghostly, into a fog of ice crystals. The man let go of Nathan, floated for a brief time unmoving, and then jerkily clamped a hand over the cut.

Inside his suit the man was screaming, but Nathan could hear nothing. He slashed at him again and again. Desperately the man tried to fend him off with his free arm, and the blade tip became snagged in the toughened fabric of the sleeve.

The second man heard his companion's cries over his suit RT and abandoned his work on the backpack. Tugging at Nathan's helmet, he guided himself over the top of the fight and pulled himself into it. As he reached downwards, the lights on his wrists illuminated the knife, which was still caught in the other man's sleeve, and he snatched for it.

By the two thin beams of light waving around him, Nathan immediately saw why the blade was stuck. It was a frictionless stiletto, precision-built to need no weight behind it. A spaceworker's weapon. Not designed to slice; designed to puncture.

When the second man plucked at it, he was already too late. Nathan stopped trying to rip the knife through the sleeve, and simply stabbed forward with it. Decompression began even before he had pulled it out. He stabbed again, to be sure. Vapour jets ripped from the holes, spinning the man away to scream in silence as his blood vessels ruptured.

The surviving attacker was paralyzed, apparently unable to decide whether to fight or make a break for it. The hesitation was fatal. Nathan thrust high, aiming between the lights which marked clearly the position of the man's arms. He punctured the centre of the chest. It was a neat, almost clinical kill.

As the man flailed despairingly, trying to stem the venting gas, one of his lights shone back on his own face cover. The sun filters were at their minimum now and Nathan saw him clearly. He expected him to be a stranger, and he *was* a stranger. What he did not expect was the feeling it gave him to see, to *really* see, that it was a stranger who had come to end his life. To kill someone known to you was ugly and savage enough, but somewhere in the shameful dark, it was human. This, though, *this* had no link with people. This was outside. This was horror. He shivered.

The dying stranger, driven by the hole in his chest, began to move away from him into the black. Before he was completely out of reach, Nathan stabbed at him again and missed and then again and again until finally the blade burned a hole through the leg of the man's spacesuit. This second vent pushed him into a tumbling cartwheel. His wrist-lights made symmetrical patterns in the darkness. Nathan watched them, fascinated. He was aware of a vague disappointment that the fight seemed to be over. He was holding the knife out in front of him and there was an odd sound echoing in his helmet. He found he had an erection. Then he recognized the sound as giggling. He was giggling.

A ripple of nausea trembled over him. He swallowed the wash of saliva in his mouth, and tasted bile at the back of his throat. He took a deep, shuddering breath, and concentrated on getting control of himself. He must not throw up. He definitely must not throw up. There were two things you *didn't* do in a spacesuit, his trainer had told him. One was vomit, and so was the other one.

Disgust took the place of nausea, and he flung the knife away from him. Almost at once, it vanished from his sight. The small action produced a small reaction and arrested the last of the slow somersaulting which the fight had been gradually eliminating.

The effect was too minor to change his line of drift, and he was anyway unsure of what that might be. Then he saw the turning lights jolt and swing as the second of the men he had killed struck the plating some distance away on the far side of the module. The lights bounced and twisted and rolled onwards into the dark.

For a moment, he had an impression of perspective and position. It was probably an illusion, but it brought him back out of the limbo in which he had lost himself. He focused on where he thought he had seen the wall and dragged his eyes across the imagined curve of it in a long, unblinking stare.

He peered for the slightest change in the darkness which would indicate the gap he had first come to. Without a reflective surface floating directly above it – as he himself had done, gathering light and shining like a target beacon – his only hope was that the sun filters of his face cover were now clear enough to let him see the difference between darkness and deep space. He stretched the look as far as his eyes would reach.

Nothing. The blackness was uniform.

Perhaps the exit was behind him. Except that he wasn't absolutely sure whether or not he was rotating – so how could he be sure where 'behind him' was?

A long way off now, the lights of the dead man flickered intermittently. It looked as though he was spinning, but that did not help Nathan to decide if *he* was too. He nudged the heads-up display back on. The readings looked okay. If the spacesuit had been damaged, it wasn't showing on any of the telltales. Everything was functioning normally. Apart from the RT. That was clearly buggered. He wondered if that was part of the plan, and decided that it must have been. "Unless you're a lover of coincidence," he said aloud, and was glad to hear his voice sounding more or less normal again.

Time-elapsed was the only immediate worry. It had run into deficit. He was past the outward maximum by several minutes. He should have started back by now. But even that was not critical. There was plenty of margin for error.

He was surprised at how quickly it had all happened. Killing two men should have taken longer.

He released the jet pack control. He would have to risk a delicate boost, a very delicate boost, to take him to the module wall so that he could really orientate himself. He touched the control and discovered to his horror that the system was registering nothing. The jet pack was dead.

"Dead? What do you mean, dead?" asked Theroux, when the general panic had subsided enough to make communication with Butler possible.

Lancine looked up from her desk terminal where she was trying to override the automatic safety lockouts, and waited to hear the reply.

"*I mean there's nothing from his suit telemetry, no voice response, and I can't find any sign of him on anything else.*" There was no trace of emotion in Butler's voice. "*I can only assume therefore that he's dead.*"

Lancine shook her head and said, "'ow many people can he lose, this base control?"

Theroux ignored her. "What the fuck sort of an assumption is that?" he demanded.

Butler's voice retained its professional calm. "*He went into the construction zone. I gave him a direct instruction not to do that.*"

Professional calm was not what Theroux wanted. "He didn't do as you told him, so you write him off? For Chrissakes, Simon!"

"*What's the alternative?*"

"Send out a team," Theroux said.

"*Stop wasting my time, David. We've got enough problems thanks to you and the climb...*" he stopped, obviously he had remembered where Theroux was calling from, and then he went on without any change of tone, "*thanks to you and Madame la directrice.*"

"What about Nathan's problems, you asshole?"

"*Before anyone got to him, he'd certainly be dead.*"

"But you don't know where he is, do you?"

"*I know where he isn't. He isn't close enough to be pulled back in the time available.*"

Theroux glared at Lancine. "How long before you crack the hatches?"

"Not long," she said.

Butler's voice cut across them. "*The question of rescue is academic since we're all stuck, yes? You in your small corner, and me in mine. Call me back when that changes.*"

Theroux floated across and watched Lancine punching in the operating codes. She did not react to the lack of etiquette or to the breach of security. He said, "My question was, how long?"

Lancine continued to work, and said without looking up, "My answer was, not long."

Theroux thought, *fuck you, bitch*, and said, "We don't have time left."

"You stand ready to discharge your responsibility when I 'ave completed this?" Lancine asked.

Theroux grunted, "Yeah."

"Perhaps there is a contingency plan for such an emergency as this?"

Theroux said, "Of course there is. You know there is."

Lancine gave a Gallic shrug of denial which was small and very dismissive. "I am only surprised the Star Cops are so well prepared."

Theroux's confusion showed. "Pardon me?"

The reaction was not lost on Lancine, whose supplementary academic specialization had been Inter-Personal Psychology in Management Structures. "I assume you 'ave not forgotten," she said, "that there is a murderer running loose on the station. And you are the only remaining policeman."

The crack rattled through Nathan's head and made his ears ring, and he knew that some part of the spacesuit had failed catastrophically. It took a minute or two for him to accept that everything was functioning and he was still in one piece, and it was several seconds more before he realized that his helmet had struck the metal skin of the module, filling the suit with vibration and his ears with noise.

He put his hands up and touched the panels. He tried to do it lightly; the last thing he needed was to push himself off again, back into the void. The suit's armoured gauntlets were not exactly sensitive, but as far as he could tell, he had stopped drifting. He badly wanted to hold on, but there was nothing to grip, and he had to fight the drowning man's impulse to clutch and thrash, and he had to force his body to relax and float. For reassurance he permitted himself an occasional numb, silent tap with a single finger but he couldn't risk anything more.

Star Cops

So. He was located. Somewhere. If he could pick up a reference point, any reference point, then there was a chance he could navigate his way out of this. This trap he had fallen into like a mouse into a bottle. Only there weren't any bloody reference points. Like a *blind* mouse into a bottle.

He was sorry now that he had stopped Theroux from coming outside by exaggerating the threat from Brownly and Goff. He could probably have trusted Theroux. He wasn't a professional copper, but he could probably have trusted him. He looked at the displays again. Everything functioning as it should. Everything optimal. Except time. He was in trouble with time. Time was getting critical. Error was claiming its margin. Everything critical then. Nothing optimal. He should be back inside the airlock in…in two minutes twenty-five…he hadn't even started the return. He cancelled the display. Maybe conserving power would help. Help what though? And how the hell was he supposed to get back anyway? Walk?

He looked down towards his feet. He could see them faintly. It did not immediately strike him that this was in any way remarkable. They were very faint. An almost indistinguishable silhouette, against an infinitesimally paler patch of darkness.

Service engineer Carl Saliero had recognized Brownly's corpse at once, even though it had been mutilated by the abortive attempts of the mess's main disposal unit to add it to one of the waste containers.

Carl had been stripping down the system, looking for whatever was jamming things up, when he uncovered the mangled remains. Before he could report the find, there were alarms and warnings and general hysteria. He was one of the few people to remain unmoved. He did not like what he had found; it disgusted him, but he knew there was nothing to be frightened of. A homicidal madman was no threat if he was dead. Brownly was not going to get much deader.

Carl was not a stupid man, but murder was outside his experience. Thinking about it did not come easily to him. In truth, he preferred not to think about it. What he preferred to do was wait calmly and patiently for the hatches to be unlocked and the communications channels to be unjammed, so that he could pass on the fact that there was no more cause for alarm.

Only when he was doing this did it occur to him to wonder how Brownly, a tall man, could have fed himself into the disposal unit. He would have to have been superhuman to stay conscious long enough to push his way through machine so that his feet reached the second-stage compactor. But who knew what a madman was capable of? Even when it was clear that Brownly must have been killed first and shoved into the unit, it did not occur to Carl to wonder why the murderer would try to dispose of the body using a machine which could not possibly do the job, as anyone on the station would have known.

But then it was not Carl Saliero's job to think of such things, and those whose job it was were not quick to think of it either.

Nathan pushed himself, feet first, towards the opening. How could he have missed it? It was vast and bright. How could it have taken him so long? Once you saw, it you couldn't *not* see it. He floated out of the module, laughing with relief. He could see again. He was out of the blind, bloody bottle. He stared around eagerly. Beyond his feet, the vastnesses of space opened up. Below him, the construction framework was vivid in the light.

Below him?

He swept a desperate arm back and managed to hook his hand over the edge of the hole and stop himself. Christ. He turned over and clamped both hands on the metalwork. It was unnecessary but it was comforting, his own personal wacsob, and he clung on until the fear subsided and he stopped feeling light-headed. Without a jet pack that worked, he'd better be bloody sure where he was pointing from now on if he didn't want a straight flight into oblivion. He had to be more careful. He had to concentrate. And he had to do it quickly. Check the readouts? No point. What was he going to do, breathe less if he was running on empty? First thing was to get back in among the construction girders and spars, then he could work his way to a return launch point.

He swivelled so that his head was aimed at the nearest section, and pulled with his hands and pushed off with his knees. The thrust was clumsy, uncoordinated, with the pull and the push almost cancelling each other out, and though he moved in the right direction, his progress was agonizingly slow, the more so because there was nothing he could do to speed it up. His arms, at first held in front of him to fend off collision, were now stretched out, anxiously reaching for a chance to grab onto something and tug.

When he finally drifted onto his target he lost more time with ill-considered, snatching rushes, pulling himself into intricate dead ends among the networks of construction. He knew he was panicking; he knew panic was swallowing the air he had, using up the time; he knew he must stop and think about what he was doing; and every instinct in him howled for action, flight, movement; and he knew reason kept you alive not bloody instinct: reason.

He stopped where he was and tried to reason.

He called up the telltale display and looked at each readout reflected in the helmet's face cover, reviewing them in turn, making sure they registered on his mind and meant something to him. He did it as though it was a routine, pre-EVA systems check and when he finished he had information on which to base rational behaviour.

The backpack gases readout said he had fourteen minutes breathing time left, though he had been taught never to rely on the last few minutes capacity in anything as crude as a suit system. The journey back to the airlock would take anything up to twenty minutes. "On the face of it the rational behaviour is panic," he said but couldn't manage the wry smile necessary to complete the heroic image.

Carefully, trying not to think about the time it took, he worked out a route through the construction zone and then picked his way along it meticulously. This time he avoided the fumbling haste and covered the distance quickly. He was only slightly out of breath when he reached the edge. But even slightly out of breath was trouble. He was using oxygen faster. Time was speeding up. He needed to be quicker to keep up with it. He had to be quicker.

The space between the construction zone and the station seemed wider than he remembered. It yawned hugely. He found he was breathing faster still. Stop it.

Stop it.

He looked around for something substantial enough to launch from. Everything within reach was tubular. There was nothing he could put both feet flat against to balance the push. He chose a crossbeam finally. It was the biggest surface available. He set his feet on it and began to draw his legs up into a crouch. This was precisely the reverse of how he had trained and practised for such a manoeuvre. The standard procedure was always to settle into your body posture, knees to your chest or whatever was required, and then position yourself relative to the fixed object. You needed above average muscle control to do it the other way round without an involuntary push floating you away.

Nathan did not have above average muscle control. Before he was ready to commit to the final thrust towards the station he found himself drifting forward, flapping and floundering like a helplessly water-logged bird. Reason pulled him back from the chasm.

Stop trying to balance. This isn't balancing, you stupid bastard. And it isn't flying for Christ's sake. You're not high up and this isn't flying and you can't balance.

He stopped flapping his arms, reached to the crossbeam with the toe of his boot and flipped himself into a somersault. It could have pushed him further off but he had developed some small skill by now so what it did was to turn him round an almost stationary axis. He was still just within glove-tip distance of a bracing spar as the half spin was completed, and he clawed himself back and tried again. This time he did everything right. When he was ready the readout said eight minutes of breathing time left. He knew it was hopeless: he was a dead man.

He launched off from the crossbeam, pushing every ounce of power his legs could develop into the kick.

Theroux made a preliminary identification of Brownly's corpse, left Lancine to deal, and made immediately for the traffic control and communications module. He got there to find it was empty.

"Simon?" he called.

There was nothing out of place. The screens were operating. Everything was normal except, unthinkably...

"Where the fuck are you?"

...the place was unmanned.

He peered round half-expecting to see Butler's lifeless body jammed between the consoles or floating in a spreading cloud of gore, but there was no sign of him.

Theroux moved to the main console to see whether he had logged off when a movement on one of the small monitors caught his eye. In the field of the exterior cameras a spacesuited figure was drifting across the side of the station in the general direction of the secondary two-man airlock.

Theroux slapped the resuscitation team alarm and keyed the communications circuit. "Blue alert, blue alert, resuscitation team to secondary EVA lock B for Baker, RS to EVA two B for Baker. This is a code one."

He glanced at Nathan's suit telemetry. Shit. "We have a suit breathout,

Star Cops

man down by minus ten. This is a code one suit breathout. Let's go, guys, let's go, let's go!"

Telemetry said Nathan was unconscious by now, or dead. Either way someone had to go out and pull him in. Leaving communications without a duty traffic controller was out of the question so one of the RS team would have to do it. He was about to issue the instruction when Vanhalsen arrived looking tense and distinctly wary. "Have you got him?" he asked.

Theroux left the console and headed for the hatch. "Take over. Nathan Spring's on empty, resus is on the way to lock B, Butler's AWOL."

Vanhalsen moved to block his way. "Have you got him?" he demanded.

"Got who?"

"Brownly, who else!"

"Brownly's been disposed of." Theroux ducked past and hopped through the hatch.

"What does that mean?" Vanhalsen called after him.

"He got himself wasted," Theroux shouted back, unsure why the ugly pun sprang so readily to mind and wondering uneasily where Simon Butler had gone.

"Jesus," Vanhalsen muttered as he keyed in to the duty log, "when did it get so dangerous out here."

Nathan was very sleepy…sleepy very…sleepy… He kept blanking out. Despite concentrating fiercely on the station surface flowing past him he could not keep his attention focused. He drifted as he drifted, his mind drawing back behind his eyes until it was so far from them there was no link could connect them, nothing –

He woke again thickly. He had to stay awake. He was not sure why. Why did he have to stay awake? He looked ahead in the direction of the airlock. Christ it was a long way away and his line of travel was not exactly right not to reach it right exactly right –

The resuscitation team and Theroux arrived together at the airlock. Butler was already there, suiting up. "I thought it was quickest," he snapped before Theroux could ask and went on, "I didn't want to lose another one." He pushed the helmet at Theroux and bent his head forward. "Who's on the monitors?"

Theroux said, "Vanhalsen."

"Get him to patch you in to the suit circuit. It'll save time."

"Why no blue code one?" Theroux asked as he hurriedly worked the helmet down into its seating. Butler's answer was too late to be heard through the sealed suit.

To Vanhalsen's eye the man was obviously trying too hard. He was making difficulties for himself. Having overshot the airlock he seemed to be trying to turn round now rather than simply reverse the movement. And manoeuvring the other man was proving to be almost beyond him.

He repeated the only instruction he could think of which might help: "Take it slower, Simon," if only the fool would listen. The body was inert but without weight intervening that should have made Spring easier to handle not more difficult.

"Stop telling me that! There isn't time to take it slower!"

Vanhalsen watched the screen helplessly as Butler shoved Spring back towards the airlock and immediately lost control of him.

"Oh shit!"

He jetted in pursuit, using too much thrust so that he pushed them both past the airlock once more. It would have been funny if the time he was taking was not costing Spring whatever chance he might have of survival. He was turning to try yet again when, quite unexpectedly, the outer hatch of the airlock closed.

"Oh for Christ's sake!" Butler bellowed. "Who in God's name is playing silly buggers with the automatics?!"

Seconds later small plumes of gas flash-clouded from the safety valves as someone used the emergency venting cycle. Then the hatch opened again and a figure emerged and made straight for where Butler was still struggling with Spring.

"Who is this, what's going on?" demanded Butler.

"I don't know," Vanhalsen said and opened a general channel. "Operative exiting secondary EVA, B for Baker, identify yourself please."

"David Theroux," was the terse response, "now shut the fuck up both of you and lets get Nathan inside."

Nathan Spring, Chief Superintendent on attachment to the ISPF, was dead when they got him through the airlock and into the station.

Chapter 12

"How do you feel?" Theroux asked.

"I've got a splitting headache," Nathan said, "apart from that…"

"Apart from that you feel like shit, right?"

Nathan wanted to pull a duvet up round his neck and turn his face into a soft pillow but the med-lab sleeping frame into which he was strapped offered none of these options. "I've had better days," he said.

"It is not likely," Lancine remarked as she peered without much comprehension at the readings on the total-body monitor to which Nathan was hooked up, "that you 'ave 'ad luckier days. Pieter estimates that you were within seconds of being irrecoverable."

"Pieter?" asked Nathan.

"Pieter Loos," said Theroux and, when Nathan did not respond, prompted, "Belgian? Biochemist? The only trained paramedic on the station."

Nathan sighed, "Yes, yes. I didn't ask for a CV."

"But you do know who I mean?" Theroux persisted.

"Yes I do know who you mean."

"Well?"

"Well what for Christ's sake?"

"Well what is it that he does?"

Nathan sighed again. "I don't know what this is about but I'm not in the mood for games."

"He leads…?" Theroux said as though questioning a very young child.

"A life of unspeakable debauchery; the off-Earth weightlifting rankings; what do you want me to say? He leads… the resuscitation team: what?"

Theroux looked relieved. "He leads the resuscitation team," he said. "And his estimate was ninety seconds to brain-death. That's a pretty good margin." He grinned and shrugged. "Hell you don't want to get back too early right, why waste the time?"

Lancine said, "It seems that there are no signs of physical injury. The impairment of brain function is 'owever a possibility. You will require periodic monitoring for a number of years to decide whether this 'as happened."

"A year," said Theroux encouragingly, "eighteen months tops," and then drawing Lancine aside lowered his voice to murmur. "Is now a real good time to be discussing this, Françoise?"

Nathan gave up any thought of comfortable infirmity, without Lee to nurse him it would be no fun anyway, and began to undo the straps and release himself from the frame.

Theroux hurried to restrain him. "Hey, whoa! Computer instruction is you remain on that monitor for twenty-four hours while it diagnoses and prescribes."

"I don't have to stay here for it do that," Nathan said and finished unstrapping. He disconnected the standby treatment lines and switched the body monitor to remote. "And could we avoid one of those cliché ridden scenes where the ill-natured patient discharges himself against advice from interfering bystanders."

"Interfering bystanders?" Theroux asked.

Lancine said, "If David 'ad not interfered you would not be alive now."

Nathan had been struggling to get free of the sleep-sack and now when he was almost out he realized that he was naked. Embarrassed he stopped moving, half in and half out of the sack, and said, "That was then, this is now. Interfering is a bad habit to get into."

"Well fuck you and the horse you rode in on," Theroux murmured, and moved to the hatch saying over his shoulder, "I've got peace officer work to do. There's two stiffs to bag-and-tag and computer forensics to agree with."

"Wait!" Nathan said, more sharply than he intended. Christ his head really hurt. It made thinking difficult and tact impossible. Theroux stopped and turned. Nathan said to Lancine, "If you'd excuse us please. This is police business." She looked for a moment as though she was going to object, then she said, "Of course."

On her way out she plucked a pair of coveralls from a locker and floated them back in Theroux's direction. She hopped through the hatch saying as she went, "Your colleague needs those. He looks ridiculous wearing that sleep-sack."

Without being asked Theroux checked the coveralls for a bug. Box registered nothing. Puzzled, Nathan said, "Box please re-scan for listening devices." The unexpected result had been confirmed by the time he had freed himself from the sack and while he struggled into the clean pair Theroux checked the coveralls still in the locker. They were not bugged either.

Nathan said, "We'll need to find out why this lot are different. Make a note, David."

"I'll add it to the list," Theroux said.

"Just don't forget, okay," said Nathan irritably. He was clammy and shivering now. The coveralls stuck to the small of his back and the backs of his legs. His face and neck were cold and slick with sweat. As well as the blinding headache, the horribly familiar nausea had returned. And this time he knew he wasn't going to be able to control it. He looked round in desperation. Wordlessly Theroux handed him a sickbag and he put it to his face and retched miserably.

Theroux said, "I have the feeling that if the computer'd said get moving you'd have stayed where you were. Like you were supposed to?"

"There are two more corpses out at the construction zone," Nathan said when he got his breath back. "They're in the main module... B7 is it?"

Theroux's reaction was muted. "I don't think we're missing anyone else. Just Brownly and Goff."

"These are strangers," Nathan said. "Strangers to me at least."

"What were they doing there?"

"They were trying to kill me."

Theroux nodded. "That's what held you up?"

"Fighting for my life wasn't included in time allowed to the outward maximum. Stupid oversight."

"And you killed these two strangers." Theroux's tone was neutral but though he tried to keep his face expressionless the scepticism was there to see.

Nathan saw it clearly but he was too preoccupied and uncomfortable to react. "I didn't have to make it look like an accident," he said. "How good are the station radars?"

"Compared to what?"

It was a reasonable question Nathan realized but it irritated him anyway. "Are they precise enough to locate an individual within a few feet?"

"Your would-be killers are not likely to have snuck past them undetected if that's what you mean."

"It isn't what I mean. Don't interpret the bloody question just answer it," Nathan snapped. "Have we got accurate, close range, small-scale radars?"

"No."

So. "So one of them was watching me." It was further confirmation if he needed it. The question was could he prove what he now knew.

"One of them was watching you, waiting for a chance to jump out."

"That wasn't what I meant either," Nathan said and yawned.

"Listen," Theroux said, "I know you're not going to want to hear this but a breathout can play weird games with your head. It's possible that none of what you remember out there really happened."

"It's possible that none of what anyone remembers really happened," Nathan said and yawned again. He was suddenly quite sleepy. "Has the machine already given me some sort of medication?"

Theroux looked at the treatment readouts and then called up the user notes. "Relaxants mostly," he said. "To counter the stuff the resus team used. Stabilize you."

"I think," said Nathan drowsily. "it overdid them. Go and retrieve those bodies, David. The thing about police work, good police work, is that it doesn't require faith. Just evidence." Then he let go and fell into sleep, floating there where he was, in the middle of the med-lab.

The orbit shuttle was on the other side of the construction zone, hidden from the main station radars by the complex geometry of building work in the foreground, and the jumble of junk which drifted through the background of any scan.

Theroux remembered.

"I didn't realize you still couldn't tell shit from shuttle."
"Without the computer nobody can, not even you."
"Don't take any bets on that, David old love,"

They must have come in slow, he thought, and on exactly the right trajectory. They went to a lot of trouble. This was a well planned crime.

The corpses were where Nathan had said they'd be. They were a mess but their IDs said they were freelance shuttle-jocks out of Moonbase. They had borrowed the transportation and the flight was neither authorized nor cleared.

This intelligence had amused Simon Butler inordinately. "How can Moonbase tell? Their traffic control is currently being fucked by one, Sally

McMasters, which is not inappropriate since rumour has it she did a lot of that to get the job in the first place."

"I hadn't heard that rumour," Theroux said.

"Every woman in a senior position is the subject of such rumours," said Lancine, resting her hands on the desk in front of her and drumming her fingers lightly.

Butler said cheerfully, "I don't start them I just pass them on," and helped himself to another squeeze-pack of the general manager's coffee. "How is it your coffee is so much better than the stuff in the mess?"

"I give sexual favours to the Beverages Department of the Quartermaster Division," she said without smiling.

"Now that rumour I had heard," Theroux said but Lancine remained unsmiling.

"'Ow much longer have we to wait for 'im?" she asked, drumming her fingers a little harder.

Theroux was not sure whether the gesture was theatrical or an uncharacteristic sign of real agitation. Before he needed to make up his mind though and frame an appropriate answer, Nathan shambled in.

"I'm sorry to have kept you waiting." He moved clumsily to the vacant seat and pulled himself onto it. "Doesn't get any easier does it?"

"Life?" asked Butler, now fully into his amused Englishman persona.

"Weightlessness."

If that were true Theroux found himself thinking, how come you took out two experienced attackers with an L-tip switchblade?

It doesn't get any easier? Nathan thought, why do I persist with these games, and said, "I expect you're wondering why I asked for this meeting."

Butler chortled. "Presumably you're going to tell us whodunnit."

"I fail to see the 'umour," Lancine said and the expression on her face left no doubt of that. "Death is not funny."

Nathan smiled at Butler. "I expect you're wondering why I've called you all here to the library – is that the idea?" he asked.

Before Butler could reply Lancine snapped, "We 'ave a serious problem here."

She looked suddenly older as she glared at Nathan. It was odd, he thought, how quickly fine bone structure became simply thin and haggard under stress.

"This station," she went on, "now 'as a death rate in excess of any of the other off-Earth installations."

"Whadya mean now ?" Theroux demanded. "Christ we've been above average for months."

"But we haven't been killing visiting celebrities or stuffing each other into waste disposal units," remarked Butler.

He really did seem to find it funny, Nathan thought. Was it funny? He wondered for a jangled moment whether he'd miscalculated all this. "That was a mistake," he said.

"A mistake?" said Lancine, expressionless with anger.

"Ill-thought out," said Nathan. "A stupid departure from a successful strategy."

"He is still on medication, I imagine," Butler said quietly, looking at Lancine.

"The system worked perfectly well," Nathan continued, "when killings were done by strangers from unrelated locations."

"What killings are these exactly?" asked Butler.

"Deaths from suit failure," Theroux said. "Deaths made to look like they were from suit failure."

Butler smiled. "Oh not that again," he said. "David old thing, does the word obsession mean anything to you?" He turned the smile towards Lancine but she was staring fixedly at Nathan.

"It was an elegant MO designed simply to fool the computers," Nathan said. "Elegance and simplicity are usually synonymous in such things."

"What things?" she asked.

"Programmes, investigations, crimes."

She nodded. "*Continuez.*"

"If the death looked like an accident; and if there was no obvious motive for anything else; and if all the safety procedures were in operation; and if everyone on the station was accounted for…"

Theroux said, "If it looked like a duck and it walked like a duck and it quacked like a duck, odds-on it was a duck."

"The computers have a weakness for probabilities," said Nathan. "Odds-on is enough for them."

"But you know better," murmured Butler. "Despite all evidence of anatidae, that's duckdom to the uninitiated, you recognize it's not a duck when you see one."

"And the mistake?" Lancine asked. "What caused that?"

"Jesus!" said Theroux looking at Nathan. "It was you right? You did it."

Butler was chortling again. "That's original anyway," he said. "The detective did it. What's the procedure in cases like this, is the arrest put out to private tender?"

"You were using Box," Theroux went on, "to feed all that stuff onto the open screens because you wanted to spook them. That's why you made such a big production about going outside. You knew you'd be a target."

All three were staring at Nathan now. It wasn't the reaction he wanted at this point and he was annoyed with himself. He hadn't got any bloody proof of what he was saying and without it he needed to develop a line as carefully as if he was conducting an interrogation. This lot was all over the sodding place. It was his own fault. He should have briefed Theroux beforehand. He couldn't really blame the man for thinking on his feet, well on his arse anyway, though he could blame him for blurting out his conclusions. Why was it that Americans never seemed to understand the advantages of discretion.

"Christ!" Obviously another thought had struck Theroux and it was not one that he liked. "Did you put the pressure on Brownly and Goff? Did you make up all that stuff about them?"

"What stuff is this?" enquired Butler politely.

"Oh right," said Theroux, "like you weren't following developments, Simon."

Butler raised innocent eyebrows. "Hacking's illegal," he said.

"So's murder," said Nathan flatly. "And no I didn't set up Brownly and Goff. Somebody did but it wasn't me. There are probably fall-guys like them on any station that's featured in the programme."

"Programme," said Butler softly, his face alive with exaggerated wonder, "it's a programme."

"Why this station?" asked Lancine. "Because of me?"

My God Nathan thought bleakly, paranoia really is rife out here, and said: "The building work made coming and going easier, and death more..."

"Odds-on," said Butler and when Nathan nodded, went on, "Is that your explanation of how Hendvorrsen was killed? Lurkers among the girders?"

Lancine snorted, "They would have 'ad to be invisible."

"Why?" asked Nathan. "Hendvorrsen wasn't on visual scan and there are no close-range radars. I don't think anyone else was reporting back on his position, were they, Simon?"

Butler shook his head.

Lancine said, "There were six people out there when 'e died."

"From a distance everyone looks the same in a spacesuit," said Nathan, "and any one person's field of vision is restricted. My guess is that there were at least seven people out there when he died."

"If he was attacked – " Butler said.

Nathan interrupted him. "Interfered with rather than attacked. You have to remember he wasn't experienced and he wasn't expecting an attempt on his life."

"Whatever," Butler said. "Why didn't he say he was in trouble? He had a suit radio which he was using pretty freely."

"The killer jammed it. Not difficult to do."

"And his suit alarm, what about that? You can't jam a suit alarm." Butler's amused detachment was becoming less amused and less detached suddenly.

"Hendvorrsen's suit alarm didn't work," said Nathan.

Butler made no attempt to keep the sneer out of his voice. "That was convenient."

"It wasn't a coincidence," Nathan said mildly. "A suit with a non-functioning alarm had been provided beforehand."

"They were all tested, Nathan," Theroux pointed out gently. "You were there when they were all tested."

Dismissively Lancine said, "Per'aps you know longer remember, but I insisted on a test before we went outside. Any fault would have shown up then."

"The fault did show up then. That was how the killer got to find out who was wearing the target suit."

Butler was smiling again. "You're saying Hendvorrsen wasn't the target? After all this highly imaginative brouhaha, they got the wrong one?"

Have I got the wrong one? thought Nathan. *It seems that there are no signs of physical injury. The impairment of brain function is 'owever a possibility...* "Hendvorrsen's presence guaranteed publicity and that was what they were interested in. The accident victim wasn't important. It could have been any one of them. That's why it worked for so long. None of the victims was ever important."

"This is nonsense," Lancine said, "the suit alarms were tested. We know they all worked."

Nathan closed his eyes. "If the tests had been carried out one at a time, the way you suggested Françoise, then the fault would have been obvious to everyone including the wearer, but it wasn't done like that was it? And why wasn't it done like that?"

Listen Françoise there's no point in doing this by numbers. They have to do it randomly paying no attention to each other.

Some will overlap.

You mean they won't panic in an orderly fashion?

I mean you will 'ave more than one at a time to deal with.

Isn't that what you're paying me for?

Very well, base control. We will do it your way... in your own time, gentlemen.

"And why wasn't it done like that?" Nathan asked again.

It was Theroux who said, "Simon wanted the tests to be realistic."

There's nothing like a good panic to waste time and energy.

Nathan opened his eyes. "There's nothing like a good panic," he said, looking at Butler, "to cover up the fact that one suit alarm was disconnected, and to find out which one it was. Until you ran the tests, you didn't know who'd drawn the short straw, did you?"

"You're not suggesting I murdered Hendvorrsen are you?" Butler asked and laughed.

"I'm suggesting that having identified the victim you informed whoever was waiting outside and they did the rest."

"Bollocks," said Butler, "total bollocks."

"You used virtually the same strategy on me," Nathan said. "You panicked everyone over Brownly, and overloaded the systems so when I yelled for help, no-one was listening – not even the computer."

"Are you just going to sit there," Butler demanded, getting out of his chair and moving towards Lancine's desk, "and let this brain-damaged groundsider ruin the career of the best in the business, the best bloody traffic controller you or any other fucker is ever likely to come across?"

Lancine stared down at her hands clenched tightly in her lap. She was blank-eyed and seemed no longer to be listening. It occurred to Nathan that she might only now be realizing that her progress in the ESA would be stalled by this; probably for good. Chances were that Butler's 'climbing frog' would get no further up the tree. He felt almost sorry for her as he said to Butler: "Loss of career is the least of your problems. In the matter of the death of Lars Hendvorrsen you're facing charges of conspiracy;

accessory to murder before and after the fact..."

Butler turned his back on Lancine and held up his arms in an elaborate gesture which was quite at odds with the low key English personality he had been displaying. Conscious of this inappropriate behaviour, Nathan tensed ready for him to make some sort of aggressive move. Psych training was very positive about such indicators, the precursors of violence. But there was nothing threatening in what Butler did next. He simply stood where he was and asked almost plaintively, "Why? Why would I have done it?"

"Money?" Theroux said. "They pay you to look the other way, Simon? They'd never have gotten past you, isn't that right? You're the best in the business. You just said that to Françoise. Shit, that's what you always said to *everyone*. Must have finally paid off, huh? Is that what happened? Did these guys buy that crap?"

"For quite large sums actually, David old love. And it isn't crap."

"So you were insurance."

Butler smiled and said, "Lloyds of London revisited," and then he back-flipped neatly over the desk, tugging himself down to stand beside Lancine. Before she or either of the Star Cops –

I'm a Star Cop for Christ's sake, Nathan was thinking, how can this be happening in front of me while I squat here like a bump on a log?

– could react, he produced a small automatic pistol from his pocket and rested the barrel lightly in Lancine's left ear.

Though he knew something was going to happen, the move took Nathan completely by surprise. It hadn't even struck him as an option. Fuck it. Weightlessness would never be instinctive, no matter how much skill he worked up. You can take the man out of gravity, but not gravity out of the man... but you can keep it light, you must keep it light, and smooth, nothing sudden, nothing dark. As casually as he could he said, "How very traditional of you, Simon. A choice of three hostages and you pick the woman."

Equally casually Butler said, "If I'm going to have to kill someone, I'd sooner it was someone I didn't like much."

Lancine shifted her head slightly, leaning a little away from the gun and trying to look at him.

"Sit still, Françoise," Butler murmured, with a small, smug smile. There was something obscene about the intimacy of his tone. He was clearly enjoying the physical power he had over the woman. Nathan

Star Cops

wondered if he was getting an erection from it.

"Madame Lancine," Lancine said coldly.

Nathan tried to catch her eye and failed. *Don't challenge him*, he thought, *not yet, not in that position. He might kill you for the climax.*

"Or *Madame la directrice*, if you would prefer." Her face and voice were stone-smooth and unyielding. The stress was gone from her features, anger made her young now.

Butler poked the gun a bit harder into her ear. "I would prefer that you remain silent and motionless, until I tell you otherwise."

Theroux said, "You can't fire that thing in here!" He was angry too and more than a little bewildered, but Nathan was relieved to see that he had enough sense to stay in his seat.

"I can fire it in here," said Butler, indicating Lancine's ear. "No danger to life-support." He leaned closer to her and lowered his voice slightly, "Apart from yours of course."

"You miserable, sick prick," said Theroux.

Butler straightened up. "There's a reduced load in the cartridges, David. I could risk putting a slug or two in your direction if it became… appropriate."

"I'm impressed, Simon. No really I am. Assholes with guns have always been tops with me."

"That's enough, David," Nathan said.

"Shut the fuck up!" Theroux blazed. "This is between him and me!"

"Shut the fuck up *sir*," Nathan said, quietly enough for the emphasis to be arresting. "And what's between him and you is a hostage, in case you hadn't noticed."

"Slow on the uptake, our coloured cousins, and given to irrational violence," smiled Butler. "I've always thought that if it wasn't for their normally sunny natures, they would make natural policemen."

"So what now?" asked Nathan, hoping to forestall any further outbursts from Theroux. Oddly though his rage seemed to have subsided into a scowling sullenness. Nathan wondered briefly at the speed of the change. Butler answered, "Unlikely as it may seem I hadn't really given it much thought." He was so relaxed and careless of what was happening that he looked to Nathan like a man who might have decided to die.

"Since this is a game of 'Simon Says'," Lancine said, "I am ready to start by suggesting what you can do wiz that gun." The woman's tone was mild, but her eyes were fierce with violation. Nathan could see she was going to do something stupid. He set himself to dive at Butler when she did. He had to try for the gun – if he could just work out the trajectory, find the right point of thrust, there might be some chance.

Theroux hunched forward in his seat, and said, "I thought we were supposed to be friends, Simon." His voice was loud with reproach and Nathan glanced across at him. He saw to his surprise, that without giving any obvious sign of it, Theroux had managed to detach himself from his seat and his slippers from the floor. It was unlikely that Butler could tell from where he was, but Theroux was floating poised on the tips of his toes. "I thought we were friends," he repeated.

"I know you did," said Butler cruelly. "And in the circumstances it would seem churlish to kill you, so I'd prefer to avoid that, if at all possible." He twisted the gun upwards in Lancine's ear in an effort to raise her from her seat. "On your feet, *Madame la directrice*." She resisted the push.

It was time to do it, Nathan thought. Now. I've got to do it now.

"A man's got to do what a man's got to do," said Theroux. Butler looked at him quickly, but he had not changed position, angle and attitude remained reassuringly down.

Butler grinned. "Fifty," he said. "The bid is fifty." He twitched the gun. "On your feet, woman or 'bang' is what you hear forever."

"Fifty?" said Theroux.

"Could be our last game," said Butler.

"Now look, I've had enough of this," Nathan protested. "You people are not beyond the law. This has got to stop." He stood up abruptly.

"Sit down, groundsider!" snapped Theroux.

Barely glancing in his direction, Butler said, "Do it, Spring."

Nathan had judged the force of his rise exactly. He was already detached from the floor and floating gently upwards. "I can't," he said, waving his arms and looking helpless. It should be convincing, he thought, because he *was* helpless – but was Butler's arrogant contempt for groundsiders enough to let him fall for this act again?

"For Christ's sake," said Butler, with mounting irritation, "if you can't control yourself you're going to get somebody killed here, and it'll be your fault!" He was still holding the gun firmly in place, but his attention was partly on Nathan now.

Lancine and Theroux stiffened to fight. Nathan could feel them tightening. Not yet, he thought, not yet. They were edging to the moment, aching to act. "No!" he said. It held them both paused for a few blinks more as he drifted onwards. "I'm sorry about this. But don't lets lose our heads because I lost my footing." He was almost within reach of the wall.

Wait...wait... wait...

And then Lancine could wait no longer. She ducked forward and down, away from the gun, at the same time slapping back at it with her left arm. She thrashed round with her other arm, furious to strike at her tormentor and smash her fear and pain into him, too angry to pick the vulnerable points and aim at them. For a moment, the abandoned ferocity of her assault disconcerted Butler. For a moment, it confused him.

For a moment he could not decide whom to kill.

Theroux had been ready to launch himself at Butler as soon as an opportunity offered, but Lancine's action was fractionally sooner than he expected. When she jumped the gun, she had jumped the gun, and he kicked off too late and flew towards the desk too late, too late goddammit goddammit *goddammit* he didn't want to die for this tight-assed bitch *too late*.

Nathan reached the top of his drift as she moved, he clapped his hands on the wall, flipped over like a turning swimmer and thrust with his legs, down towards the gun.

Butler saw Theroux coming. Caught the movement as he had flown from his seat and looked as he loomed, arms outstretched, face set and staring with strain and fear. The woman's frantic battering was no threat. He pulled the gun away from her and turned it into Theroux's face.

Too late goddammit.

"Honky *motherfucker!*"

"Fuck you, *nigger!*"

And he pulled the trigger. As the hammer dropped, Nathan smashed down onto the gun. The shot burned and bit into Butler's thigh, a bone-bruising punch which thumped the gun loose, spinning it away. Theroux rolled to one side and caught it.

"That's another dollar you owe the fund, Simon," he said.

The security restraints that held Butler on the med-lab sleeping frame were the type that could only be released by someone else, and he made no effort to struggle against them. He listened passively as Theroux went through a formal reading of the arrest warrant. "...accessory after the fact in the murder of Auguste Goff. You are further charged that on that date you murdered Liam Brownly. These charges are not exclusive and do not preclude further charges being brought. Do you understand?"

Butler nodded. Theroux read on, "Nothing you say will be noted to be used in evidence until recording and representation have been arranged. Do you understand?"

Again Butler nodded. Theroux folded the warrant and handed it to Nathan who said, "Right then, we'll leave you to get some rest."

Butler yawned. "You'll never prove I killed Brownly," he said.

Theroux said, "We'll prove it."

"If he was crazy enough to kill his best friend and hide his body –"

"With your help."

"You're not serious."

"You knew exactly where that body was. You sent me right to it."

"Lucky guess, David old thing. And I repeat, if he was crazy enough to do all that, who knows what else he was capable of?"

"He wasn't crazy enough to commit suicide feet first in the waste disposal," said Theroux.

"Are you sure?"

Nathan interrupted before Theroux could give any more free information to the prisoner. "We're sure," he said. "Let's go, David."

"I don't see what he expected to gain from it," Theroux said as they made their way to a table in the mess.

"Time maybe," said Nathan, "who knows?"

"Yeah, yeah, motive's always the difficult part."

"And not always necessary. If they did it and you can prove they did it…" He sat, and settled down to eat. He was hungry now, and for the moment he had forgotten to feel nauseous.

Theroux said, "Shouldn't we make the effort, at least?" He looked tired and depressed. "If *we* don't understand, what hope is there?"

Nathan thought about saying that he understood how he must be feeling, betrayed by a friend, but then decided it was none of his business. Besides, he probably *didn't* understand how he must be feeling. He said instead, "I'm not sure but I think he was probably hoping I'd be suspected of killing both Brownly and Goff. Everybody knew I'd had a fight with them. Maybe I was another victim of cabin fever. Maybe afterwards I went outside and killed myself. It would have been neat. Discredit my investigations, get him off the hook, maybe even earn him a bonus from whichever multinational is behind it all…"

"Shit, he really thought of me as a major investigative threat, didn't he?"

"He thought of you as a friend."

Theroux smiled tiredly. "You heard what he thought of me as."

"You frightened him," said Nathan. "Frightened people say things like 'honky motherfucker'. Or was that you?"

Theroux didn't smile. "Can we prove any of it?"

"Absolutely."

"I mean I'll buy the trick that you claim stopped us from spotting that Hendvorrsen's suit had a non-functioning alarm, but how come Forensic didn't spot it afterwards?"

"How did they check that the alarm was working?"

"They removed the unit for test."

"The unit worked. What didn't work was the connection, and Forensic—"

"Disconnected the unit for test…" Theroux shook his head in small appreciation. "If you're right, those bastards took a lot of chances."

"Suit-servicing contract's worth a lot of money," Nathan said, "and I am right. Relax David, there aren't going to be any mistakes on this one. I've waited my entire career for a case like this. You must have been born lucky to get one first crack out of the bag."

"Pardon me?"

"Well, think about it. It's a classic, every detective's dream."

Theroux thought for a moment, then shook his head and shrugged.

Nathan said, "Butler did it." And smiled his best smile.

Simon Butler rolled over on his contacts, who in turn rolled over on theirs, and Earthside arrests were being made by the time Nathan was ready to return with his prisoner. The news networks reflected a general relief that Hendvorrsen's end had been planned and not caused by some malign chance, arbitrary and inexplicable as death itself. The painstaking work by European and US federal agencies which would lead eventually to the arrest of the senior executives of Pancontel, a Kuwait-based conglomerate, was of no interest to them.

"I can't say it's been a pleasure," Nathan said, as he and Theroux shook hands at the airlock, "but it has been an experience."

"Can I ask you something?" said Theroux.

"You can ask."

"Where did you get Box?"

Nathan smiled. "Why? Do you want one?"

Theroux looked him in the eyes. "I could never afford it," he said.

Nathan stared back, and then said, "My father gave it to me. He was in the business. Even so, I don't know how he came by it, and I could never think of a graceful way to ask."

"Policemen are supposed to be more tough-minded than that, aren't they?"

Nathan looked thoughtful. "Did you know," he said, "that when the Taj Mahal was completed Shah Jahan ordered the arms of the craftsmen cut off? So they could never make anything more beautiful."

"They should have had a better union," said Theroux, wondering whether Nathan was showing the first signs of brain-damage.

"You do remember Box's lecture at the restaurant?" Nathan asked.

"Sure I do, yeah."

"Well, why was that detail not in it?"

"Beats the shit out of me."

"Obviously," said Nathan cheerfully, "nobody's perfect. What about those bugged coveralls?"

Theroux noted the abrupt change of direction, was it strategy or symptom? "We got them by mistake," he said, "the consignment was intended for one of the Moonbase installations. Outpost Nine."

"What do they do there?"

"It's classified."

"Might be worth looking into," Nathan said.

"You looking for another case?" Theroux asked.

"Shit, no. I'm going home."

Chapter 13

Since walking was recommended therapy in the re-adaptation to a one-G environment, Nathan walked through the park towards the inner city monorail link which would take him to Europol headquarters. It was strange how heavy he still felt, how thick the air still was; and he walked slowly, despite the colour of rain which was filling in the sky. Around him people were picking up their pace, not ready to run yet, but anxious to be closer to shelter as the weather threatened.

It was one of the clouds that turn the light a pale greenish colour, as though everything is already under water. It struck Nathan that being a ground-dweller with the trees stirring in the wind around him was like living in the bottom of a river. Weeds of many kinds grew towards the surface though even the tallest trees did not break through it to where breathing was alien. Squirrels scuttled up and down through the dark, drifting beds, and the birds swam above him. He and his kind grubbed around in the mud, rapacious as dragonfly larvae and about as appealing. It seemed suddenly that going into space was like being scooped out of the river into thin, alien air, suffocating, and giddy as a falling bird.

"How long did it take you to get over the motion sickness?" asked the Commander.

"About another week, I should think," said Nathan washing down his midday medication with a cup of the indifferent coffee they served on the thirty-fourth floor.

"It can't have been that bad."

"Yes, it can. Trust me."

"It was a first rate job. First rate. I don't think there's anyone else who could have done what you did."

"I can think of several," said Nathan, though in fact he could not, and he was slightly ashamed to realize that he felt the compliment was no more than appropriate. "But it's kind of you to say so."

The Commander's eyes narrowed, and he contrived for a moment to look both shifty and hunted. He was not used to such routine courtesy from Nathan and was obviously waiting for the punchline, but when it did not come, he relaxed and said, "You'll need some time to yourself I expect. To sort everything out."

"A couple of days would be useful, yes. Get my breath back; catch up with things."

The Commander smiled benignly. "Take as long as you need. Nobody will expect you to pick up the reins straightaway." He stood up and held out his hand. "In the meantime what can I say, except: Congratulations."

Nathan rose and shook the proffered hand. Puzzled, he asked, "Was that all you wanted to see me for?"

"Not quite." The Commander opened his desk drawer, and with something of a flourish produced from it a small box. "I wanted to give you this in person."

Nathan lifted the top carefully. He half-expected an explosion and a shower of soot or paper snakes, but what he found was a thick, leather wallet. He took it out of the box and flipped it open. On one side was a new ID plate – at least, the hologram looked new, though he had no recollection of posing for it. Separate from it on the other side was a heavy gold shield reminiscent of the badges once carried by officers in major police forces across the world. Behind the shield, a silver and blue hologram of the ISPF logo had been etched into the soft leather. The holograms flashed and glowed as Nathan examined the wallet. He swung the badge on its finely-wrought, gold-retaining bar. "What is this?" he asked.

"It's twenty-two carat gold," said the Commander. "In my opinion, they never should have dropped the detective's gold shield. Of course, it wasn't real gold, but it might just as well have been. It stood for something. It was an emblem. Good idea to revive it for out there. Take some tradition into a new environment. Symbols matter."

"I don't understand," Nathan said quietly, "at least I hope I don't understand."

The Commander frowned, and then made a production out of the sudden realization. "You haven't been told, have you?" he said and beamed, offering his hand again. "You got the job. You are the new Commander of the International Space Police Force."

Nathan ignored the hand and tossed the wallet towards the Commander. For a second he was surprised when it fell onto the desk instead of floating onwards. "I don't think so," he said, without emphasis.

"You haven't got any choice," said the Commander, his smile unwavering, but draining of warmth.

Nathan said, "There's always a choice."

The Commander sat down and dropped the smile. "The Carmodie case has already finished your career in this force," he said.

"I beg your pardon?"

"You countermanded a departmental order. You compromised a departmental budget. And you cocked-up. That's the unforgivable one of course."

"I didn't cock-up."

"You got it wrong. You arrested an innocent woman. Not just an innocent woman but the grieving, bloody widow for Christ's sake!"

Nathan still did not raise his voice. "You made the only cock-up when you released the murderous bitch."

"She was released," said the Commander, delicately distancing himself from personal involvement in the decision, "because of lack of evidence."

"She confessed," said Nathan.

"Lack of hard evidence," said the Commander.

"The cash?"

"You know what happened to the cash. She gave it back. The identical notes. She couldn't have used them as you claimed and then paid back the loan by selling the husband's antique collection."

"The stuff was sold."

"The husband sold it himself because he was in debt to the sharks and they wanted his business."

"Evidence?"

"We'll get it."

"As a matter of interest, why did she confess?"

The Commander looked suitably disapproving. "She was alone, she was shocked and frightened, and you harassed her. You used unacceptable pressure to force a confession from an obviously vulnerable and totally innocent bystander. I expected better than that from you."

"Spare me the pained disappointment."

"Take the job," the Commander said mildly. "It's your only real option."

"You devious bastard," said Nathan.

"The Psych department tell me that she may be emotionally crippled by what you did."

"Psych need a new computer," Nathan said. "Preferably one that sweats, farts and pukes. If it had some idea of what fucking was, that might be useful too."

"What are you suggesting? That you understand the Carmodie woman better than Psych do?" asked the Commander.

"I'm suggesting," said Nathan, "that Psych are a poor cover for bad police work. That's why I've always ignored them and you never have."

But the Commander was not to be provoked. "Don't be a poor loser," he said.

Nathan said, "I haven't lost yet."

"That's true," said the Commander. "It isn't everyone who gets promoted out of trouble. You're being a poor winner, Nathan."

"So what are you going to do, my love?"

The question startled him. She had her back to him, and he had thought she was asleep. He turned on his side and reached for her. "I can't leave it like that," Nathan said. Lee did not turn as he drew her to him, but shifted so that her buttocks were cradled against his lap. The warm pressure and the smooth roundness aroused him and he ran his hand down her belly and pushed it between her legs. Their lovemaking lasted longer this time and they finished face to face, climaxing together, loud and uninhibited.

"Third time lucky," she breathed.

He sighed and murmured, "Luck had nothing to do with it." He began to drift off to sleep.

"You could resign," Lee said.

Nathan yawned. "And do what?"

"You could get another job."

Nathan kissed her lightly. "Gigolo, you mean? Nathan Spring, love-machine."

"I'm serious."

"Oh, thanks a lot."

"You don't even need another job. You've got enough time in. The pension's reasonable."

"I'm not ready to retire," Nathan said, suddenly irritable. "I'm not that old, for Christ's sake."

Lee smiled. "I can testify to that," she said. "Relax, love-machine, you have nothing to prove."

Nathan was only half-listening. "I have to prove I was right about the Carmodie case," he said. "Then let's see the bastard force me out. I can tell them to stuff the Star Cop job."

"So what are you going to do, my love?"

The woman did not seem unduly put out to see him. Nathan said, "I hope I'm not disturbing you, Ms. Carmodie," and offered his best smile.

"No, you're not disturbing me, Detective Chief Superintendent Spring."

Policemen and liars need good memories, he thought and saw that her eyes were as intelligent and watchful as he remembered. "May I come in?" he asked.

"Of course," she said and opened the door wider.

"I uh, I wanted to apologize," Nathan said as he crossed the threshold. "It seems that I was misled when we talked before."

"Misled?" she asked solemnly.

"Mistaken. There was new evidence I gather. While I was out of the country."

She smiled for the first time. "You were out of the world, weren't you? I've been reading all about it." And she turned and led the way through the house.

She was slimmer, Nathan noticed and though her clothes were not flamboyant, they were definitely more stylish now. "Fame at last. I'm flattered," he said, looking around for possible places to conceal the half-dozen thread transmitters he had brought back with him from the *Charles De Gaulle*.

"I do not believe that you have gone on harassing these people!!" the Commander raged. "Sweet mother of God, what do you imagine you are doing?! Are you *entirely* insane??"

"He's visited her four times this week," Nathan said. "Always after dark."

The Commander leaned forward, trying yet again for a screen-dominating close-up. "You must have been brain-damaged out there, is that it?"

Had the bastard been given access to his confidential medical file? Nathan wondered. "They weren't harassed," he said. "They knew nothing about it. That's the point." He got up from the workstation, and went to get himself more coffee.

"You called at the house," the Commander accused, as Nathan moved out of range of the screen.

Nathan filled his mug. Damn. He hadn't allowed for the possibility that he might be being watched. He hadn't spotted them, either. He moved back into the scanner field. "To apologize for my mistake," he said, wondering who'd been assigned; hoping it wasn't Lincoln.

The Commander was momentarily taken aback. "You went to apologize?" That option had obviously not occurred to him – but recovering quickly, he snarled, "You expect me to believe that?"

"Why not? What did the tail tell you I was doing?" Nathan asked mildly.

On the screen, the Commander pointedly ignored the question. He shrugged. "Alright, so he visits her, so what? He was her husband's business partner. He's probably concerned for her welfare."

Nathan keyed a screen window and played the time-coded surveillance video he had shot. "It only seems to occur to him late at night. And he leaves just before dawn." Nathan enlarged the inset picture slightly. The figure was clearly identifiable on the day-bright, enhanced night-vision: a small, chubby man in his sixties scurrying in and out through the grounds at the back of the house. "Fairly furtive, wouldn't you say? I mean, look at him," said Nathan. "More philanderer than philanthropist, surely."

The Commander's curiosity was piqued despite the circumstances and he watched the screen antics, which seemed simultaneously pathetic, absurd and somehow sinister. When the man had come and gone a couple of times the Commander got bored and said, "Oh come on. He's small and fat and a good twenty-five years older than her."

"She's fucking his brains out," said Nathan matter-of-factly, thinking the expression had more than just a crude truth to it, and as he spoke the surveillance camera caught the woman waiting at a side door. Their embrace was passionate, and she was pulling at the man's clothes before the door closed behind them.

"Proves nothing," said the Commander, sounding more positive than he looked.

"They became lovers just before the husband's death. At her instigation."

"How do you know? You *can't* possibly know that."

"I don't think you can charge him with murder and make it stick. But accessory after the fact should be no problem, conspiracy to pervert the course of justice, and so on."

"Charge him?"

"He loaned her the money, just as he said. When he found out what she'd spent it on he provided her with an alibi. A nice uncomplicated alibi. Something obvious that didn't require too much checking."

"Balls!" bellowed the Commander. "This is all guesswork!"

Nathan sipped his coffee and said nothing. The Commander glared out of the screen. "What do you think it's going to get you? Do you think it's going to get you off the hook, is that what you think?"

Nathan thought, *So what are you going to do, my love?* that's exactly what I think, I get off the hook and you take my place on it, *So what are you going to do, my love?* and I'm going to enjoy telling you, and watching you squirm *So what are you going to do, my love?* and he said, "It's not going to get me anything." *So what are you going to do, my love?* "I'm taking the Star Cops job. So I'm not on the hook any more, am I? This is a parting gift. I've left all the information for Lincoln. He's a good man, he won't be able to resist going after those two. I suggest you make sure your code is on an authorizing order dated now. That way when he busts them, you won't end up on your own hook."

The Commander stared suspiciously at Nathan. "What are you up to?" he asked eventually.

Nathan said, "We Commanders have got to stick together, don't you think?" and smiled.

Neela Shah, the acting Liaison Co-ordinator of the Candidate Selection Board, said, "*After your smashing success with the case, whom else could we have chosen?*" She shrugged, a small asymmetrical movement of shoulders and head which seemed to Nathan to be the essence of Indian grace and elegance, and smiled. "*I must be honest though, there was a small question-mark over your...attitude?*"

Nathan smiled back, and wondered what her perfume would be like. "Only a small one?" he asked.

"*I think my approach to reality as a scientist, would not be unlike yours as a detective. We are both perhaps disinclined to judge except by results. Are you ready to receive the contract now?*"

Nathan hesitated. He could still turn it down. He could still avoid having to tell Lee.

"Yes," he said.

At one side of his workstation, the printer accepted the document and envelope instructions. Glancing at the freshly minted, sealed envelope which dropped into the document tray, he asked, "What have the Russians done about that maintenance technician they arrested? Svetlana Tereshcova."

Neela Shah looked away from her screen. "*They executed her,*" she said. "*They're not admitting it, of course, but that's what they've done.*" She looked back into the screen and caught his eye. "*They were going to announce it, I think, but now there is nothing to be gained. You rather spoiled their show.*"

"I don't imagine the Kuwaitis and their American masters were particularly pleased with the PR either," Nathan said and took the hard copy of his employment contract from the envelope. "It's strange how all systems seem to work in more or less the same way. They have the same ends; they use the same means; they produce the same victims."

"*That is the sort of attitude,*" remarked the acting Liaison Co-ordinator of the Candidate Selection Board, gently, "*which gave rise to my colleagues' doubts about your temperamental suitability for the job.*"

Nathan signed the contract and had the computer notarize his signature. "Well, it's too damn late now, isn't it?" he said.

Conversations With The Dead

They were both asleep when they were finally murdered, but that did not make it painless. In a way, it hurt more. It was one last mistake for them to live with; one last mistake in a history of carelessness, which they woke up to only when they were dead.

Most cargo-jocks took some of the operating short-cuts which Mike and Lara had been taking since they began to fly together, but no-one else took them all at once. Even the laziest and least professional member of the Guild of Pilots and Co-pilots would have regarded that as an unacceptable risk.

Not that Mike and Lara were particularly lazy or unprofessional. They were simply distracted. And ironically if there had been as the manual specified, 'an officer in designated watch position' when everything caught up with them, it probably would have made no difference. As it was though they were tangled around each other in the double frame they had rigged and they were both asleep when the *Dædalus*, en route to Mars, began a totally unscheduled main-engine burn.

As the chemical fire drove the inter-orbit freighter into the soundless dark, the low vibration of the blaze resonated in the light-framed metalwork of the ship, and sang through the air of the pressurized sections where the crew lived and worked.

Lara woke first. She was confused, disoriented and struggling for the where and when of the Earth dreams which follow all long-haul spaceworkers. Then she snapped awake.

"It can't be," she said aloud, knowing that this was still a dream, though not of home, but sharply here and now. She disentangled herself from Mike and looked around the cramped living compartment for some anomaly she could identify as dream. She stared for something to bring on the rush of waking-up relief that grief and fear were imagined; there was no tragedy, love and the world was not lost. Food dispenser, waste disposal, recreation console, ablutions stall, exercise wheel: it was all there, all as it had been, is now and ever shall be, world without end. "What time is it?" she asked Mike, who had not woken. She pulled at one of his long, pale arms and he stirred. "What time is it?" she repeated.

"It's your watch," he muttered. "Can't be mine again already."

"Wake up, Mike!"

"I'm not doing the log and I'm not making the coffee. I wasn't properly compensated last time." He yawned and wrapped his arms back round her. "You owe me, bitch."

"Mike?" Her voice was quiet now, as if fearing to wake him in case she herself could not wake. "Wake up?" she asked softly.

"What is it?"

"The engines have kicked in."

"Can't have," he said, sleepily calm, knowing that it could not be true. "It's four days to the correction point."

"Listen."

Mike listened.

It sounded like the engines. It sounded like a major burn. But they didn't have the fuel for a major burn. Fuel for course correction. Fuel for orbit attainment. Fuel for a small safety margin. But a main engine burn? Oh, Christ, no!

"Oh, Christ, no!" he shouted at her. "What have you done?"

"I haven't done anything! What do you mean, what have I done?"

They scrambled apart and dived out of the frame.

"It's your watch!" he shouted, as they thrust themselves down the tube towards the control and navigation bay.

"Fuck you!" she shouted back at him.

"Engines don't fire themselves," he accused under his breath, adding more loudly, "Something set them off."

"You're the pilot," she snapped.

By the time they reached the bay, the fuel was critical. They keyed the overrides and tried to abort the firing programme. The computer rejected the instruction. The machine's safety systems would not accept an unplanned interruption to a precisely projected flight pattern. The outcome would be random. A random outcome could not be optimized.

"Engine cut-off is dead," Lara chanted.

"Re-try," intoned Mike, punching in the code again.

The engines surged on.

"Confirm non-function," Lara chanted.

In desperation, they tried to cut off the fuel at source.

"Engage emergency fuel bypass," Mike said and then hesitated. "It could blow us to hell."

"That's where we're heading anyway," Lara said.

But when Mike tried to punch it in, the computer immediately closed the board.

Two minutes later, the engines shut down.

In the half-heard silence, Mike said, "I'm sorry I was such an asshole. What I said. I don't know why I said that."

Lara said, "It doesn't matter."

"I didn't mean to have a go at you. I knew it wasn't your fault."

"It's not important," said Lara.

"I was scared."

"I think we're dead, Mike."

"It is important," Mike said. "I thought I'd die better. And if I was going to lose you I'd sooner it hadn't happened till I'd stopped living."

"If you were going to lose me by being an asshole, Mike love, I'd have been gone long enough before this," Lara said, and keyed the mayday circuit on the communications rig.

He was walking on the top of a high bridge. The water below him was so far away that he could barely see it. And he knew that at some point he was expected to jump. The bridge was gigantic but incomplete. Just beyond its highest point where the span began to slope downwards again, there was nothing but empty air. And he knew that at some point he was expected to jump. He felt as though the bridge was rising under his feet, getting further and further away from the water all the time, getting more and more precarious. And he knew that at some point he was expected to jump. All around on other parts of the bridge there were people moving purposefully to and fro. Some jumped; no-one seemed afraid.

He was afraid, though. The huge bridge was beginning to sway. And he knew that at some point, he was expected to jump. As he moved reluctantly towards the swaying end of the unfinished bridge, he realized it was so high now that he could not see the water at all. He stumbled and tried to grab on but he was slipping so he jumped. He jumped and the sinking lurch took his breath away. He gasped a deep gasp. He was falling and tipping back as he went so that his legs were rising and he could no longer look in the direction he was travelling. He was helplessly rushing down, helplessly sucking air. As he hit the water the voice said:

"*...the crew of the stricken vessel, believed to be a man and a woman, have not yet been identified. This is WBC News on the hour. Staying with the High Frontier...*"

and he opened his eyes and stared groggily at a viewing screen which was showing pictures of an Earth orbit station rising with brooding menace above the curve of the planetary horizon.

"*...in Geneva today,*" the newscast continued, "*all the major space powers have made formal protests at the US refusal to allow inspection of its latest unmanned orbital station. Speculation that it's military and a treaty violation has been fuelled by the sophistication of the communications screening with which the station appears to have been fitted.*"

"Screen off," murmured Nathan Spring, newly created commander and boss of the International Space Police Force. The screen went blank and silent. "Did you set that thing going?" he muttered at David Theroux who was floating near the hatchway entrance of the sleeping quarters.

"Stopped you falling," said the youthful-looking, black American. "That is what you were doing, right?"

The sensation was suddenly vivid in the muscles of Nathan's back and in the pit of his stomach. "Only forever," he said and began to extricate himself from the sleeping frame. "I thought these bloody papoose-carriers were supposed to help with that."

Theroux proffered a squeeze-pack of coffee and said, "Some people get over it."

"Some people?" Nathan accepted the coffee gratefully, though he still doubted that drinking it through a straw would ever take the place of self-mutilation as a recreational pursuit. "I wonder if it's too late to get a refund on my ticket."

Without pausing in his efforts to get out of the frame, he took a pull at the coffee and fumbled the pack. It floated away from him and though he quickly retrieved it, Theroux said, "I don't think you'll be able to afford to go back Earthside. Unless you get a major hike in the Star Cop budget."

"Oh come on," Nathan protested wearily, "you're not going to fine me for that one. I was half-asleep. Play fair."

"No problem," Theroux said. "Shit, nothing's gonna kill you when you're half-asleep. You can rely on space to play fair."

Nathan's irritation got the better of him. "All right, Inspector, let's not be a smart arse," he snapped. "I hate a smart arse first thing in the morning." Immediately regretting his outburst, as he always did, he added without much change of tone, "Assuming that's what this is?"

Theroux nodded. "Close enough. You've been asleep for ten hours, give or take."

"You can fall a long way in ten hours," Nathan said.

"Get a shower," said Theroux. "I'll bring some breakfast to the office."

Farlane Wibbs was not unattractive physically, but she affected a soft-voiced, fluffy innocence which would have been inappropriate in a woman half her age. Theroux had always found her irritating, especially as he was fairly sure that underneath all the English sweetness she was a blue-steel bitch.

She was leaning now into the half module office allocated to the ISPF on the European orbit station *Charles De Gaulle*, and frowning with earnest concern. "It looks like machine failure," she was saying, "that's everyone's best guess. Engine control programme perhaps, or the navigation computer. It's a Euro-flight, obviously, so we'll get access to the data as soon as Moonbase gets it. But it's so horrible, I'm not sure that I want to know really."

"Not a question of wanting to know," said Theroux brusquely.

"Mike and Lara were such a lovely couple. They'll be badly missed, won't they?"

"I didn't know them that well," Theroux said.

Wibbs' eyes widened in mild surprise. "I thought everyone knew them," she said, the sweet tone of voice managing to suggest that Theroux must be some sort of social isolate, a groundsider even.

"Everyone knew *of* them, s'not the same thing," said Theroux, and then could not resist asking: "They were friends of yours, huh?"

"You could say that."

"Tough break."

"You're doing police work full-time now, are you?" Wibbs asked and when Theroux nodded said: "You'll be wanting all the official frills and furbelows on the case for your new boss, I expect?"

"Hell, no. Time enough for all that crap if we're called in for real."

"For this relief, much thanks. We're on doubles and standard alert as it is."

"Double shifts?"

"They still haven't replaced the Murderous Movie Buff. Oh, I'm sorry." Wibbs held out a hand towards him, and looked for a moment as though her heart might break. "I forgot. You two were close, weren't you?" She smiled a warm, sympathetic smile.

Theroux grinned, he hoped wryly, and said, "Till he pulled the gun, anyway. And the SA – what's that all about?"

Wibbs looked a bit put out that Theroux wouldn't play. She shrugged. "Routine reaction to all the fuss in Geneva. The US un-manned that's got the Treaty powers all of a tiswas? Typical American arrogance of course, that's really all it is."

Theroux recognized the cue for some more role-playing and to forestall a display of niceness about forgetting that he was an American he said, "Keep us updated, okay?" and keyed a communication screen.

Wibbs was not ready to be dismissed that easily. "Are you sure your Commander Spring isn't going to want chapter and verse on Mike and Lara?" she asked. "Only I thought he was supposed to be a by-the-book type of guy."

"There's all kind of books," Theroux said.

"Very well. If you say so." She turned and moved off down the corridor tube, passing Nathan on his way into the office. "If you say he doesn't need to know, he doesn't need to know," she said over her shoulder.

"Who doesn't need to know what?" asked Nathan as he heel-and-toed smoothly across the Velcro walking strip and pulled himself down onto the vacant seat fixture.

Theroux indicated several brightly wrapped food packs clipped to the console. "Breakfast."

Nathan said, "I'm not actually very hungry."

"Falling's easier with something in your stomach."

"A ritual disembowelling sword comes to mind. You know the odd thing is that I actually feel worse now than the first time I came out here."

"It could be your age."

Nathan scowled. "Late-flowering for a spaceman?" He tore the access tab from a pack marked 'Little Red Hen Scrambled Eggs', and waited for the contents to heat and expand. "The original pioneers were my age. Older, some of them."

"They were explorers. We're settlers. Settlers are different. They don't have the romance and excitement to keep them going. They need to be tougher."

"They need strong stomachs, certainly," Nathan said as the egg pack began to extrude a livid yellow paste. He shoved it quickly into the waste disposal. "Who doesn't need to know what?" he asked again.

"You. You don't need the fine print on the latest accident on the Mars run."

Star Cops

"Depends how fine it is."

"There's a two man freighter gone rogue. Headed for the dark. Flight crew's dead."

"How did that happen?"

Theroux said, "Investigations are proceeding. Standard cop-speak for 'we're unlikely ever to know', right?"

Nathan frowned. "What investigations? Who exactly's doing these investigations?"

"The flight crew, obviously."

"Obviously. This is the flight crew you said were dead?"

"Yeah, technically speaking they're dead, but that's just a way of –"

Before he could get any further Nathan interrupted him. "Inspector Theroux, in case it has escaped your notice," he said without raising his voice, "I am feeling a little below par. That makes me irritable. When I am irritable it ill-behoves subordinates to start playing silly buggers."

"They've got limited life-support," said Theroux coldly, "and no fuel left to correct their course. They'll run out of air before they run out of space. That's standard crewspeak for 'they're dead and everyone knows it, including them'."

"I see," said Nathan.

"Do you?"

"I still have things to learn."

"Yeah."

Nathan smiled. "But then, doesn't everybody?" he said, and thought there must come a time when the open, boyish smile wouldn't work any more, and he would have to start apologizing for his pompous ill-temper.

Theroux was certain by now that his new boss used that charming smile of his in a totally calculating way, but it was a killer and it was difficult to stop himself from smiling back. "I guess so," he said, and smiled anyway.

"Box?" Nathan unclipped the hand-size black box from his equipment belt. "There must be something I can do about the way I feel."

"Transfer to an environment which is blessed with gravity," Box replied, in a voice which Theroux still found impossible to distinguish from Nathan's. "After detailed consideration," it continued, "the conclusion must be: there is no significant probability that you will ever adapt to prolonged weightlessness."

"It's too soon to be sure of that," commented Theroux, finding himself unsure whether to talk to the man or directly to the machine.

"Is it a question of time, Box?" asked Nathan.

"Not according to the projections," Box answered. "Do you want to see them?"

Nathan looked at Theroux. "Do *you* want to see them?"

Theroux shook his head. "There's Moonbase. We could probably get an office allocation," he said. "They don't have a Star Cop based there, so…"

"So they owe us one," said Nathan. "Good. We'll take a look."

"Be more expensive as a base. You'd need a one-sixth rated launch vehicle at your immediate disposal if you wanted a rapid response time," Theroux said, then looked at Box. "Wait, wait just a cotton-pickin' minute here."

"Problem?" Nathan asked.

"Box couldn't have put that together from your question. You telling me it was listening, assuming stuff, using intuition?"

"Not if you won't believe that, no."

"It's just a machine."

Nathan nodded. "And it takes a human being to do those things effectively. What took you so long?"

"I had no reason to expect that you'd primed Box to respond the way you wanted."

"A little more scepticism, a little faster, and maybe we can make a copper out of you," Nathan said.

Theroux looked sour. "You'll let me know when I've got to take the written quiz."

The first time he had seen one of the all-purpose orbit shuttles, Nathan had fancied that it was pitching and rolling very slightly. It reminded him of the dinghy he once borrowed on a childhood holiday. He still remembered the weird, bouncing dip as he stepped down into it, and the slithering water pushed his weight back up at him. It was odd that a small shuttle craft should have triggered that memory, since it did not move in the same way, and boarding it produced no reaction to speak of. Nevertheless, the fibreglass boat on the tall, transparent sea now seemed inextricably linked in his mind with the squat, utility space-transports – and riding this one to Moonbase, recollections nudged each other forward.

"My old man," he said, the forgotten image of his father suddenly complete and unexpectedly clear to him, "always maintained that the greatest discovery made by the systems manufacturers was that people would accept any damn-fool thing provided there was a computer involved somewhere. *You want 'em to believe it*, he'd say, *stick it on a VDU screen.*"

"I thought he was a computer salesman?" said Theroux.

Nathan shrugged though the gesture was lost in the bulk of the unhelmeted spacesuit he was wearing. "Do you have to believe in everything you do?"

"Only if it's on the screen."

"He didn't believe what he said, anyway. Which was a pity, really."

Theroux said, "Don't feel too badly about it. Kids mostly expect too much of their fathers."

"He was right, though, that was the point."

"You sure you want to continue with this trip?" Theroux asked. "I'm the designated pilot, but there's a computer doing all the flying."

"I'm serious," said Nathan. "Gospel according to Spring: anything that can be used to stop people thinking for themselves –

Message.

In the darkened room the communications console activated a window in the top left-hand corner of its main screen.

Message.

Theroux interrupted, "Does this come before or after 'where there's living, there's policemen' in the order of service?"

"Before," said Nathan. "And it was written: Anything that can be used to stop people thinking for themselves, *will* be used to stop people thinking for themselves. Sooner or later."

Message was the only light, tiny and indistinct in the blackness, like an afterimage on tightly closed eyelids. But there was no-one to receive it. The apartment was unoccupied.

All messages should have been re-routed to the European Earth Orbit Station *Charles De Gaulle*, that was the instruction Nathan had programmed into his workstation the day he left, but somehow this one had bypassed the system. After a few moments, the message window began to pulse with a steady urgency. Not until the door of the apartment elevator opened, however, and the lights came on, did it add a soft chime to this flashing and announce in a polite voice, "*There is a message.*"

Lee Jones shed her outdoor jacket and said, "All messages for the keyholder are to be re-routed up to...or should that be out to...well whatever –"

"*There is a message*," the pager, ignoring the wrong cue, interrupted in the same polite tones.

Unlike Nathan, Lee had no ideological objection to depending on machines – so she usually found them far more irritating than he did. "Who... is... the... message... for?" she asked, enunciating each word with exaggerated care.

"*The message is for Lee Jones*," said the machine, at the same time displaying the name **LEE JONES** and her personal identity code on the main screen. This combination of the visual and oral was designed to make such transactions less impersonal, avoid misunderstandings, and allow for the possibility of SF or 'screen-phobia', which was the latest corporate euphemism for illiteracy. Inevitably, the overall effect was that the user was treated like a retarded infant.

Puzzled, Lee crossed to the screen and checked the PIC. "I left no instruction for re-routing," she said.

"*For further information, please enter your confidential personal identity code*," instructed the machine blandly, and printed up the instruction: **ENTER CPI CODE NOW**.

Lee tapped out the five digit code on the workstation's auxiliary number pad – standard, so that SF sufferers could memorize finger positions – and waited for the message to be transmitted.

"*Thank you Lee Jones*," said the machine. "*The message is coded for your eyes only. It will be necessary –*"

"Oh for God's sake," muttered Lee and was already tapping in her secure personal identity code by the time the machine said, " *– for you to enter your secure personal identity code*," and printed: **ENTER SPI CODE NOW**.

"*Thank you Lee Jones. And as a final safeguard your confidential keyword must be entered before the message can be transmitted.*" **ENTER KEYWORD NOW**.

She punched in 'pandashit', and briefly wondered how the functionally illiterate really coped with all this nonsense. "I hope," she said, "this is not one of your dumb jokes, Nathan. A professional caretaker would be a lot less obliging than me."

But in a way, she hoped it *was* one of his jokes. She had agreed to keep an eye on the apartment because they both recognized it as an uncomplicated way to stay in touch, and so when the machine assured her: "*In a very short while your message will be unscrambled and relayed to you,*" she smiled. "Or as we say round here…" she murmured and watched the screen display the single word: **WAIT**. "But not too long, my love," she added. "The clock is running. Besides, jokes are all about timing are they not?"

The theme tune of telecommunications corporation jingled at her and the machine said, "*This service has been brought to you by Unitel, the Secure Communications Link, a wholly-owned subsidiary of Wideworld Supranational. Thank you for patronizing Unitel.*"

Lee left the workstation, saying, "You're entirely welcome. Imagine my surprise: all this time I thought you were patronizing me," and crossed to the drinks cabinet where she poured herself three fingers of one of Nathan's better malts. "Just goes to show how easy it is to misjudge the ordinary warm-hearted multinational corporation." She sipped the smooth, smoky liquor and then, because she knew it would have annoyed Nathan had he been there, and he should have been there, damn him, she held the glass under the ice-maker and pressed for finely crushed. Nothing happened. Even the ice-maker fell in line with Nathan's wishes. Even when he'd run away to space taking her life with him like a selfish kid, like the selfish kids there might not be time for, even then he got his own bloody way. She looked at the gauge. The thing was empty. She knew she was being irrational but she was going to have ice in her sodding drink. She would wait for it. However long it took. She snatched up a glass jug from the drinks cabinet and went into the kitchen to get water for the ice-maker.

On the main communications screen the message began to print up.

FROM: NATHAN SPRING
TO: LEE JONES
YOUR LIFE IS IN DANGER. REMAIN WHERE YOU ARE. UNDER NO CIRCUMSTANCES MUST YOU LEAVE. LOCK OFF THE ENTRY ELEVATOR.
MORE FOLLOWS.

The last two words flashed insistently.

In the kitchen, Lee was beginning to feel petulant and just a little silly. At major inconvenience to herself, she was going to ruin good Scotch to score a minor point off a lover who wouldn't know she'd done it anyway.

And *Nathan* she called childish? She reached forward to flick off the water tap and suddenly all the lights in the apartment went out.

Her first thought was that the control programme had degraded a bit through lack of use. "Lights!" she called loudly to reset it. When the lights did not come back on she muttered, "What's this, a punishment? All right, I *won't* put ice in the Macallan," and then shouted, "Lights!" She waited a moment and then turned in what she hoped was the direction of the nearest control sensor and instructed in a clear, even voice, "Central control, central control check lighting fault please!"

In the pressing blackness, she waited for the computer to respond. She waited for the response and tried to be objective about how long it was taking. She was conscious of how quickly the dark stripped her sense of time and space and frightened her. But there was nothing to be frightened of. There was no life-threatening difference between the light and now, there was no reasonable reason to be frightened of the dark. She was in no danger from the dark.

She decided to go back into the living area and use the workstation to call block maintenance. Putting the jug down on the drainer, she felt her way towards the doorway. The jug crashed to the floor. Fear shocked through her, jagged as a fever spike. Realizing that she must have left the jug teetering on the edge of the sink she said, "Worried I'd change my mind about the ice, is that it?" and groped her way on.

The living area was a slight improvement. There was a faint light coming from the screen. Of course, she'd forgotten there was a message; thank God for Unitel and bureaucratic pandashit. Gratefully, she started to fumble her way towards the workstation.

She was still several yards from it when the elevator door opened on the other side of the room. The momentary brightness was dazzling. As she turned to look, an indistinct silhouette on the corner of the white flare side-stepped out beyond the light.

Lee froze.

The elevator door closed and the darkness was darker than before, but confused now, with the fading patterns of retinal overload. "Nathan?" she asked, and then more softly, "Nathan, is that you?" But she knew that it wasn't. Who was he? Where was he? Why did she think it was a man? Maybe she imagined it; could just be the computer playing silly buggers and her imagination playing tricks and something moved by the screen *oh God no*.

Star Cops

A voice from near the workstation whispered, a loud stage whisper, strange and threatening, "You didn't read your message."

Lee couldn't help herself. "Who is that? Who are you, what do you want?"

"You should have read your message," the whisper said.

Then he was moving, coming towards her. "*From Nathan Spring to Lee Jones,*" he whispered in the same flat, lifeless whisper, "*your life is in danger...*"

Lee backed away, and blundered into a seating platform. She tried to hold herself together. She tried not to let go. Oh please oh please oh please don't.

"*...remain where you are...*"

Lee felt her way along the edge of the cushions. Why was he whispering? Where was he?

"*...under no circumstances must you leave.*"

Lee scrambled across the cushions. Was he still moving? Where, oh Christ, where?

"*Lock off the entry elevator.*"

She couldn't picture where she was and what was between her and the elevator and there was still no light at all except from the screen. She tripped and fell. Sobbing, she crawled and scrambled towards where she thought the elevator was. She cannoned into something. Somebody grabbed her by the hair, and hauled her to her feet. She tried to scream. Close to her face, the voice whispered, "*More follows.*"

"Obviously," Detective Chief Inspector Colin Devis said nodding at the steadily flashing MORE FOLLOWS on the workstation screen, "that was intended to keep her sitting there, so the killer would know precisely where she was even in the dark."

Nathan sat in Crimescene Forensic Studio 437 while the recording was played back for his appraisal. Although what he was looking at was a close-up which Devis had zoomed in on and frozen for a moment to make his point, Nathan couldn't shake the illogical thought that just out of frame the paramedics were still bagging and tagging Lee's corpse. "Why is that obvious?" he asked.

Before Devis could answer, his sergeant said, "It's what the Scenes of Crime computer suggested."

Devis looked at her with obvious distaste. He was a heavyset man with a round, deceptively cheerful face. Only a sour narrowness about his eyes and mouth gave any indication of the deep cynicism with which he viewed the world. "Thank you Sergeant Corman," he said. "When I want your input, I'll ask for it."

Corman was pretty in an unspectacular, even-featured way and, at maybe thirty years old, she was at least twenty years younger than Devis. She was clearly not to his taste, and the feeling seemed to be mutual. Despite an unreal feeling of blank incomprehension, Nathan registered this routine assessment quite automatically and wondered in passing why these two were teamed.

"Sorry sir," Corman said, without sounding particularly apologetic.

"Try to remember you're new around here," said Devis, "and I'll try to do the same."

"Did it suggest why the message was left on the screen so it could be found by the investigating team?" Nathan asked and thought, *so it could be found by the investigating team.*

"You tell us," said Devis, cueing the playback to continue.

The cameras swept every part of the crime scene. Nathan couldn't see it as his apartment. It was a crime scene. Not familiar or personal. The paramedics were working. Lee.

He watched Lee disappear, enfolded in the black body bag, as though she was falling backwards into the dark waters of his dreams. "I didn't send it, Chief Inspector," he said.

Devis said, "Unitel have charged it to your account."

"I haven't got an account with Unitel."

"They'll be disappointed about that. Especially as they seem to have all your right numbers."

"One of his right numbers, sir," Corman put in. "The rest they issue themselves when they open the account."

"Corman," Devis said threateningly.

She ignored the warning and went on, "It's not difficult to get a CPI code, sir."

"As frames go, it's fairly crude," said Nathan.

"As killings go, it wasn't exactly neat," said Devis.

"Yes it was." This from Corman again.

"I won't tell you again, Corman," Devis said. And then in the same tone of voice asked, "Why would anyone want to frame you, Spring?"

"Commander Spring, Chief Inspector!" snapped Nathan. "You may

Star Cops

not be bright, but you can at least be civil!"

Devis looked bored as he waited for the rest of the tongue-lashing.

Nathan said, "I'm sorry that wasn't bright or civil was it? I'm having trouble adjusting to gravity…and death."

Devis paid as little attention to the apology as he had to the outburst. "How long had you known Miss Jones?" he asked.

Nathan hesitated. How long had he known her? How long would he have to live without knowing her, with her gone into the past, him here alone…?

"Did you hear what I asked?"

"Ten years?" Nathan said at last.

"Aren't you sure?"

"I can't remember ever not knowing her." He thought, I can't imagine not knowing her for all that's left of forever. The only person who doesn't know you're dead is you… Oh God, Lee, you are dead.

"Sir?" murmured Corman to Devis, who gave her a baleful look which she ignored as she drew him to one side. "The man's obviously in shock. Don't you think maybe we should give him a little time…?"

Devis glanced across at Nathan, who stared unseeing at the playback screen. "Just star temperament, that," he said and smiled at the pun. Corman was not amused.

Devis switched off the playback and said to Nathan, "I don't think there's much point in going on with this at the moment. I shall want to talk to you again."

"Yes," said Nathan. "I'll want to talk to you once I've cleared my head. There's something not kosher about this whole thing."

"You think not?"

"They left a message on the screen, the place still in darkness with the light and elevator system overrides still there for us to find. I can't believe they carried out such a careful plan so carelessly."

Devis frowned and said, "Yeah, well, you can safely leave us to worry about that."

"Leave you to worry about it?"

"That's what I said."

"Someone walks into my home," Nathan said getting to his feet, "and kills the only real friend I ever had, and I should leave it to *you* to worry about it?" He began to climb the steps towards the exit at the back of the tiered seats.

"Unless you'd prefer a charge of obstructing justice?" Devis called after him.

Nathan turned back down the steps towards him. "I'd prefer some cooperation," he raged, "so that I can catch the bastard who did this!"

"So that *you* can catch the bastard who did this?" Devis shouted and started up the steps. "Listen, glory boy. You might be flashy as all hell up there, but down here you're just another citizen."

"Like fuck I am. I'm a copper. I paid my dues at the door."

"Brotherhood of the Job?" Devis sneered. "I don't think so, Commander Spring."

They were facing each other now. Nathan could see the dull resentment in the other man's eyes. "No neither do I, Chief Inspector Devis," he said.

"This is my case," said Devis. "I suggest you be very careful to remember that."

"I just want them caught," said Nathan flatly. Somehow he didn't have the energy to fight with this fool any more. He didn't even want to listen to him.

"They will be," Devis was saying. "All you've got to do is answer the rest of my questions. Then you can hop on a shuttle and go back to playing spaceman with that public relations exercise you call a police force. Leave detective work to real policemen."

Nathan turned away from him. "Let me know when you've checked with the computer and found out what the rest of your questions are," he said as he headed for the exit again. "And I'd suggest a hard copy, listing them in order of importance. You won't want to overtax yourself, will you?"

"You've run the full list? Asked all the questions," Theroux had asked, "and there's nothing? No fault of any kind? That just leaves us with a glitch in the system. A million to one shot. Is that what we're saying here?" He had touched the key and an electronic signal indicated that his mic was now deactivated and the communications console had switched to receive.

On the small screen Mike's face continued to stare at him without reaction. "Knock once for yes, twice for no," Theroux muttered to it, aware that this was in poor taste considering the guy really was dead. It would be minutes before the frozen face could respond. The outgoing transmission had to reach *Dædalus*, where it would animate Theroux's blankly staring face on its communications screen, then Mike's answer had to make the return trip here to Moonbase and the open console.

The delays inherent in talking over such distances made for halting conversations, which in turn made for occasional misunderstandings and wanderings from the point. For this reason, most off-Earth communications consoles incorporated Longcom-Prog which built up a record of developing exchanges and made available an ongoing summary or a full transcription, and even offered prompts to guide a dialogue back to the course it had identified and analyzed. Not everyone was comfortable with this, but most people used the system, as Theroux used it now, because it was there and because if you didn't and you fucked up it was that much harder to justify yourself. Longcom-Prog was a major solution to a minor problem and, Theroux thought in passing, it was a classic example of Nathan Spring's 'anything that can be used to stop people thinking for themselves'…

"*That's about the strength of it,*" Mike said from the screen. "*Everything is faultless, as far as we can tell. The good ship Dædalus is as sound as the day she was commissioned. A million to one shot. Wouldn't you bloody know it? I never won a thing in my life before.*"

Lara stuck her face into scanner range and said, "*Oh, thanks a lot.*" Despite her shaved head, or maybe because of it, she looked very young and vulnerable. Theroux felt a sudden urge to protect her, a strangely sexual longing, almost an ache.

Mike said, "*I never thought of you as a prize. More of a just reward for a clean and virtuous life.*"

Lara said, "*I can see the logic of that from your point of view, but look at it from my side. I've always been clean and virtuous, so how come I ended up with you?*"

Theroux watched them play-acting. He couldn't decide whether to be touched or irritated by the ritual performance of grace under pressure. Cargo-jock stereotypes joking with death. Why bother, for Chrissakes? Who was it for? Surely not for him, a fast receding stranger, a red-shifted cop assigned the shitty job of accident investigator because he happened to be there. He guessed it must be for other people they knew would be watching. And for the record. And for posterity. It's a good day to die. No blindfold. Long live freedom! Viva Zapata, viva Mexico! Shit, what a fucking waste.

"*This is not relevant to the matter in hand,*" prompted the flat, unhuman tones of Longcom-Prog. "*A reminder of the questions still to be addressed will precede your responding transmission.*"

"Shut the fuck up," Theroux muttered, and disconnected the system abruptly. It queried the disconnection and chimed a warning alarm which Theroux also disconnected. The technicians on duty in the European Operations Suite looked up and glanced in his direction but none of them stared or spoke. Etiquette required they give the impression that they were not listening, though obviously they were. Theroux was aware too that there was a certain coolness towards him, but now he was a full-time copper he was getting used to that.

On the screen, Mike turned his attention back to camera and spoke directly at Theroux. "*Listen, we know this isn't what you want to hear. We know it would make things easier for you if we could find a reason why this happened.*" He shrugged and grinned. "*Christ, it might even make things easier for us.*"

"*I don't see how,*" Lara put in.

"*Be nice to know it wasn't our fault,*" he said.

Lara said, "*Dead's dead.*"

"*So?*"

"*So don't you think that's too late for blame, love?*"

No, Theroux thought, I don't think so. There may not be life after death, but there's blame without question and without end. Guilt goes on.

"*We'll go on while you run the accident simulations and whatever else,*" said Mike. "*For whatever reason. You've got one last chance to see if we missed something. Only don't take too long, David. We haven't decided whether to wait it out or not.*"

Lara's face pushed into frame again as she said, "*Let's not rush it all right? I'm barely used to being dead, and already the experience leaves me cold. This is nothing like what it said in the brochure.*"

The electronic bleep ended the transmission, and the faces of Mike and Lara froze on the screen; she smiling, he looking pensive, both of them looking lost.

"What will you tell them?"

Theroux had no idea. He looked up to find it was the Base Co-ordinator, Roland Paton who had asked the dumb damn question. He must have wandered through from the Secretariat while the message was coming in, and he was standing now at Theroux's shoulder peering intently at the images of Mike and Lara. Paton was a slightly built, dapper Frenchman. Why in the hell was it that all Frenchmen were dapper, just as all Frenchwomen were elegant? And how did the guy contrive to look so neat and well-groomed in a standard issue coverall? P'raps it was the job. Just an illusion because he was as close to a CEO as the Moonbase set-up had. It wasn't only the Brits who bred the habit of deference into their people. "I don't know, sir," Theroux said.

"Will they self-destruct?"

Fox, the duty Traffic and Logistics Officer – a Scot who seemed to Theroux to be constantly on the verge of violence – jumped up from his workstation and two-hopped to the coffee dispenser. "Their options are a bit limited, wouldn't you say?" he remarked harshly, as he drew coffee into a tall beaker.

Theroux noticed the polite fiction that no-one had been listening to the communications with *Dædalus* had been unceremoniously dropped. Paton glared in the direction of Fox, but otherwise ignored the comment. "I meant, of course, immediately. Is it your opinion that they might do it immediately?"

"I hope not, sir," said Theroux, "but it is a matter for them. I don't feel I should even try to influence their decision."

Paton nodded unhappily. "Yes." He moved towards the passageway which connected EOS to where the Secretariat had its offices, in the central hub of the wheel-shaped underground complex.

Unlike on the Earth orbit stations, in the Moon's one sixth-G environment it was not the convention to keep the feet in contact with the floor. Velcro walking strips and slippers were provided in all the installations just as they were on the zero-G stations, but unlike the heel-and-toe skill of weightless walking, control-hopping was what separated an off-Earther from a groundsider here on Moonbase. Smooth soled footwear was the mark of the lunar professional.

Paton was a slighter man than Fox, his movements less extravagant, but his looping strides showed the same basic technique. Since it was this technique that everyone used, Theroux had been quietly trying to perfect it ever since he arrived, and now he watched the casual expertise of the Frenchman's departure with some small envy.

"I will be in my office should you need me, Inspector Theroux," Paton said, as he disappeared through the bulkhead pressure doors.

"As if anyone could possibly need him. Man's pathetic," Fox said loudly. "I cannot understand how he came to be in that job."

Gina Andreotti looked up from logging communications traffic and said, "You cannot understand how he came to be in that job and you did not, is this not so?"

"Senior management? *Moi*? Christ, no, this is not so. Not me, sweetheart, I'm strictly a labourer in the vineyard."

"Sally McMasters thinks you want her job."

"That's different. I think whoever's in that job should do good work, not just give good head."

"Sexist Neanderthal," Ernst Kohl muttered, as he ran the calculations of the life-support refunds accruing to the European operation over the previous month.

Fox looked across at the Section Quartermaster. "Did you speak, Ernst?" he asked.

"I find your manners are not good," said Kohl, his thin face pinched with disapproval and not a little anxiety.

"You sanctimonious little shite," Fox said amiably, "you wouldn't know good manners if they threw up in your lap."

"You see, that is exactly what I mean. You are crude, Guy."

"He was joking, Ernst," Gina said, shaking her head and smiling.

"Does Roland Paton have a personal connection with the *Dædalus* crew?" Theroux asked of no-one in particular, glancing round the wide but claustrophobic room.

There was a moment's silence, then Fox said, "Lara's his love-child. That the sort of thing you have in mind?"

"I wondered why he was so concerned," said Theroux. "I wondered if anyone had any ideas?"

"You're the detective," Fox sneered.

"*Dædalus* is carrying a lot of Professor Paton's most recent work," Kohl said. "It must be..." He gestured with his hands as he reached for the appropriate words.

"A real sickener," Fox finished for him.

"Paton's a biologist, right?" Theroux asked.

"Current specialization: cryogenics," Fox said. "So at a guess, that's one part of the *Dædalus*'s cargo that a colony on a freezing hellhole like Mars can manage without."

"Mars is a logical location to pursue ultra-low temperature research," said Kohl primly.

Fox sipped his coffee. "Life support supplies would have been more use to them. But it's largely academic now."

"We haven't checked the cargo yet," Theroux said, more or less thinking aloud.

"We haven't?" asked Fox. "Who 'we', exactly?"

Theroux was conscious that the man seemed to be getting more aggressive. He wondered if the coffee was affecting him. "I didn't ask Mike and Lara to check the cargo. I guess I should've done."

"Why, for God's sake?" Fox demanded. "Do you like pestering the dead? Do you get some sort of kick out of it?" A single stride brought him to the communications console and he stared down at Theroux as if he was only waiting for an answer to begin the fight.

"Stop it, Guy," said Gina quietly. "He's doing his job."

"It's a shitty job!" Fox snarled.

Theroux nodded sombrely. "You got that right."

"Then why do it? Let them go in peace, man."

"I can't. You know I can't. It's standard operating procedure. Policy." Theroux regretted the word as soon as he said it.

"Policy? What's the fuck is 'policy' supposed to mean?!"

"It means," Gina interrupted calmly, "that we all need to know if there is a design fault in that ship."

Fox turned to look at Gina. "Design fault, my arse," he said finally, as though he had suddenly become very weary. "You know as well as I do the only design fault in that ship won't be investigated at all."

"Oh yeah," Theroux asked, "why's that?"

Fox headed towards the other passageway which led from the European Operations Suite, this one linking it to the outer ring where the mess and recreation areas were located. "I'm taking a break, Gina," he said.

Theroux raised his voice. "You didn't answer my question, Mr. Fox."

Fox did not look back. "Question?"

"Why won't it be investigated?"

"Because your average Star Cop," said Fox, "couldn't find his bum with both hands." Still without looking back, he went out through the pressure doors.

Theroux got up from the communications console and hopped rather clumsily to where Gina was sitting. "Was it something I said?" he asked.

She was a good-looking woman, short dark curls framing a squarish face, big eyes, big breasts, legs that wouldn't quit, all the things he found attractive except for the most important one: she obviously wasn't attracted to him in the slightest.

"He and Mike were friends," she said.

"That's it?"

She shrugged. "I don't know him that well."

"He seemed to think you understood what he was talking about. You know as well as I do, that's what he said."

"He was wrong."

"You sure?"

"Are you interrogating me, Inspector?"

Theroux smiled his best smile. He had been practising that, too. He was never going to do it as well as Nathan Spring did, but half as effective would still make it a pretty useful device. "Were Mike and Lara popular?" he asked.

Gina said, "They were famous."

"That isn't what I asked."

She considered for a moment then she said, "They were lovers. Lovers are popular at a distance. Distance is difficult, in a place like this."

Theroux thought, *it's not difficult any more – not for them, that's for damn sure.*

Gina said, "They will be more popular than before."

"Could you patch a call through to Earth Central for me?" Theroux asked.

"You could do that for yourself," she said. "It's a standard console."

"To the one in our new office," he jerked a thumb in the direction of the inner complex. "It isn't fully plumbed in yet, but I figured if anyone could manage it…" He tried the smile again.

She didn't react, but she did say, "I'll see what I can do."

Without looking up from his workstation Ernst Kohl murmured, low but distinct, "Does he have call authorization codes?"

"Muttering's ill-mannered, Ernst," Theroux said loudly. "And yes, I do have authorization codes." He waved his ID from the ISPF, unexpectedly enjoying the feeling of power. "It's police business."

Nathan sipped his coffee and frowned at Theroux on the main screen. "A glitch in the system?"

"*Standard engineer-speak for: could happen to anyone, don't uncross your fingers,*" Theroux said, shifting his position a bit, trying instinctively, and pointlessly, to get a better view from the scanner.

Nathan realized that on Moonbase his screen image would be partial and irritating but he couldn't bring himself to sit in the optimum position at the workstation. Lee hadn't sat there, he knew, but it made no difference. The truth was, he couldn't sit anywhere in the apartment. It was irrational, but he felt that if he sat down, he would be accepting something, moving on, and he wasn't ready to do that. "No, that's not good enough, David," he said.

On the screen, Theroux smiled. "*How did I know you were going to say that?*"

The short time-lag in communication between Earth and Moon made it necessary for speakers to finish positively and indicate by their expression that they were waiting for the reply. Without these almost subliminal signals, the tendency would be to speak across one another. Nathan realized that for Theroux, unable to see him fully, it would be hard to be absolutely sure when to speak so he decided to keep things succinct, which wasn't difficult since he didn't feel particularly chatty anyway. "What's unusual about the *Dædalus*?"

"*Standard General Dynamics freighter. Nothing remarkable about it.*"

"It kicked in the engine at an unprogrammed time and killed the crew. I'd say that was moderately remarkable, wouldn't you?"

Theroux shrugged. "*I'd say that was Sod's Law of Technology. The more there is to go wrong, the more there is to go wrong.*"

As if to make the point, the image on the screen broke up as he spoke. Nathan leaned forward and fiddled with the tuning. When nothing changed he banged the console sharply and got a sudden rock-steady picture of Theroux waiting for him to speak. Nathan said, "Something fairly specific would have to go wrong to produce that particular effect, surely?"

"*Blocked up washing facilities wouldn't do it, if that's what you're asking.*"

"A limited number of things could have caused it, all of which the crew have checked, is that right?"

On screen, Theroux looked momentarily unsure. "*Yeah, I guess so. They say they have.*"

"You don't trust their expertise?"

"*I don't trust their motivation. I mean, hell, how reliable would your work be, under those circumstances?*"

Nathan thought, *if I was the victim, already dead but with a chance to find out why...* "I'd want to know," he said.

Theroux nodded. "*You're a cop.*"

Stupid comment. "So are you." Why is everybody being stupid?

"Sooner or later." Or am I just... "Anyway there's no point in second-guessing them. If they say there's no fault to be found then as far as I'm concerned there's no fault to be found. What we've got to do – what *you've* got to do – is find out all there is to know about that ship. Who worked on it, when, what it's carrying, everything. And the same goes for the crew. There's an answer there somewhere. I expect you to find it."

Theroux's pause was slightly longer than before, then he said, "*Okay Nathan, you're the man. It would help some if I knew what the question was, though.*"

"You have only two real alternatives, David. If you rule out the accidental, then what you're left with is deliberate."

This did not seem to have occurred to Theroux. He looked genuinely surprised by the thought. "*Someone set out to kill them?*"

"Eliminate the impossible and whatever's left, however improbable, must be the truth."

"*Jeez, I wish I'd had a classical education,*" Theroux said wryly.

"And Sherlock Holmes always did have the advantage of knowing the answers right from the off. How's the office?"

Theroux glanced around at what was out of scanner range. "*Coming together. We'll have most of what we need before long.*" A brief pause, then, "*How's the apartment?*"

Nathan appreciated the comparative delicacy of the question. "Strange. Something not right about it. I feel as though I'm being...picked on."

"*Shuttle-lag,*" Theroux said. "*And shit, you're bound to be paranoid under the circumstances.*"

Paranoid? Perhaps that was it. "They've assigned Devis as investigating officer."

"*Should I have heard of him?*"

"He's one of the department's all time great cretins. British Native and All-Comers record holder. A cretin's cretin, in fact."

"*Sounds like natural Star Cop material. You going to recruit him?*"

Nathan smiled a little. "I'm going to dump you, if you don't find the anomaly that explains what happened to the *Dædalus*. Keep in touch, yes?"

He killed the screen before Theroux could answer. It was only when he leaned back, that he realized he was sitting at the workstation.

"Box?" he said.

From the kitchen his own voice answered him. "Yes Nathan?"

"Book my usual table at the Lotus Garden."

"Should I confirm a time with Miss Jones?"

"Miss Jones is dead."

"Do you want me to adjust the reference framework and remove her?"

"No."

"Then that datum is meaningless."

Talking to himself. Talking to the air, it was too close to madness when the world, when the bloody reference framework, wasn't whole anymore, wasn't real anymore. *Who else do you trust love.*

Nathan got up from the workstation and went to retrieve Box from where he left it by the coffee percolator. It might be just a box but he had to have it in front of him if he was going to talk to it; he had to know which one of them was talking. *If you don't count that creepy Box, there's no-one to talk to apart from me.*

When he had Box in his hand, he asked, "Does the regional crime computer have a manageable list of suspects yet?"

Box said, "There are one hundred names still on the list."

"Front runner?"

"Remains the same."

He put Box down again, and poured himself another cup of coffee. The voice didn't sound like him. Was that really how he sounded, even to her? "Odds?" he asked.

"The possibility of error remains significant."

"Let me know when there's someone worth lifting."

"Have you decided whether to eat alone?"

Without thinking, he had ordered for two, and with their customary discretion, the waiters at the Lotus Garden had not commented, assuming simply that he was greedy, and caring only that he paid his bill. Carefully, he had helped himself from dishes set out in the centre of the table, leaving enough of each for Lee.

He was sure that if he didn't think about it, her face and voice would come more clearly to him. At the moment he couldn't picture her at all. What he had to do was stop thinking about her. It was like trying to recall a forgotten name, you had to stop thinking about it. You had to stop thinking. If you could. You had to stop thinking about her dying. You had to stop thinking about her terror, her dying alone and in terror. You had to stop thinking. You had to stop wanting to make it better. You had to stop wanting to say you were sorry. You had to stop thinking.

"Am I disturbing you, Commander?" He looked up from his untouched food. Sergeant Corman was standing by the table, looking slightly embarrassed. "It'll keep," she went on. "I can come back when you've finished."

"That's all right, Sergeant, have a seat," Nathan said, indicating the chair opposite, where Lee would have been sitting. When Corman had sat down, he asked, "How did you know where to find me?"

"This was listed as an eating place for you and Lee Jones."

"Detective work?" He couldn't quite keep the sarcastic edge out of his voice.

Corman did not seem to notice. "It's what they pay me for," she said.

"It's what they pay your boss for," Nathan said. "You they pay as a gofer." Why, he wondered, was he being gratuitously unpleasant to this woman?

"My mistake, sir," she said stiffly.

That had obviously hurt. He said, "Their mistake, I'd say," and smiled his best smile. She relaxed again, as he knew she would. "How many places did you try?"

"This is the first," she said, managing not to sound smug about it. "It's a routine sort of place. You'd want to remember routine things, if you wanted to remember at all."

"She hated this place. I never noticed," Nathan said, the picture of Lee clear in his mind, scowling at the panda on the wallzac. "Are you hungry? I can get another plate."

"No, thanks."

No explanation? No polite 'I've already eaten, thank you, sir'? Clearly a very self-possessed young woman. "So, if you're not looking for excellent Chinese food, what are you looking for?" He picked up his chopsticks, lifted his rice bowl to just below his chin, and began to eat.

"Advice. As you know, we've been processing a fairly comprehensive list of psychopaths –"

He interrupted her, gesturing with his chopsticks, "How would I know that?"

"You've been monitoring our computer."

"Who says?"

"I do. I may be a gofer, sir but I'm not a fool."

"Does anyone else think I've been breaking the law?"

She looked him straight in the eye. "Just me."

Star Cops

"Then my advice –" Nathan said.

Corman cut in quickly, "Is to keep my mouth shut, yes. I fully intend to."

"I was going to say, report me to your superiors."

Her smile was politely sceptical. "Without proof, sir?"

What was she up to? Was she ambitious, what? "What is it you want, Sergeant?"

"I got the impression you thought the crime had an extra dimension. Something that was almost obvious but…not quite."

Nathan returned to his eating. "Yes, well, it's hard to think clearly under those circumstances."

"You mean, you've changed your mind?"

"I don't entirely trust my mind at the moment."

Corman looked disappointed. "That's a pity, because I think you were right."

"You sure you won't have something to eat?" Nathan asked.

She leaned forward and said earnestly, "There's no recognizable motive, sir."

Nathan couldn't help noticing the front of her tunic was unbuttoned enough to show off her small, pale-skinned breasts. "So you look for someone whose motive wouldn't be recognizable," he said.

She saw him looking, and held her position for just long enough to make it obvious, though to make what obvious he wasn't entirely sure. Then she sat back and said, "A psycho."

"That's the logic of it."

"But no psycho is that elaborate in his preparations."

"Are you serious? I've had some who were positively theatrical."

"If all they were going to do was kill?" she said. "That's all he did. He killed, fast and efficiently. And then he left."

Fast and efficiently? *Oh Christ, I hope so, Lee. No fear. No pain. Lee, I'm sorry.* "A professional wouldn't leave all those loose ends. Not unless he was interrupted."

"He wasn't, but maybe he thought he was."

"A professional wouldn't spook," Nathan said. "Which brings you back to the psycho."

"Yes, I know," Corman said dejectedly. "I was hoping you'd have some new suggestions. You used to be a brilliant detective."

"How long have you been with Devis?" Nathan asked.

"Not long."

"Does he know you're here?"

Corman shook her head. "I don't think it would strike the Chief Inspector as a very good idea."

"He'd be right."

Corman said deadpan, "There has to be a first time for everything."

Nathan put down the bowl and chopsticks, wiped his mouth carefully with his napkin, poured himself a glass of wine and sipped it. Finally, as he began to help himself to more food, he said, "It's getting late, Sergeant."

She frowned. "And I've overstepped the mark, I know. But I'm good, and sick of being told what to do by people who are stupider and less talented than I am."

"You'd be surprised how many people feel like that, Sergeant," Nathan said, without looking up from what he was doing.

Coldly angry she said, "I wouldn't be remotely surprised. Don't patronize me, Commander. Get me fired by all means but don't patronize me, I don't deserve that and I won't sit still for it." She made no move to get up from the table, however.

Nathan drank some more wine, sipping it slowly. "I'm outside my jurisdiction, as your Chief Inspector pointed out," he said. The wine was a Dowchem Medoc, the most expensive the restaurant mixed and a guaranteed perfect copy of his favourite 1970 vintage. Everything about it was right, and still it tasted like shit. "I couldn't get you fired, even if I wanted to. And if you're as shit-hot as you think you are, you'll have worked out beforehand that I'd be unlikely to want to. Yet."

"I'm not that calculating," Corman said.

"Then you're not that good. Why 'used to be'?"

"Used to be?"

"You said I 'used to be' a good detective."

"I said brilliant."

"You flattered me.

"I don't think so."

"So what's changed?"

She lifted her face towards the ceiling. "You're up there," she said.

"Out there," said Nathan. "We space types say 'out there'."

"No offence, sir," Corman said, "but we detective types say, 'what the hell is there out there to detect?'"

Star Cops

The office was much bigger than the quarter of a basic module the ISPF was allocated on the *Charles De Gaulle*. The room, like several others now used for storage, had been intended as a research facility until it became clear that many of the scientific teams assembled to work on the Moon, whether funded by governments or multinational corporations, were paranoid and competitive enough to prefer the less accessible Outposts to the laboratories of the Science Annex in Moonbase itself.

"Nothing but the best for you lads, eh?" remarked Fox, looking round the sparsely furnished chaos of the half-finished office.

Theroux tossed the remains of the cold pizza he had been eating into the organics disposal and said, "We got a good union."

"Makes you wonder why anyone would volunteer to be a cop," Fox said and tested the negative-pressure double door, which was part of the original lab specification.

"As I remember it, no-one on Moonbase did," said Theroux.

"A high IQ was one of the entry requirements," Fox said and then smirked and added, "to Moonbase, that is."

"The test was always unreliable," said Theroux.

Fox stopped playing with the door. "Negative pressure cycle," he said. "That'd be standard on all Star Cop offices, I suppose? Wouldn't want anything nasty to get out and contaminate people." When Theroux offered no reaction he asked, "What was it you wanted to see me about?"

"Quote, 'the only design fault in that ship won't be investigated at all', unquote."

"Liars and policemen need good memories, isn't that what they say?"

"That's what they say. What did you mean by it?"

Fox moved to look at the screen where Theroux had been working when he came in. "The cargo manifest," he said, adding conversationally, "You know the Mars colony will never be economic. What in God's name do they do with all this stuff?" Without asking, he scrolled down the list for a while then said, "Why are you interested in what the *Dædalus* was carrying, can you tell me that?"

"I'm looking for anomalies," said Theroux.

"Anomalies?"

"That's where you find your bum with one hand but not the other, and you know something's wrong."

"Sounds half-arsed to me," Fox said, unsmiling.

Finally beginning to lose patience, Theroux said, "All right, enough of this shit."

"You really don't intend to let them rest, do you?" Fox asked.

"You didn't answer the question," Theroux said.

"What question was that?"

"Quit jerking me around and answer the fucking question."

"Or you'll what?"

"Or I'll arrest you, charge you with a whole series of technical offences and have you shipped back to Earth for trial."

For the first time, Fox looked rattled. "Are you threatening me?"

"You'd better believe it."

"Get stuffed." He took one light, hopping stride towards the door.

"Fox, if you're charged with anything," Theroux said matter-of-factly, "anything at all, your career is over out here. You realize that, huh?"

Fox turned back. "Like hell I do!" His voice got harsher suddenly, and his face flushed. "The police state bully boys haven't taken over yet. Not out here, they haven't."

Theroux gestured round the room, and smiled. "No, but the branch office is open for business," he said mockingly.

"You think it's funny?" Fox raged.

Theroux stopped smiling. "I'm conducting a murder investigation."

Fox seemed genuinely taken aback. "You're kidding," he said.

"Just tell me what you meant?"

"A murder investigation?" Fox shuffled back into the room, the looping stride technique forgotten. "Since when?"

"Parkinson's Law of Criminology, that's what Nathan Spring calls it."

"I'm sorry?" Fox asked uncertainly, still shocked, it seemed, by the idea of murder.

"Crime expands to occupy the number of cops available to deal with it," said Theroux. "Now what exactly is it that you know about a design fault on the *Dædalus*?"

Fox said, "I was talking about the crew roster." All his furious anger was gone now.

It was Theroux's turn to be perplexed. "The crew roster?"

"Those two should never have been allowed to fly together," Fox said, his voice and face set to express outrage, but showing a pained resentment as well. "It's against operating procedures, against the rules and it's dumb. Handling a freighter is dangerous work. Hell, all work out here is dangerous. You can't afford distractions."

"They've been flying together for a while," Theroux said.

Fox snorted with contempt. "And everyone's been doing numbers about how romantic it is."

"Everyone except you?"

"I don't find taking stupid risks particularly romantic. I find death even less so. Do you know, people actually bloody helped them to juggle the roster?"

"Why didn't you stop it?" Theroux asked. "You could have blown the whistle on them – how come you didn't?"

"You think I haven't asked myself that question?"

"Did you give yourself an answer?"

Fox shrugged and looked Theroux in the eyes. "Mike was a friend of mine."

Is he gay? Theroux wondered. *Is that what the violence is?* "All the more reason," he said.

Fox said, "I suppose I didn't want people to think I was..." He shook his head, and shrugged again.

"Jealous?" suggested Theroux, without emphasis.

"Christ," Fox said, "Mike was careless at the best of times. With her as a distraction, sooner or later he was bound to foul something up."

"And that's what you were talking about?"

"I reckoned the people who screwed around with crew planning caused a design fault. Mix the personal and the professional, and what you get are mistakes. People are part of the design. It's dangerous to forget that."

On Nathan's main screen, the midnight news summary was running a routine bite on the spat between the Treaty powers.

"...Secretary of State Francis has stated quite categorically that the unmanned station is a civilian project..."

There were no new pictures of the US station, which had been shuttled into orbit and assembled under the tightest possible security. What was showing now was the same mixture of simulation and computer enhanced, very long lens material that had been used on all the previous bulletins.

"...but is nonetheless of the utmost secrecy..."

Nathan could see that by starving the networks of sexy, live visuals the PR blackout was ensuring the story would die of malnutrition before anything too embarrassing happened.

"...and any attempt to penetrate its security screens would be regarded as an act of war."

"Can't get much more civilian than that," he muttered, taking a long pull from a generous glass of malt. Alcohol was probably a mistake, he realized. I mean, Christ, how badly could he need a depressant under the circumstances? Then again, there wasn't much chance of feeling better, so sod it.

The visuals mixed through to Corporate PR footage of General Dynamics freighters, and the bulletin moved on to Theroux's case.

"The European Space Colonization Bureau tonight denied rumours that their Martian colony will run dangerously short of vital stores as a result of the tragic accident to the supply ship Dædalus."

In the top left-hand corner of the screen the **MESSAGE WAITING** cue began to flash. Nathan keyed the PRINT code, and on the black screen appeared the words:

LEE JONES HAS BEEN DEALT WITH. SHE WAS A SILLY BITCH BUT IT WAS A PLEASURE DOING BUSINESS WITH HER. NOW WE COME TO THE MAIN EVENT. NOW IT'S YOUR TURN, SPRING. YOU ARE NEXT.

Belatedly, Nathan fumbled Box against the processing unit. "Trace message," he said.

Box said, "Tracing."

The message began to fade from the screen, but it did not disappear completely. **YOU ARE NEXT** remained when all the rest had gone.

"Box?"

"It was on a delayed relay," Box said.

"How long a delay?"

"The message was registered one hour ago in a public access booth."

"Who was it charged to?"

"You."

Nathan slammed his fist down on the workstation. "Bastard!" he shouted. Then the analgesic effects of the alcohol began to wear off and he grunted "Shit!" and rubbed his stinging hand.

He was trying to decide what to do next when the lights in the apartment went out. Only the workstation was active, and in the darkness **YOU ARE NEXT** suddenly expanded to fill up the screen. And then the words began to pulse slowly.

"All right, Box, check the power control circuits," Nathan said.

"A remote breaker has been installed."

Another one? Nathan could hardly believe it. If the source of the information had been anything other than Box, he wouldn't have believed it.

"Only the screen and the elevator remain operational," Box went on. "The elevator is on its way up."

Nathan swivelled in the chair so that he was facing the elevator door. If the message was meant to keep him in the chair then at least he knew where the assassin would make for. Unless whoever it was had a gun. Nathan slipped out of the chair and crouched to one side of it. The booze was making him slow and muddled. He concentrated fiercely. He'd only get one chance at this. If he could just get a hand on the bastard. One chance. One chance was all he wanted. One chance to break his fucking back.

Across the room, the elevator door sighed open. Its brightly light interior was stark in the darkness. It was empty. No movement. Nothing. The door stayed open. Then the apartment lights came back on again, and the workstation screen went blank.

Nathan got to his feet, feeling stupid and angry and relieved. He checked in the elevator, not knowing quite what he expected to find and finding nothing. An incoming call chime drew his attention back to the workstation. The cue spot was flashing in the top left-hand corner of the screen. "Accept call," he said.

The cue spot darkened, but the screen remained blank. "*Commander Spring?*" the voice said, in a flat whisper that would have been inaudible if the system had not automatically adjusted the volume to Nathan's optimum hearing level.

"Yes," Nathan said, annoyed with himself for accepting the call before he was back at the workstation where he had left Box.

"*I have information which I think will interest you,*" the whisperer went on.

Nathan slipped back into his seat and said, "I'm not getting vision at this end."

"*I prefer to remain unseen for the moment.*"

"And unidentified, presumably," Nathan said wryly, as he used Box's keypad to initiate a trace. "What's this anonymous tip you have for me?"

"*I know who killed your lady,*" the voice whispered.

Nathan hesitated fractionally; he couldn't help himself. As he said, "Is that right?" he tried to keep his tone noncommittal – bored, even.

"I also know why she was killed. There was a reason. If you're interested, I will tell you in person. Only in person. Only face to face."

"Is that right?" Hell's teeth, couldn't he think of something else to say?

"I will wait for you at the east end of Victoria Park, but not for long."

"The east end? At this time of night?"

"Are you afraid?"

Nathan said, "Absolutely. My mother didn't have any stupid children." On the screen Box was displaying the progress of the trace: it was a public access booth…

It was somewhere local…

"Neither did mine," the whisperer said. *"By the lake. Thirty minutes,"* and broke the connection. The trace was incomplete. Box had only narrowed it to a choice of three booths. "Bugger it," Nathan said. "I'm losing my touch. Box, did you get a charge code?"

Switching to voice in response to the verbal cue, Box said, "There is no personal identification. The call was charged to the account of the Adam Smith Nexus. It is a senior management authorization."

"I want the authorized user list. I also want any level one confidential information there is about the company or its staff. Start with the Police Intelligence Databank. Store for retrieval, no hard copy, no outside access."

While he gave Box these instructions, he dug out the Beretta 98S handgun he kept locked in the safe-drawer at the back of the drinks cabinet. In the time since he had been issued with the lightweight police automatic he had only ever used it on the practice range, never before feeling the need to carry it.

Nathan left the apartment using the emergency exit chute rather than the still-unexamined elevator. The gun was uncomfortable in the pocket of his jacket. At the workstation where he had left it Box was already using all the available communications channels for the illegal data search.

In the background the newscast chattered quietly to itself without disturbing Theroux.

"…and it was emphasized in the strongest possible terms that any unauthorized attempt to…"

He was not even stirred from his doze by the arrival of Roland Paton in the office.

"…approach the unmanned station…"

He slept the sleep of the bored and exhausted.

"... would have the gravest possible consequences."

His feet were propped up on a packing case, his head was lolled forward at a neck-crippling angle, while the screen at which he had been working had switched automatically to a power-down hold.

"Suggestions that the security radars were of a state-of-the-art military pattern have meanwhile been dismissed..."

Paton touched his shoulder and murmured, *"Monsieur L'Inspecteur?* David?"

"...as quote unquote 'absurd fantasy'."

Theroux woke with a start. "I'm sorry, what?"

"I apologize to disturb you at this late hour."

"This is BBCNN global news..."

"Screen off," Theroux said, yawning and trying to straighten his neck.

"May I talk wiz you?" Paton asked.

"Of course." Theroux yawned again. "Excuse me, it's been a long shift. Won't you sit down, sir? Can I get you some coffee?" Paton did not seem to hear. He paced around the room with those small looping strides, which struck Theroux abruptly as being absurd affectation.

"Your scientific background," Paton said, "is as a flight engineer I think, yes?"

Theroux went to the coffee dispenser without attempting such controlled hops, resolving not to bother with any more professional bullshit. Fuck it, the man looked like a half-witted rabbit. "I was a flight engineer." He poured two coffees. "Still am, I guess. My boss doesn't quite see it like that, though." He proffered the tall beaker. "Coffee sir?"

Paton shook his head. *"Non, merci."*

Theroux shrugged, and took both beakers back to his seat. Paton continued fidgeting and hopping about like an agitated cottontail. "I have an idea," he said, "of which I would like your opinion before... I am a biochemist."

"I was told you were a biologist."

"This is a general term. My specialist training is biochemistry; my recent research, cryogenics."

"Ultra-low temperature stuff."

"Oui, ç'est ça. Specifically, I work on the freezing of living organisms and then the restoration to normal temperature and function without cell damage."

Theroux drank his coffee, thinking he didn't want to know this, what he wanted was to call it a day and go get some real sleep. "Suspended animation," he said.

"Exactly," said Paton. "Now what I wanted to ask you about is this. It is not possible to reverse the course of the *Dædalus*, but if it were possible to divert it a little…"

"Divert it? Divert it where, for Chrissakes?"

"Back into our system. To allow the eventual recovery of the ship. After many years per'aps but even so…"

"But even so," Theroux said, "the crew would be long dead. What's the point?"

"The point is that they could go into frozen hibernation," said Paton eagerly, "suspended animation, yes, using my equipment."

"The stuff you've got on that ship is ready to work?" Theroux was wide-awake now, with the itchy feeling that there was a possible hope here, a way back from death.

Paton stopped hopping about, and shrugged sadly. "It is of no consequence. You need a source of propulsion to change course and they 'ave none."

And then Theroux saw it. There was one. *There was one.*

"They don't need air to breathe, right?" Paton nodded. "But what about pressure?" Theroux went on. "Do they need air pressure? I mean, even frozen, they couldn't survive the vacuum could they."

Paton said, "The units are pressurized with inert gas mixtures. They are completely self-contained."

Theroux got to his feet excitedly. "Then there is a possible way to change the course of the *Dædalus*," he said.

Nathan left the deserted monorail, and stepped down the spiral stairway into Victoria Park. Once away from the brightly lit elevated platform with its moulded acrylic rain shelter and location hologram, he found the park got dark quickly. The distant lights in the bright corporate towers made no impression on the night at this eastern end of the city's wildlife sanctuary.

He knew the lake was maybe ten minutes walk from where he was – and that was all to the good, he thought, give him a chance to finish sobering up. Not that he'd really been drunk, not *really* drunk, not nearly drunk, not nearly drunk enough really. But it wouldn't do any harm to clear his head. He took a couple of deep breaths, and set off at a brisk pace in the direction of the lake.

Before he had gone far the noise of his footsteps began to bother him. God, if this was a trap, he was making it very easy for whoever set it up: they'd be able to hear him coming all over the bloody park. And not only them.

He made an effort to walk more quietly, but his feet still scrunched and crackled on the gravel path. He tried walking on tiptoe, but it was difficult and slow, and besides he felt like a fool. He considered leaving the path altogether but, since he could see almost nothing, the prospect of getting stealthily lost, or of softly breaking a leg, looked promising. A torch would have been a bright idea. He should have brought a bloody torch, for Christ's sake. Bright ideas weren't coming thick and fast to him just at the moment. Without Lee, they probably never would again.

Without Lee... A shock of intense loneliness took him by surprise and his eyes filled with tears. He blinked, and wiped them clear with the heel of his hand. He looked up. It was a cool, cloudless night. The sky was high and full of stars. Why wasn't there a moon? Why was there never a bloody moon when you needed one? He dried his cheeks on the sleeve of his jacket, and walked on more slowly.

He found his eyes were adjusting to the gloom now, and he could distinguish the shapes of trees and bushes, darker shades against the darkness. He was not sure that it helped, because with the shapes came movements, lurking and stealthy, and every-fucking-where. It was only his imagination, of course, only fearful and adrenaline-rich hallucination. He tried to rationalize it away, to concentrate on ignoring what he saw, but without getting careless and missing something.

Fighting an urgent impulse to take out the gun and fire indiscriminately in all directions, he pushed on, and at last a flat wide space opened out in front of him, glimmering blackly. The air was colder here, and he could smell the green, silt smell of standing water.

It was a fairly small lake, but when he reached the edge Nathan realized that as a rendezvous point it was still big enough to be a problem, especially in the dark. He stood for a moment wondering where he was supposed to wait for his whispering friend. Assuming he *was* a friend, which was a largish assumption under the circumstances. And he didn't much fancy being in the open even if the man was kosher. You could catch your death in Victoria Park once the sun had gone down.

He decided to keep moving round the lake until the informant showed himself or he found some way to cover his back, and he began slowly and carefully to walk along the bank side path. The light seemed better here. He glanced back. A first quarter moon was rising above the trees behind him and now he could see enough to step off the gravel.

He was irritated to find that walking on the grass verge still made noise so when he came upon the derelict building, he decided at once that this was the place to wait. The overgrown, roofless shell had been a cottage or a large boathouse perhaps, though more likely it was a purpose-built ruin. The wall looked old in the moonlight, the bricks were rough and powdery to the touch. Set in one section, facing the lake, was a wood-finish, plastic bench. Nathan almost sat down on it, but then sitting suddenly seemed risky. He leaned his back against the wall instead. Straining to concentrate, he peered down the dark path and listened intently for any sign of approach.

After half an hour, it was clear that no-one was coming. Nathan pushed himself off from the wall, and stretched his stiff shoulders. The call had to be a hoax of some sort, to get him out of the apartment. He began to walk away. But why did they want him out of the apartment, for Christ's sake? The sudden crashing weight leaned into his back and onto his shoulders heaving him forward. He fell onto his hands and knees. There was no pain, not much sensation of any kind, as his disoriented brain rejected most of the initial inputs. The weight stayed until he hit the ground, then the impact jarred it loose. Abruptly, sense and pain came together. Gravel bit into the palms of his hands and tore at his knees. There was a wrenching ache in his neck. Snarling at him was a heavyset youth with a shaven head and a tattooed face, and the fancy-dress of a comic book redskin warrior. Dimly, he registered the uniform of an urban apache, though his immediate attention focused on the hatchet the murderous little bastard was clutching. Nathan struggled to get to his feet and thought, with bizarre detachment, *the hatchet's why he lost his grip on me when he jumped from the wall.*

The youth rushed at him, left shoulder down, hatchet raised in his right hand. The silent charge caught him before he was fully upright, hitting him in the ribs, knocking the breath out of him, and spinning him back down so that a savage swipe with the hatchet missed him only narrowly.

Nathan scrambled away and snatched the gun from his pocket.

Star Cops

While he was searching for the safety catch, he fumbled, juggled with it desperately, and then dropped it on the ground. In the flat moonlit shadows, the gun vanished. He bent quickly to feel for it. It wasn't there. As he groped around he shouted breathlessly, "I'm a copper! Fuck off, kid, before I run you in!"

This time he didn't even see the attack coming. He looked up just as a feint with the hatchet flashed at his face. He jerked his head away and lurched upright. The kick to his groin ended any thought of fighting back and he doubled over. The youth kneed him in the face, then kicked him in the stomach, and kicked his legs out from under him.

Nathan fell hard, but he was a long way past feeling that. He would have been sick if it wasn't for the pain; if there'd been anything left to be sick with. He retched weakly. "Oh Christ," he whispered. He wanted to curl up round the agony, but there was too much of it. He wanted to curl up and die, but if he did, he *would* die – he knew that much. He knew he couldn't lie there. He had to move, because if he didn't move, he would be chopped up and scalped and whatever else this little brute could think of. He pushed at the path, dragged his knees under him and heaved himself onto all fours. "Don't make me hurt you, kid," he mumbled as he began to lose control and tilt to one side. He shoved his hand out a long way to correct the imbalance and put it on the gun. Hope surged through him. He grabbed up the gun and waved it about unsteadily. "I've got a gun here! Don't make me use it!" he croaked. He struggled back into a more or less upright position, and stood swaying and peering around. He couldn't see the urban apache. Where the fucking hell was he? "Where the fucking hell are you?" Had he run off? Please God let him have run off.

He took a few shuffling steps. He was giddy and nauseous. New pains seared out of his guts, spreading down through his legs and cramping up his arms. He remembered the seat. He badly wanted to sit down. Unsteadily, he made his way towards the wall and he had almost reached it when he fell over the body.

The urban apache was lying on his back, stretched out and staring blankly at the stars. One hand was clenched into a fist, the other still gripped the hatchet. Holding the pistol pointed squarely between the unblinking eyes, Nathan gingerly felt the neck for any sign of a pulse, but the youth was safely dead. He looked smaller now, already old and helpless. Nathan pushed him over. There was a warm, wet hole, small and about a hand's breadth below the left shoulder-blade.

"All right, where are you?" Nathan said. "Hullo? Come out, come out wherever you are? Whoever you are?" He sat back on his heels, as the temporarily forgotten pains surged back. "Oh shit," he said, "I think I'm going to be sick," and he retched until he was sobbing for breath.

When he finally stopped, a voice close by whispered, "Sorry about all that, Commander. I didn't bring you here for someone else to kill you."

Still breathless, Nathan managed to say, "Come out where I can see you."

"Why should I?" the voice whispered, and with what could have been a snigger added, "I can see you perfectly well."

Abruptly Nathan was sure that the urban apache had been a playful child compared to whoever this was. Clutching the gun tightly, he stumbled the short distance to the wall and pressed his back against it. Carefully, he raised the gun in front of him and arranged his hands in the correct combat position on the grip.

"Don't bother," sneered the whisperer. "You've already demonstrated your expertise with our friend there."

"We all have our off-days," said Nathan, trying to decide where the voice was coming from. The whispering made it hard to pinpoint. Was that why he was doing it? Or was it some sort of theatrical scare tactic?

"Even on my worst day, a UA would have been no more than a casual irritant."

"Did you kill him?" Nathan asked, glancing backwards and forwards along the front of the ruin, making himself giddy in the process.

"Yes."

He was behind the wall, Nathan decided. It was the only place he could be. Nathan he tried to see which end was the easiest to get round. "Speak softly and carry a pig-sticker, right?" he said, reminding himself that without Lee, there was no-one to recognize the wordplay, reminding himself that without Lee there was no-one… He chose the more overgrown end of the wall – because he hoped it was the less obvious approach – and crept towards it.

"Now we come to the main event," whispered the voice. "Now it's your turn, Spring. You are next."

Nathan stopped. He should have known. Actually, it wasn't that much of a surprise; perhaps he did know. He moved on.

"Yes, that's right," the whisper gloated. "Even you must have worked out by now that it was me killed your lady."

Nathan reached the end of the wall. Whoever it was did not seem to have moved position. What tone there was in the voice did not seem to have changed either. Maybe he'd outflanked him; maybe the bastard had underestimated him enough to give him a chance. If killing the bastard was his only chance... Something in him hoped that killing the bastard *was* his only chance. He checked the settings on the gun and took three slow, deep breaths. He was ready for the final plunge round the wall, ready as he'd ever be, ready or not here I come. He tensed himself.

Before he could move, there was a loud shout from the lakeside path. "Armed police officer! Freeze!"

A burst of shots crackled and small calibre slugs spattered off the top of the wall somewhere behind Nathan. Without thinking, he crashed forward through the brambles and evergreen scrub, and ducked round the corner of the ruin. Someone was running away, up a shallow slope towards a stand of spindly pines. He fired a couple of shots after the indistinct figure and watched helplessly as it disappeared into the trees.

When he came back out from behind the wall, he found Sergeant Corman bending over the corpse. He leaned his shoulder against the rough brickwork and asked, "What are you doing here?"

"I was following you," she said.

"Oh, that was you, was it?"

Corman looked up. "You mean you lost me deliberately?"

In fact, Nathan had not been aware of anyone following him. He had made a routine double shuffle but that was all. "Did you see him?" he asked. "Did you see the suspect?" The adrenaline rush was subsiding rapidly, and exhausting pain was draining back.

"No," she said.

"Then what in God's name were you shooting at?"

"I saw a movement."

"Probably me," he said tiredly. "You were probably shooting at me."

"It was on the wall above you," she said. "A figure. Something."

"Get away from that," said Nathan as she turned her attention back to the dead youth. "You know better than to interfere with a crime scene."

She stood up and moved away from the body. Nathan made his way to the bench and sat down. "Tape off the area," he said, leaning his elbows on his knees and putting his head in his hands. "I want a category A forensic. Everybody here, the whole turnout and double fucking quick."

* * *

Chris Boucher

Almost everybody had turned out. Technicians from most of the shifts offered their services, and for a while the European Operations Suite had ground to an over-manned halt. It had been Paton, demonstrating an unexpected taste for management, who had rapidly pulled together a project team and got all the specialist parts of it concentrating on every necessary aspect of the problem. Once they were working, however, he reverted immediately to his normal ineffectual behaviour, and by the time Theroux came back from his meal break, he was hopping nervously about on the edge of things, largely ignored by the busy groups gathered at the various workstations.

Theroux sat back down at the communications console. He stared again at the frozen hope on the faces of Mike and Lara, as they had signed off to go and locate the cryogenic equipment in the cargo pods and begin preliminary modifications and hook-ups. In some ways, he found the optimism they couldn't hide was harder to take than their previous desperate laughter. They looked to him like the victims of some dumb practical joke, who were doing their best not to be bad sports about it. Why was he more uncomfortable with their situation than they seemed to be? It couldn't be because the chance of a rescue had overwhelmed any investigation? Jesus, surely not. Did becoming a cop make you that much different from a regular human being? Just because I'm a cop, it doesn't mean I'm a bad person. I guess it does mean I assume everyone else is though...

Gina interrupted his thoughts as she hurried across from the huddle of propulsion experts. "We have just finished the full simulation," she said. "Theoretically, it works, okay? An explosive release of all the remaining air out of the ship does alter the *Dædalus*'s trajectory enough to bring it back into the solar system." She paused slightly now and frowned. "Eventually."

"How eventually?" Theroux asked.

"Retrieval in six, perhaps seven years."

"Well, shit, that's a lot less eventually than dead would be, huh?"

If she found the comparison encouraging, she gave no sign of it. "The manoeuvre must be carried out within the next thirty hours to have a realistic chance of success," she said, still frowning.

"That's the margin for error?" Theroux said. "How long for the cryogenics package?"

"With the setup they are putting together, they must be at least twelve hours in the capsules for their body temperatures to reach the required minimum. And that will be pushing the safety limits on the schedule for administering the drugs."

"So they may not be ready in time," said Theroux. "It's lucky Professor Paton didn't wait any longer to mention the idea."

Gina glanced towards the fidgeting Paton. "Luck favours the prepared, they say."

"I hope not, because so far we haven't been," Theroux remarked, as he debated whether to waste precious time summoning Mike and Lara to the communications screen so that he could urge them to hurry.

Paton, meantime, had caught Gina's eye and, mistaking her gaze, he had smiled and started towards her. As he neared the communications console, he was intercepted by a scowling Guy Fox.

"Not now, Guy," Gina muttered.

Theroux heard her, and looked up to see the two men facing each other. Gimme a break here, he thought. Fox punching out the Base Co-ordinator in the middle of this shit? This is all I fucking need. But before he could get to his feet to part them, Fox smiled and stuck out his hand to Paton.

"Congratulations, Professor Paton," he said. "I underestimated your worth – the worth of your work, I mean."

Paton accepted the gesture gracefully. "You are most kind." They shook hands.

"Those freezing chambers of yours could have been designed for the *Dædalus*," Fox enthused.

Paton said quickly, "They are not ideal, I fear."

"I'm just glad the things happened to be there at all."

"They are intended primarily for use in larger ships. Ultimately, of course, the aim is to freeze a crew, to put them into suspended animation, thus at last making possible genuine deep space exploration."

"If it works," said Gina.

"It is a melancholy way to test my theories."

"Cheer up, man," Fox said. "At least they've got a chance now. A chance is all anyone can ask for."

Gina said, "And there's a chance at a place in history for the scientist who is successful in this field." She had stopped frowning but, unlike Fox, she was not smiling either.

* * *

Death had come between them. It had separated them, so that each had forgotten why they had been obsessed with the other's face and body and touch and voice, why their presence had been essential to life. Somehow, an infinity of nothing was too all-embracing to cope with as a couple. Dying was not something you could share, unless perhaps you had shared most of living, which Mike and Lara had not. Secretly, too, some small part of each of them blamed the other for the advancing darkness.

So they had joked with the investigating Star Cop – but in between transmissions, they had hardly spoken except where the work had called for it. While they carried out the accident procedures and systems checks together and with calm professionalism, they faced death alone and disordered.

Then the new offer of life came and brought back all the old feelings, with a renewed intensity. They were close again, they were dependant again, they were in love again, but, live or die, loneliness would never leave them again.

As they finished buckling down the webbing which strapped the cryogenic capsules against a bulkhead, Mike said what they were both thinking. "They look like coffins, don't they? Let's hope that's not what they turn out to be."

"I wasn't scared before," Lara said. "Not as scared as I am now."

Mike took her hand and kissed the palm. "Me too."

"Some chance is better than no chance," she said. "Isn't it?"

"It's got to be," he said. "At least I think it's got to be. I mean, I suppose it is possible that we could wake up in six years time with frost-bitten extremities."

"I'll try and love you even if your nose does drop off," she said.

"The way my luck's running, it won't be my nose that drops off."

"An extremity?"

"What would you call it?"

"I'd call it bragging."

"Penis envy, that's what this is. A bad case of penis envy."

"Penis envy?" Lara said scornfully. "Why should I be envious of that? I own it anyway," and she grabbed at his crotch.

"We haven't got time for this," he protested, but he already had the beginnings of an erection, and he wrapped his arms round her, and ran his hands over her small, tight buttocks.

* * *

"You stupid fucker!" yelled Devis.

Nathan leaned his head back into the cushions of his favourite seating and moved the ice pack over onto the bridge of his nose. He winced. "It wasn't bright, I'll allow," he murmured, through lips that were swollen and stiff.

"Bright?" glowered Devis. "All I need to make this a perfect case is for you to go and get yourself killed as well!"

"So you'd have two – three – unsolved murders, instead of one. So?"

Devis sneered, "You're not counting that urban apache, are you? The more of those little scumbags that kill each other off the better."

Why is it that the biggest reactionaries are always *fat* reactionaries? Nathan wondered. Or do they just look the biggest?

He said, "He was killed by the same man who killed Lee."

"If you say so."

"I do say so. And I almost had him."

Devis moved closer, and peered at his injuries. "Looks like it," he said dryly. "Pity Corman's such a lousy shot. We'll never know now, will we?"

Nathan said, "Forensic'll confirm it."

Devis did his best to look unconcerned. "I called that off," he said.

"You called it off?" Nathan sat up abruptly, tossing the ice pack onto the coffee table.

"Star Cops might have unlimited budgets, but we don't," Devis said, managing to sound accusing rather than defensive.

Nathan's head was spinning. He poured himself a Scotch from the bottle on the table, drank it quickly and poured himself another. The liquor burned in his throat and stomach. It did nothing for his spinning head, but a warm glow began to spread through him. He'd pay later; for the time being, he'd settle for the relief. He sipped the second drink, and said, "What are you talking about?"

"I'm talking about wasting Category A resources on investigating the sort of killing that happens every night in that area," Devis snapped. "Victoria Park is fucking Psycho Central, or didn't you know that?!"

Was it possible the man was really that stupid? Nathan thought. Maybe he was in on it; maybe he was devious rather than stupid; devious Devis, a bent copper. "Are you doing it deliberately, Devis?" he asked.

Devis looked at him with obvious pity. "The computer gave it a double F," he explained, patiently irritated. "Who can argue with that?"

No, he *was* probably just stupid, Nathan thought, and said, "*I* can.

I'll lay odds it was the same man, and probably the same weapon, that killed Lee."

"Difficult things, probabilities," Devis said, mildly patronizing now. "Best left to computers, all that sort of thing."

Best left to computers, Jesus Christ. "It could have been the breakthrough you'll never come up with," Nathan said, furiously.

"Oh yes!" Devis mocked. "With one mighty bound. Am I right? A crank call, you rush off and get seven shades of shit kicked out of you, and abraca-fucking-dabra the case is solved. That's real talent, Commander, I'm definitely impressed. I can certainly see why *you* got to be such a high-flyer."

Nathan stared at him and saw the disappointed man, overweight for a career copper, overage for a rank he was never likely to better, and faced with a murder he didn't have the equipment to solve. A high-flyer? That wasn't bad under the circumstances. "Do you want a drink?" he asked, indicating the Scotch.

"Thank you," Devis said, looking round for a glass.

Nathan got up and went, a little unsteadily, to fetch one. When he sat back down and slid it across the table with the bottle he said, "He claimed to have done it."

Devis pulled up a seat. "Ask yourself: is it likely?" he said, and poured himself a very generous measure.

Nathan felt a sudden kinship with this unsubtle man. It seemed like a compliment, in some obscure way, that Devis didn't feel he had to be polite. Never trust a man who doesn't drink – was that W.C. Fields? Well, whoever it was, it was his father who had added, especially if it's your liquor he doesn't drink. Nathan topped up both their glasses, spilling Scotch on the table. I'm missing something, he thought – apart from the glass, something basic to all this has got past me. "I'm missing something. Apart from the glass," he said.

"You lost a friend," Devis said, draining his glass and pushing it back towards the bottle. "That's good stuff. Single malts are on the pricey side for me."

Nathan filled the glass again. "No point in cheap vices," he said. "If you're going to hell in a handcart, it should at least be well-sprung."

"I'll drink to that," said Devis, creasing his face into what passed for a smile.

"D'you ever get the feeling you're being *pushed*, Devis?" Nathan asked.

Star Cops

"All the time. Why?"

Nathan sighed and thought, *No, he wouldn't know what I was talking about. I don't know what I'm talking about.* He said, "Are you going to need me for anything more?"

Devis shook his head. "Not really."

"I think I'll go back to my high flying, then," Nathan said.

Devis took the bottle and filled up both their glasses. "That's what I'd do in your place."

"Leave the ground work to you?"

Devis raised his glass in a small salute. "You're not as stupid as you look, Commander," he said.

Nathan raised his glass in acknowledgement, and said with a tired smile that hurt his swollen mouth, "I wish I could say the same for you, Detective Chief Inspector."

For the first time, Devis smiled a genuine smile. It gave his face an unlikely, cherubic look.

It proved to be impossible to persuade the *Dædalus*'s onboard computer to permit an explosive release of atmospheric pressure. The safety systems would not even allow a controlled cracking of the airlock's outer seal while the inner hatch was open. But the cargo pods once again provided the solution. A whole case of seismic cartridges intended for the next phase of the Martian Geological Survey were primed and placed, half of them against the outer hatch and half against the inner. The microwave triggers were parallel-linked, so that the jury-rigged program would set them all off at the same instant. It was crude, but analysis suggested that the computer would interfere with any more precisely engineered firing sequence as it tried to compensate for a first disastrous failure.

Mike and Lara had said their goodbyes to Moonbase.

"And David, you might suggest to Professor Paton that when he works on the Mark 2 units, he gives some thought to a double capsule. These things look lonely."

"If your happy band of boffins have miscalculated this lot we're going to be severely miffed, you understand. We may never speak to any of you again."

"I can't think of a dream that'll last seven years without getting boring. Unless it's a nightmare…"

"We'll see you when we see you. On my mark, time to firing will be twelve hours twenty-five minutes and counting... Mark."

Then, leaving the communications link open, they had finally gone from vision.

After that there was no way to tell whether the cryogenic capsules worked. The explosion worked though. At the completion of the countdown the detonation thudded through the ship, followed briefly by the strident hootings of the *Airlock Failure* and the *Major Life-support Integrity Failure* warnings. When the atmosphere had fully vented, the klaxons ceased to be audible. The simulation had estimated this interval at two minutes nine-point-three seconds.

"We timed it at two minutes ten-point-four. After that, the automatics started broadcasting the standard mayday. And that was all she wrote." Theroux switched off the recording and waited.

Nathan was wandering round his new headquarters wondering if the ISPF Establishment budget would run to full eavesdrop screening. "The rescue beacon's on self-contained power?" he asked to cover the fact that he hadn't really been listening.

"Twenty year's worth. Capsules'll run for twenty-five. If they run. And long range tracking claim seventy percent that they've got the ship picked out and on the predicted course. If that's true, then there's only one thing we know nothing about. Whether Mike and Lara are just cargo-jocksicles—"

"Or the first successfully preserved adult human beings, yes," said Nathan, who for the moment had lost his sense of humour about death. "It's a pity that. Seven years is a long time to wait to decide on what the charge should be."

Theroux said, "That's how come I almost missed it. I was looking for the wrong crime."

Nathan shook his head. "Right crime, wrong motive," he said and thought, *Come on you got it right, don't spoil things by misreading what you did.* And then it struck him: that's what he'd been doing himself. "Fuck," he said softly.

"What?" asked Theroux. "What is it? Did I miss something anyway?"

"I did," Nathan said. "I missed it." *Motive*, he thought. *That had to be it. Whatever's left, however improbable...* "They've deliberately been keeping me off-balance. That has to have something to do with the motive."

"It does?"

"It has to. It's all that's left. It's got to be the key to Lee's death."

Theroux frowned. "You lost me," he said.

Nathan stared into the middle distance. "Motives are never simple," he said vaguely, unaware of Theroux's growing concern at his ramblings, "and sometimes there isn't a motive for the act, because sometimes the act is the motive. What look like cause and effect are the same thing. Cause. We're still waiting for the effect."

"You want to float that by me again?" Theroux asked, loudly enough to get Nathan's attention back.

"Case in point," Nathan said – but then he was interrupted by the door sliding open. Got to get some way of controlling access to this place, he thought, as Roland Paton hopped elegantly across the threshold. "Co-ordinator," he said, rising to his feet. "I've been hearing all about your giant leap for spacemankind. Congratulations."

Paton inclined his head slightly. "Thank you indeed, Commander. But I did very little."

"You're too modest. David tells me it was all your idea."

"Oh, *mais non*. David thought of the mode of propulsion. Is that not correct, David?"

"With a little prompting from you, sir," Theroux said and smiled.

"When did the possibility first occur to you?" Nathan asked, his interest polite, casual.

Paton grimaced slightly, and shrugged a small but eloquent, Gallic shrug. "At the eleventh hour, as you would say."

Still polite, Nathan said, "No, I don't think that's what I would say. Please sit down." He indicated a workstation seat which had been pulled out from behind the unit.

Paton declined, with a slight shake of the head. "I think better on my feet."

"Sit down, M'sieur Paton," Nathan said, his voice suddenly harder.

Paton hesitated, then sat down. "I was told there was something you wished me to see." Theroux perched on the end of the workstation. Nathan remained standing where he was. Paton found he could no longer take in both of them with the same look, but would have to turn his head from one to the other if he wanted the conversation to be three sided. "As Moonbase Co-ordinator," he went on, "I have no time to waste on –"

Nathan cut across him. "As a biochemist, I assume you must be aware of the Brussels Accords – on animal and human experimentation?"

"Of course. Why do you ask?"

"You'll be familiar with the regulations arising," Theroux said, offering him a flimsy volume of official hard copy.

Paton said, "Yes," but he did not take the book or even acknowledge it was there.

Theroux dropped it onto the workstation. "Under which regulations, you were refused a license for the human experiments that you are currently —"

"It is not an experiment!" Paton interrupted.

"The crew of the *Dædalus* will be glad to hear that," Nathan said.

Paton turned to him. "It was an emergency. It was their only chance."

"So it was. I repeat: when did the possibility first occur to you?"

"What possibility?"

"That ship didn't go rogue," Theroux said. "The main engine burn happened exactly as it was supposed to happen. Someone had reprogrammed the navigation computer."

"This is not a possibility," Paton remarked contemptuously. "This is an absurd fantasy."

"That someone, whoever it was," said Nathan, "had enough authority for unquestioned and unremarked access to the ship, to cargo assembly areas, to the computer that was putting together the manifest..."

"*C'est ridicule, ça!*"

"As ridiculous as sending experimental cryogenic equipment to the Mars colony?" Nathan asked.

Theroux punched up the *Dædalus*'s cargo listing on the workstation screen and said, "Not exactly essential stores."

"It was my intention to go to Mars when my tour here is over," Paton said.

Theroux set the list scrolling. "Could be, you should have told *them*," he said. "You see, sir, the stuff's on the ship's manifest okay but it's not on the Mars colony's print out."

"They don't seem to be expecting you, or your equipment," Nathan said.

Another shrug from Paton, this time disdainfully dismissive. "A computer failure."

"A flaw in the plan, Professor," said Theroux. "Our theory is that you didn't update their end, because you didn't want to risk drawing attention to what you were doing."

Nathan said, "Otherwise, it wasn't a bad try. You targeted a notoriously careless crew. There wasn't much chance of them noticing anything anomalous about the cargo."

Theroux said, "And when the shit hit the life-support, it didn't matter."

Nathan said, "Until it did matter."

Theroux said, "Then everyone was – 'just glad the things happened to be there at all' – isn't that the way your friend Fox put it?"

Nathan said, "And to encourage a policeman to come up with the possibility of a rescue. That was inspired."

Theroux said, "That was pushing it. That you're going to pay for Paton."

Paton did not look at either man, but stared steadfastly at a midpoint somewhere between the two of them. "Even if what you said was true, and it is not, no-one has been hurt."

Theroux's expression was incredulous. "No-one has been *hurt*?" he said softly, his voice a fierce whisper.

For a shuddering moment, Nathan was back in the park, back in the apartment, back at the time when Lee stopped being. He cleared his throat and said harshly, "If they turn out to be dead, you *will* be charged with murder."

"They are not dead," Paton stated flatly. "And what you do not understand is that this work is of major importance. It is a breakthrough. Those people will be famous."

"If they turn out to be alive," said Nathan, "I imagine they will bring civil suit against you. Whatever *they* decide to do, *I* shall certainly bring the appropriate criminal charges."

Paton got to his feet. "I did not expect men of your profession to appreciate the significance of what is happening."

Nathan smiled. "I'm sorry we disappointed you."

Paton began to lose his temper. "You can prove none of this," he said, his voice rising. "None of it!"

"Oh, we'll prove it," said Nathan.

"I warn you, Commander Spring, I am a man of influence. If you pursue this, or if you speak of your ridiculous theories to anyone, your career will be over. *Tu comprends?*"

"Perfectly."

"Be sure that you do."

Nathan watched Paton hop haughtily towards the door, and as he reached it, said, "In the meantime, it would save a lot of unpleasantness if you'd keep us informed of any journeys you might plan. In the next six or seven years."

Paton left without comment and without looking back. When the door had shut behind him, Theroux snorted. "Yeah, right. Keep tabs on him for seven years? What did you have in mind: tag his butt with a tracer chip?"

"He's a man of influence, David. Like the prize-fighters used to say, he can run but he can't hide."

"Well, perhaps hiding is not quite accurate." Vanhalsen looked mildly embarrassed. It was during his shift as duty controller that whoever was now holed up in the orbit station's Star Cop office had got onto the *Charles De Gaulle*. "But they won't identify themselves, and they won't come out."

"You've no idea what they want?" Nathan asked.

"I don't even know how they got in there."

"Okay, we'll leave as soon as we can get launch clearance. Nobody goes near them in the meantime, all right?"

"Don't worry, Commander," Vanhalsen said. "You're the professionals. Everyone here is more than happy to leave dealing with an armed intruder entirely in your hands."

During the flight from Moonbase, they discussed ways of dealing with what Vanhalsen had referred to as 'a situation', but they both knew that neither of them had much idea of what to do. Tactics for handling an armed siege in the weightlessness of a space station were not included in any of the training courses that Nathan's had been obliged to attend. Theroux's experiences with weapons had been mercifully limited and had convinced him of only one thing: they were fucking dangerous. It had become an article of faith with him that anyone who seriously believed 'guns don't kill people, only people kill people' was a sad asshole with a tenuous hold on reality.

"I was never much good with these things," Nathan remarked as he checked the clip in the small automatic again. It was the pistol that they had taken from Simon Butler, and as it turned out, it was the only gun to which the ISPF presently had access. "It still doesn't seem like a sensible weapon. Our options could be a bit limited, though."

Theroux nodded and said, "And I got the strong feeling that swearing in a batch of deputies is not among them." He mimicked Vanhalsen's well-spoken, reserved, and apologetically ironic tones, "Everyone here is more than happy to leave dealing with an armed intruder entirely in your hands."

"You don't buy a dog and bark yourself, as Brian Lincoln used to say."

"Simon Butler used to say that since the Dutch spent their formative years below sea-level, it was hardly surprising they were wet."

Vanhalsen was waiting for them at the main entry lock. "They are still in there," he said.

"Have they said what they want?"

"There's been no further contact."

Nathan checked the automatic's clip once more. He suddenly felt self-conscious about it. It was a silly little gun, but a bigger gun would be even sillier. "Okay. I'll want that area cleared of personnel. If anything goes wrong, you may have to seal off the damage." Probably better not to think too closely about what that means, he thought.

"It was cleared as soon as you were confirmed in transit," Vanhalsen said.

Theroux said, "Five'll get you ten there's at least two pressure hatches between there and the nearest civilian." He was surprised that a word which separated him and them came so easily now.

"I should like to go with you," Vanhalsen said.

"I don't think so," said Nathan, glancing at Theroux for a reaction to the offer.

"I can distract them, maybe, while you make the arrest," the Dutchman persisted.

"We use you as a shield, is that it, Willem?" asked Theroux.

"That's not quite what I had in mind."

"You sure? It works for me," Theroux said, and grinned at him.

Vanhalsen smiled unhappily. "I am not pretending to be a hero, David," he said. "I feel responsible, that's all. It seems unjust that I should not share the risk arising from my mistake."

Nathan said, "We appreciate the offer," and thought, Christ he really means it – *unjust* – "but you'd better stay in the communications center, and act as base control."

Then, to forestall further argument, he pushed himself off and floated down the link-tube in the direction of the module which contained the ISPF office.

"The thing of it is, we're not insured for volunteers, Willem," Theroux said, and set off after Nathan.

"What the fucking hell are you doing here?" Nathan demanded, furiously relieved when he ducked a look through the office doorway and found that Sergeant Corman was the armed intruder. She was asleep at the workstation, held in place by the Velcro seat pads while her upper body floated, arms outstretched, head lolling. She looked as though she had drowned in dry water. "Corman?"

Corman woke up with a start. "You're here at last, sir," she said and got to her feet. She came loose from the seat, began to drift upwards. "Oh no. How do you cope with this?"

"I don't," Nathan said curtly. "You're not still trying to follow me, are you, Sergeant?"

"I feel so sick."

Theroux took a pack of chocolate from the breast pocket of his coverall and proffered it. "Eat some," he said, "you'll feel better."

Corman peered at the label suspiciously. "Sweets?" she said. "Do I know you?"

At the communications console Nathan said, "Inspector Theroux; Sergeant Corman," then keyed the direct line to traffic control. "Okay, Willem, it was a false alarm."

"Thanks," said Corman, and accepted the chocolate. Out of the corner of his eye, Nathan watched her break open the packet and begin to eat hungrily.

"A false alarm? I don't understand."

"That's it exactly: a misunderstanding. Everything will be explained in due course." He killed the connection, and looked directly at Corman. "Like now?" he said.

"I was following the killer."

Nathan concentrated on keeping his face and voice expressionless. "You've identified him?"

Corman took another bite of chocolate and said, "He came here."

"To the station?" said Theroux.

"To this office. He came to this office."

Theroux was making no effort to disguise his scepticism. "Why would he do that, for Chrissakes?"

Nathan said quietly, "Looking for me, d'you think? Where is he now?"

She shrugged helplessly. "He's vanished."

"What's his name?" Nathan asked.

"Smith."

"Smith?" Theroux commented, with heavy irony.

"John Smith," said Corman.

Theroux said, "That's original."

"It's his real name, apparently."

Nathan asked, "What's he got against me?"

"He was a construction engineer working on some project out here."

"He's one of ours," said Theroux.

"He's not a Star Cop, no."

"I meant, he's high frontier. A spacejock."

She nodded. "Until a Moonbase Star Cop busted him." Then it was her turn to be derisive. "A spacejock?"

Theroux ignored it. "When was this?" he asked.

"A while ago. The details are a bit vague."

"Yeah. Right."

"As far as we can find out your part-time policeman charged him with some sort of misdemeanour and that was the end of his career out here. Even though he was ultimately cleared."

Nathan said thoughtfully, "He blames the Star Cops. Decides to revenge himself on the headman." It was a motive, of sorts. Who could tell with a psychopath? Maybe it was even a bit too rational.

Theroux looked at Nathan, and raised one eyebrow. He couldn't really mean what he just said. Shit, it was ludicrous. But Nathan wouldn't catch his eye.

"That's what it looks like," Corman said. "Listen I'm sorry to have been so melodramatic, sir." She gestured vaguely at the office. "I needed to get you here quickly, without a lot of arguments and explanations."

"Why?" Theroux asked.

"I should have thought that was obvious," she said.

"Not to me."

Before she could respond Vanhalsen was back on the communicator. "*Commander Spring?*"

"Yes, Willem?"

"*There is an orbit shuttle heading out from the station. It is unauthorized and not cleared for transit. It refuses to acknowledge my signals.*"

"It's him," said Corman eagerly. "It's our man."

Nathan's reaction seemed almost automatic. "David? Take Sergeant Corman and get us a shuttle prepped. Willem, we shall need transit clearance to follow him."

For the first time since they had arrived, Theroux used the walking strip, and he indicated that Corman should do the same.

"*I'll get onto it.*" Vanhalsen sounded pleased. "*Real cops-and-robbers stuff, eh?*"

"We're an old-fashioned outfit at heart," Nathan said.

When Corman had made her uncertain way into the link-tube, Theroux said, "You carry on walking in that direction, slow and easy. I'll be right with you," and he turned back into the office.

"Something wrong?" Nathan asked.

Theroux glanced out of the doorway and, satisfied that she was still moving, slid the door curtain closed, and said softly, "Yeah, there's something wrong. None of these stations are secure but you can't just wander in, Nathan. They had to have some kind of authorization, she and this Smith guy both."

"His would be forged but why hers, is that what you mean?"

"And Moonbase never had any Star Cops."

Nathan nodded. "She's certainly faking space sickness," he said, and smiled tiredly. "Take it from one who knows."

"So what do you want me to do?"

"Just what I said. Seems she's gone to a lot of trouble to get us to chase that shuttle. Be a shame to disappoint her at this late stage."

"Okay," Theroux said. "I hope you know what you're doing."

Nathan said, "I always know what I'm doing, David," and thought, *I'm just not sure why I'm doing it any more.*

When Nathan hopped through the entrance hatch into the traffic control and communications module, he was relieved to find Vanhalsen was working alone; it made things simpler. "No back-up, Willem?" he asked.

Vanhalsen looked up from his mixer-screen. "I have logged your clearance, Commander. I should have confirmation by the time you are suited up."

"I wasn't pushing."

"The standard alert has made things difficult. If the Americans would only give a little, then maybe we could all get some sleep."

"I wanted a private word with you," said Nathan.

"The explanation at last?" Vanhalsen asked.

Nathan shrugged and said, "Soon, I think. No, at the moment I'm recruiting. I want you to give serious consideration to joining the ISPF."

The Dutchman frowned slightly. "I don't think I would make a good policeman."

"It's a decent enough profession," said Nathan. "If it's pursued decently by decent men. Think about it. In the meantime, I need a favour."

Vanhalsen's smile was mildly mournful. "Is this a test?" he asked.

"This is a theory."

"I don't do auditions, Commander."

"Nathan," said Nathan. "Call me Nathan."

"I don't do auditions, Nathan."

"I have a theory Willem, about where our friend in the shuttle is heading. I want you to arrange a reception for them."

"Is there a reason you do not you do it yourself?" Vanhalsen asked politely.

Nathan smiled. Maybe recruiting this man wouldn't be such a bright idea after all.

Soundlessly, the fuel burned and the orbit shuttle accelerated silently out from the station. From inside the small craft the chemical reaction in the drive was audible as a low rushing, like dust on a drum.

"How long before we see him?" Corman asked, peering first at the screens and then directly out through the forward observation ports. She was sitting, lightly strapped in place, in the auxiliary observation frame – known as the Kibitzer's Cradle – just behind and between the pilot and co-pilot positions. Like Nathan and Theroux, she was fully space-suited apart from the helmet which was clipped in a rack within the regulation reach of either arm.

Theroux killed the engine burn and said, "Depends how good your eyes are."

"*Burn confirmed, trajectory is stable, fuel status is positive sixty-seven percent, board is green confirm please,*" Vanhalsen intoned from the pilot's communications screen.

"Confirmed all green," said Theroux. "Thank you Eurostat Control."

Nathan cut in the co-pilot's mic and said, "We'll be in touch, Willem."

"*Take care, Nathan. Eurostat Control listening out.*"

"I didn't realize it was a silly question," Corman said. "I'm new to all this."

"I don't mind sacrificing fuel margin, David," Nathan said. "Get a sight of him as early as possible."

"You sure? It's risky."

"Not as risky as what he's trying to do." Nathan turned his head to look Corman in the face. "Wouldn't you say so, Sergeant?"

"I might," she said. "If I knew what that was."

She said it without the slightest hesitation or change of expression that Nathan could detect. Not a flicker, he thought. Have I got this wrong too? Can she really be that controlled about it?

The second burn used up most of the fuel in the safety reserve, but it was only a matter of minutes before their onboard radar showed that they were rapidly overhauling the other shuttle. It was Corman, watching fixedly through the forward ports, who got the first naked-eye sighting. "There he is," she said, and then dropping her voice, "There. Look."

The fleeing shuttle was tiny, bright against the sharp blackness. Almost motionless with distance, it seemed to hang just above the long curve of the planet.

"It is him, isn't it?" She was whispering now.

"It's him okay," said Theroux.

Nathan glanced back at Corman. Why was she whispering? Was it for his benefit? Was it a coincidence? Was it genuine excitement? What?

"What do you want to do, Nathan?" Theroux asked. "You want me to plot an intercept? We got fuel margin for manoeuvre. Some."

"No rush," said Nathan.

"Now there's no rush? Did I miss something?"

"He's almost where he wants to be. That is right isn't it, Corman?"

Corman looked puzzled. "I don't understand, sir."

Nathan rubbed his eyes and yawned. God he was so tired. Not so much tired of games and tired of bullshit, though he *was* tired of them, but more just bone bloody weary. He yawned again. "No? It's coming above the horizon now," he said.

"Jesus H Christ," Theroux said as he looked up from the instruments and stared ahead. "It's the US unmanned."

Given the fuss it was causing, the secret station was not a particularly impressive piece of hardware. The original, graphically-enhanced news visuals had done it more than justice, making it appear large and bristling with hidden menace.

"Looks bigger on screen, huh?" said Theroux ironically.

In reality, it was the equivalent of maybe three standard modules; not big enough to house even a small working crew for more than a routine maintenance tour.

"The news bulletins made it look more threatening, too," murmured Corman.

Its appearance gave no sign of what its function might be, and heavy security screening made it impossible to penetrate electronically. The radar profile was a blank exclusion zone.

"Secrets are always threatening," said Nathan. "The unknown terrifies, but you can't be frightened of what you understand."

"What I don't understand is why this guy Smith is headed there," Theroux said, since it was becoming obvious now that the other shuttle was on a direct course for the station.

"What does it matter?" Corman's voice was suddenly harder. "You've got the bastard!"

"Which one of us is stupid, Corman, you or me?" Nathan asked without looking at her. And then, without waiting for an answer, he said to Theroux, "This is as close as we want to go. Can you hold us here more or less?"

Theroux said, "Sure, no problem," and began the braking manoeuvres.

"What?" demanded Corman. "You mean you're going to let him get away?" Her reaction had just the right mixture of shocked puzzlement and hurt disbelief. Nathan was ready to believe her, to accept that it was all just a paranoid fantasy, and then she said, "After all he's done to you?"

He thought, *after all he's done to me*, and he flicked on the co-pilot's communication set and told it, "Link one, Eurostat *Charles De Gaulle*, Commander Spring for Duty Traffic Controller." While he waited for the signal to be relayed, by whatever priority satellite or ground station channels were available, he said calmly, "That's the reason for all he's done to me, isn't it? So that he could go to ground on that station, and be absolutely certain that the Star Cop would go in and arrest him."

"You're not serious, are you?" said Theroux, realizing as he said it that he could have chosen his words better. Christ, the man wouldn't joke about it, would he?

"Do you think I'd joke about it?" Nathan asked, still calm.

"So what are my countrymen going to do about a sudden rush of day-trippers arriving at one of their most sensitive locations?"

"Not one damn thing. We're the police. Politically neutral. With a legitimate reason for going in there."

"*Eurostat Charles De Gaulle, Duty Controller Vanhalsen, yes Commander?*"

"It's a go, Willem. Repeat: It's a *go*, Willem."

"*Very well. Eurostat listening out.*"

"You see, David," Nathan went on, "the Americans could protest till they were red white and blue in the face, but that's all folks, and by now I should be loony-toons enough to do it. Shouldn't I, Corman?" As he spoke it occurred to him that he should be angry, but there was nothing. The sensation he had was weirdly detached, the oddest feeling of objectivity. It wasn't deliberate and it wasn't correct, it was simply that all this didn't touch him, it seemed to have no connection with him. Then he turned to look at Corman and found that in the same detached, unconnected way, he wanted to kill her with his bare hands. "Speak to me, Corman," he said softly. "Say something careful. Your life is hanging by a thread."

Theroux reached out and touched Nathan's arm. "Nathan? Take it easy."

Nathan saw the nervous concern in his eyes and said, "Yes. I'm all right."

Theroux said, "I'm still not sure I see the point, Nathan?"

Is he humouring me, Nathan thought, or does he really not see it? Surely it's obvious. "We bring him out. He brings out what he's learned about the station."

"You mean he's a spy?"

"When did you spot it?" Corman asked, suddenly relaxed and businesslike.

Nathan matched her tone. "Box traced one of the calls he made to me. It was charged to the Adam Smith Nexus. It's a cultural foundation."

Corman nodded. "It's a Japanese cover."

"That was Box's estimation. But then Box is just a computer."

Corman frowned. "It is theirs, I promise you."

Nathan smiled thinly. "And if anything went wrong, they could be blamed – but it was all too messy and complicated for them. They work at elaborate simplicity. That bastard's not a Japanese agent, is he? He's one of ours. A Brit. Just like you are."

Corman took out her Europol ID and thumbed the corner. The

Star Cops

standard format disappeared and in its place her security service credentials were displayed. Nathan used the authentication loop in his own ID to confirm what was there.

"It seems that Sergeant Corman has authority over us and all our works, David," Nathan said showing him the plate.

"If you're satisfied, gentlemen," said Corman, "shall we go and arrest John Smith?" The request was an order, casual enough to show that she was used to unhesitating obedience.

Theroux was unmoved. "It's your call, Nathan," he said.

"I need to know more about him," said Nathan.

Corman said, "No you don't, Commander."

Nathan was struck by the way the use of his rank was now, without any change of inflexion, a deliberate reminder of her authority. *Did she know how close to death she might be?* he wondered. "You want me to justify my actions, presumably?" he said.

She thought for a moment, and then clearly came to the conclusion that she could afford to indulge him. "All right. He's one of our best. A borderline psychotic, but then all the good ones are."

"Christ, I'd say this guy went south of the border a while back," Theroux muttered.

"The whole strategy was his. He's sharp. Of course, he did almost blow it, that night in the park. Killing has always... over-excited him."

Before she could go on, a vivid flash of white light splashed into the shuttle cabin through the forward ports. Instinctively, she and Theroux both glanced away from the brightness, but Nathan gazed into it.

"That must have been a real thrill, then," he said, and laughed a short, mirthless laugh. "The Americans seem to have killed him."

Theroux looked and saw in the distance where the other orbit shuttle had been, a smear of vapour and small particles was fading outwards to nothing. "Lucky we didn't get any closer," he said.

"One of those ground controlled defence satellites," Nathan said. "Way over to the left there, I think. See it?"

Theroux had already picked out what he thought it was from the jumble on the pilot's radar. "Must be right at the edge of its range," he said.

"My God," Corman said, "they didn't even hesitate." Then obviously calculating what could be salvaged from the mess she went on grimly, "At least we've got some idea of the lengths they'll go to."

"They didn't have much choice," said Nathan, matter-of-factly. "They were dealing with a dangerous criminal."

"They didn't know that," she said.

Nathan kept his tone even, unchanged. "Yes they did. I arranged for them to be told. In fact, I used my authority to ask for their assistance. If he got to where he got to, and my chances of apprehending him seemed remote, then I requested them to stop him. At all costs."

"Do you realize what you've done?" Corman demanded furiously.

"Yes." *I've had a man executed because he killed me, the better part of me,* Nathan thought. *Was it revenge?*

"We need to know about that station."

Or was it retribution, or just to stop him winning, and it made no difference, I don't feel any different... and I still want to kill you.

"Because of you it's been for nothing. The woman died for nothing."

Theroux stared at Corman, horrified. "You're crazy, you know that?" he said. "You are crazy. 'The woman died for nothing'? You're fucking right the woman died for nothing!"

"We need to know about that station. Knowing about it could make the world safer."

"Jesus, Nathan," Theroux said, "are you going to kill this rabid bitch or do you want me to do it?"

The earth had sunk a little, but it was still mounded up on the grave. It would be several weeks, apparently, before it had settled enough for the marble gravestone Nathan had chosen to be placed over her. He thought perhaps he should remove the wreath, which was decaying now, but then he decided against it. He had nothing to put in its place, and the bare soil was too lonely to leave unmarked.

In the old cemetery, the only light was the soft glow from the solar charged globes which illuminated the pathways. He wondered why he couldn't cry, not even here in this private darkness where he was closest to her silence.

A voice behind him asked, "You normally visit cemeteries at night?"

Nathan turned to see Colin Devis strolling towards him. "What are you doing here?" he asked ungraciously.

"Looking for you." Devis looked at the grave, and shook his head appreciatively. "Traditional interment. And in a place like this. Must have cost you an arm and a leg."

"What do you want?"

Devis seemed impervious to Nathan's obvious irritation. "I wanted to apologize," he said mildly, "for that bitch Corman. For not knowing about her."

"I didn't spot her either," said Nathan. "Not until it was too late." He stared down at the grave. "I've got a real gift for that."

Devis said, "Yeah well. I didn't spot her at all. A fortnight late and a quid short, as usual." He nodded thoughtfully. "That's why I was on it. That's why the spooks arranged to have me put on it. But then, I expect you'd worked that out, hadn't you?"

"I'm finding it hard to believe that they killed Lee just to put pressure on me. It's not a good enough reason to kill someone."

"Not someone you know anyway," said Devis.

Nathan took an angry step closer to him and peered into his face. It was set in its habitual slightly sour smile. He didn't look as though he was being sarcastic, but simply stating a fact as he saw it. Nathan said flatly, "Not anyone."

Devis showed no inclination to argue, confining himself to saying, "Difficult to feel much for strangers, I find," before getting down to what he really came to say. "Listen, I'm going to bring charges against Corman. Accessory before and after, conspiracy, perversion of justice, impersonating a police officer... anything I can take into court."

"You won't get a conviction."

"I know." Devis smiled the small, sour smile. "But I'll embarrass the hell out of her and her masters. Shine a little light on them. Maybe they'll dry up and blow away."

Nathan said, "I'll be glad to give evidence if that's what you're going to ask." He began to walk away from the grave.

Devis fell into step beside him. "No, what I was going to ask was whether you'd give me a job. When they sling me out."

"Can't promise anything," said Nathan.

"Thought I'd mention it," Devis said, without any sign of resentment.

They reached a path and Nathan quickened his pace, uneasy in the comforting artificial twilight, and obscurely shamed by the other man's unconditional honesty.

"Why were you visiting her grave at this time of night?" Devis asked.

"I thought maybe you could see the stars," said Nathan. "It seemed an appropriate way to say goodbye." It struck him then that he hadn't said goodbye, that he would never come back to this graveyard, that if he cried it would be for himself, that missing her would be something he'd get used to living with…

"Bit sentimental for my taste," said Devis.

"I'm old fashioned at heart," Nathan said. "I'm going to change that."

"Last time I looked up at the stars," said Devis, "something nasty dropped in my eye. I think it was bat shit…"

Intelligent Listening For Beginners

Despite the high security which isolated Outpost Nine from the rest of Moonbase – itself fairly isolated – Dr. Michael Chandri still felt exposed as he sat in his office deep inside the secret installation. He was thinking about the smooth and effortlessly superior Dafyd Talor, and what he had said. The request that had been made – oh, very *politely* made, of course – was quite obviously a test. Did the sponsors back on Earth think he was such a fool that he couldn't see it? They expected him to fail. They had always expected him to fail, he knew that. He knew what the assumptions about him were: that he wasn't of the top scientific rank; a second rate mind from a third world background; an inferior, whose credentials could never be entirely trusted. He knew that without his father's reputation and wealth no-one would have paid him serious attention. Were he not the son of his father, there would have been few academic honours, little or no advancement. He would certainly never have been given control of the project. Under such circumstances, the shame of failure would be too great to bear. He could not fail. Whatever happened, he must not be seen to fail.

Dr. Michael Chandri loved and respected his father. He determined now, with a renewed fervour, to bring honour to the name of Chandri. Or to die in the attempt. Then, as was his habit when panic pushed his thoughts to dark spiralling despair, he turned to his books for comfort. To get them to the Moon had entailed monstrous freight costs, but without the touch of them he would certainly have gone mad. He took a volume of poetry from the small shelf, let it fall open at random, and began to read aloud.

> *"O Rose, thou art sick!*
> *The invisible worm*
> *That flies in the night,*
> *In the howling storm,*
> *Has found out thy bed*
> *Of crimson joy:*
> *And his dark secret love*
> *Does thy life destroy."*

Chris Boucher

As always, the familiar textures and the remembered sounds, gentle reminders of the secure happiness of childhood, comforted him.

With the upgrade, the central control room of the expanded rail tunnel complex linking the United Kingdom with mainland Europe had become entirely independent of the people who were nominally in charge of it. This made no difference to the staffing levels, of course.

To their frustration, the directors of the company discovered that the majority of the travelling public could not be persuaded to use an unmanned undersea transport link. It should have been a plus-point that the network was operated by tireless machinery, but sales surveys and focus groups had shown that without a human presence, the great unwashed would stay away in droves.

Inevitably, the ads showed tall, handsome and confident men and women, unblemished specimens of physical perfection – 'a team of highly trained and motivated technicians, round-the-clock guardians of your comfort and safety…' – working and walking and smiling to the corporate jingle.

When the confidential market research was leaked to the Guild of Transport Engineers, they used it to negotiate a generous employment package for the workers. Senior management found this even more frustrating and they were provoked into pressing for 'a maximum-plus' return on company assets. Roughly translated, this meant doubling the volume of tunnel traffic.

During the Public Enquiry, management and union blamed each other's greed for the system overload which escalated a small accident into a major disaster. While it was in no-one's interest to point out that 'a small accident' was a contradiction in terms, what did become clear from the testimony was that the employees were sharply divided about their purpose. Despite the pay and conditions, the corporate uniforms, the huge operations monitor screen in the underground central control room and all the rest of the paraphernalia, for some workers, the token nature of their jobs was unmistakable. It was not lost on them that the routes to the control room started high in the main passenger concourses on all-singing-all-dancing monorails. Other workers could not see themselves as just a public relations exercise; for them, such expensive embellishments were proof that what they did was important.

It was a coincidence – the kind which suggests to the gullible there is some symmetry to existence – that Ben Rykker and Leo Pond were both there on the day it happened. Of all the shift managers – 'shift manager' was the inflated title given to each lone watchman at the big screen – these two best typified the opposing attitudes to CRC manning policy. Ben was the type who knew it was all bullshit. Leo knew that it wasn't. Ben spent most of his shifts working on an investment portfolio. Leo spent his worrying over what the multi-input screen was reporting about tunnel operations.

At first, in the moments before the horror began, the shift changeover seemed routine as ever. "Okay Leo," Ben had said as he thumb-printed the lock and the inner door closed behind him, "you're relieved," and he had crossed to where Leo was sitting. Neither man noticed that, although the door mechanism chimed softly before it flashed up *Access: Secure. Environment: Closed cycle* – which was normal – the indicator flickered – which was not.

Leo had looked at his replacement, but he made no attempt to vacate the impressively padded swivel chair. "I am too," he had said, then added, "Relieved I mean."

Ben dropped the leather case containing the emergency radio link beside the chair and shed his quasi-military, uniform jacket. "That's what I just said," he said.

"They put sixteen extra trains through this shift," Leo whinged. "Sixteen! Bloody board was flashing like a flock of fucking fruit machines."

Ben glanced up at the big screen, on which direct visuals from fixed cameras at the tunnel entrances and all the crossover points was combined with continuously updated digital readouts of temperature, atmospheric pressure, air contaminant levels, train weights, speeds, and relative distances. It made a vivid show but only the computer could get a useable overview from so much data, and its current assessment of the immediate situation was indicated by the blocks of green lights lined up across the bottom of the display.

"You shouldn't keep staring at it, you know. You'll go blind," Ben said.

Leo stood up and stretched his cramped muscles. "You can laugh."

"Pity you can't."

As they busied themselves with the small tasks, petty rituals and pointless bickering involved in the shift handover, Ben and Leo were too absorbed to observe the second, more bizarre sign of trouble. Five of the screen's green sit-rep lights went out, one after the other, and in their place in each of the darkened panels a single word was flashed up: *O – Rose – thou – art – sick*. When the sentence was complete, the words faded and the green lights were restored. It happened quickly enough to be overlooked – and it was.

Leo was pontificating. "The Company's got to be made to realize that profit isn't everything."

"Yeah well," Ben said, "loss isn't anything," and he chortled to himself at the joke.

"A lot of good it's going to do you and the rest of the shareholders," Leo lectured, warming to his theme, "if there's an overload and the computer crashes."

Ben shrugged. "I've got some stock in a couple of hospitals and three medical supply houses," he said, and took his place in the chair.

"You can forget medical supplies if that happens. They'll all be well beyond medical help and you know it."

"You're right," Ben said solemnly. "Heavy lifting plant, tunnelling equipment, funeral parlours – that's where the smart money should be. Wonder what price they're quoting..."

"I'm serious, Ben."

"Yes, Leo."

"Safety? They've got no bloody idea."

"Yes, Leo."

"I've warned them."

"Yes, Leo."

"I'm sick of warning them."

"Did you ever think," Ben asked, rummaging around in the emergency radio case for his notepad, his lunch and various other personal odds-and-ends he had stashed there, "maybe they're sick of it, too? I know I am."

Leo stopped fastening his jacket. He turned on Ben angrily, but then he forgot what he was going to say, because behind the other man, he glimpsed the unthinkable. The whole of the giant screen blinked. For the briefest time, there was nothing on it. His voice squeezed with shock, he said, "Did you see that? It blinked. The screen blinked."

"If I didn't know you better," Ben said dryly, "I'd think you were playing silly persons with me, Leo."

"The whole fucking thing just blinked off."

"Why don't you do the same?" Ben snapped the case shut and put it back on the floor. "Your shift's over," he said. "Blink off." He looked at

Star Cops

Leo, who was staring at the screen as if transfixed. "For Christ's sake, Leo," he went on, still suspecting a gag, "you're not the world's wittiest, you know what I mean?" And then he looked at the screen.

It was blank.

Ben punched the desk communicator open and reported almost calmly, "This is central control to engineering, we have a perceived malfunction on the main screen, do you copy?" There was no response, but he pressed on. "All data input is down, switch to alternate, I repeat switch to back-up systems and confirm please?"

There was still nothing.

"I told you," said Leo. "The computer's gone down. Everything's out. Communications, everything. I told you this was going to happen."

"Shut the fuck up!" Ben shouted snatching for the emergency radio.

In the tunnels, two trains were already decelerating and two accelerating as they approached the switching points which would cross them from the high speed line to passing loops and then back again. At either end of the system, two more trains were entering, each on primary acceleration, and behind them two more had stopped boarding passengers and were cleared to follow within minutes.

Such intricately co-ordinated movements allowed two way streams of traffic, local cross-Channel trains and a staggered succession of city-to-city expresses to use the same line and pass safely without losing vital speed.

Of the six trains committed to the tunnels when the computer failed – four local plus the London Bullet and the Brussels Flier – none survived. Only the two locals – loaded and cleared, but delayed and still above ground – were not wrecked.

It was over in slightly less than an hour. Fifteen hundred and thirty-seven passengers were killed in the tunnel-constricted impacts and the suffocating fires which followed.

Trapped in the central control room, Ben and Leo could only guess at what was happening. From the panic-stricken gibberish coming over the emergency radio, it seemed that everything was breaking down. Not even the simplest and most basic of the safety back-ups were working. Nothing that involved the main computer in any way could be relied upon.

"Listen," Ben said holding up his hand, straining to hear the mutterings of distant vibration. "Did you hear that, Leo?"

But Leo wasn't listening. He paced up and down. "It wasn't my fault," he said. "It wasn't my fault, Ben. I didn't… I mean I warned them to pay

Chris Boucher

more attention to safety…not to keep pushing the computer."

"This isn't an overload," Ben said. "An overload wouldn't take out the secondary systems at the same time. I mean look at the board." He gestured at the blank screen. "Do you see any sign of them kicking in?"

Leo stopped pacing abruptly and looked at the screen. "Terrorists? You think it was terrorists? How would they have done it?" And then, answering himself, he said, "Bomb. A fucking big bomb."

Ben said, "Stop babbling, Leo. Christ, they'd have had to nuke the place. Even then, it wouldn't have been like this."

Suddenly, eight of the sit-rep light blocks glowed black at the bottom of the grey screen, and a word faded up and shone in each: *O – Rose – thou – art – sick – The – invisible – worm –*. The words were briefly bright, then they and the blocks faded back into the overall blankness.

"Did you see that?" Ben said, and when Leo did not answer, said again, "Did you see that?"

Leo said, "I didn't see anything."

"You must have seen it," said Ben tearing his gaze from the screen long enough to glance at him.

Leo's eyes were tightly closed. "I didn't see it," he said. "I didn't see anything. There was nothing to see."

"Leo?" Ben said, almost pleading.

"No!"

A few minutes later, the lights failed in the central control room. The atmosphere recycling system stopped about the same time. Over the emergency radio, Ben described what they had seen on the screen. Leo reluctantly confirmed the details. By the time the rescue services reached them, both men were dead.

The Public Enquiry discounted and suppressed the more lurid aspects of their story, and found Ben and Leo each to be negligent. This was unfair, but inevitable. It was unfair, because they were helpless to affect anything. It was inevitable because taking the blame was, finally, all they were there for.

The offices no longer looked like an unused research lab in the undersubscribed Science Annexe on Moonbase – but they didn't look much like the headquarters of a police force, either, not even one as currently disreputable as the Star Cops. Nathan was aware that the delays in filling his requisitions for equipment and personnel were not entirely due to the supply difficulties all off-Earth installations experienced. He knew that he would have to make the ISPF a success before it would be given what it needed to succeed. But like they used to say back in Europol, if you've got no sense of humour, you shouldn't have joined. Not a lot of laughs in cleaning house though, he thought, as he waited for Box to finish the analysis. He wasn't sure which part of it was more unpleasant: discovering the corruption, or having to deal with it.

"Another example has come to light that meets the stated criteria," said Box, with Nathan's voice, which didn't sound to him like him, but did to everyone else, apparently.

"Christ," Nathan said, "there'll be no-one left."

"Do you wish to see the data?"

He sat down at his workstation. "Yes, please. Run it through for me. Let's see if there's a flaw."

Box began to feed the figures to the screen and outline the logic. Nathan tried to concentrate on what he was seeing. His chance of finding an error in the deductions was not good. Zero, pretty much. So why was he wasting the time? He hated the idea of letting a machine make up his mind for him, even Box – especially Box – but was that a good enough reason? Lee said he was irrational about computers, trying to compete, but she was dead, so what did she know? And these were decisions about people, and people should make decisions about people...

"You ready?" Theroux said behind him.

Nathan's attention snapped back to the screen. "In a minute," he said irritably. What the hell had happened to his attention span these days?

"It's a longish drive to Outpost Nine," said Theroux mildly, and when Nathan ignored this he wandered over to the newly installed communications screen. "News," he instructed quietly. The screen responded, switching slowly through the available news channels, with each offered broadcast precisely adjusted to match the volume of his voice command. "This," he said, as slow-motion footage of a sequence of train wrecks filled the screen with vicious power.

"*...said as yet there appears to be no explanation of the computer failure which caused the multiple wreck in the tunnel under the English Channel.*" If the newscaster was aware of the pictures the station was transmitting, his upbeat commentating style showed no sign of it. "*These pictures taken direct from the accident monitors, the only pictures of the disaster as it happened, are brought to you exclusively by TWBC. If it's news, you'll see it first on TWBC,* *the all new News Channel."*

The images came from the surface units linked to hundreds of self-contained black box accident recorders in the tunnels. Visuals were just a small part of what these crude automatics were designed to relay so the quality was poor. To compensate for this, a skilfully intercut sequence had been assembled, a montage of the destruction: collapsing trains engulfed by each other; sudden bursts of flame; glimpses of what might have been people falling, crawling, smashed in the heaving concussion waves; black billows of fiery smoke exploding with tightened power through the containing tunnels. Theroux watched with fascinated horror, then caught himself, and said, "Screen off!" As it blanked he said, "I cannot believe those bastards getting away with that stuff."

"What?" Nathan asked vaguely.

"TWBC. They must have greased some palms to get hold of those pictures."

"It's what makes the world go round," Nathan said, staring at the last of Box's evidence.

"I thought it was against the law," Theroux said.

Nathan leaned back in his seat and sighed. "You might try telling that to Inspector Hubble."

"Hubble, as in Kirk 'Boldly-go' Hubble? Our token American?"

"Our token bent American," Nathan said flatly.

Theroux looked unimpressed. "I hope the evidence is better than what you've got against Kenzy."

"It's virtually the same."

"Hubble has more money than he should have. Various characters he's been involved with have less."

Nathan killed his workscreen and pocketed Box. Moving towards the door he said, "Now tell me what a good poker player he is." The sarcasm was understated, and the more cutting for that. Theroux said nothing as he followed Nathan out.

The Moonrover was the best piece of basic engineering to come out of the Moonbase Technology Section. In fact, it was the only basic engineering they completed. Their other projects, like a purpose-built lunar shuttle, got no further than the planning stage before international co-operation broke down and funding dried up. The MoRo was a triumph though. A pressurized cabin was slung between eight shock-absorbing wheels each

Star Cops

fitted with a giant, soft-compound solid tyre measuring fourteen feet in diameter. Simple computer controls smoothed the ride further by raising and lowering the vehicle on its suspension in response to the terrain. All the wheels were driven and steered independently, with the computer co-ordinating the system. In an emergency, however, the automatics could be overridden and the MoRo then became a standard eight-wheel drive crater-buggy. Inside the cabin was a shirtsleeve environment with room for six people and the Earth-weight equivalent of one and three-quarter tonnes of freight. The motive power, atmosphere and temperature maintenance came from fuel cells with a twenty-six hour reserve and solar panel recharge. The driving controls were a simple directional joystick with integrated accelerator and a dead-man brake. Direct forward vision was supplemented by all-round video, ground radar and beacon-grid navigation. Alternatively, the computer had a full autopilot option. The MoRo was robust, flexible and safe. It was designed to be the ideal work horse vehicle for its operating environment, and of the sixteen currently in use around and about on the lunar surface, none had ever been the cause of a moment's anxiety.

None of this made the slightest difference to Nathan. He hated riding the things with a white-knuckled passion. Once he left Earth, being afraid was, like feeling nauseous, a routine experience for him – but this was different. He felt this fear was shaming, somehow, since it was so clearly irrational. He had tried to think it away, but reasoning it through wasn't easy when he couldn't decide if it was the vehicle with its seasick-soft ride which frightened him, or the vivid moonscape, harsh and discomfiting, to which it clung. He wondered whether it was precisely because the Moon's surface was less alien than space itself that it actually seemed more disorienting than weightlessness. Maybe it was the too-jagged rockscapes, drab even when they were bright enough to hurt your eyes; or the dust that kicked up but didn't cloud and blow about and didn't fall back naturally; or black sky with blazing light, and the same black sky with freezing dark; or Earth seen clearly from the surface of not-Earth. Maybe it was the way things played to your instincts, and then used those instincts to make you uneasy – which was frightening, like the beginnings of madness. The MoRo lurched gently, and Nathan realized that his mind had been wandering again.

Theroux eased up on the acceleration a little and said, "Sorry about that."

"No problem," Nathan said and checked that the helmet and gloves which he needed to complete the spacesuit he was wearing were still within easy reach.

"So what do you think?" Theroux asked conversationally.

"I think I prefer the autopilot. It doesn't have designs on the Trans-lunar Rally."

"Hubble and Kenzy? That is what you were trying to decide, yeah?"

Look thoughtful, Nathan thought and, people – bright people like Theroux – assume you're reasoning through some urgent problem, rather than wondering why you feel sick or how to stop your arse itching. "It's not a difficult decision," he said. "They're out. See? Easy-peasy."

"Okay," Theroux said, turning to Nathan to make his point, "I guess on past performance, they're not our most reliable people."

"True. Understated, but true," said Nathan, conscious that although Theroux's hand moved on the joystick he was no longer paying any attention to where the MoRo was heading. "You want to keep an eye on the road?" he suggested.

Theroux leaned forward slightly to look out. "But don't you think maybe you should give them a second chance?"

"No."

Theroux took his hand off the joystick altogether, and Nathan braced himself for the sudden stop. It was only when the dead-man brake did not kick in that he noticed the autopilot indicator was showing at the top of the navigation screen.

"We're almost down off the scarp now," Theroux said. "Shouldn't be any problems. Crater floor is pretty smooth. You can just about see Outpost Nine from here. Way over the far side. Tucked in below the rim." He pointed. "See?"

Nathan steeled himself, and peered across the wide, shallow basin. It was a nightmare desert of coarse dust, rock pocked and vacuum stark. There was something in the distance that might have been a dome. The navigation screen said it was the half-buried entrance to one of the general purpose research facilities and living quarters which Moonbase continued to spawn. His eyes said it was an unfocused speck a nervously long way away. As he stared, the MoRo whined on down the slope, its gyroscopes labouring to keep the cabin straight and level. It felt like the damn thing was trying to pull itself free and glide off from a slope of thick treacle. "Yeah," he said, and had to stop himself from grabbing for his helmet and gloves.

"You've decided, then?" Theroux persisted. "You're going to fire two of the longest serving officers in your command? No warning: just 'thanks, guys, and goodbye'?"

"I wasn't going to thank them, actually," Nathan said, without smiling.

"Those two have got friends, did you think about that?"

"I'm aware that you're a fan of Kenzy's, if that's what you mean," Nathan said and thought, cheap shot, shouldn't take cheap shots at friends. So he fancies the woman. Being corrupt doesn't necessarily make her repulsive, and there's no accounting for lust.

"I mean people with power," Theroux was saying. "Influential friends."

"I never knew a successful crook yet who hadn't got friends like that," Nathan said.

Theroux said, "And you don't have any real proof against either one."

"Hubble and Kenzy are dirty. Both of them."

"It'd never stand up in court."

"Which is the only reason I'm not insisting *they* do."

"Come on, Nathan." Theroux was getting exasperated. "Even if they were a bit –"

"Corrupt," said Nathan.

"It's not that unusual."

"It's going to be, David. In the Star Cops, it's fucking well going to be."

Theroux looked thoughtful. "What do you call corrupt?" he asked.

"Using your power to steal from people."

"That's sort of a loose definition. You could end up as a chief with no Indians."

Nathan thought, *You're not trying to confess, are you, David? Christ, I hope not*, and he said, "It's only Hubble and Kenzy. So far."

The MoRo reached the bottom of the crater wall and speeded up a little as it levelled out and set off across the plain.

"You picked the most difficult first, that's for sure," Theroux said. "Kenzy's a national figure."

"Only in Australia." Nathan smiled. "And what have they done for us recently?"

"Hubble's the only American we have on the *Ronald Reagan*."

"For what that's worth," Nathan said. "We should have at least three men on that station. Two permanently based there, one seconded to us here."

Theroux snorted. "You do know what the State Department thinks of us?"

"Does someone in the State Department think? As far as I'm aware, they haven't got anyone who can read without moving their lips."

"It's my experience they don't have anyone who can look at the pictures without moving their lips, but where does it say you gotta be bright to be powerful?"

The MoRo was accelerating steadily now. Nathan glanced at the screens but there was no indication of any problems that he could see. The autopilot was still in control and Theroux seemed unconcerned. He tried to relax. The first step to feeling relaxed is to act relaxed. That's what the trainers had told him. It was bullshit, of course. He shrugged. "Wasn't it one of their tame journos who came up with the 'Star Cops' tag?"

Theroux inclined his head and pointed with his index finger, his thumb cocked like the hammer of a gun. "And that's when we had a US cop," he said. "You want to guess what'll happen *after* you can him?"

"We've still got you," said Nathan.

Theroux said, "Shit, are we in trouble…"

A moment later, the MoRo ground jerkily to a halt. As the motors cut out and the cabin rocked gently, the movement slowly damped by the computer, Nathan murmured, "Are we in trouble?"

The navigation screen was flashing a small warning symbol and a soft electronic klaxon drew attention to the legend: *Brake override – ID check*. Theroux touched the icon and the klaxon stopped. "Security perimeter," he said casually. "Automatic cut-off while they check us out."

"Just routine?"

"Yeah."

Nathan rubbed his eyes lightly, and sighed. "It won't upset anything if I scream, then?"

"I'm sorry," Theroux said. "I should have warned you what was going to happen."

"You did," said Nathan, surprised to find his relaxed pose still more or less intact. "So did all the training people. Leave Earth and anything you forgot to bring with you will kill you. And anything you remembered to bring with you that doesn't work properly will kill you. When in doubt, assume everything is going to kill you."

"I thought you didn't believe all that stuff."

"That's the trouble with training. Even when you don't believe it, you believe it."

From the communications system a warm, sincere voice interrupted them. The unnaturally charming inflections identified the speaker as the security computer. *"Moonrover Seven, please prepare for voice identification as a preliminary to security clearance for access to Outpost Nine."*

Theroux said, "This is MoRo Seven ready for –"

"Please speak now," the voice said, speaking over him.

"It used to take talent and the right sort of upbringing," Nathan said, "to be polite and have shitty manners at the same time. Now all it takes is a computer."

"Commander Nathan Spring is identified, thank you."

"A man's gotta do what a man's gotta do," Theroux said.

"Inspector David Theroux is identified, thank you. International Space Police Force personnel journey authorization codes have been confirmed." The navigation screen returned to normal, the drive units hummed back into life and, with a barely discernible shudder, the MoRo began to move again.

"D'you know who said 'A man's gotta do what a man's gotta do'?" Theroux asked settling back in his seat.

"Just about every drunk who ever went for a piss and thought he was funny," Nathan said.

Theroux looked smug. "A movie buff should really know the answer."

"Are you sure I don't?"

"I'm ready to bet money you don't."

"You wouldn't be trying to box me in here would you?" said Nathan. He hadn't leaned on the word 'box', but simply saying it should have been enough to activate Box.

"Ten bucks says you don't know," said Theroux.

"I have to know what movie character said: A man's gotta do what a man's gotta do."

"Right."

"For twenty bucks," Nathan said.

"You're on."

"Let me think' now."

"Either you know it or you don't."

Nathan ran his hand down over his face and was just rubbing it over his mouth and chin, when Box – muffled by the coverall pocket – said: "It was *Shane*, though it is a paraphrase."

"That's twenty you owe me," Nathan said. "Do you want to pay now, or would you prefer to run a tab?"

Before Theroux could answer, the MoRo heaved to a stop again with the same sequence of warning icon, klaxon and screen message – this time: *Brake override – Clearance violation.*

"What the hell's gone wrong now?" Nathan demanded, abandoning all pretence to being relaxed.

Theroux looked mildly rattled himself. "I don't know."

"*Moonrover Seven,*" said the computer, as charmlessly charming as before, "*an unauthorized communications device has been operated –*"

"You used Box to tap into the Base amusementfile," Theroux accused, a little shocked.

"*-from your vehicle. Clarification is required before your journey can continue.*"

"You cheated, you sonofabitch."

Nathan said, "Security? I had occasion to use a multifunction, self-selecting system interface."

"*There is no such device registered to Moonrover Seven,*" said the computer.

"It's my personal property."

"*There is no such device registered to Commander Spring.*"

"Listen, I'm not going to argue this with an officious bag of bolts. Refer it to the Outpost Controller please. ISPF Code three four."

While they waited, Nathan took the twenty from his pocket and offered it to Theroux, who took the note and snapped it a couple of times and then held it up to the light. "Seems okay," he said.

"I'm not sure that was cheating," Nathan said. "I knew the answer."

"Not when I asked the question."

Deadpan, Nathan asked, "Did we specify a time frame?" and then before Theroux could protest, as he was clearly about to, said, "That's a lot of very efficient security for one small research outpost, don't you think? All this and bugged coveralls too. Be interesting to hear the official explanation."

"We have certain military involvements, as I am sure you do yourselves."

Why was it, Nathan wondered, that the gestures and mannerisms he found so elegantly charming in Indian women he found irritating in Indian men? Clearly racism did have a sexual element. Maybe that's what racism was: a simple perversion of the sex drive. "Involvements, Mr. Chandri?" he asked, struggling to finish shedding his spacesuit, thinking it was a bloody stupid convention, ten minutes to get unsuited, ten minutes to get suited-up again, just to be polite. But then, of course, the man was probably less confident here in the reception chamber than he would be in his own office, so you might get more out of him. The time might not be entirely wasted.

Chandri rocked his head a little in a delicate shrug. "Difficult to avoid out here," he said. He was engrossed in an examination of Box, and Nathan took the chance to study him carefully. He was perhaps thirty-five years old, with black hair worn longer than was customary off-Earth: was that vanity? He had a round face whose olive-dark complexion made its tendency to puffiness less immediately obvious, and there were bags under his heavy-lidded brown eyes; signs of stress – but how bad?

"We seem to manage it," Theroux remarked.

Chandri looked up, and Nathan had to switch his attention to putting some conspicuous effort into getting the suit boots off.

"It's a question of funding, as much as anything," Chandri said and then, referring to Box, went on, "Interesting toy. Itel never went into production with it, did they?"

Nathan shook his head. "Box was one of the prototypes."

"Expensive toy as well, then," Chandri said and handed it back to Nathan. "My apologies."

"For what?" Nathan asked.

Again the small shrug. "For… inconveniencing you."

"What exactly do you do here, Dr. Chandri?" Theroux asked briskly. He had already clipped his spacesuit into the storage rack and put on the soft indoor galoshes, and was ready to go.

"You didn't bother to check?"

"You're listed as Communications R&D, which doesn't tell us a whole hell of a lot."

"It tells you as much as you need to know," Chandri said politely. "As much as we want anyone to know, in fact."

"Even us?" Theroux said.

"Especially you, perhaps," Chandri said and smiled. He was ready to go now, too.

Nathan had the feeling that he had lost an opportunity, but there was nothing more to be gained from delay. While he stowed the suit, he said, "You lead a civilian project team. You're a physicist by training, most of your people appear to be mathematicians or computer development engineers. You've got a lot of security and 'certain military involvements'. At a guess, you're working in digital cryptography, new ciphers for old, code making or breaking of some sort." He pulled the fresh galoshes from the locker at the bottom of the rack and unbagged them. "But that's as much time as I intend to waste guessing."

"As I said..." Chandri murmured.

Nathan slipped his feet into the sterile overshoes and nodded. "...we know as much as we need to know about what you do." He wriggled his toes appreciatively. The boots had pinched a little. He made a mental note to check that his feet were not swelling more than was normal. "Perhaps you'd like to tell us what we do, in that case?"

Chandri frowned. "I am sorry?" His accent, which had shown almost no trace of his national origin before, was noticeably more pronounced.

Nathan smiled his best smile. "Why did you send for us?"

"Oh yes, of course," Chandri said. He sounded relieved. "This is not a very secure area. I have some excellent coffee in my office. Perhaps you will follow me, gentlemen?"

As they followed him through the pressure sensitive inner door Theroux murmured to Nathan, "The Sherlock Holmes act was impressive," and grinned.

"Let's hope it was impressive enough to stop him playing games," Nathan muttered, resisting the impulse to add, *and to stop you talking incessantly.*

The office was unexpected. There were the usual flimsy desk and chairs, the standard multiple work and communications screens, the conventional decor: pastel shades of palest yellows, and blues, and greens with multi-source indirect lighting, but not much else was in the average run of lunar provision. Exotic plants were carefully lit and nurtured in the sort of terrarium normally found only in those areas of Moonbase designed to impress visiting politicians. Even more carefully assembled and lit was an elaborate gallery of family holograms, and tiny, exquisitely-fashioned household gods. Most impressive of all however, was a bookcase filled with real printed-on-paper books, each one a beautifully bound hardback edition.

Nathan surveyed all these luxuries with undisguised admiration. Theroux paid them no obvious attention, and it struck Nathan that his American subordinate had a slightly puritanical streak when it came to money. It made his reaction to Hubble's and Kenzy's corruption seem decidedly incongruous. Perhaps he was subtler than Nathan was giving him credit for, but there wasn't much sign of it. At the moment he was staring pointedly at the bank of blank screens and asking, "You have a screen maintenance problem, sir?"

Unperturbed, Chandri continued to pour coffee from the old-fashioned percolator into white china mugs. "How do you like your coffee, Inspector?"

"Black, no sweeteners, thanks."

"And for you, Commander?"

"The same, thank you."

"We could send one of the main base repair guys," Theroux persisted, "if you've no-one on site."

"Inspector Theroux, you know quite well why those screens are off," Chandri said smiling. "You won't embarrass me about our security you know."

A little embarrassed himself, Theroux said, "I wasn't looking to, Dr. Chandri."

Chandri handed him his coffee and carried the second mug to where Nathan was reading the spines of the books. "I see you're impressed with my library, Commander," he said.

Nathan took the coffee carefully. "Yes indeed, sir. And I'm impressed with the weight allocation it took to bring them from Earth. You must have friends in the space freight business." He smiled, in case it should sound like an accusation.

"It was all paid for, I assure you," Chandri said quickly. "All above board."

Nathan nodded and sipped his coffee. He watched Chandri move to the books. The guy was strung tighter than piano wire, and his every response was guilty. Or was that paranoid?

"I don't like electronic books you see," Chandri was saying. "They are adequate for technical works yes, but for art… There's something about poetry particularly which must be read from the printed page. It dies when you put it on a viewing screen." Absently, he plucked a volume from the shelves and opened it, then realizing made to return it.

Nathan peered at the book. "You have a particular fondness for Blake?"

Chandri carefully put the book in its place. "I suppose I have." He went back and sat down at his desk. "It is something from my childhood perhaps. *Tyger! Tyger! burning bright / In the forests of the night...*" He smiled sadly.

"Blake was some kind of lunatic, wasn't he?" Theroux said, looking at the books for the first time.

"Lunacy," said Chandri. "Madness brought on by the Moon. Did you know that's where the word came from originally?"

Theroux ignored the question, and said, "I don't think I ever met a genuine billionaire before." He looked directly at Chandri so that the comment became a challenge.

"If it causes you concern, Inspector," Chandri murmured, "I am only a multimillionaire."

"How can we help you, sir?" Nathan interrupted, irritated with Theroux for his unsophisticated suspicions.

Chandri said, "Actually, you can't help me. However, we can help you, I believe."

"We're always grateful for that."

"Some intelligence has come into our possession which we feel is properly the concern of the space police." Chandri paused, as if he was suddenly undecided whether to pass on the information after all.

"Yes?" Nathan prompted.

"A group of extremists is planning to hijack one of the Earth-Moon shuttles," said Chandri and paused again.

Nathan frowned. Why was the man so hesitant? "When exactly is this supposed to happen?" he asked.

"Fairly soon, we think."

"And which group is it?"

"The Organisation of Pan-Continental Anarchists is behind it."

Theroux smiled and said, "Organizations of anarchists. Sounds like a contradiction in terms, doesn't it? Like military intelligence. Is that what this is, sir? Military intelligence?"

This time it was Chandri who ignored the question. "In fact 'anarchism' means 'without ruler,'" he said. "It doesn't mean 'without order'."

"That's interesting, sir, but you didn't answer my question."

"The group involved call themselves the BHG. Apparently that stands for the Black Hand Gang, but we can't identify any of the members at this stage."

"The Black Hand Gang?" Theroux made no attempt to hide his amusement.

Chandri said, "It's no joke, I assure you."

"Is the source of this military?" asked Nathan.

Again, Chandri gave the delicate, head-rocking shrug. "The information is reliable."

"You do realize," Nathan said, "that it's too little to act on, but too much to ignore."

"Leaves worrying as our only option," said Theroux.

"You could put men on the flights," Chandri suggested.

"Sky marshals?" Theroux shook his head dismissively. "They were always a lousy idea."

"I haven't the manpower, anyway," Nathan said then added, "One other question, Dr. Chandri, if I may."

"I have nothing more to say, Commander."

Nathan persisted. "Why did you send for us? Why did you want to see us in person?"

Chandri looked uncertain. He said, "To impress upon you the importance…" and then his voice trailed off into silence. He stared at Nathan, who thought he saw quite clearly in the man's eyes a wish to tell becoming a need to confess becoming a decision to speak.

"You could have done that over the communicator circuit," Theroux said.

And Nathan saw the decision change abruptly as the uncertainty disappeared behind a suave smile. "I was probably being overcautious," Chandri said. "It's just that it was slightly sensitive material and in my field one is aware of the… shall we say the vulnerability of carrier waves."

Nathan knew there was no way to salvage the lost confession, whatever it had been, but he realized that in his haste to bury a larger truth, the man had uncovered a smaller one. Casually he said, "So that's what you do here."

Chandri recognized the mistake. "It would not be wise to read too much into a casual remark, Commander."

"Your principal research area will be communications monitoring," Nathan went on.

"Not more buggers and super-snoopers?" asked Theroux.

Nathan said, "More impressive than that."

For the first time since they arrived, Chandri's deferential charm seemed to desert him. "I must suggest," he said, coldly polite, "that to go on would be foolish of you." The words were mild enough but his tone made the threat unmistakable.

Theroux was too surprised to be immediately hostile. "Is that a threat, Doctor?" he asked.

Still cold Chandri said, "An observation, merely."

Nathan felt he had no choice now but to press on. "We've always been able to hear more than we can listen to. You'll be working on intelligent listening systems."

"Sounds impressive, certainly," commented Theroux taking his cue from Nathan.

"Machines that listen to everything and decide for themselves what's worth passing on. Machines that don't need the normal, precisely defined criteria."

Theroux said, "What, you just say: look for the bad guys?"

"Is that where this BHG information came from, Dr. Chandri? A test running? Did one of your new computers pick it out from the babble of all the world?"

Chandri stood up. "Commander, it has been a pleasure meeting you," he said, coming out from behind his desk. He shook hands with both men and then said "I'll show you out, gentlemen."

Theroux said, "We can find our own way, sir."

"I wouldn't dream of being so discourteous," Chandri said. "The thought of you wandering lost and alone around our establishment would be most distressing to me."

Because the boots were a bit tight, it took Nathan longer than ten minutes to suit-up again but Chandri waited, patient and helpful, clearly doing his best to make up for the previous lapse.

As happened when they arrived, Theroux was ready first. "Tireless attention to every word spoken?" he said, still in the mood to chat. "No possibility of human error? You tell it to listen for subversives and it listens to everyone and identifies the ones it assumes you won't like?"

His expression and tone deliberately amiable, Chandri said, "I'm afraid I have no more time to waste on such idle speculation."

"It can't be quite that successful, anyway," Nathan remarked, pulling

Star Cops

on and sealing his inner gloves.

"You think not?" asked Chandri levelly.

"We can't identify any of the members at this stage. Isn't that what you said?"

Chandri smiled. "Ah, yes. But then, one would hesitate to develop something which would do you people out of a job."

"There's not much danger of that, I'm afraid," Nathan said.

Chandri's smile became cool and fixed. "Perhaps I seem to you incapable of such complex work. Is that what you think, Commander?"

Theroux said, "He thinks that where there's living there's policemen. One of nature's rules," and he put on his helmet, secured it, and checked the suit telltales. Satisfied, he signalled his readiness to move through the access lock. Nathan waved him on and Chandri raised his hand, palm outward, for Theroux to touch with his open gauntlet in the professional gesture of farewell.

"Where there's living. there's policemen," Chandri said, handing Nathan his helmet. "It must be very restful to be sure of one's place in the world."

Nathan watched the atmosphere recycling gauge register the evacuation of the airlock. "It would be restful to be sure one was going to get back to it," he said, mindful once more of just how life-threatening everything had become.

Chandri's soft face creased into a frown of concern. "We are on the same side, you know," he said.

Does he think I'm afraid of him? Nathan wondered. It struck him that if he did, then there might be good reason to be afraid of him, and he said, "Not too long ago my closest friend died."

Chandri's expression became sympathetic. "I am sorry for you," he said. "Death is a lonely business."

"She was killed by someone who was also on our side."

The look of sympathy remained unchanged but it was uninvolved. Chandri was thinking about something else now. "You will keep me informed of anything you discover about the hijacking?" he asked. "I should be most interested to hear of your progress."

Nathan nodded. "Is there anything else you want to tell me, Dr. Chandri?" he said – though he wasn't sure what question he was really asking.

Chandri said, "There is nothing I can tell you."

Nathan lifted the helmet and bent his head towards it.

"My world," Chandri said, "the world I came from, reveres all life."

"This is a dead world, sir," Nathan said and slotted the helmet into position, cutting himself off from further talk. It was not until the airlock hatch closed on him that he wondered why he had allowed himself to be so stupid, so glib. What the hell was it about Chandri that had irritated him – was it the self-pity? Or was it that the man had made him nervous? Or maybe it was all just his own paranoia brought on by blind panic about claustrophobic fucking airlocks. He looked at the vent gauge and the hatch locking mechanism. Both showed normal function indicators. There was no reason for him to look at either for a maker's name and the thought did not even occur to him.

On the other side of the airlock, Dr. Michael Chandri glanced at the same indicators before turning away and heading back to his office. It had not occurred to him to look at the maker's names either but there was a reason for that.

Nathan stepped through into the cargo bay. The MoRo door was open, and he hopped carefully up the steps and scrambled into the cab. Theroux was sitting with the controls fired up and ready. "*What kept you?*" he asked over the suit-to-suit radio circuit.

Nathan set the steps retracting and slid the cab door closed. "Not sure," he said, checking the seals and getting a green light on them. "Might have been promises of safe conduct." Another green light showed the steps were stowed. "Steps and seals are green."

"*You getting paranoid again?*"

"Don't knock it. Without paranoia how are you going to know who your enemies are?"

While Theroux began the cabin pressurization Nathan opened a main communications channel and said, "This is MoRo Seven, all checks are complete, request surface access please."

Moving slowly on its dustproof nylon runners, the access cover rolled aside and harsh lunar daylight spilled into the bay and overwhelmed the fluorescents. As the sharply shadowed rockscape outside the dome was revealed, Theroux said, "A view that never fails to move me."

The MoRo lurched gently into motion and Nathan had to swallow hard against the trickle of bile that immediately rose in his throat. "Explains one of the more pervasive smells associated with space travel," he said.

Theroux did his best to sound hurt. "The privileges of rank don't extend to stealing jokes."

"Who's joking?"

"Scares the crap out of you too, huh?"

The MoRo was still accelerating down towards the crater floor when the cabin pressure light came up. "Cabin is fully pressurized, suit systems can be closed down whenever you're ready," Theroux said, and began to release the seals on his helmet.

Nathan was deliberately slower to remove his own helmet. The meeting with Chandri had been a complete shambles and once they could talk face to face he was going to have to tell Theroux exactly whose fault that was.

Back at his desk, Chandri had reactivated the surveillance screens. He watched the seven members of his team, each in their separate cubicle, each struggling with their part of the problem. It was a good team. That was the pity of it. He had assembled them with great care. What more could he have done?

"Have we received the location signal?" he asked.

"The unit has been identified," the computer replied.

Was he justified in this? What other choice did he have? They had forced him to it. It was not his fault that they wanted him to fail. What more could he have done?

"What more could I have done?" Theroux protested angrily.

"It should have been less," Nathan said, doing his best to be patient without sounding like a training school lecturer. "Chandri was hiding something,"

"Gee, do you really think so?"

Nathan thought, *it's odd the way Americans never quite master irony*, and said, "I'm not talking about the work they're doing there."

"So what the fuck are you talking about?"

"I don't know, but if you'd talked less and listened more I might have found out."

The cabin lifted smoothly as the MoRo straddled a boulder and Nathan's stomach tensed. Was the bloody thing still accelerating or did it just feel like it? He glanced at the rear screen. The Outpost still seemed quite close. Surely they had travelled further than that. He said, "Didn't you feel how close he was to…?"

"To what, for Chrissakes?" Nathan looked at Theroux without speaking, and Theroux nodded. "If I'd talked less and listened more you might have found out."

"He had some sort of guilty secret," Nathan said.

Theroux grinned slightly. "He'd better enjoy it while he can," he said. "Doesn't sound like it's going to be possible to hide anything for much longer."

"And he was scared," said Nathan. "He wanted to tell us, but finally he couldn't bring himself to trust us enough."

Theroux shook his head and grinned more broadly. "What do you base that on? Reading the coffee grounds? You know what I love about your intuition? Your detective's instinct?"

"Nose, David," Nathan said, tapping the side of his nose. "The preferred professional expression is 'detective's nose'."

"By the law of averages, you've got to be right fifty percent of the time," Theroux said.

Unsmiling, Nathan said, "It's a comforting thought, isn't it?"

"Simple goddam guesswork."

"Not exactly."

"Well what would you call it?"

"An intelligent listening system," said Nathan. "For beginners. Failing that: just goddam guesswork. Nothing involving people is ever simple." As soon as he'd said it he thought, *More bumper-sticker philosophy, why do I trot out this trite shit?*

"How come you didn't ask Chandri why he's got his people's coveralls bugged?" Theroux asked suddenly.

"You think he'd have told me?"

"I doubt it."

Nathan said, "Not much point in letting him know we knew, then."

"Not much point in knowing unless we use it," Theroux said.

In the huge production complex which Seal Sands Chemicals operated at the mouth of the river Tees near Seaton Carew in the North-East of England, the dozen or so process workers who oversaw the systems were not prepared for the non-routine. They were prepared for everything else, fully trained for every predictable emergency. They were drilled in the procedures for dealing with everything which might go wrong between the off-loading of crude feedstock through catalyzers, crackers, distillers, fermenters, separators, settlers, driers, packers and the on-loading of the sale products. They were familiar with all the various combinations and reactions of which the plant was capable and, in the unlikely event that the computer needed back-up, they were ready.

But not for poetry. There was nothing in the manuals about poetry on the screens. There was no procedure for poetry.

"'That flies in the night'? What does that mean?" the shift foreman demanded, staring at the screen which should have been showing main reaction readouts but wasn't, and then was again. "Fucking hell." He had paid no attention to the slight shudder of the automatic doors when he came into the process monitoring suite a few moments before, and he had no reason to link it with the words, especially as he wasn't sure he believed in the words. He scowled. "I saw it. It showed up on here. I saw it." He glared round at the other process workers. "Alright, who's the joker?" Nobody answered him. They often didn't. He hadn't asked to be put in charge. The money was useful, but he was uncomfortable telling people what to do. "Come on, I like a laugh as much as anybody, but this is going too fucking far!"

One of the others said, "There's a problem."

He turned on him and snapped, "You've got that right. If head office ever hear about this…"

The man did not look up from his screen, and sounding nervous, he said, "The second line is out of phase."

The shift foreman crossed to his console, saying, "Well, balance it, for Christ's sake."

"I can't. Computer's not responding."

"It must be." The shift foreman touched the man's shoulder. "Here, let me." The man moved out of the way, relieved to hand over the responsibility. The shift foreman deftly adjusted the flows and watched as the readouts registered. "Nothing. There's no bloody difference." Another man called out, "We're losing three!" and another shouted, "Four's running out of control!" Everyone looked at the shift foreman. It was for him to call it. He hesitated. It was obvious that if they gave up on it now, the place would tear itself apart. The readings kept on slipping. "Hit the switches," he said. "Let's get the fuck out of here!" Each man flicked on a control-failure alarm and as klaxons howled and hooted in the complex they ran for their lives.

On the main reaction screen the words: *That – flies – in – the – night – In – the – howling – storm –* flashed up just before the firestorm roared through and blew everything out.

"*She said she was one of yours, and she had the ISPF clearance code.*" The voice of the security woman sounded slightly defensive. "*We did try to check with you, but Outpost Nine is tricky to contact.*"

"Okay, no problem," Nathan said. "Thanks for letting me know. Seven out." He looked at Theroux. "How did she get hold of the new code?"

"She probably used her old one as authority to ask for it," Theroux said, choosing now to switch the MoRo to manual control and accelerate past the Moonbase perimeter checks. The excess speed icon flashed on the navigation screen and audible warnings chimed. Nathan reached out and cancelled them. He felt unable to let such an obvious diversion go unremarked. "Makes changing it a bit pointless," he said.

"She wasn't suspended. Shit, she wasn't even under suspicion – except by you," said Theroux, then he smiled. "That's the trouble with security. Nobody knows what the fuck's going on until it's too late."

She was watching a newscast when they got back to the Star Cop office. Pictures of billowing fire and a mid-Atlantic voice selling the news like a commercial. "*The destruction of the chemical plant has been put down to computer failure.*"

She had her back to the door. "*Rumours of sabotage which link this incident to the failure of the Channel Tunnel traffic computer –* "

She stood and turned as they came in. Nathan got an impression of startlingly blue eyes and a small vivid mouth. "*– have been dismissed as quote simple fantasy unquote.*"

She was slim and lightly muscled. Her hair was almost white, close cropped for free-fall, and her skin was so pale it seemed as though a bright light must shine straight through it. "*Bizarre stories of poetry preceding disaster are circulating –* "

She smiled. Christ, Nathan thought, feeling guilty in some obscure way, she is beautiful. " *– though to date no-one seems able –* "

"Pal Kenzy, Commander," she said holding out her hand.

" *– to pin down exactly –* "

"Screen off," Nathan said, and shook hands.

Star Cops

She said, "I hope you don't mind my waiting in here, only they said you were on your way back from one of the outposts." Her voice was slightly husky with just the trace of an Australian accent.

"Do you know David Theroux?" said Nathan, keeping it formal, coldly polite.

Theroux smiled warmly, "Yeah, we have met," and started to offer his hand.

She didn't seem to notice the gesture, just nodding and saying, "Yeah hi," before turning her full attention back to Nathan. "I was on leave when you were first appointed, and since then I've been catching up on the backlog."

What the hell is she trying to do? Nathan wondered. Did she know? Did she expect to change his mind? "Yes, so I understand," he said still not returning her smile, which did not falter for a second.

"I'm currently based on the Coral Sun. That's the fixed orbit station run by –"

Nathan interrupted her, "The Pacific Basin Consortium, yes, I know. What is it you want, Kenzy?" It was more abrupt than he had intended, but it didn't faze her at all. Obviously her skin was thicker than it looked.

"This is the first chance I've had to pay my respects and welcome you to the Star Cops," she said.

"Thank you."

"I realize now is probably not the time, but there was something I wanted you to see." She picked up a small black case, opened it with a flourish and offered it to Nathan. In the padded interior was a handgun. It was about the size of a nine millimetre automatic but it was single moulded out of plastic and was clearly no sort of percussion weapon.

Nathan left her holding the case, and with barely a glance at it said, "You're right, Kenzy. Now is not the time."

Her smile was less confident, suddenly. "You don't understand, Commander."

"That's possible," Nathan said.

"This weapon has been developed for use on the high frontier."

"And your interest is?"

"It's manufactured in Australia by the Consortium. Commander, this really is the weapon we need if we're to keep control out here." She took it out of its case and began what sounded like a rehearsed sales pitch. "The wavelength of this laser can be adjusted for a variety of organic materials."

"You mean like flesh," Theroux put in.

Kenzy said, "Well, of course like flesh. You can even pick the pigmentation of the skin. And this little beauty won't touch anything else."

Theroux took the gun from her, and turned it over in his hands. "Fuck," he murmured. "The bastards finally came up with a racist weapon."

"We're not interested in your gun, Kenzy," Nathan said.

"Think about it," she said. "You can hardly use your police special out on the stations."

"I don't usually carry a gun at all," said Nathan.

Kenzy said, "That'll be good news to the scum who'll be pouring out here to build the Big Ring."

"That's three, maybe four years down the line," Theroux said, handing back the laser pistol. "If they ever come up with the funding. Off-world space colonies ain't sexy right now – or hadn't you noticed?"

For a moment she looked ready to demonstrate the gun on both of them, then, putting it back in the case she said, "So what about the people who're already out here?" She was angry, and it made her voice sharper, her accent broader. "They're gonna love the idea of unarmed cops looking after their interests."

"I'm impressed with your concern for other people's interests," Nathan said, thinking that his accent must change when he got angry and wondering, in passing, how exactly.

"Meaning?" Kenzy demanded.

"Not your strong suit, surely?" And he crossed to a workstation and punched up a playback channel onto a main screen. A close-up of Kenzy's face appeared glaring directly at them. "*I don't give a rat's arse about your family,*" the face snarled. "*I'll heave you straight back Earthside and you can starve right along with them.*"

Just out of the picture a man said, "*I'm not rubbishing you, honest I'm not. My kid's sick. I can't pay the hospital bills. I wouldn't have risked my neck out here otherwise.*"

"*Some things never change, do they?*" the recording of Kenzy said. "*And whinging poms are one of them.*"

The unseen man's voice became more pathetic, taking on an almost tearful edge, "*You send me back to Earth now and I don't know what I'll do. My son could die.*"

Kenzy's face showed her distaste for the man. "*Tough break. He shouldn't have picked a loser for a father.*"

"*Look…*" the voice said, "*maybe we could come to some arrangement?*"

"*Arrangement?*"

"*I had to pay a recruiter to get this job in the first place. An agent's fee, he called it. I think maybe I was cheated, don't you?*"

"*Looks a lot like it.*"

"*Okay, so if I could pay someone to make sure I wasn't cheated any more…*"

The recording of Kenzy appeared to think about this then said, "*These things cost money. And we're talking cash money, you understand.*"

"*I understand,*" the unseen man said eagerly. "*And I'm ready. I'm ready to pay to be protected.*"

The picture of Kenzy's face froze on the screen.

Nathan said, "You're already paid to protect him." Kenzy and Theroux both turned from staring at the picture to look at him.

"What is all this?" asked Kenzy.

Nathan left the image of Kenzy up and switched a subsidiary workstation screen to personnel and payroll records. Scrolling through these he said, "We pay you."

"What's going on here?" Kenzy demanded. She looked at Theroux. "Do you know what's going on here? Did you know about this?"

Theroux was tempted to say that this was as much of a shock to him as it was to her, because this part of it was, but he said nothing and, hoping his face was expressionless, held her accusing stare.

"At least, we used to pay you," Nathan said and amended her file. "Not any more."

"Oh no," Kenzy said, shaking her head and smiling sardonically. "You think I just rode over the rim on a sputnik?"

Nathan said flatly, "You're fired, Kenzy."

She moved to face him, a direct challenge. "You can't," she said. "Not on evidence like that, you can't. Some small-time crim sets out to smear my good name?"

"With some success, wouldn't you say?" Nathan snapped, getting a jolt of angry pleasure when he saw the thrust go home.

"Don't get toffee-nosed with me, you stuck up pommy bastard."

Was that how his accent went when he was angry? Nathan thought, clipped and pseudo middle-class?

"Listen, you one-minute wonder," Kenzy raged on, "I was stringing him along so I could add attempting to bribe an officer to all the other counts I'd got him on."

"And very convincing you were too, ex-officer Kenzy," a voice said from the doorway. It was the voice from the recording – only now it was confident, cheerful even. Kenzy turned slowly to confront a large plump man, whose narrow eyes belied a chubby grin. "You set me up," she said.

"Doesn't take much doing, when they're as greedy as you are," he said.

Kenzy said, "I should've known those bloody eye shades weren't kosher."

"They're good, aren't they?" he said taking the fashionable sun glasses from his coverall pocket and pointing out the eye-focused video system incorporated in the frames.

"This is Inspector Devis," Nathan said. "One of the more recent recruits."

"I was formerly Detective Chief Inspector Devis. Till my sergeant got me into bother." He smiled with evident satisfaction. "She's due for sentencing quite soon, I believe."

Nathan said, "And unless you want to find yourself in a similar situation, I suggest you get the first available shuttle back to Earth."

Kenzy closed up the gun case. "Oh, don't worry, I intend to. There's some people in Canberra who'll be really interested in how you're running things out here."

"Goodbye, Kenzy."

"Don't count on it, Spring," she said, and left the office without a backward glance.

Devis watched her go. "Not a bad looking woman, for all that," he said when the negative pressure double door – a constant reminder that the office was just a surplus laboratory – closed behind her.

Nathan thought, not as beautiful as Lee. Never as beautiful as Lee again.

"Nice tight little arse," Devis said to Theroux. "Sorry we haven't been introduced. Not properly. Colin Devis. We did meet briefly."

Theroux ignored his outstretched hand. "Yeah. I processed your documentation. When I passed you for the Coral Sun I had no idea who you were." He looked at Nathan. "Were you testing me as well?"

"I can tell you he was straight as a die. No hint of gummy digits," Devis said.

"Listen Jack," Theroux said angrily. "When I need a character reference I'll call you okay?"

Devis' eyes narrowed to slits, the smile disappeared and he straightened up to become a much more imposing figure. "It's Colin, not Jack," he said.

Nathan said, "Give us a couple of minutes, will you Colin?"

Devis nodded, and relaxed a little. "Word of advice, David," he said. "Nobody loves a smart arse. Least of all me." As he left the office, he was wondering aloud, "Have I blown my chances with Kenzy, do you think? I suppose a fuck's out of the question now…"

Nathan waited until he and Theroux were alone, and then said, "Get it off your chest."

Theroux was furiously angry. "Don't patronize me, you supercilious bastard."

"I wasn't."

"You couldn't tell me, could you? You couldn't trust me."

"You never believed she was bent."

"I didn't realize it was a condition of employment," Theroux said bitterly.

"I needed a clean approach," Nathan said – and thought, *I could have put that better*.

"And you thought I'd give your grubby little scheme away."

Stung, Nathan snapped, "Alright, that's enough. I meant what I said. There's going to be no corruption," and thought immediately, that helped a lot.

"There's gonna be no Star Cops," Theroux said.

"I run this outfit and I do it according to my own lights," Nathan said.

"And alone." Theroux pivoted on his heel, and control-hopped a long looping stride to the door.

"David," Nathan said sharply, making him turn back. "Sometimes those lights aren't as bright as they should be." He took a small leather wallet from his workstation locker and tossed it in Theroux's direction. "Sue me." The throw was not particularly accurate. It would take more practice before Nathan could be spontaneous in one-sixth G, and he was mildly irritated to see that Theroux had mastered the lunar professional's control-hop and was moving effortlessly to where the wallet was falling short of its target.

Looking at the badge and ID, Theroux asked, "What is it?"

"Your promotion came through. You did a good job on the *Dædalus* case. You're now officially my second-in-command."

"I didn't know you planned to promote me." Theroux examined the badge without any obvious enthusiasm.

"Chief Superintendent. Big jump from Inspector," said Nathan and when Theroux continued to look unconvinced, added, "It's a helluva good pension," and waited with the beginnings of irritation.

"Who lives long enough for a pension?" Theroux said finally, and pocketed the wallet.

Nathan found he was vastly relieved that Theroux hadn't rejected the promotion out of hand; somehow that would have undermined him completely. With Lee gone, there was only the job left and if someone threw that back at him there'd be nothing. With Lee gone. Unless there had only ever been the job. Unless that was how Lee came to see him, finally. Too late to think about that. All of it too late. "Get Colin back, will you?" he said. "I want him to find out exactly who produces that gun."

"I thought we weren't interested."

"We weren't interested in *her* gun. But *that* gun is just what we need."

Theroux control-hopped to the door. "She's probably got shares in the company, you realize."

Nathan shrugged, and said without smiling, "You can carry principle too far."

Theroux opened the first part of the door. "I never know when you're serious and when you're joking," he complained, as he stepped on the pressure pad to release the second part. In the corridor outside, Devis was unselfconsciously hopping backwards and forwards like a tourist. Theroux gestured at him to come back.

"When in doubt, don't smile," Nathan said.

"Don't smile?" Devis asked as he shambled in.

Theroux smiled and said, "It's the secret of advancement in the Star Cops."

"Useful to know. What's next, then?" He looked at Nathan. "There was an Officer Hubble you wanted sorted, yes?"

Nathan yawned. "You and Chief Superintendent Theroux can handle that one. I've got a more urgent priority."

Devis nodded to Theroux. "Congratulations. That makes you two-I-C, I suppose. Do I call you 'sir'?"

"David'll do."

"Just so long as you remember that when you're pissed off with me."

"I'm going to get my head down," Nathan said. "I am knackered."

When he had gone Devis said, "The urgent priorities of rank, eh, David?"

Star Cops

Theroux wondered if the informality was going to turn out to be a mistake.

Devis flexed his shoulders. "I could do with some sleep myself, mind," he went on.

"Ever have one of those days when nothing goes your way, Colin?" Theroux asked.

"Frequently."

"I think you're having another one."

Nathan stepped out of the mist shower clean, dry and regretting that he couldn't have a proper bath. He scooped up his coveralls and hurried from the ablutions unit into the bright corridor which led to the sleep block where he had been allocated a cell. No-one ever put their clothes back on to make this short trip and Nathan knew that to do so would be inappropriate behaviour, best avoided in the narrow confines of off-Earth living. He concentrated on moving more slowly. *When you're nervous, do everything as slowly as you can bear to,* his father had told him once, *self-conscious people move too quickly and that makes them conspicuous, which is exactly what they're trying to avoid.* He remembered being surprised that his father knew he was shy. He remembered too thinking that one day he'd be a grown-up and relaxed and confident just like his father was. It took a long time to realize that nothing was going to change, that all he could hope for was to hide his feelings well enough to look relaxed and confident... just like his father was. Now he successfully covered his embarrassment at public nakedness and routinely gave no clue that the casual intimacies of communal living made him uncomfortable. So he did not allow his pleasure that the other eight sleep cells in the stack were already sealed to show, and he resisted the impulse to hurry the last few yards to privacy.

Slow and deliberate, he climbed up to the number seven tube and crawled inside. As he pulled the hatch closed behind him, the light and the air-conditioning, pre-set to his preference, came on automatically. He shoved his coveralls and his slippers into the personal effects drawer and sat back on the sleeping couch, leaning against the gel-filled padding which slowly adjusted itself to his position.

The design theory was that your sleep cell was somewhere you could feel totally secure and relaxed. In the unrelentingly hostile lunar environment everyone needed such a place. Even crater bunnies, the hardened professionals for whom the Moon was home, needed relief from the constant background stress. The cells were basically steel tubes which had built in to them a measure of self-contained life-support, protection against disastrous decompression in other parts of the base. The diameter of each one was not quite large enough to let a man stand up, but they were fully upholstered, provided with snacks and drinks dispensers, an entertainments centre, and an all-enveloping video projection system – virtual reality was too isolating – which, with a little imagination, took you to wherever the library had on file. In the sleep cells. nostalgia for Earth could be soothed, yearning for the childhood planet could be calmed. Universally, the sleep cell was known as 'a womb with a view'…

Nathan opened the drawer again and disentangled Box from the discarded coverall. He propped it up at the foot of the couch and said, "Box, there are days I feel as though I've missed every trick."

Box answered him in the voice which was identical to his. "And today was like that?" it asked.

"Since Lee died, they've all been like that. I'm not as fast or as clear as I was."

"Tomorrow is another day," Box said.

"When did I programme you for platitudes?"

"The programme merely reflects a slightly degraded version of your own speech patterns," Box said, telling him what he already knew and reminding him that what he was really doing was talking to himself.

"Access the history data bank and find me a reference to the Black Hand Gang."

"Is there a cross-reference?"

"Anarchists."

"Checking."

"The BHG is supposed to be an anarchist splinter group."

"Supposed to be?"

"There's remarkably little information about it."

"It is a secret organization, perhaps."

"It has enormous power focused on it, and yet it remains hidden."

"What power?"

"Technology."

"You have said: 'The more powerful the technology, the smaller the error needed to defeat it'."

"You're right about the platitudes."

"You have also said: 'people are too unreliable to be successfully replaced by machines'."

"I hope I only said all this crap to you."

"The Black Hand Gang was a criminal organisation formed in the United States of America around 1868. Do you require a detailed history?"

"Was it political?"

"It is not listed as political."

"Not anarchist?"

"No. The Black Hand were Spanish anarchists repressed in 1883."

"Not the Black Hand Gang. If they've named themselves for the wrong outfit how bright can they be?"

"How bright must they be?"

"Bright enough to avoid being found by Dr. Chandri's machines. Box, please see what you can find out about Dr. Michael Chandri that isn't in his base personnel file." Nathan stretched out on the couch. He felt ready to sleep. Maybe this time the dreams would not be so drab. "Have it ready for me when I wake up."

"You have completed your thinking?"

It would be nice to think so, Nathan thought and said, "Shut up, Box." Briefly he considered trying to get to sleep without help, but then couldn't see the point of it, and cued the cell's video. "Sleepcircuit." The light began a slow fade to twilight paleness. "Seascape," he instructed, "sunset, small waves lapping a shingle beach." Dreamlike, the gloom resolved itself into a view of perfect unspoilt coast, the half-remembered picture of some childhood holiday. The system filled the tube so that wherever Nathan turned to look the illusion was coherent, and a new refinement which linked the air conditioning to a fragrance dispenser brought a hint of the salt and seaweed taste to his nose. He lay watching for a moment and his vision blurred with tears. "I miss you," he said, and closed his eyes. "I miss you Lee." The sound and smell of the ocean continued to wash over him as the sensors waited for him to fall asleep.

When the UK air-traffic control computer went down, all four London airports managed to avoid casualties thanks to the quick thinking of the four duty controllers at Heathrow Central. Diverting incoming flights. However. overloaded French, Dutch and Irish airspace resulting in two mid-air collisions and five landing accidents of which three were without survivors. All four British controllers saw the words: *Has – found*

– *out* – *thy* – *bed* followed, just after all machine function ceased, by: *Has – found – out – thy – bed – of – crimson – joy.*

"*How does it feel to be back on Earth?*" Nathan asked from the screen.

Devis reduced the illumination in the tollbooth. He was fairly sure he looked like shit. The previous night's session had been uninhibited and the booze had not mixed well with the shuttle-lag medication. Still, with Corman going down for a seven, old colleagues expected to celebrate – and so, come to that, did he. "I'm sorry?" he asked, playing for time without really being sure why – except that he doubted whether his new boss would sympathize with a sod of a hangover which Star Cops expenses had paid for.

"*I said, how does it feel to be back on Earth?*"

"It's exhausting. You forget how bloody heavy you are down here," Devis said, thinking not bad, Colin, not bad for an old and seriously liquidized brain.

"*At least the scenery's green.*"

"So's vomit."

Theroux stuck his head into the field of vision. "*Very poetic, Colin,*" he said. "*Good party, was it?*" Then he ducked away, leaving Nathan staring expressionlessly.

Fuck.

"Listen, was there something in particular you wanted? Only I haven't closed the deal yet and I don't want to give their sales guy too long to think about the discount he's been offering."

Nathan nodded. "*I want you to double the order.*"

"A hundred guns? Did somebody declare war out there?"

A shrug. "*We need more people.*"

"You planning to invade Poland or what?" Devis said suddenly feeling better. A discount now looked like a definite possibility. "Hey, how would you feel about my taking a small commission on the deal?"

Still expressionless Nathan said, "*Short one inspector.*"

That's what I thought, thought Devis and said, "Just a thought."

"*Do the business and get back, all right? We're spread a bit thin out here.*"

"You will keep sacking people."

Nathan smiled for the first time. "*Yes. Bear it in mind.*"

Devis called up the Moon shuttle times and downloaded the schedule onto his wrist-sec. "I'll catch the next shuttle," he said, adding,

"Incidentally, you do realize who developed the original of this gun, don't you?"

"*Should I?*"

"Word is, it was your mate Chandri. The guy with the useless information about hijackers?"

Nathan looked mildly surprised. "*Score one for the man who reveres all life,*" he said.

Devis was pleased with the reaction. "Rich boy makes good, eh?" He grinned. "Is that it?"

"*Yes, that's it.*"

"See you then."

Devis was still smiling that narrow-eyed chubby smirk of his when he broke the connection. Nathan turned from the communication screen. Box hadn't found anything in Michael Chandri's records about weapons development. Michael wasn't the technology buff.

"It was Chandri's father who was the inventor in the family," Theroux remarked, as if speaking the thought. "Or did I miss something?" He was watching a news update on the UK's latest computer disaster. At least one cameraman had managed to get sexy footage of airliners plunging from the sky and this was being replayed, or so it seemed, on whatever pretext the station editor could think of: "*…at this time the problem seems confined to the United Kingdom, quite why this should be is as much of mystery as precisely how it's happening.*"

"It was his old man who made the money," Nathan agreed. "Build a better locking system and the world beats a path to your door."

"And can't get in, huh?" Theroux said, but found the joke was spoiled by yet another slow motion replay of the falling aircraft. "*…the world holds its breath as it waits to see where the horror will strike next…*"

"Screen off," Theroux said and turned to look at Nathan. "I've been listening to that stuff for a while now. You want to know an interesting coincidence? It's a Blake poem that's featuring in machine failures."

Nathan was wondering if Box would have missed anything as obvious as a weapons patent. "A Blake poem?"

"'Poetry precedes disaster?' They're suggesting it's some weirdness of Blake's."

"So?"

"So Chandri said he was a Blake fan, didn't he?"

"That's what he said."

Theroux hesitated. "There's another one."

"Another poem?"

"Another coincidence. Chandri Security Systems had supply contracts with all the companies who've been hit."

"They're a big outfit," Nathan said. "They've got contracts all over. Why the sudden interest?"

Theroux looked slightly embarrassed, as though he'd been discovered indulging in some private vice. He shrugged. "I noticed them on the lists in the background briefing Box put together. I guess two coincidences are just two coincidences..." His voice trailed off, and he turned back to his screen and punched up the latest batch of work permit applications.

"Three, actually," Nathan said. "If you count the gun."

"The gun isn't a coincidence," said Theroux. "Leastways it doesn't fit with the other two."

"It doesn't fit with anything," Nathan said, his interest piqued now. He was getting that feeling again – something was wrong, or rather something was not right. "Perhaps there are a couple more questions I should put to the good doctor."

"You figure he'll answer? You heard how he feels about communications circuits."

"Forget communications circuits," Nathan said. "Questions have to be face to face. We're coppers, not market researchers. You can't tell they're sweating –"

Theroux interrupted, "-if you can't smell they're sweating, yeah, you did mention it."

Nathan smiled. "Notify Outpost Nine that I'm on my way, will you?"

"You can't go now," Theroux said.

"I can't?"

"Did you forget? Hubble's coming. So you can meet him, greet him, and fire him?"

"You do it."

"Me? Why me?"

"Privilege of rank, Chief Superintendent," Nathan said, and smiled.

"It's a privilege I can do without, thanks."

Nathan shook his head. "A privilege of my rank, not yours," he said, and smiled more broadly.

* * *

The MoRo was slower. Nathan had never been tempted to try his driving skills and this time was no different. He had fed the destination co-ordinates into the navigation computer and given the go-command and that was his only contribution to the journey. Oddly enough, he found such machine-run solo trips less stressful than travelling with other people. He put this down to not having to worry about disgracing himself. He had never considered the other possibility – that despite what he thought he believed, he actually trusted computers more than human beings. Whatever the reason though, talking to Theroux now on the communications screen while the MoRo hummed steadily onwards, he felt relaxed and in control.

"*Hubble is history,*" Theroux was saying. He looked pleased with himself.

"Just like that?"

"*He couldn't wait to resign.*"

Nathan nodded. He'd been corrupt, why would he put up a fight? "Gutless too then?"

Theroux said, "*Pal Kenzy's twice the man he'll ever be.*"

"We need replacements for both of them," Nathan said, suppressing his irritation that Theroux was still pushing the bloody woman.

Theroux's face began to fade and break up. "*And then some,*" was the last thing that got through before the Outpost Nine security computer isolated the MoRo. "The man's security obsessed," muttered Nathan, as his relaxed control faltered. The communications screen was filled with white noise. The static hiss sounded like tension.

Devis climbed up the steeply sloping central aisle of the Earth-Moon shuttle looking for unoccupied seats – preferably two, so he could spread himself a bit. He was not hopeful. All the sleeping cubicles had been booked, which suggested that there were not going to be many empty places on this flight. He hadn't expected the Temple Bay Spaceport, stuck out on the Cape York Peninsula in Northern Queensland, to be as popular as this. He hefted the three day cabin kit – '*Everything you need to stay comfortably human without weight or volume penalties*' – which he had just bought in the terminal, and pressed on past another set of the rigid, red brocade curtains which separated each block of seating from each much narrower block of couchettes.

All the seats in the next section looked to be taken too, and he was beginning to get a little out of breath. This was unlikely to be a problem for his fellow passengers, he thought, since most of them were younger than him and slimmer, still, what the fuck. Once you got off-Earth, weight and volume penalties didn't count as much – but that would be then and this was now, and the launch pad tilt was definitely getting to him. The time to be choosy was over. He decided to take whatever presented itself. And then he saw her.

"Is this one taken?" he asked, waiting politely for her to remove the flight bag from the seat beside her.

Pal Kenzy glared up at him. "You have got some kind of nerve," she said.

"You mean, it isn't," he said, and when she made no move to shift the bag, picked it up. "Allow me," he said, and stowed it in the overhead locker.

Kenzy leaned back and closed her eyes. "Security must really be shit on this run if they let ratbags like you on board," she said, as he sank gratefully into the seat and sighed his relief.

"Feel like I climbed halfway there already," he complained conversationally, then asked, "Did you manage to get a berth? Only I was too late. If you got one, maybe we could share? Turn and turn about and split the cost?"

Kenzy opened her eyes and turned to stare at him.

Devis smiled. "Or," he said, "we could use it together even. I'm very cuddly when you get to know me." Kenzy looked as though she couldn't quite believe what was happening. She seemed to struggle briefly for the right reaction. Then she laughed. To Devis it sounded like male laughter, unforced, nothing hidden in it. "Devis, you are a miserable pig," she said.

"That's better," he said. "I didn't think a fine looking woman like you would be the type to bear a grudge."

"I got the impression you didn't like women much," Kenzy said.

"Women police officers," Devis said.

"And I'm not a police officer any more."

"Unless your trip to Canberra was everything you hoped?" he asked, knowing it hadn't been.

Kenzy did her best to sound positive. "They're going to bring pressure."

Nodding, Devis said, "Are they indeed?"

"I've got contacts working on it," she said.

"Arms manufacturers and the like?"

"Yeah well you cut me out of that loop. And doubling the order just like that? Your boss plays dirty."

"He's had some ugly teachers."

"Him and me both. And it's not over yet."

Devis decided it wasn't only her arse and her laugh that he liked about this woman. "Is that why you're going back up there?"

"Out there."

"Sorry?"

"We say 'out there' not 'up there'."

"So we do, I keep forgetting. Is that why?"

"I'm entitled." For the first time, Kenzy looked genuinely defensive. "I can still find a job out there. I used to be a pretty good engineer."

"Before you discovered money?"

"I haven't been charged with anything," she said flatly.

"Push it, and that's what he'll do," Devis said seriously. "Nathan'll charge you."

She shrugged. "I can't help that."

As she said it, Devis thought he saw finally what it was that mattered to this bold woman. "You really like it out there, don't you?" he said.

"Yeah. I really like it out there."

"I can understand that."

"It's a flat-out sort of life. No whinging, no cringing."

"No weakness," Devis offered.

She shook her head. "It's not about strength or weakness, it's about… living till you die. No excuses. I reckon you can cling to life so tightly that you strangle it. Groundsiders never see that."

And then he really could understand it. "That's why you didn't care about ripping him off? The bloke I was pretending to be?"

"He didn't belong out there." It was a statement of fact.

"No sympathy for him at all."

"Sympathy'll get you killed." She looked into his face. Her eyes were bright, the vivid blue quite startling against her pale skin. "What do *you* think of it out there?" she asked.

"This is a trick question, isn't it?" he said. "Is there a prize? Rampant sex if I get it right?" But something in her expression told him he had already got it wrong. He frowned, and grunted noncommittally. "Pay's good and there's no heavy lifting." Then he couldn't help himself, and he smiled. "And it's amazing. I've been enjoying the novelty, I've got to admit."

On the seat screen, a flight attendant began an announcement. The unnatural clarity and the perfectly bland face suggested that she was probably computer-generated. *"Ladies and gentlemen, Pacific Spacelines welcome you aboard their Earth-Moon shuttle…"*

"A thrill seeker?" Kenzy was clearly not impressed with this either.

"…final countdown will begin in twenty minutes. In the meantime drinks are still being served in the main lounge…"

"What's wrong with thrills?" Devis asked, opening his travel kit and rummaging around to see if it provided anything in the way of booze. It didn't.

"It's a dumb reason for doing anything. Are you married, Devis?"

"Is this a proposal?"

"…seats are still available in sections seven and nine."

"Is this an evasion?"

"I'm not married at the moment."

"But you have been?"

"Five times. I told you I was cuddly."

"Five times and you still don't know the value of money?" Kenzy said, looking at the kit. "I can't believe you actually bought that crap."

When Nathan came out of the airlock, Chandri was waiting and fidgeting. He made no move to help with the suit helmet. This did not seem to be out of discourtesy but rather because he was distracted, totally preoccupied with his own thoughts. Free of the helmet finally, Nathan said, "I hope I'm not interrupting you, sir," and began working on his gauntlets.

"A little. You are a little," Chandri said.

Nathan frowned. On a bad day, the gauntlets could be more of a problem than the helmet – and this looked to be a bad day. "I won't take up much of your time. It's quite a minor matter. An error in your personnel file."

Chandri chortled suddenly. "You expect me to swallow that?"

"It is an offence, sir."

The amusement ended as abruptly as it had begun. "Of sufficient importance to be dealt with by the Commander of the Star Cops?"

"We're not quite up to establishment yet."

"I am of the opinion that you are on a fishing expedition," Chandri said, walking out of the reception chamber.

Nathan finished the gauntlets, and wondered whether he should take off the rest of his suit or follow as he was.

"This way if you please, Commander Spring!" Chandri called from the corridor. Clearly Nathan was not expected to waste any time. Feeling clumsy and uncomfortable, he shambled out.

In Chandri's office, nothing had changed. Plants, gods, holograms and books: everything was in its place, and the screens were still carefully blank. On the desk, an optical enhancing frame had been set up and within it were some partially analyzed electronics. Chandri sat down and gestured Nathan to a chair. "Why have you *really* come here?" he asked.

"I wanted to ask you about the laser pistol."

Chandri was silent. Nathan let the silence hang, waiting, half-expecting the man to feign ignorance. Eventually Chandri said, very softly, "Ah. That."

"You did develop it, then?"

"Of course."

"Why?"

"Because I could."

"It's a vicious thing for a man of your background."

"Weapons aren't vicious." Chandri said it without much conviction, the empty repetition of a lobbyist's paid-for argument. "Only the people who use them are vicious."

"That's the sort of drivel," Nathan said, surprised by his own anger, "that idiot gun-freaks and bomb-happy monsters like Edward Teller used to peddle. You're ashamed of it, aren't you? That's why it isn't in your records."

"My father said it was the cleverest device he'd ever seen," Chandri said.

"You made it to please your father?"

Again, the small head-turning shrug. "He is never pleased."

"They never are," Nathan said, recognizing the man's pain.

Perhaps there was sympathy in his voice. Perhaps Chandri heard it and for a second or two forgot the plan, departed a little from the carefully prepared text. Perhaps sympathy was just too much for him to leave unchallenged. "I have made a momentous discovery," he bragged, indicating the electronics on the desk. "It is of profound significance to the whole of mankind. Look."

Nathan leaned forward to peer at the small analyzer screen. "What is it you're examining?" he asked.

"This is the standard door control developed by I.T. Chandri."

"Your father."

"My father." He pointed with a micro-probe and the analyzer screen switched briefly to a visual of part of a control chip. "Do you see it?"

"What am I looking for?"

"The threat."

"I'm sorry, I don't understand."

"The invisible worm," Chandri said softly, "that flies in the night."

The shuttle had reached its preliminary orbit without incident. *"Passengers are further reminded that the remainder of the flight will be in zero-gravity. For your own safety, you are requested to remain in your seats until weightless procedures have been fully demonstrated."*

Devis slowly unclenched his buttocks and his teeth, and relaxed into post adrenaline-rush euphoria. "Lift-off's the most telling argument I've come across yet for staying out there," he said grinning.

Kenzy was smiling too. "Out *here*. 'Out there' starts here."

"Christ, we just rode the fireball, how come the computer still talks to us like we're idiots?"

Across the aisle a nondescript man in his late twenties released himself from his seat harness and floated forward along the hand grips towards the stiff curtain at the end of the section. Watching him Kenzy said, "Because some of us are."

"Obviously a man who's unimpressed by demonstrations," Devis remarked.

"I hope he knows how to use a weightless toilet," Kenzy said. "Otherwise that'll be one place to avoid for the rest of the flight."

Devis sniggered. "And one unsavoury passenger I should think," he said, leaning against his harness and reaching down into the seat pocket to pull out the Velcro soled overshoes, so that he could fit them before the instruction tape started its lecture by telling him to reach down into the seat pocket, pull out the Velcro soled overshoes, and fit them.

"The original concept of the worm programs," Chandri said, carefully manipulating the probe, "was worked out by Shoch and Hupp fifty years ago; more. Like most brilliant ideas, it was developed and perverted by the military. It became an anti-computer weapon." Nathan sipped the coffee that had been pressed on him when the mood changed, and let Chandri talk. The man seemed calmer now, almost happy as he worked and lectured. He went on, "It was like one of those hideous parasites that invade the human brain and render it useless and irredeemable. The programmes could be made self-replicating, self-defending. They could multiply and spread like any other disease."

"Computer viruses were banned by the Tokyo treaty," Nathan interrupted, "and most of them were eliminated within five years. As far as I remember almost all the signatories have retained the death penalty for, lets see, 'any person deemed to have created or aided in the creation, development, or passage of any machine virus as defined by said treaty'."

Chandri smiled without looking up from what he was doing. "All Tokyo did was to weed out the amateurs, the techno-anarchists, the cyber-biologists, the hobbyists and the inadequates. But make no mistake about what went on in government laboratories. There was a classic arms race. Development, counter development, back and forth. More and more powerful; more and more expensive. A sort of stalemate exists now within the strategic military computers. Only *they* are defended."

Nathan said, "Everything else is open to attack? Is that what you're saying?"

The skinny brunette heel-and-toed her way carefully along the central aisle from one of the rear sections. Neither Devis nor Kenzy paid her much attention as she passed through, though afterwards when Kenzy thought about it she realized that the young woman had walked with a movement that was practised but not expert, as if she'd done it before but never for real. She wondered too if that was why the announcement was not a total surprise.

"*There is a message for passenger Wilberforce.*" The computer voice was as bland as ever. "*Will passenger Wilberforce report to the flight deck, please. Passenger Wilberforce to the flight deck, please.*"

"What's the matter?" Devis asked, as Kenzy stirred in her seat. She was frowning. "That's a security code," she said.

"What is?"

"'Wilberforce'."

"You sure?"

"Crime in progress," she said.

"'Passenger Wilberforce to the flight deck'? Christ, you know what that sounds like, don't you?" said Devis.

Kenzy said, "Nobody hijacks these things. Where the fuck is there to go?"

"Rich boy makes good again," Devis said, more or less to himself.

"There it is." Chandri extracted the speck from the control system and placed it in the analyzer beam. He watched the screen for a moment, and then said, "As I thought. It is silicon. Old fashioned, uncomplicated, robust. A chip which sits in the door lock, waiting for a code message to activate it. The code is Blake's poem, a line from which prompts the chip to use power from the unit to send programming instructions to the main computer down this." He indicated an optical fibre. "One of my father's innovations was a simple, control interface between his lock and any computer."

"It's an old fashioned virus programme?" Nathan asked.

Chandri inclined his head in a small nod. "It kills the computer and then it self-destructs with a second line from the poem." He looked up. "Elegant." His tone asked for approval.

Devis had released himself from the seat harness and drifted upwards to peer round the section. "What sort of security have they got on this thing?" he asked.

"What do you think?" Kenzy said pulling the gun case from the under seat locker and unclipping the laser pistol.

Devis tugged himself down. "No reaction so far," he said, and then he saw the pistol. "Christ, how did you get that on board?"

"I used my Star Cop ID."

"That's been cancelled." She shrugged and adjusted the setting on the pistol. He nodded. "The lazy bastards didn't bother to check, did they? You know impersonating a police officer is an offence."

"Yeah, I was worried about that."

He held out his hand. "I'll take the gun, Kenzy."

"Go fuck yourself," she said, concealing the pistol carefully in the knee pouch of her coveralls.

"You've got no official standing here," he said.

She pushed out of her seat, floated neatly past him and tugged herself down onto the aisle's Velcro strip. "Your standing's pretty shaky too by the look of it. I'm the one with the experience in zero-G."

Devis knew that arguing would be a waste of time – and anyway, she was right. "Okay," he said, "but we've got to decide what we're going to do."

"What do you expect me to do?" Nathan asked.

"Crimes have been committed," Chandri said. "A railway tunnel, a chemical complex, airports. People have been killed."

Nathan looked at him steadily, and said, "To what end, Dr. Chandri?"

"Soon, perhaps, someone will say 'do as we tell you or more people will die'."

"And how did you find all this out?"

Chandri began to rummage through the drawers of his desk. "It was the last thing our intelligent listening system discovered."

Nathan nodded. "Before that virus programme got in and destroyed your machines?"

"Yes."

It was time, Nathan thought, to confront him. He had led him as far towards confession as he could, now he had to accuse. "No," Nathan said flatly.

Chandri straightened up and pointed a laser pistol at him. "Yes," he said equally flatly.

Devis and Kenzy slid the curtain aside just enough to get a look into the next section. Passengers were stretching and relaxing much as they themselves had been doing before the security alert. Devis set his face in a scowl and then folded the curtain back with a flourish. As he began to heel-and-toe his way through, he glanced back over his shoulder and said in a loud voice, "I don't care what your ticket said, madam, that berth is mine."

Following behind him Kenzy snarled theatrically, "I'm not going to argue with you, no-neck. Let's just find us a flight attendant and *they* can sort it out."

No-one in the section showed them anything more than casual curiosity. If the hijackers had left anyone on watch, they obviously weren't this far back from the action.

"Why could you not just take my word and go?" Chandri asked. "I suppose you knew all along that the intelligent listening project was a failure." He was having difficulty holding the gun on Nathan while tapping in the verse line that he needed.

And –

Nathan tried to edge closer. "The information you gave us was what the military had given you wasn't it? They wanted you to find that anarchist group as a demonstration of your progress."

– his –

Chandri gestured him back with the gun. "But we had made none," he said. "I had the briefest hope that you might buy us a little time."

"Dr. Chandri, this is pointless," Nathan said, trying to keep the tension out of his voice. "I mean, how would you explain all this if one of your project team walked in right now?"

– dark –

Chandri stopped touching out the code and switched on the screen links with the rest of the outpost. In various work cubicles what had been four men and three women were sprawled and stiffening. Most of them had been shot in the back. "*You* did that?" Nathan asked and when Chandri did not reply asked, "*Why* did you do that?"

"I had no choice. I knew what they thought. They had begun to question my authority." Chandri returned his attention to loading the code.

"Is that why you bugged them?" Nathan asked sharply, hoping to get his full attention. "Bugged coveralls? A bit paranoid that, surely?"

Chandri looked up, surprised. "You knew about that?"

"Of course. You were right. I didn't come here because of your personnel file. We know all about you and what you've done." *It sounds thin*, Nathan thought, *he's a long way from sane, but he's further from stupid... keep talking*. "The engineers who installed those chips for you are being arrested right now."

"I installed them myself. And I tracked the consignments."

You don't lie with specifics, you idiot, he's not stupid, keep talking, "Tokyo makes them responsible."

But Chandri had already gone back to the code.

– secret –

"Why are you doing this?" Nathan almost shouted. "It can't be because you're afraid of failure."

Chandri looked up again and smiled. "But I won't fail, don't you see? There are already rumours linking what has happened in the tunnel with the chemical plant and the airports. A conspiracy is suspected."

"So they've asked you to find the conspirators," Nathan said, the realization clear in his voice, "I see."

"Do you also see that when my computers are destroyed in an identical way it will prove that we found what we were looking for. We found the worm and it killed us. It will prove that we were a success."

"And at the same time, eliminate all evidence of failure. Bravo." Nathan clapped ironically. "Your father would be proud of you. If he didn't already know what a pathetic and feeble failure you are and if he wasn't already deeply disappointed in you."

Chandri looked stricken. He lowered the pistol. Then, as pain turned to rage and he raised his aim again, Nathan jumped at him and grabbed the hand holding the pistol and slammed it down onto the desk top and held it there while he punched and smashed furiously at Chandri's wrist and arm. When Chandri's hold loosened Nathan stopped hitting and wrenched the pistol away from him. He stepped back breathing hard. "Right," he said. "Enough of this shit."

Ignoring him Chandri completed the code line.

– *love* –

"Every system in this outpost," he said, "is linked to my computers. When they die..." He made a small gesture with his hands like releasing a bird – and then, before Nathan could react, he cued the transmission signal.

In the reception chamber the normal function indicator on the airlock hatch flickered.

Nathan tugged at Chandri's arm in a vain attempt to get him to his feet. "We have to get out of here. If the control systems do fail, explosive decompression will take this place apart." Chandri leaned back in his chair like a wayward child. "You are too late, Commander Spring," he muttered stubbornly.

Nathan reached past him and keyed the main control. "Open the surface access lock," he instructed. "Security computer, open the cargo bay surface access lock." There was no acknowledgement from the machine and he watched in horror as on the monitor screen was flashed up: *And – his – dark – secret – love –* each word fading into the next.

Without warning, Chandri snatched at the pistol and pulled it to him, holding it against his chest. Nathan felt his soft fingers pluck at the trigger. The flash was barely discernible even when Chandri dragged the muzzle across his chest cutting through tissue and bone, puncturing his lungs, searing his heart.

"I count three," Kenzy whispered.

Devis looked over her shoulder. There were three that he could see; two men and a woman. One of the men was talking over the bulkhead communicator to the flight crew, obviously demanding access to the control deck, which – equally obviously – he was not about to get. The second man was watching the silent passengers in the crowded section. Devis swayed around, trying to see more through the tiny crack in the curtain. His view was obscured and he couldn't see what exactly was happening. *What did these scumbags have to negotiate with? Why was everyone so still and silent?* "I can't see any weapons," he murmured. As he said this, the man at the communicator gestured angrily at the girl, and she hauled a female flight attendant into view, and shoved some sort of transparent blade at her throat. So that was it. "I bet the security scanners don't look for glass."

"The operatives should," Kenzy breathed.

Devis smiled. "Nobody's perfect. You of all people should know that," he said softly, and thought, *but one crystal blade's not enough for all this attention.*

Nathan shambled with clumsy haste down the corridor. He couldn't control-hop, and his attempts to run bounced him against the sides, and stumbled him onto his knees. The spacesuit was hot and awkward and he was already breathing hard and sweating. Around him, the lights dimmed briefly and then brightened again. Was it real or was it just the sweat dripping into his eyes?

He reached the reception chamber and pressed the airlock hatch release. Nothing. He pressed it again, and without waiting to see the result, turned away and crossed to where he had left his gauntlets and helmet. He struggled to push his shaking hands into the stiff gloves. Calm, he thought, be calm. He fumbled at the first of the wrist seals. He was desperate to turn and look and see whether the hatch had opened. Pointless. If it hadn't, he was dead anyway. If it had and he couldn't get these fucking gloves on, he was dead anyway. "Stop it!" he said aloud. "Stop thinking like that, and get the fuck on with it!" The lights dimmed. This time there was no doubt about it.

* * *

Star Cops

Devis flexed his neck and took a couple of deep breaths. "You ready?"

Kenzy nodded. "Let's do it."

Devis started forward then paused and looked back at her. "And listen," he said softly, "don't bother with any of that 'armed police officer, drop your weapons' bullshit, right? Just shoot the fuckers."

She held the pistol vertically in front of her in the ready position, and nodded again.

Devis took a last peek at what was going on. The frightened flight attendant was talking into the communicator.

At the third attempt, Nathan sealed the second gauntlet. The lights were bright again. And getting brighter. He lifted the helmet, ducked his head into it, slotted it home. He switched on the suit systems, glanced at the telltales, all green, he was ready, he had to turn now, and look, and see if he was dead. He turned. The airlock hatch was still closed.

Devis pushed his way past the curtain, sliding it only half way open so that Kenzy remained hidden. "Look, what the fuck is going on here?" he demanded loudly as he heel-and-toed his way uncertainly towards the hijackers. He avoided looking at them by concentrating owlishly on his unmanageable feet, and he declaimed as he struggled to make progress, "I'm dying for a drink and bursting for a piss and some disembodied voice tells me to stay in my seat. Then they go away for fucking ever."

The man by the communicator shouted, "Hold it!"

"That's just my point, I can't," Devis complained still watching his feet. "And a man's gotta do what a man's gotta do, right? How the fuck do you walk on this stuff?"

Nathan felt nothing. The rush of panic and despair did not come. The worst had happened and it was a sort of relief. There was nothing he could do. Slowly he walked across to the hatch. Behind him a lighting circuit blew out as the systems began overloading. He stared at the airlock hatch, and it opened. He continued to stare at it. He still had a chance. He might just be able to outrun the explosion. He stood transfixed, paralyzed with hope. And then terror hit him. He plunged into the airlock and stabbed furiously at the controls.

Devis approached the hijackers and finally looked up. "Well, I'm buggered!" he said, affecting to see the flight attendant for the first time. "A hostess. I began to think there weren't any." Now that he wasn't looking at his feet, he deliberately tangled them up and got himself detached from the aisle. "Oh fuck it!" he yelled, flailing his arms.

The three hijackers were momentarily mesmerized by the performance. They did nothing as Devis grabbed at the flight attendant and used a seat grip to pull himself and her to one side. Kenzy's shout from the other end of the section took them completely by surprise.

"Freeze! Nobody move!" she yelled.

Only the girl reacted. Without any change of expression, she thrust the blade at the flight attendant. Devis twisted to deflect the blow with his arm. Kenzy fired. The shot was a tiny flare on the side of the girl's head, and the force went out of the blade as she died.

Nathan clambered into the cab of the MoRo. He was shaking with exhaustion. He didn't wait for the greens on steps and door seals but strapped himself straight in and powered up the systems. Only when the motors were humming did he acknowledge to himself that the cargo bay access cover had not fully retracted. Tension ached through him. He opened a communications channel. "This is Moonrover Seven, Moonrover Seven, open main cargo hatch please." To his surprise, the cover started to move. It rolled back a little, it rolled slowly and jerkily, and then it jammed.

"Shit!" he shouted. "Shit!" He pounded numbly on the joystick. "Stop fucking me about, you bastard!"

With a flash and a spray of dull sparks, the bay lights went out and the movement died.

The corpse of the girl slouched over Devis like a sullen drunk at a bad party. He pushed her aside. "Thanks a lot, Kenzy," he complained. "Why didn't you do like I said?"

Kenzy was holding the weightless pistol parallel with her shoulder and sighting down her arm at a point midway between the two remaining hijackers. "Give it up!" she shouted at them. "I'll kill you where you stand!"

The tension went out of the two men, and they raised their arms in surrender. Devis noticed for the first time how young they both were. Not a good sign, normally. Testosterone was not the reasoning hormone.

"Get their weapons," Kenzy said.

Throughout the section, passengers began to unbuckle themselves from their seat harnesses. "Everybody stay where you are," Devis ordered loudly, grabbing the closer of the two young men and binding his arms behind his back with self-tightening plastic wristlinks. "Stay in your seats! It's not over yet!"

"You got that right," the other one said and held out his fist towards Devis.

"Move again and you're dead and gone!" Kenzy shouted, aiming the pistol.

Unmoved, the man opened his fist a little and Devis saw for the first time the real threat. "Easy!" he called to Kenzy. "Take it easy. He goes, we all go."

Nathan heaved. The cover wouldn't budge. He didn't dare put his shoulder against it for fear of damaging the suit, so he put his gauntlets flat against the leading edge, braced his arms and pushed. Almost imperceptibly, the cover began to roll back. Behind him, he could hear the airlock doors collapsing. It was impossible; this was a vacuum, and there could be no sound in a vacuum, but it made no difference – he could hear the terrifying roar, he could feel the ripping force of the shattering burst. He pushed more frantically.

The bomb was a delicate glass sphere about the size of a golf ball. On the street, it was known as a nitro globe, and though Devis couldn't remember the technical name for the colourless liquid inside it, he knew that if it was exposed to oxygen the bang was hot and huge. The young man made a cage of his fingers and bounced the globe around inside it.

"Christ," Kenzy said, "they really didn't scan for glass, did they?"

Devis moved towards him. "Easy, son," he said. "You don't want to kill all these people. What would that achieve? Give that to me now."

The arm flexed, as if to throw. "I'm not your son."

Devis stopped trying to get near him.

On the screen in Chandri's office, the poem ended: *And – his – dark – secret – love – Does – thy – life – destroy.* And as the last word disappeared, so did every control system in Outpost Nine. Nathan jammed the joystick forward and gunned the MoRo at the gap left by the partially open access hatch.

* * *

"Give it up! Do it, you little fucker! Do it *now*!" Kenzy yelled aiming the pistol squarely between the hijacker's eyes. He did not hesitate. His arm arced forward. Kenzy shot him through the forehead. It was too late to stop the action. Already dead, he threw the bomb at her.

With maximum power to every wheel, the MoRo heaved into the opening. Nathan felt the wrenching impact, a soundless jarring through the unpressurized cabin. He ignored the collision damage lights and kept the drives on full.

Kenzy saw the nitro globe spinning at her, flashing and glistening like a soap bubble, rising high as it came, high towards the top of the bulkhead. She lost sight of it against the lights.

The MoRo lurched free and out into the rockscape. Nathan cancelled the safety overrides. Accelerating hard, he plunged it down the side of the crater. He glanced at the rear-view screen. A plume of vapour was venting through the coarse dust and rock covering the outpost. It could only be seconds before everything blew. "Faster, you bastard," he muttered. "Faster." It would be over in seconds. He would be dead in seconds. He could do nothing to escape it.

The globe flew away from Devis, smaller and smaller. He saw Kenzy raise her arm. Was she waving? Death was high beyond her outstretched arm.

The MoRo lunged and pitched. *Faster, you bastard, faster.*

Kenzy couldn't see it. It was there, but she couldn't see it. She detached herself, floated upwards arm out. It was there flashing in the light. She reached for it stretching her arm stretching her fingers too fast too far.
The flash was fierce and gone. Shock wave and debris smashed through the dark.
Kenzy's fingers pulled the globe into her hand. She barely resisted the urge to clutch it tightly in her relief and triumph. "Yes!" Devis yelled and passengers began to applaud.

The MoRo was far enough away and low enough down onto the

crater floor to survive the explosion which had destroyed Outpost Nine. Nathan applied the brakes and sat in the gently swaying cab feeling sick and exhilarated. He found he was breathless as though he had just stopped running. He was laughing as he checked the systems for damage.

"Are you all right?" Devis asked taking the nitro globe carefully – very, very carefully.

Kenzy was quietly gleeful. "I'm better than all right," she said. "I'm a bloody hero. When the press get hold of this, you and I are *both* going to be bloody heroes. Let's see that mongrel Spring try to fire me then."

"Always assuming they let the press get hold of it," Devis said. "Pacific Spacelines are a pretty rich outfit, if you know what I mean."

"Michael Chandri's younger brother Sajiit, now sole heir to the Chandri fortune, said tonight that his father would have been very proud of the sacrifice that Michael had made." The picture of Michael Chandri was flatteringly youthful. *"Investigations continue into what exactly happened –"*

"Sound off," Nathan said, and the newscast was silent.

"How long do you think they can keep it away from the press?" Theroux asked.

Nathan poured himself another coffee and shrugged. "The man was a mass murderer," he said. "Difficult to keep that in the family."

Theroux frowned. "I'm still not sure I buy the motive." He smiled. "No offence. I mean it's pretty damned elaborate wouldn't you say?"

"He had the resources to make it work," Nathan said. "And an abiding horror of falling short of what his father expected of him."

"Yeah but he must have set the whole thing up at the first sign of difficulty with that intelligent listening project."

"At the first hint of the possibility of failure," Nathan agreed. He sipped his coffee. For some reason Lee was in his mind. He was thinking that death was infinite. Forever, lonely, terrifying, empty, never again. He felt his heart flop in his chest like a suffocating fish. He took a deep breath. Too much coffee, he thought, have to watch that.

"No," Theroux said. "I could accept it maybe if his father was still alive. Old man Chandri's been dead for how long–?"

"Five years," Nathan said. "Death doesn't stop you trying to please your father. It just makes it a bit more difficult."

Theroux grinned, and nodded at the mute but still running newscast.

"Hey they're on again," he said. "Sound."

"*We'd had a tip-off about a possible hijack attempt,*" Kenzy was saying to one of the scrum of reporters fighting for her attention as she and Devis made their triumphal way through the Temple Bay Spaceport. "*Commander Spring was responsible for us being on the flight.*"

"She's quick," Theroux said. "You've got to allow she's quick."

"Incompetent shuttle security," said Nathan grimly, "and I'm stuck with a corrupt cop."

"*The ISPF will be pressing for a general reorganization of shuttle security,*" Kenzy went on.

"You going to reinstate her, then?" Theroux asked.

"She's reinstating herself," Nathan said. "Listen to the bloody woman!"

"*And now that Nathan Spring is running things, the Star Cops can get the job done. Can't we, Colin?*"

"*Oh absolutely, Pal,*" said Devis, with a perfectly straight face.

Trivial Games and Paranoid Pursuits

It was there. Lauter resisted the urge to say I told you so, but only until they got visual confirmation. "Now what do you think of my drunken journo?" she crowed, as they watched the module tumbling slowly against the blackness.

Marty still looked unconvinced and unenthusiastic. His round, pale face remained irritatingly expressionless. "I think she was lucky they didn't deport her," he said. "I would have done."

Lauter smiled and snorted but her violet eyes never left the screen. "You didn't like her because she fancied me."

"I've got nothing against the odd muff-muncher," he said. "But that one was decidedly odd."

"Like you would know," Lauter chortled. "And anyway there wouldn't have been a scrap hauler left on Moonbase if the alcohol regs had been enforced. Half the Guild were blind that night."

"Some of them probably still are," Marty said. "Rocket fuel tends to do that to your visual cortex." He punched up a computer simulation of the cylinder's motion and its dimensions relative to the salvage shuttle's cargo bay. "Can we stop it, do you think?"

Lauter hadn't come this far to go back empty. She sighed patiently. "Be serious, dear heart," she said.

"Can we stop it *safely*? That's what I mean. And get it in the hold? It's a big bugger."

"It's a standard module." Lauter was getting impatient. "No bigger than she said it would be. It'll fit. You know it'll fit."

"Don't tell me what I know. You know I hate it when you do that," Marty said.

Lauter ignored the prompt to further bickering. "Is the trajectory right?"

Marty already had the confirmation from the navcom. "It'll drop into the sun eventually."

Lauter closed her eyes and sighed. Everything was definitely right. "Everything's definitely right," she crooned. This was better than sex. "This is better than sex."

"If you say so."

"She promised us a jackpot, lover."

"A possible jackpot," Marty said. "Sorry a possh-ible shack-pot." He burped loudly. "Shhcushe me, doll."

"She wasn't that pissed."

"It was meant to be you," he said, without smiling.

Lauter reached over and pinched the soft flesh on the inside of his right thigh. "Listen, misery-guts, we've got them every which way to Christmas, and you know it."

He pulled her hand away. "You're doing it again."

"One." She held up a finger. "It could be a fuck-up and someone wants it back," she said, rehearsing again the arguments for the retrieval.

"Even though it's not on anyone's list," he said, more or less automatically.

She held up a second finger. "Two. It could be stuffed with goodies." It was like a litany.

He said, "Even though it's not on anyone's list." An almost ritual response.

A third finger. "Three. There's the scrap value."

"Wouldn't be worth the fuel to haul it back," he said.

"And four." She held up a fourth finger and Marty looked at her in surprise. There shouldn't have been any more. "Last, but a long way short of least, there's the hazard to navigation premium."

"It's a long way short of navigation too," Marty said scornfully. "All those commercial flights into the sun? They'll pay top whack for getting this thing out of their way, won't they? Your reasoning is flawless, as ever. How does she do it, I ask myself?"

"Well we're not going to tell them precisely *where* we picked it up," she said, in the purring voice he claimed irritated him but she knew made him horny. "That would be silly wouldn't it, Marty dear heart?"

"And how do you propose we get away with that?"

"I will lie through my teeth. You will falsify the computer records. It's called teamwork."

"You're a bad person, Lauter," he said.

"And you're putty in my hands," she said, this time stroking the inside of his thigh.

They had stabilized the module quite easily using the strap-on jet packs which Marty had attached on his first EVA. Now, on his second stint outside, he was attempting to manoeuvre it into the cargo bay. Despite the bulk of the thing the procedure should have presented no real problem but for some reason he was having trouble lining up the remote handling arm.

Lauter was not being much help. "*Marty, sweetness? How much longer is it going to take to secure the fucking thing?*" she murmured over the suit radio. Marty suspected she thought he was trying to abort this pickup because he was nervous about it. She was always complaining that he was overcautious. Wimpy, she called it. "If you can do it faster," he grumbled, "get suited-up and get your arse out here."

"*Such tantrums,*" she chided.

"I shouldn't have let you talk me into this," he said, straining to see what was snagging the huge cylinder and keeping it out of the holding cradles.

"*Your mother must have told you there'd be women like me.*"

He couldn't see any reason why it didn't come straight in. It was just a standard construction module. No sign of any major damage. Access was sealed off and a couple of long-burn directional drives had been bolted onto the equipment lugs. It was odd, but there was nothing obviously sinister about it. "I don't like this," he said. "There's something not good about this, Lauter."

"*You can be good or you can be rich, Marty my love,*" she purred. "*You can't be both.*"

"So it seems." Only he hadn't been talking about the ethics of Lauter's plan. He'd been talking about the feeling he was getting. She'd really have thought he was wimpy if he'd said it out loud. But there was no escaping it. The thing was creeping him out. It was spooky as fuck.

Odile Goodman waited with growing impatience for the corporate logo to finish playing. The fanfare from *Also Sprach Zarathustra* accompanied a montage of station graphics, grainy footage of pioneers Armstrong and Aldrin, and a mechanically enhanced old glory waving clumsily in space. It was finally replaced by the perfect receptionist announcing, with just the right mix of pride and eagerness to be of service, "*This is the United States Space Station Ronald Reagan. My name is Suzette, how may I help you?*"

Odile sat back down at the house's main console and said brusquely, "Connect me with Section OMZ 13."

The receptionist's response was immediate. "*I'm sorry, but there is no section of that designation.*"

"You sure?" Odile asked – then thought better of the question, and said, "Just connect me with Dr. Goodman."

"*I'm sorry but there is no Dr. Goodman presently on the station.*"

"Dr. Harvey Goodman."

"*I'm sorry,*" the receptionist repeated and smiled encouragingly. "*Is there someone else I may contact for you?*"

"Dr. Harvey Goodman," Odile enunciated slowly and clearly, as though talking to a deaf child, "has been working on the station for more than a year."

The receptionist did not take offence at the tone. "*I can find no listing for a Dr. Harvey Goodman.*"

"Transfer me to a human being," Odile instructed.

"*The information I have given you has been checked and rechecked and is correct,*" the computer-generated receptionist confirmed politely.

"I don't want to argue with a PR graphic. Connect me with a human being," Odile said. "Now, Suzette. Now. Do it *now*." She was pleased to see the receptionist's smiling face freeze-frame briefly before it faded. It was always satisfying to induce failures, however small, in the smooth running of marketing machines. Another face appeared on the screen. There was no logical reason to assume that this was the human being she had insisted on but Odile was reassured to see that the man looked tired and a touch irritable. A superimposed caption identified him as Pete Lennox, Duty Personnel Controller. "*Yes ma'am, how can I help you?*" he said without bothering to smile.

"There's some sort of computer foul-up," Odile began.

"*When is there not?*" Lennox interrupted wearily. "*And your name is?*"

"Goodman. Odile Goodman."

"*Well, Ms. Goodman, if this involves salary allocation, I am going to have to ask you to be patient with us.*"

Odile said, "I'm trying to contact Dr. Harvey Goodman. Your communications computer doesn't have a listing."

Lennox yawned and rubbed his eyes. "*I'll cross-check it for you.*" He yawned again. "*Sorry, it's been a long day. How are you spelling Goodman?*"

Odile spelled the name and Lennox looked away from the screen. When he looked back he said, "*Nope.*"

"What do you mean, no?"

"*No reference to arrival, departure, allocation of resources, nothing.*"

"He has to be there."

Star Cops

"*Do you have a section for him?*" Lennox asked. "*A designated work area?*"

"OMZ 13?"

"*We don't have any outer modules designated thirteen. On account of it's an unlucky number.*" He thought for a moment and then said, "*This Dr. Goodman… would he be, uh… would he be your husband ma'am?*"

"Harvey's my brother," Odile said.

Lennox looked relieved. "*I see. Is it possible you've got the wrong station, Ms. Goodman?*"

"Anything's possible, Mr. Lennox," Odile said. "Thank you for your time."

"*You're quite welcome.*"

Odile stared unseeingly as the smiling receptionist came back on the screen. "*Thank you for calling Ronald Reagan, the station which works to keep your peace of mind in mind,*" it said.

"Right now, someone, somewhere, is committing a crime," Kenzy said to no-one in particular as Theroux went through the main office on his way to the Moonbase central complex. He paused to check that his new ID tag was straight on the breast pocket of his dress coveralls. He was pleased with 'Chief Superintendent David Theroux'. It looked pretty good, if a little long. "Some friend of yours?" he asked.

"Oh that's very funny," Kenzy said. She jabbed at her screen's hold icon. "My job description reads 'cop' not filing clerk."

Theroux ignored the complaint. "I'll be a couple of hours, okay?"

Kenzy got up from the workstation and went to pour herself some coffee. "You going to ask how come they sent the guy out from Earth instead of nominating one of their base people?"

Theroux shrugged. "It's not against the rules."

"It's against custom and practice," Kenzy said. "And those bastards never do anything without a reason."

"Does anyone?" he said. "Pretty much by definition."

"Something wily and oriental," Kenzy said, and shook her head pityingly. "Probably too subtle for the American mind."

Theroux shrugged, and sighed. "So, if making this guy Base Co-ordinator is the first step on the road to world domination, and they don't come right out and admit it, right there over the soya snacks and fruit juice, then basically I'm screwed." He started towards the doors. "Any unsubtle messages, you know where I'll be."

"Listen, I'm a hero, not a fucking receptionist and filing clerk," Kenzy complained again.

"You've got to stop playing those press conferences vids," Theroux said without looking back.

"Maybe I should give another one," Kenzy called after him, "tell the world how our beloved leader is treating the Moon Shuttle hijack hero."

"Bent cop reinstated, praises tolerance of boss, that sort of thing?"

"Fuck you, smart arse," Kenzy muttered.

Theroux stopped in the doorway. "Fuck you, *Chief Superintendent* smartass." He was grinning. "Unless you want to join Kirk Hubble in the ranks of the ex-cops?"

"Hubble was gutless," Kenzy said. "And witless. Even for an American."

"He was smart enough to recognize a losing hand when he was dealt one."

"Meaning I'm not?"

"Are you?"

"I'll play these."

Theroux nodded. "I had a feeling you weren't."

"No-one pushes me into resigning."

"I'm impressed."

"And in charge," Kenzy mocked. "And there was me thinking the good Commander had no sense of humour."

"Where you're concerned, he doesn't, Kenzy."

"Unlike you. You think it's all a big joke, don't you?"

"Frankly my dear," Theroux said doing his best Clark Gable imitation, "I don't give a damn." Then, stepping past the first door, he continued in the same voice, "Strange girl. Only one I ever met who enjoyed filing enough to spend the rest of their life doing it."

"Yes, Kenzy?" Nathan peered at the small face which glowered out at him from the screen on the orbit shuttle's instrument panel.

"*I'm going to resign, sir.*"

"Fine," Nathan said. This was his preferred solution to the problem she posed but he was surprised that she had given up so easily. "Get a hard copy, sign it and have the signature witnessed, leave it on my workstation." The pilot, pretending not to listen, looked surprised and Nathan realized that his response must have sounded pretty casual, brutal even.

Star Cops

"You didn't let me finish, Commander," Kenzy protested. *"What I was about to say is that I'm going to resign unless I get something more interesting to do."*

Nathan was even more offhand. "Fine. Get a hard copy, sign it and have the signature witnessed, leave it on my workstation." He could have told himself he was being cruel to be kind, but he suspected he was just being cruel. Truth was, he resented the woman. There was corruption in every organisation, it was natural, but just because it was natural that didn't mean you had to live with it. Except that because of her, it seemed, he did.

"Yeah, well, that's obviously shaken you to the core," she said.

"I don't want you to have any illusions about your future."

"I reckon the press might find your attitude interesting."

"I think the press are about as reliable as you are."

"I'm not resigning, Commander."

"And about as consistent."

"If you want to get rid of me you're going to have to fire me."

"Yes," Nathan said and leaned away to look out of the forward observation port. He didn't expect to be able to see the *Ronald Reagan* yet, the signal from the radar beacon put it well beyond line of sight, but the move took him out of screen vision. Without bothering to move back, he asked, "Now, is there something else, Kenzy, or did you call simply to play musical resignations?"

"Your ETA?"

"As logged."

"Any other orders?"

"Theroux's giving the orders. If you've got a problem with that –"

"Get a hard copy, sign it and have the signature witnessed, leave it on your workstation."

Nathan leaned back and glared at the screen. "And Kenzy, I don't want any more nonsense like this while I'm talking to the Americans."

"You don't want me to call you at work, dear?"

"Don't push it, Inspector," Nathan said. "I let you off once but I don't intend to make a habit of it," and he broke the connection.

"You smug bastard!" Kenzy raged at the blank screen.

Behind her a voice said, "Unforgiving soul, our Commander Spring."

Kenzy turned to find Colin Devis smirking his chubby smile. "How long have you been there?" she demanded.

"Private row, was it?"

"There's one thing I really don't like about you, Colin," she said.

Devis said, "Only one? This could be the start of a beautiful friendship."

"You're one of nature's lurkers."

"That's it?" His smile broadened and his eyes almost disappeared. "I married five wives with more objections to my character than that."

"Not all women are bright," Kenzy said and cued her workscreen.

"Be nice to me," said Devis, moving close behind her and breathing on her neck, "and I'll put in a word for you with the Man."

Kenzy did not react, but said flatly, "I can put in my own word, thanks all the same."

Devis shrugged, and went to get coffee. "Suit yourself, but I can't see 'smug bastard' having the effect you're looking for," he said. "Try waggling your bum, that's probably your best bet."

"Worked for you did it?" she said, adding, "Get that, will you?" as the message icon began to flash on the main communications screen.

"Sorry," Devis said, "I'm off-shift. Don't start for another four hours. I only came in hoping for a grope."

"A lazy pervert," Kenzy said.

"Cuddly, though. Very cuddly," said Devis, leaving with his coffee.

Kenzy keyed the communications link and said automatically, "Star Cops Headquarters, Inspector Pal Kenzy –" and stopped as Theroux appeared on screen.

"*Listen,*" he said, keeping his voice low and leaning in so that his face almost filled the frame, "*he wants to visit us.*"

Behind him, Kenzy caught glimpses of the guests milling about in the Secretariat reception suite. Among the token efforts to give the occasion the appropriate look, several Chinese had been drafted in from somewhere to act as waiters, and she could see them scurrying about with trays of ethnic looking snacks. "Do we care a lot?" she asked.

"*Just warning you, is all,*" he said quietly.

She bristled. "Warning me?"

Theroux looked exasperated. "*Alerting you, for Chrissakes. Don't be so touchy.*"

"Okay, so I'm alerted. What do you expect me to do now, rush round with a duster, change my underwear, what?"

"*Try looking busy,*" Theroux said, and broke the connection.

* * *

Star Cops

The *Ronald Reagan* was more imposing than its computer-manipulated graphic, which made Nathan wonder why their publicity people hadn't used actual images. Presumably there was a reason, just as there would be a reason why his shuttle had been routed to red three-four, one of the outermost docking locks, normally used for off-loading construction materials.

"If you'd put us any further out," the pilot had remarked when he received his instructions, "we'd be building the damn dock ourselves." But the irritation was wasted on a traffic control computer that was only following orders, as it politely pointed out.

"Can you get resupplied from here?" Nathan asked as he disembarked.

"Oh yeah, that's no problem," the pilot said. "The problem is it's a major trek to administration, or any of the messes, or anywhere. Always assuming you can find what you're looking for. They keep adding to the damn place. It's a regular labyrinth."

Nathan pushed his bag through the hatch and floated feet first after it. "I imagine they've got indicators of some sort," he said.

"Only the *strictly no entry* kind."

"Whatever's left must be the way, then," Nathan said, and smiled. "Sherlock Holmes school of navigation."

The pilot grinned. "Good luck, Commander."

Minutes later, Nathan was lost.

As lost as he could ever remember being.

Jiang Li Ho was more than six feet tall, heavyset and cheerfully extrovert: a combination which tended to disconcert people, most of whom, it seemed, still thought of Chinese as short, skinny and inscrutable. In his sixty years, Ho had learned to exploit the surprise his appearance engendered and he used it shamelessly to take the initiative in meetings and negotiations. It helped to make him a successful career scientist and a formidable politician. Now, as he followed Theroux into the main office, he was chuckling disarmingly.

Kenzy took her feet off the workstation just quickly enough to avoid being obviously discourteous, and stood up slowly.

Ho beamed and bustled across to her. "You are Inspector Pal Kenzy. I saw your news conference and read of your bravery," he said, taking her hand and making a small formal bow. "I am Jiang Li Ho and it is my great honour to meet you in, if you will pardon my boldness, the flesh."

He managed, without leering or stressing the word, to make 'flesh' sound disgraceful and funny. Kenzy was struck by how big the man was – and how cheering. She smiled. "I'm pleased to meet you, sir," she said, and was surprised to find that she actually meant it.

Ho looked serious. "It has long been my view," he said, "that popular entertainment has trivialized courage to the point that we no longer value it as we should."

"Can't argue with that," Kenzy said. "I'm certainly undervalued."

Ho said, "Most people who come out here are," and, turning with practised charm to include Theroux in the conversation, added, "Are they not, David?"

Theroux looked at Kenzy and said, "Some more than others."

Ho began to wander about the office, peering unselfconsciously at the equipment. "The ISPF is a most important organisation," he said, "most important. There is always a criminal element. In all societies. This one is no different."

"Where there's living, there's policemen," said Theroux. "The gospel according to Nathan Spring."

"Ah yes," said Ho pausing in his examination of a workstation. "You said the reason for Commander Spring's absence...?"

Theroux said, "He's away working, sir."

"On the Americans," Kenzy put in.

"Is there a problem with your countrymen, David?"

The question was a delicate combination of curiosity and polite concern. It fooled Theroux completely. "No, sir, no problem. It's just a routine meeting," he said.

"I see," Ho said gravely. "So a routine meeting with the Americans is more important than a first meeting with me." It was an awkward moment. Theroux wasn't sure whether Ho was serious or not. He hesitated. Kenzy caught his eye. She looked amused at his discomfiture.

"Is that what you are telling me?" Ho continued.

Theroux said, "Well, it's not entirely routine, sir. There's a slight problem about putting Star Cops on American stations."

"They won't let us," Kenzy said grinning.

Ho looked towards the coffee percolator. "It is said," he said, "that this office has the best coffee on Moonbase."

"May we offer you a cup?" Theroux asked, his relief obvious.

"That would be most pleasant," said Jiang Li Ho smiling.

Theroux glanced at Kenzy, but thought better of it and hurried to pour the coffee himself.

It had taken Nathan nearly two hours to find his way to the administration office and then to Mess Room One. Here, he was told, he would find the station commander, a former air force colonel named Max Moriarty, playing pool. It was Colonel Moriarty's unswerving habit to play pool at this time every day; apparently he was the undefeated station champion and he practised hard to maintain his position.

Nathan floated just inside the entrance and looked round. The mess was certainly a strikingly large and luxurious set-up. A lot of effort and launch weight had been wasted in what was obviously intended to be a demonstration of power and success. It was designed to be an exact replica of an Earthside saloon. The decor, furniture and fittings all looked authentic, indeed most of them were, and no expense had been spared to disguise all the effects of weightlessness. Gimmicks abounded: from the simplest fixing down of beer mats to mechanically reactive light fittings which swung if pushed. There was even low alcohol beer on tap with an ingenious system of shaped tubes and sealed glasses that allowed it to look as though it was being drawn and served normally. The ultimate triumph, however, was a pool table which stood in the centre of the room and played exactly as though it was in a one-G environment. Nathan realized that with all this attention to detail, his remaining in the doorway without bothering to stand on the floor would probably look impolite; it might even look like mockery. Several people glanced in his direction. "You wanna ground your feet there buddy?" one of them called out to a ragged chorus of agreement from around the room. Nathan ignored them, and deliberately tugged himself forward into a slow drift towards the pool table. A short stocky man, square headed and thick necked was bent over it practising shots. When Nathan reached the table, the man said, without looking up, "Welcome to the *Ronald Reagan*, Commander Spring. I apologize for not being at the airlock to greet you personally."

"No need to apologize, Colonel Moriarty," Nathan said. "I can see you're busy." Moriarty missed his shot and as he straightened up Nathan added, "Besides, it was a fairly remote airlock," and smiled his best smile.

"Remote?" Moriarty exclaimed unconvincingly. "goddammit, I gave instructions that your shuttle was to get a priority docking." He stared fiercely round the room and then shouted at a young black woman who was standing at the bar. "Billy! What the hell is it with you people in traffic?"

"Is there a problem, M-M?" she asked politely.

"This man is an important European police officer. How come he gets routed to a cargo dock? I mean for Chrissakes, red three-four?" He smiled at Nathan. "That is where you said you were sent, Commander?"

They both knew he hadn't, of course, and as a way of putting him in his place it was a bit crude Nathan thought. "Don't concern yourself, Colonel," he said, and nodded in the woman's direction. "No problem."

"If you're sure, sir," she said wryly.

An exhausted looking man joined them at the table and Moriarty introduced him as Pete Lennox. "You ready to give the Commander the ten cent tour?" Moriarty asked him.

"Not yet, M-M," Lennox said. "I still have to get clearances from some of the contractors."

"Well get on it, Pete. Christ, do I have to do everything myself?"

Lennox smiled tiredly. Nathan noticed that although the man was obviously dog-weary, he was careful to walk out. Watching him leave Moriarty said to Nathan, "A few of our clients are nervous about who sees what they're working on."

"Don't frighten them on my account," Nathan said.

"This is a high-profile, multi-use station," said Moriarty, "but one of the few things we're not really able to cope with is tourists."

"That's all right, sir," Nathan said. "I didn't bring any."

Moriarty rolled a ball across the pool table. "Do you play this game?" he asked.

Nathan smiled. "I'm still trying to work out how you do," he said.

"It's neat don't you think? One of the original specialities of the station."

"Artificial gravity for pool tables?"

Mildly irritated Moriarty said, "Solutions to the problems of weightlessness."

Nathan aimed a ball at a pocket. It did not go down. "So how does this one work?" he asked.

"The table generates an electromagnetic field which the modified balls react to. The whole system's balanced by an analogue computer, and the whole damn thing is totally self-contained."

Nathan was impressed and showed it. "The control programme must be a monster," he said.

"You'd better believe it," said Moriarty. "That is American technology, boy, and I tell you we are still the best."

Lennox came back into the room. He looked harassed.

"She's on the circuit again," he said to Moriarty.

"Not now, Pete," Moriarty said angrily.

Lennox said, almost pleading, "She's very insistent."

"Christ," said Moriarty glancing at Nathan.

"Don't let me interrupt your work," Nathan said.

Moriarty said, "I don't plan to, Commander." He heel-and-toed towards the door followed by Lennox, and added over his shoulder, "I'll be right back."

"I'll be right here," Nathan said, and when they had gone immediately began an ostentatiously awe-struck examination of the pool table. He rolled the balls, he felt the cushions, he carefully looked into all the pockets. It was a slightly exaggerated impersonation of the superstitious primitive confronted by a marvel of science. No-one in the room who noticed the performance was at all surprised when he crouched down to peer about underneath the table. No-one saw him place Box on the underside and murmur, "Box, I want you to tell me very quietly what we have here, and how much of an edge you can give me."

"I don't know what else I can tell you, Ms. Goodman," Moriarty said smiling patiently. Behind him, positioned so that any call to the office always had it in the field of vision, the image of the 'see, hear, recall no evil' president after whom the station had been named was smiling too, albeit vacantly. Even Pete Lennox had a weary smile on his face.

Odile was not smiling. After a brief signal delay, she snapped, "*You can tell me where my brother is, that's what else you can tell me.*"

Moriarty looked at Lennox and gave a small shrug.

"*And never mind signalling your shit-heeled henchman,*" Odile raged from the screen, though the inescapable pause took a little of the bite out of it.

"My what?" Moriarty chuckled. "Ma'am we never heard of your brother. My... uh... my henchman has been through the records right back to when this station was first commissioned."

"*What does that prove?*" Odile demanded.

"It proves he's never been on the administration staff; he's never leased a work module; there's never been a Harvey Goodman here," Lennox said. "As I tried to tell you."

"*You'll be trying to tell me next there's never been a Harvey Goodman.*"

"Let us take a hypothetical example," Jiang Li Ho said. "Let us say there has been a kidnapping."

Devis who, coming for more coffee, had stumbled into the official visit and was now stuck with it, said, "You mean taking someone against their will and holding them for ransom."

"Or for politics perhaps," said Ho.

"It's not a very common crime out here for any reason," Theroux said.

Ho beamed. "That is why I chose it."

"I'm not totally sure," Theroux floundered. "I think we'd need to discover the purpose behind the crime."

"Not necessarily," Devis said, taking a malicious pleasure in making things difficult for Theroux, "a crime is a crime." Maybe he'd think twice next time before he invited bloody politicians to the office.

Ho seemed oblivious to Theroux's difficulty. "But the purpose would be obvious, don't you think?"

Theroux hated this. What was he supposed to say? What was he supposed to know? He wasn't trained in police procedure, whatever that was. You used your brain and you did what you had to do. He tried to sound more positive. "Only if the disappearance was accompanied by a demand. Without that, you might not be looking at a crime at all."

Ho would not be put off. "A kidnapping with a demand for money then. What are the first steps that you would take?"

On the main communications screen, a message icon began to flash. "Saved by the bell," Kenzy murmured as the soft electronic chime sounded a reminder.

"Perhaps this will not be a hypothetical crime," Ho suggested, moving quickly to stand behind Kenzy and watch her key the screen.

"Star cops Headquarters," she said. "How can I help you?"

In the short delay between speech and response, Kenzy studied the face of the young black woman on the screen. While she waited, her face was thoughtful but then, when she spoke, her expression switched suddenly to anger. "*My name is Odile Goodman,*" she said. "*I'm calling from Earth and I want to report the disappearance of my brother.*"

* * *

Star Cops

"Goddam woman keeps pestering us," Moriarty said, "I don't think she's playing with a full deck." He played a confident shot to break the balls which Nathan had set up. Nothing went down.

"If it's a problem," Nathan said, "maybe we could deal with it for you."

"Hell, no, she's an American."

Nathan smiled. "Thought I'd make the offer anyway."

"Nice try, Commander. It's your shot."

Nathan made a tentative effort and watched a ball roll into a pocket.

"Were you practising while I was gone?" Moriarty asked, grinning.

"My dad used to say," Nathan said, "that computers are solutions without problems."

"Weightlessness is a problem."

Nathan nodded. "Especially for pool players."

"It does have other applications," said Moriarty, a touch defensively.

"Pinball?"

"It's popular with our people. Don't underestimate the importance of that."

"I don't. Especially as I'm not. Popular with your people I mean." Nathan surveyed the table. "What happens next?" he asked.

Kenzy tried again. "You must understand, we have very limited powers to deal with runaways if they're out here on legal work contracts. It would depend on his age, of course. How old is Harvey?"

Now Odile looked genuinely confused. "*How old is he?*"

"He's disappeared from home and you reckon he's run away to space, yes? You have checked with the Earthside authorities, have you? Only most kids change their minds and never make it out here at all."

"*What is it with you people? Do you patronize all groundsiders, or just the women?*" Odile snapped – and it struck Kenzy that this time the anger was different somehow.

"I'm sorry, madam," Kenzy said. "I seem to have misunderstood."

"*My brother is forty-seven years old. He's a scientist and he's disappeared from the space station where he was working.*"

"What do they say about it?" Kenzy asked.

Ho nodded excitedly at Theroux and Devis. "This is fascinating, is it not?" he whispered. "Perhaps I shall see at first hand your method of working."

On the screen, Odile said, "*The guys I talked to said he was never there.*"

They seemed to think I was some kind of flake."

"What station was this?" Kenzy asked.

"Lucky you were here, Dr. Ho," Devis whispered, with a small narrow eyed smile.

"Indeed, yes," Ho agreed softly.

"*It was the Ronald Reagan.*"

"That's the main American station," Kenzy said, glancing back towards Ho with a slight frown.

"With a hypothetical all ready for discussion, too," Devis went on.

Odile said, "*We're Americans, where else would he have been working?*" Then she paused, and asked suspiciously, "*Is someone monitoring this? Someone there with you?*"

"Just give me all the details," Kenzy said. "I'll get it looked into for you."

"You did say a disappearance?" murmured Devis.

"I believe I said a kidnapping," smiled Ho.

Devis looked thoughtful. "So you did." He was no longer bothering to smile.

"Once you get the hang of it, it's not really a very complicated game, is it?" said Nathan, as he sank another shot. "Snooker for the tactically challenged."

Moriarty was getting irritated again. "Hubble was an American national working on an American station."

"Hubble was a Star Cop working for me," Nathan said.

"You people had no right to fire his ass without consultation."

"We consulted him. And I didn't fire him, he resigned."

Moriarty snorted. "So did Richard Nixon."

"Not a bad parallel actually." Nathan pointed at a ball with his cue. "They were both crooks. Four in the corner?"

"They might have been sons-of-bitches, but they were *our* sons-of-bitches."

Nathan cued the four ball, and it rolled accurately into the pocket. "My country right or wrong?"

"There are worse philosophies," said Moriarty.

"And most of them start with that," Nathan said. "Six ball, centre."

"You and Theroux should get on real well," Moriarty commented, just as Nathan was about to make the shot.

Nathan straightened up. "I'm sorry?"

"Your second-in-command is a little short on patriotism."

"I knew there was something I liked about him."

"He was a student radical, did you know that?"

Nathan bent down to the shot. "Wasn't everybody?"

"No."

"If you're not radical as a kid, where is there to go in your reactionary old age?"

"Well, not onto our space program, that's for fucking sure," Moriarty said.

Nathan struck the nominated ball harder that he had intended, but it hurtled unerringly into the pocket, scattering the remaining balls into clear shooting positions. "Your loss, maybe," he said, trying to look modestly pleased.

Moriarty was trying to look unconcerned. "This table's really running for you, isn't it?" he said.

"Theroux's developing into a good copper," Nathan said.

Moriarty said, "I preferred Hubble."

"Hubble wasn't even a good crook. Seven ball, top left. The stupid bastard got caught." Nathan lined up the shot carefully. "If you're going to pay someone off you should always be sure they're bright enough to make it worthwhile." He struck the ball and again made the pot.

"Someone paid him off?" Moriarty asked. "Why would they do that?"

"To keep him quiet, I imagine."

"You don't know?"

"Eight ball, centre," Nathan said and potted the final ball.

Moriarty stared at the table. "I do believe you're the first person to beat me on this," he said.

For a moment, it seemed as though he might start to look for reasons for this setback. Nathan wasn't sure how he would react to finding Box attached to the underside of the table monitoring and modifying the control system responses. "Best of three, Colonel?" he suggested quickly.

Lauter came awake slowly. She knew she had snorted and that was what had woken her. She had suspected for a while that she snored these days, and she found it rather touching that Marty had said nothing about it. She yawned. "How are we doing, my lovely?" she asked.

He switched off the book he was reading and said, "The trouble with long hauls without the fuel for a decent burn is that they turn into very long hauls indeed."

Lauter stretched and yawned again. "I just had a terrific dream about that module. We made enough off it to buy a nice little business back on Earth. A nice little agribusiness."

"We know sod-all about farming," Marty said as the six hour warning chimed and he started to run the routine function checks.

"We weren't born knowing the scrap salvage business," Lauter said.

"No, we spent years learning it."

"A little house. Roses round the door. Chickens scratching in the yard."

"Years of grafting and we still can't make a straight living."

"Oh stop moaning. We make a living."

Marty confirmed a full set of greens to the flight computer and accepted its acknowledgement. "You call this living? And anyway I said a *straight* living."

"You really are a guilt-ridden little soul, aren't you?" Lauter said.

Marty said, "It's no fun winning if you have to cheat."

"Winning's not supposed to be fun, sweetie," she said. "If it was fun, everybody would be at it. No it's just something you have to do. And it is something we are about to do in a big way."

"Yeah, right; chickens round the door, roses scratching in the yard."

Lauter switched on the cargo bay remote monitor camera. "I've got a feeling," she said gazing at the module which filled the screen, "a definite feeling."

Marty looked at it too. "So what was in it?" he asked. "In the dream? What was in it?"

"I never got to see," she said. "But it was the end of all our troubles, I know that."

They both stared at the anonymous container they had gambled so much to find and reclaim. There was nothing to show where it came from, nothing to indicate what might be in it. They had deciphered some partially obliterated lettering on the welded-up hatch but Marty hadn't been able to relate it to anything on the most recent Guild database – the most recent they could afford anyway – so it was no help. Of course, Lauter, determined to be optimistic, insisted that thirteen was a very lucky number, but Marty had always resisted such superstitious nonsense. If the cylinder, which he had come to think of as monstrous rather than

Star Cops

huge, had been stencilled it must mean something but if that something wasn't important enough to be registered anywhere... And whatever else it meant, of one thing he was sure: the marking OMZ 13 had nothing to do with luck.

Though Nathan still disliked weightless showers – 'boil-in-the-bag' in current slang – he used them almost routinely now. Like weightless lavatories they were uncomfortable, inconvenient and potentially messy, but with practice you could cope. Experience did not help with some problems, however.

"Morning, Commander," Moriarty said, around a mouthful of breakfastburger. "You look like shit."

Nathan slotted into the seat opposite him and dialled up coffee and a blueberry muffin on the dispenser. "I'll never get used to sleeping weightless, I'm afraid."

"We got a couple of guys working on that."

"Government research?"

"Christ, no. They're both from pharmaceutical houses. They're probably duplicating each other's research but, hell, they've got the funding." He shrugged.

"Do you do any government work?" Nathan asked, taking a bite out of the soft sweet sponge cake.

"There's some research funding," Moriarty said, and then before Nathan could pursue the question, asked, "Say, what's the story on this Chinese of yours?"

"Chinese of mine?"

"Jangley Ho."

"The Moonbase Co-ordinator?" He shook his head. "I've never even met the man."

Moriarty looked sceptical. He sucked on his drink pack. It was tea, Nathan noticed. The label proclaimed it to be British Breakfast Blend, and Nathan wondered if this was for his benefit. "You got the last guy fired," Moriarty said.

"Paton was a murderer. *Possible* murderer," Nathan said.

"So it was you got the Chinese his job."

"It was their turn."

Moriarty said, "You got it for them early. They're in place two years early."

"Does that matter?"

"Damn right it matters. We weren't ready."

"What were you planning, Colonel?" Nathan smiled. "A ticker-tape parade perhaps?"

Moriarty didn't smile. "They were ready though. They had a guy trained and waiting back on Earth."

"Dr. Ho is a Nobel Laureate. His field is space medicine. It's largely due to his work that we can come and go between Earth and space the way we do without major bone damage. You think the man's a spy?"

"Crude word," said Moriarty. "They're cleverer than that."

"You think I'm a spy?" asked Nathan.

"I think you've been used."

"In other words, I'm *stupider* than that," Nathan said. Then he added without pause or change of tone, "So what exactly *is* this government research that you do?"

Moriarty's reaction to a momentary confusion was aggression. "Say what?" he demanded.

Nathan smiled again. "Any word from the State Department?" he asked mildly.

"They turned you down flat."

Nathan nodded. "I can't even replace Hubble. Any reason?"

"They are, quote, 'not in favour of international policing', unquote." Moriarty was smiling now.

"They changed their minds," Nathan said, "when they looked up 'international' and discovered that it didn't just mean 'Americans abroad'."

Moriarty detached himself from his seat. "You ready for the tour?" he asked.

Dumping the remains of the muffin in the disposal, Nathan drained his coffee and said, "You need us, Colonel."

"We can take care of our own crime."

Nathan released himself from the seat and followed Moriarty across the mess. No-one was bothering with the walking Velcro here, clearly the floating taboo only applied to Mess Room One, so Nathan carefully heel-and-toed his way to the exit hatch and high-hopped through it.

Moriarty was waiting in the corridor link. "Do you always do the opposite to everyone else?" he asked.

Nathan took his feet off the floor and glided along beside him. "Suppose I prove that you can't take care of your own crime?"

Star Cops

"You give me real good odds, and I still wouldn't bet money on it."

"You're a gambling man," Nathan said.

"Goes with the territory. You don't know that, you got a lot to learn about the people who come out here."

"Ever play cards with Hubble?"

"Couldn't say offhand. I've played poker with a lot of guys."

"You'd remember playing Hubble. He has to be the best there is."

"That right?"

"What other explanation could there be for the way he took so much money from people? And so regularly."

They drifted up through a cross link and into a half module office decorated with patriotic emblems and air force souvenirs. Behind the desk was a large holographic image of *Ronald Reagan*.

"This is the station commander's office," Moriarty said.

Nathan looked round, nodding politely. He glanced at the workstation. Given the briefest access, Box should be able to use the residuals and wear on the keys to get him Moriarty's access codes. There might be something in the station computer which would be useful. Something to give him another edge. It was unlikely, but there might even be a connection to Hubble. "Tell me Colonel, just how good a poker player are you?" he asked.

Marty had a fever. It wasn't serious, as far as Lauter could tell, but it was unusual for him. He was never ill. It was part of his reliability somehow, it went with his caution. She checked the time, reset the flight computer a few minutes early, and got him a couple more aspirins from the medical kit.

"Do you feel any better?" she asked. He looked better for the sleep, but he seemed to be sleeping a lot.

"I'm fine," he said.

"You're not fine," she snapped. "And we're a bloody long way from a medic."

"It's just a virus infection."

"Where's that supposed to have come from? We're weeks from contact."

Marty undid the sleep webbing and floated to the ablutions unit. "It doesn't work like that," he said, as he started to sponge himself off. "You know it doesn't work like that. Viruses don't have timetables."

"It has to have come from somewhere," she insisted.

Marty said, "You could have been carrying it. *I* could. It might have been in the suit. This isn't what you'd call a sterile environment, is it?" He smiled gloomily. "We sift shit for a living, Lauter. We're crap collectors, you and me."

Lauter watched him wiping over his pale skinny arms and bony legs. What the hell did she see in him? It wasn't his body, that was for sure. And he was a miserable sod when he wasn't being an irritating little know-all. Still, he did look a lot better…

"You're supposed to be Earthside, interviewing recruits," Nathan said. "Why are you still in the office, David?"

Theroux held up his travel bag so that it was visible on screen. "*There's a small problem come up since you've been away.*"

"Yes?"

"*It's not something I can talk about over an open circuit.*"

Nathan said irritably, "My mind-reading's a little rusty."

Theroux looked concerned. "*You look like shit,*" he said. "*Still finding it difficult to sleep without gravity, huh?*"

"Don't understand me, David, just tell me what the fuck it is you want."

Theroux leaned into his monitor and peered out of the screen. "*Is that Ronald Reagan behind you?*" he asked. "*Christ, isn't it bad enough they named the thing after that asshole without having pictures of him about the place?*"

He's stalling, Nathan thought, and said, "You're stalling, David. Stop pissing about and tell me what it is that's happened."

"*Kenzy's done the preliminary work on the case, she's got all the details.*"

"What case? What details?"

"*She'll explain it all when she gets there.*"

So that was it. Kenzy had got off the leash. "I thought I made it very clear," he said flatly, "that she does not leave that desk."

"*You also made it clear that I was running things in your absence,*" Theroux said with calm assurance.

It was a fair point, but the poor sod was obviously no match for the bloody woman. "I forgot you were smitten," said Nathan and smiled. "What did she do, waggle her bum at you?"

Theroux grinned. "*If she'd done that I'd have taken her Earthside with me, not sent her to you."*

"The woman's a menace."

"*I think the case could be too. There may be…*" He paused for a moment, obviously trying to think of some discreet way to put it, then said, "*…a political dimension?*"

Nathan thought, *a political dimension? How many dimensions are there out here, for God's sake?* He never should have taken this bloody job. It was vanity and ambition – which were the same thing. He should have told them to shove it when he had the chance. Lee would still be alive and he wouldn't be alone in a giddy paranoid limbo full of floating weirdoes.

"*Nathan?*"

He said, without smiling, "A political dimension? Kenzy should be ideal casting in this case. Whatever this case is."

"*She'll be less of an embarrassment there than I would be. Trust me.*"

"I did, and look what it's got me. I seem to have been making a lot of mistakes recently."

"*Listen, Nathan.*" Theroux leaned forward and lowered his voice slightly, "*I think what we're seeing here is a definite game plan. Our problem is we don't know who's coaching the play.*"

Nathan shook his head. "Your problem is, this better be important enough to justify sending that woman here."

For Devis the novelty still had not really worn off, although he was more self-conscious now. That was why he liked to be left alone in the office sometimes. While no-one was watching he could play the little hand eye co-ordination games which were beyond him on Earth but which one-sixth-G made easy. Here on the Moon he could juggle, up to six small objects at a time; he could bounce a small ball, brought back from Earth for the purpose, off at least three different surfaces and still catch it; and when he was sure he was alone he even did the occasional handstand. He was working on balancing a coffee cup on top of a pen which he was balancing on a spoon held between his teeth, when Jiang Li Ho bounded into the office and caught him at it.

"I see," said Ho, as Devis dropped the cup and the pen but deftly caught them both before they hit the floor, "that we share a delight in this new environment." He beamed, and moved to look at the screen on which Devis had been working. "Have you found out anything yet?"

Devis spat out the spoon and said, "I'm sorry sir, I'm afraid Chief

Superintendent Theroux just left."

"I came only to enquire about the case," Ho said.

Devis crossed to the workstation and switched the screen to standby. "You missed him by a matter of minutes."

Ho's smile did not falter. "Do I understand that you have found out nothing so far?"

"I personally," said Devis, "have found out that the Moon is not made of green cheese, and that Santa Claus does not live on the darkside." He smiled a thin sour smile. "There's a lot to be said for seeing for yourself, I've always thought."

"This has been the philosophy of my life too," said Ho. "Unfortunately, it is not always possible." He picked up a hard copy file and opened it.

"Some societies make it more possible than others," Devis said, politely taking the file from him and closing it firmly. If he was aware of the irony he showed no sign of it.

"You overestimate the difference, Colin. Tell me now, what progress is there with our case?"

"Forgive me, Dr. Ho, but this is not our case. It is *our* case."

"Why are you so unfriendly?" Ho asked, looking puzzled rather than hurt or annoyed.

"Maybe because you're not," Devis said.

"Have you always been so paranoid?"

"Have you always been so nosy?"

"Curiosity is what makes me a scientist."

"Suspicion is what makes me a policeman."

Ho stared at him for what felt to Devis like a long time, then he said, "It would appear that we can have nothing to say to each other." He bowed a small smiling bow, no more than a nod of the head, and left as abruptly as he had arrived.

As Devis watched the inner door closing, it struck him that Ho was not disappointed with the way things had gone, which either meant he had found out what he wanted to know... or else he hadn't actually wanted to know anything.

It was unlikely and not something Nathan wanted to admit to himself, but he was pleased to see her. That was probably what had made him angry. That and her casual confidence.

"You're the one who says 'look for anomalies'," she was saying now, looking past him at the comings and goings in the ersatz saloon. "Well, you couldn't have a more glaring one than that, could you?"

"She says he's missing. You can't find any evidence that he exists at all," Nathan prompted expressionlessly and when Kenzy looked back at him he asked, "So what exactly have you checked?"

"He has no social welfare or security ID number. No birth, marriage or death registration. No credit classification. No transportation licences, no passport number or travel ID. No medical, educational or military certification." She waited, obviously satisfied that she had missed nothing.

"Has she?" Nathan asked.

Kenzy was ready for that question. "Oh yeah. And a Harvey Goodman is listed as her next of kin – but that's the only place he *is* listed."

"What do you think this is all about?"

"I think Odile Goodman could be an *agent provocateur*."

"I see," Nathan said. "Or rather, I don't see. Have you checked with the people here?"

"Christ, no," she exclaimed softly. "If someone is trying to stir up trouble, that would play straight into their hands."

Nathan sighed. "Kenzy, tell me this isn't the yellow peril and the threat to civilization as we know it," he said.

But she was not to be deflected by sarcasm. "Ho was there when the call came through. He even predicted it."

Nathan tried again. "Clever of him. To avoid suspicion like that."

"It was arrogance. He couldn't resist playing games with us."

She was so sure that he almost began to think there might be something to it. "What did the Goodman woman say her brother was?" he asked.

Kenzy said, "A microbiologist. He graduated from Caltech, did postgrad at MIT." She was obviously pleased with her theory and the evidence she had found to support it.

He nodded, waiting for the mistake. "But not according to their computers presumably," he said.

"No Goodman H., in fact no Goodmans of any kind listed at either one."

"For how long?"

She shrugged. "Eight years straight."

Nathan nodded again. So there it was. He said, "Is that the longest period?"

"How do you mean?"

"Were there *usually* Goodmans?"

For the first time, she looked uncertain. "It's a common enough name," she said.

"Exactly; Caltech and MIT are vast institutions – so what are the odds –"

Kenzy interrupted: "On eight years in a row without a single registration in that name."

"And happening," Nathan said, "just when your boy *would* have been there."

"Fuck it!" She seemed genuinely annoyed with herself. "The records have been got at."

Nathan said, "It's possible, anyway. If someone had to do a fast, dirty job, they might erase all references to the name Goodman and rely on nobody spotting it."

"Which I didn't," Kenzy said. "I'm sorry, that was fucking stupid of me."

"Yes," Nathan said, realizing suddenly just how much he was enjoying her discomfiture, and trying to keep the smugness out of his voice, "stupid and careless."

"Do you find being perfect a problem, sir?"

Clearly he had not succeeded. "I find being patient a problem, Kenzy," he snapped, and wondered why the hell he was on the defensive all the time. "Where is Goodman supposed to have worked?"

"Is this another trick question?"

"People who use this station do so on what the Yanks are pleased to call a say-and-pay basis," Nathan said and thought, she must know this already and I'm lecturing, for God's sake. But he couldn't find a way to stop, so he ploughed on. "They say what work they plan to do, and then they pay for the right to do it in some appropriate part."

"They book a room," Kenzy said.

Unsure whether she was being sarcastic, Nathan said, "Roughly speaking, yes."

"Yeah well, roughly speaking I don't know what room he was supposed to have booked. The sister was told that OMZ 13, the one she was trying to reach, never existed. Unlucky number."

"Presumably you plan to check," Nathan said.

Kenzy nodded and said, "Presumably."

"What else?"

Star Cops

"David Theroux is going to visit the Goodman woman while he's Earthside."

"Always useful," Nathan said.

Kenzy smiled. "You can't tell they're sweating if you can't smell they're sweating, right?"

Nathan noticed that although the mouth was as he remembered, small and vivid in her pale face, her lips seemed fuller somehow. "Too late to be of much use in the investigation," he said coldly, "and no use at all to you here."

Kenzy said, "I can tell you're impressed by the moves I've made so far."

"It's not a game, Kenzy," Nathan said.

She nodded and stood up. "Do you want a beer?" she asked.

Nathan watched her heel-and-toe her way expertly towards the bar. She did have a very attractive backside, he thought. And was it his imagination, or was she waggling it more than usual?

"Check," Marty said as he moved his knight and revealed the attacking bishop.

"What?" Lauter demanded. She stared at the small magnetic board which Marty dragged along on every trip insisting it was the only real way to play chess. "You miserable rat."

"You never think far enough ahead," he said gloomily.

She stared into his eyes, clear now with no sign of fever. "You're lucky we're together, sweetness. You think so far ahead you'd never actually do anything if it wasn't for me."

"Checkmate in two," he said.

Lauter stretched and yawned. She released herself from the acceleration couch where she had been lying with Marty, and drifted across the flight deck. An empty food carton and the tear-off backing from a spacesuit repair patch were floating in front of the control console. She flicked them away. The cabin had long since degenerated into the scruffy chaos which developed over any long haul. Marty made occasional attempts to tidy up but Lauter hardly noticed the mess any more. She switched on the cargo bay remote camera and stared at the screen.

Marty said, "Don't you think you've wasted enough power watching that thing?"

"Why don't we take a look inside and see what we've got?" Lauter said.

Marty was irritated. "Are you that bored?"

"Aren't you?"

"Not bored enough to be stupid."

Lauter kicked off from the bulkhead and dived back towards the couch, lunging at his crotch as she cannoned into him. "Who are you calling stupid, buggerlugs?"

Marty struggled to protect himself. "Suppose whatever's in there's explosive?" he gasped.

"Compromise," offered Lauter. "We'll stick the video probe into the vision socket and see what we can see."

"Nothing," countered Marty. "No light."

"We'll use the self-illuminating probe," she persisted.

"There's no access for it," he said, "and you know it. And even if there was, it's too bloody dim. It's for close-up stuff."

Lauter pouted. "I want to see what's in there."

"Wanting isn't enough. You still need light."

"I'm going to get suited up and try it anyway," she challenged.

Marty said nothing. It was a stupid waste of resources, but at least it wasn't too dangerous and if it kept her happy, well then, *he* was happy.

"I am happy to meet you, Pal," Moriarty said. "It will be my honour to put at your disposal all the pleasures I have to offer." Not letting go of Kenzy's hand and still gazing deep into her eyes, he asked, "Have you played with your pretty assistant on our pool table, Commander?"

"She's not my assistant," Nathan said.

Kenzy did not flinch either from the grip or the gaze but smiled politely and said, "I'm not very good on pool tables, Colonel."

Moriarty smirked. "I'm too much of a gentleman to make the obvious comment," he murmured.

"But not to think it," Kenzy said.

"A man's thoughts are his own," said Moriarty, and held her hand in both of his and pulled it against his chest.

Kenzy said, "Only if he keeps them to himself, sir," and extricated her hand.

Nathan was conscious that he seemed more uncomfortable with Moriarty's behaviour than Kenzy did, but he could think of no rational explanation for this. Odder still was the passing annoyance he felt towards her.

"I'm a tactile kind of guy," Moriarty was saying. "I believe communication is helped by direct physical contact."

Kenzy glanced towards Nathan. "That's why you're keeping quiet is it, sir? You don't want Colonel Moriarty holding your hand in front of all these people?"

Nathan smiled thinly, "Is that where I've been making my mistake? Not tactile enough?"

"You Brits are pretty reserved," Moriarty agreed, signalling to the bar for drinks to be brought. "But I don't think that's going to be a problem for you and me, is it, Pal?" He slid onto the bench and moved very close to her, so that his thigh was pressing against hers.

Nathan noticed that the girl on mess duty was not amused at what was going on. Was that because Moriarty had treated her as a waitress, or was it something more personal? He stopped listening to the station commander's ponderous overtures to Kenzy and watched the girl moving very slowly to get the beers.

"Supposing I wanted to book a room?" Kenzy asked.

"You can share mine," Moriarty said. "Anytime."

"You should get together with a guy called Colin Devis," Kenzy said. "You obviously went to the same charm school." She smiled. "Pity neither of you passed the course."

"I think I'm in love," said Moriarty.

"If I booked workspace on the *Ronald Reagan*," Kenzy asked interestedly, "where it was would depend on what I did, right?"

Moriarty put on a serious face. "Pretty much."

Nathan stopped watching the girl behind the bar. Book a room? What the hell did Kenzy think she was doing? The woman was as subtle as a sock full of sand. "Kenzy," he warned, "I don't think this is really the time or the place."

Kenzy looked at him. "Sir?" Her expression was exaggeratedly innocent.

Nathan glanced at Moriarty. He was frowning towards the bar, trying to catch the mess girl's attention. Perhaps the damn fool really was in thrall to his glands. Hormone rush could make people stupid. Moriarty snapped his fingers a couple of times, but the girl continued to ignore him. "No, it doesn't matter," Nathan said. "You carry on."

"Suppose I was a microbiologist, Colonel," Kenzy asked, while Moriarty was still concentrating on getting the drinks, "where would I go?"

Without any sign of a pause for thought Moriarty said, "Somewhere else."

"You've got something against microbiologists?" Nathan asked, and saw Moriarty's uncertainty – as, for the briefest moment, the man avoided meeting his eye.

"There's a standing directive," Moriarty said. "No research involving bacteria, viruses, protozoan. Nothing for the buggies to play with out here. We leave those games to the Reds."

"The Chinese play dirty pool?" Kenzy suggested.

"Can you name me a worse weapon, little lady?" Moriarty said.

"What about medical research?" Nathan asked quickly to forestall Kenzy's reaction.

Moriarty said, "How do you tell what that is?"

"A blanket ban then. The good with the bad."

"It's the simple answer."

"I thought we'd grown out of simple answers," Nathan said.

"Not where that stuff is concerned," Moriarty said as the girl finally arrived with the drinks. "When there's nowhere else to go, you keep it the hell away. It's just too goddam dangerous." Then he looked at the girl.

"Thank you, Betsanne, put it on my tab."

It struck Nathan that if there had been any possible way to dump three sealed glasses of low alcohol beer on a suction surface tray over Moriarty's head, then Betsanne would have done it. "Yes, sir, Colonel, sir," she said in a soft Southern lilt. "Is there anything else I can do for the Colonel before I goes back to the fields?"

To Nathan's surprise, Moriarty grinned and said in a passably similar accent, "Why thank you, child, I'm sure I'll think of something," and tried to pat her behind as she left.

Nathan sipped the insipid beer. He needed to get to the computer in Moriarty's office. If Kenzy played her part, now might be the time. "If you don't mind, Colonel," he said, standing, "I think I'll go and catch up on some sleep."

"Mind? Hell, no, I don't mind. Question is, do you mind leaving this pretty lady with me?"

Kenzy started to stand too. "Well as it happens, sir…"

Nathan said, "She can take care of herself. Can't you, Kenzy?" He put his hand on her shoulder. "Don't get up."

* * *

Lauter screwed the camera probe into the vision receptor socket slowly and with difficulty. The gauntlets made it impossible to get a good grip, so she had to use both hands and, as she could not find any way to brace her feet, this meant taking most of the strain on her stomach muscles. The module's umbilical junction was supposed to have been designed for spacesuited working, but that was using standard fittings on a properly set up construction site, not jury-rigged odds and ends in a cramped cargo bay. By the time she had finished, Lauter was aching and greasy with sweat.

She would have given up long since if it hadn't been for Marty. She knew damn well that since the probe could not physically get into the module, the small light round the head of the camera would be useless. Just as Marty had said it would be, the smug little bugger. And it was unlikely that the computer's dark-vision system would be able to interpret as pictures whatever residual energy there was inside the thing.

"Try it," she instructed over the suit radio.

"*There's a loose link somewhere,*" Marty said. "*All I get is black and noise.*"

Lauter grasped the silver bundle of armoured cables and yanked it back and forth. "Is that any better?" she demanded.

In the cabin, Marty fiddled with the screen adjustments but white noise and occasional flashes of darkness were all he could get. "Still black and noise," he said.

"*Concentrate!*" Even allowing for radio distort, Lauter's voice was thin and tired.

Marty said, "It's no substitute for light."

"*Anything now?*"

"No, nothing." Marty knew she would think he wasn't trying because he had a point to make. He re-prompted the computer subroutine to further enhance the picture that wasn't there.

"*Are you really trying, Marty?*"

"Of course I'm trying," he said. "Why wouldn't I be trying? I don't want you out there any longer than is absolutely necessary, you silly bitch."

"*Don't you call me names, you smug little bugger.*"

"Look, I'm sorry for being right, all right?" Marty said. He turned away from the screen to check her systems readouts. Everything looked to be functioning normally, but the ambient temperature was up and her breathing rate was high. There was no sign of any CO_2 build, but it could happen – and suddenly – in cheap reconditioned suits. "I'm not happy with your suit telemetry, Lauter."

Unnoticed behind Marty the screen had started to change, apparently in response to the computer's stepped-up imaging sequence. A vague shape began resolving itself, a ghost in the intermittent noise and darkness.

"*Stop fussing, Marty,*" Lauter said.

It was there! The first indication that her backpack might not be coping. "I don't like the risks you're taking," Marty said as he monitored the waste gas levels edging very slightly closer to the danger thresholds.

On the unwatched screen, the strange shadow floated forward until it seemed to press itself against the crystal surface, filling the visual field with a huge unblinking eye.

"*One more whack at it,*" Lauter said, and Marty heard her grunt as she kicked at it or heaved at it or whatever the hell she did.

"There's nothing!" he said urgently.

"*You're sure?*" she asked, almost plaintive. "*I can't tell you how much I hate having sod-all to show for this much work.*"

Marty glanced back at the screen. She'd made it worse, there was nothing at all now – not even the brief intervals of hopeful darkness, just blank white noise. "For fuck's sake, stop pressing your luck and get yourself back in here. I don't want to lose you," he said matching her tone.

Nathan had tried every variation he could think of. But there was nothing anywhere in the data banks which linked ex-Inspector Kirk Hubble to Moriarty. Or either of them to anyone named Goodman. And there was no record of an Outer Module Series Z number 13. "Box, are there any security codes I haven't got?" he asked, because he couldn't think of anything else.

"The codes you are using will access all data available to the station commander from this terminal," Box confirmed, reducing the general question to the specifics Nathan had originally requested.

Nathan stared at the workstation screen. He was out of ideas and rapidly running out of time. Sooner or later, someone was going to come in. Sooner, he realized, as the door control activated. He killed the workscreen and said quickly, "Light off," plunging Moriarty's office into darkness. The automatic door slid open and in the light from the corridor he saw Kenzy float in.

"Commander? Commander?" she called out softly, when the door had closed and it was dark again.

"Lights," Nathan said, and pulled himself out from behind the workstation.

"Sorry, did I startle you?" Kenzy asked.

Feeling slightly foolish Nathan said, scowling, "You're supposed to be keeping our host occupied."

"I did figure that out."

"So what are you doing here?"

"When he realized I wasn't about to let him into my coveralls and I'd faked the orgasm over his pool prowess, he sort of lost interest."

"Is he still playing?" Nathan asked, reactivating the screen.

She shook her head. "He wandered off. You weren't in your quarters," she shrugged, "so I thought I should come and warn you."

"Watch the door," Nathan said and thought, *that was gracious of me.*

"Don't bother to thank me," Kenzy said. "It's all in a day's work."

"That's right, it is," said Nathan. "A day's work which, in your case, should only involve filing and taking messages."

Kenzy moved to the doorway. "And watching doors."

"Just do it."

He watched her force the automatics on the unnecessarily elaborate entrance mechanism so that the door slid open a crack. She was bright; was that his problem with her? He'd always disliked bright crooks more than stupid ones because if the bright weren't honest, what was the point of it all?

"Have you found any of what you were looking for?" Kenzy asked.

"It would help if I knew what that was," Nathan said.

"Nothing on my bug specialist?"

"Never here."

"And the Outer Module Z series ends at twelve?"

"Yes."

"I suppose it has occurred to you that if he was here and they thought his work might be risky they'd have pushed him out to the furthest available module," she said.

"Z 13," Nathan agreed. "Unlucky for some. It's not evidence."

"Any of the other series get as far as thirteen?"

The other series. He hadn't thought to check that. He punched in the questions.

"All the outer modules are prefixed Z yes?" Kenzy went on. "I mean there's got to be other series hasn't there. Two, maybe three, with different prefixes?"

Irritated with himself Nathan said, reading off the screen, "Inner, Central and Core. Prefixed M, G, and A."

"Okay, so you thought of it already," Kenzy said, misinterpreting his tone. "I'm sorry."

"No, I hadn't thought of it," Nathan said. "A runs to sixteen, G to nineteen, M to twenty and none of them miss out thirteen."

Kenzy looked back at Nathan, and said with a small frown, "We've only got Goodman's word that they said it to her."

"Why would she lie?"

"It makes her story more plausible?" Kenzy suggested.

Nathan switched off the power. "Let's get out of here," he said and pushed himself up over the workstation. As he reached for the edge of the unit to slow himself he saw Kenzy duck back from the door and jam the mechanism closed.

"Someone's coming," she whispered urgently.

"Shit." Nathan missed his hold, and his momentum carried him on towards her.

Kenzy propelled herself back gently. "Lights off," she said.

In the blinding darkness Nathan put out his hands to protect himself, unsure how close he was to colliding with the wall. "Oh, that was fucking clever," he muttered, and was surprised at how close Kenzy's voice sounded when she asked softly, "Are you okay?" and then said, "Sorry. Didn't mean to strand you like that."

He felt her hand catch his arm and, more or less instinctively, he grabbed for her. Her other hand gripped his shoulder. He pulled her in clumsily and hugged himself to her. She squirmed, so he released her hastily and found that her legs were wrapped round the back of his. Her arms slid round his neck. He held her again. It was odd to feel the balance of a woman in his arms. He knew he missed Lee but he hadn't realized how desperately he missed touching, holding someone against him. She brushed her cheek against his and the feeling was vivid, almost painful.

"You're a weird bloke," she murmured. "I mean how come you let me know that you missed it?"

Close up she smelled of shower gel and her breath was peppermint and beer. "Missed it?" He wanted to kiss her. "How do you mean?" What the hell was he doing here in the darkness? This was stupid. Stupid and wrong. This was Kenzy.

"The thirteen business. You admitted it right off," she said.

"Oh, that," Nathan said. "I *had* missed it." He took his arms from round her and pushed gently to detach her arms from his neck. "I don't think anyone's coming, do you?" he said, and thought, *welcome to the wonderful world of Freud.*

"You're too much of a gentleman to make the obvious comment, right?"

"I'm sorry?" Nathan said, feeling like a hypocrite. "Lights."

The lights felt brighter. "I guess I must have been mistaken," Kenzy muttered as she disentangled her legs from his.

"Can't you do any bloody thing right?" Nathan demanded. It was intended to be a joke, it started out as a joke anyway, but somehow the humour got lost between thought and voice.

"Obviously not," Kenzy said. "You want to get your hand off my arse?"

Nathan said, "I haven't touched your arse."

"Not a tactile kind of guy," she said wryly.

"We communicate perfectly without it," he snapped.

Careful not to touch each other, they each kicked off towards the door. Kenzy said, "It was an honest mistake."

Nathan said, "That's got to be a first for you."

"Cheap shot," she said.

"Yes it was, I'm sorry," he said.

When they reached the door Kenzy said, "Anyone can make a mistake."

As they drifted out and slipped the door closed behind them Nathan said, "You make too fucking many." By the time he realized that he had left Box on Moriarty's workstation, it was too late to do anything much about it.

It was the sort of quiet, middle-class neighbourhood Theroux had expected. The house was early post-millennium, but well maintained, with a top of the range communications dish on the front lawn. He identified himself to the door and asked for Odile Goodman. The door informed him politely that there was no-one there of that name. Theroux looked at the reference address from the routine call trace he had gotten before he left Moonbase. He instructed the door to check again. "*There is no-one here of that name,*" the door repeated, adding automatically, "*Please consult the Town Registry on Civic Plaza.*"

"What you have got to understand, Door," Theroux said, turning away, "is that you are not dealing with the delivery boy here. You are dealing with the Man." There was a path running along the side of the house. Still a little shaky and uncoordinated by the return to full gravity, he strode unsteadily towards it. "Civic Plaza, yeah right," he muttered.

The private garden was neat but anonymous. It looked to Theroux like corporate landscaping on a small scale, budget contract stuff. He stood and peered at the back of the house, trying to see into the rear windows. He hesitated to go further because the truth was, he didn't know how to react if he was challenged. Though he had done his best to develop the attitude appropriate to his promotion to senior police officer, so far what he felt like was an impostor and a not very convincing one. And the problem he had right now wasn't only because he had no Earthside authority. He was sure that wouldn't have bothered Nathan much, and Colin not one damn bit. He just wasn't a real cop, and that was all there was about it.

He walked a little further round the house. There didn't seem to be anyone moving inside. The place looked to be deserted. Then he noticed that the patio access was standing open. He moved towards it. To his surprise, it stayed open, and the security system did not respond to his approach. He reached the open wall and stretched an arm across the threshold. Still nothing from house security. He stepped inside. "Anyone home?" he called. "Ms. Goodman?"

There was no answer. In fact, there was no noise at all except what he was making. The garden room was completely empty. There were none of the usual orchids, palms, rattan chairs for that extra tropical touch. "Are you here, Ms. Goodman?" he called, moving into the main part of the house. The sound of his voice was unnaturally loud, and his footsteps seemed to echo slightly.

As he walked through the other rooms, the reason for the odd acoustics was obvious. The place had been stripped bare. No furniture, no carpets, no pictures, nothing. The upper levels were the same. Someone had done a very thorough job of cleaning the place out.

The communications console in the kitchen was still connected and working. Theroux queried the account and found that it was user-charged. He gave it his Star Cop authorization and asked for the Moonbase office. The abrupt pain was a jagged flash behind his eyes then everything went blank.

Devis's face appeared briefly on the console screen. "*Star Cops, how can I help you?*" was all he said before the connection was sharply broken.

* * *

Moriarty continued fiddling with Box in the hope that he could get it to do more than identify itself as the property of Nathan Spring. Not that there was much doubt about that – it sounded exactly like the guy. Finally he gave up, and said, "It's getting away from us, Pete."

Lennox frowned wearily from the screen. "Without the woman, they can't prove a thing."

"We underestimated this guy. I should have realized when he pretended he couldn't play pool. Sonofabitch is a hustler."

"There's no evidence. I've been real careful."

"There's always something left to find," Moriarty said, pocketing Box. "This guy Spring knows I paid off Hubble. I think he knows it all."

"He's bluffing, M-M," said Lennox. "What's his second-in-command doing here?"

"Following you, dummy."

"Yeah, right. It sure looked like he was expecting me."

"I don't imagine he was expecting you to bounce a bottle on his head. Is he going to be okay?"

"I didn't hit him that hard."

"What are you going say when he comes to?"

"I thought he was an intruder."

"That's real convincing."

"He had no business in the house."

"And you do?"

"Okay so what do you suggest?"

Moriarty paused, as if giving the question thought. It was one of his conceits. In reality, they both knew that he had made up his mind already. "All bets are off, Pete," he said. "Time to make a deal."

Nathan accepted Box with a small nod of thanks, but otherwise without comment or reaction. Moriarty, floating in the entrance hatch to the cabin, could not maintain a similar poker face when he saw Kenzy. She was working at the free-access personal computer terminal but he was clearly unimpressed by that. Leering he called to her, "Unit in your cabin non-functional, honey? Should've said. Could've used mine. I got the biggest on the station." He smirked conspiratorially at Nathan and murmured, "You didn't say she was a private game. Hell, I wouldn't blow on another man's dice." Nathan remained expressionless. Moriarty's smile faltered slightly. "I've been thinking about the replacement for Inspector

Hubble," he said.

"You've decided it's a good idea," suggested Nathan.

"Absolutely."

Nathan smiled to hide his surprise, and said, "Come inside, Colonel."

Moriarty glided past him and tried to get a look at the computer screen. Kenzy closed down the link to the Moonbase files she had been searching on the off-chance of a reference to Odile Goodman, and said, "Are you saying you'll support our case, Colonel?"

"That's what I'm saying."

"For three officers," Nathan said.

"Two."

"Three."

Moriarty gave a small shrug. "Three."

Nathan offered his hand. "I knew you were a reasonable man."

Moriarty shook hands warmly. "So if I support you, I assume I can rely on you to support me?"

Nathan said, "That's why we're here. I can't think of a better summary of what it is we're about, M-M. May I call you M-M?"

"Okay, Nathan, we're talking mutual support generally, and Goodman investigation in particular, am I right?"

"What Goodman investigation?" Nathan asked casually.

Moriarty nodded. "So we're both reasonable men," he said.

"I'm not." Kenzy was looking directly at Moriarty. "The Goodman investigation is mine," she said. "And I'm not a reasonable man."

"Nathan, do we have a deal or not?" asked Moriarty, suddenly uncertain.

"A deal as in…" Nathan prompted.

"As in you stay the hell away from the Harvey Goodman thing, or your outfit stays the hell away from this station."

"I think we can do better than that, sir," Kenzy said politely and took the micro-recorder from the breast pocket of her coverall. Carefully she disconnected the optic thread which linked it to the lens in the name tag above the pocket.

"*As in you stay the hell away from the Harvey Goodman thing, or your outfit stays the hell away from this station,*" the laser-clear image of Moriarty said on playback through the free-access terminal.

"That is unauthorized surveillance," Moriarty blustered. "Illegal recording and a major violation of my civil rights."

Kenzy said to Nathan, "I try to learn from my mistakes. Even the really stupid ones."

"You fucking people are in deep shit," shouted Moriarty, as he snatched the bugging kit from Kenzy. "And this is state-of-the-ark. I cannot believe you got this piece of crap onto my station. I want to know how you got it past the security scan."

Nathan smiled thinly, "Red thirty-four is a construction cargo bay," he said. "It's so far out, there *is* no security scan."

"You have to be careful when you're scoring cheap points, sir," Kenzy said. "You can get to like them so much they can cost you the game."

"You can't authenticate it," Moriarty offered. "An obvious fake? Christ, you couldn't buy a court that'd accept it."

"I'm prepared to give it a go," Kenzy said, pokerfaced. "If that's what you want, sir?" Moriarty's momentary hesitation betrayed him and she pressed home her advantage. "So, do you want to volunteer your version of what happened to Harvey Goodman? Or would you prefer something more formal, sir?"

Harvey Goodman loaded the next sample into the small electron microscope and adjusted the screen brightness. He yawned. "Sample two seventy-four," he said.

The picture quality was reasonable but the high angle made it difficult to see the detail of what he was doing and it was impossible to see what the microscope was showing.

"Why didn't you have the computer do a feature and enhance?" Kenzy asked.

Moriarty said, "Oh, sure. We were looking to give as many people as possible a chance to get in on this."

Goodman was peering at the microscope screen. After a moment he began to dictate, "And after twenty-four hours exposure to the full vacuum what we've got are endospores..."

Nathan said, "But you kept the accident monitor pictures?"

"Insurance," said Moriarty. "Some gambles you don't take."

"...no wait, strike that...those aren't endospores those are clusters..."

"You understand what he's doing?" Moriarty asked.

Kenzy said flatly, "A space bug. He's engineering a space bug."

Nathan wondered if she was as certain as she sounded and whether he himself had already spotted it, or had he realized only now that she said it?

"A virus that would survive the vacuum," he suggested.

Moriarty shook his head. "A bacterium," he said. "A killer that thrives in the vacuum."

"...*mycoplasmas?... strain two seventy-four?... can't be...*" Goodman was saying as he adjusted the microscope again.

"The process," Moriarty went on, "is called transduction. He used a specially engineered bacteriophage..."

"*No they are bacteria...*"

"...that's a virus that invades bacteria, to transfer genetic material from one strain of bacterium to another."

"*The strain has continued fission in the vacuum but the daughter cells are greatly reduced in size. My God you were tough little suckers, weren't you..?*"

"You seem to know a lot about it," Nathan said.

"Only because he kept notes in his cabin," Moriarty said.

"Only convenient," said Kenzy.

"You ain't seen nothing yet," Moriarty said and nodded at the screen.

"*Whoa,*" Goodman's posture was suddenly tense. "*What's happening here? My God, they're still dividing...*"

"The specimen was still alive?" Kenzy asked, incredulously.

Moriarty smiled sourly. "Seems it didn't register on the stupid bastard that if he bred a superbug, it might be tough to kill."

Goodman began to dictate more urgently. "*Fission continues and now at an accelerating rate...an exponential rate...oh Christ, they're...*"

"And that was all she wrote," Moriarty said as they watched Goodman's corpse drift away from the microscope. "Can you imagine what would have happened if whatever it was he developed in there had gotten out into the station?"

"What did you do with the module?" Nathan asked.

"Had it detached and welded tight. Dropped it towards the sun."

"Nobody queried that?"

"Contract workers don't give a shit so long as they're paid, and records can be amended."

Kenzy frowned. "I still don't understand why all the secrecy."

For a moment Moriarty looked uncertain whether to laugh or cry. "Jesus," he said finally. "Lennox was right. You really were bluffing."

Nathan said, "You didn't want Goodman's work made public."

"That stuff wasn't official. The bastard was supposed to be doing research in protein crystallography. Something to do with immunotoxin molecules. The sonofabitch wasn't supposed to be working on germ warfare, for Chrissakes."

"No problem, then," Kenzy said.

"Do you think anyone would have believed us if the story had gotten out?" Moriarty demanded. "Your Chinese buddies would've had a field day."

Nathan nodded and said, "So you decide to make Goodman a non-person. He doesn't exist. He never existed."

"It's not as dumb as it sounds. Man had no family. No-one would miss him enough to check, and even if they did," he shrugged, "it was a computer bug. It's happened before."

"Might never get sorted out," Nathan agreed. "You thought of everything, didn't you? You even paid off our man Hubble to make sure he kept his mouth shut. Pity about that. It was your payments to him that interested me in the first place."

Kenzy said, "The sister must have been a major embarrassment."

"Yes," Nathan said. "How did you miss her?"

Theroux still looked groggy, despite the intravenous medication which the health centre's computer was administering as they talked. "It was where she called from," he said, "but she doesn't live there."

Pete Lennox moved so that he was in the field of vision and said, "She never lived there. The place has been up for sale for more than a year. I talked to the realtor, the neighbours."

"Nobody's ever met the woman," Theroux said. "Odile Goodman doesn't exist."

On the bedside communications screen Kenzy, clearly impatient, shook her head. "*The computers say she does,*" she said.

Beside her Nathan said, "*And Harvey Goodman does exist, and the computers say he doesn't.*"

Theroux rubbed his aching eyes. "If she's not his sister, then who the fuck is she?"

"*Someone who wants the incident out in the open?*" Nathan said. "*Who would benefit from that, I wonder?*"

Ho was playing games – that much was obvious to Devis. The 'charming Chinese' routine was being pushed for all it was worth, which was not a hell of a lot as far as he was concerned. Privately, he had already christened the Base Co-ordinator 'Wangley Ho'. "The Commander has not yet returned, sir," he said stiffly.

Ho's smile was unwavering, as always. "Is he still with the Americans? Has something occurred to delay him?"

"Was your business urgent, sir? Perhaps I can help?" Devis said.

"Assuming he is still with the Americans," Ho said.

"Assuming you need to assume." Devis interrupted, barely polite.

"Is his return imminent?" Ho finished.

"When he gets back I'm sure you'll be the first to know, sir," Devis said watching to see if this time the man would take offence. But the smiling good humour was unaffected and Devis's mistrust grew accordingly.

"If you truly believe that I know everything, Colin," Ho beamed, "why do you make such an effort to give nothing away?"

"It's no effort, sir."

Ho said, "I am here to enquire of the developments in the Goodman case. Have there been developments?"

"I can offer you coffee," Devis said, going to the percolator.

"I am tempted, but regretfully there is insufficient time for such a pleasure."

Devis poured himself a cup. "Don't let me delay you then, sir," he said.

The burn was a risk, but Marty calculated the delay would have been more dangerous. As things had been going, he was fairly sure that Lauter's impatience would get the better of her eventually, at which point she would take a portable cutting torch to the module and end up killing them both. He had no more idea than she had what was inside the thing, but he didn't share her eager optimism about it. When they opened that monster up he wanted his feet on rock, his hands on a fully remote cutting rig, and all of him behind as much blast protection as he could get. So under the circumstances it seemed reasonable to use their remaining fuel reserves getting back to Moonbase as fast as possible, even though it did leave them without the legally required safety margins. That should have been no problem. Until now, they had always got a straight orbit injection on line and synch for immediate download to the workshops. Until fucking now.

"*Approach vectors and orbit are allocated,*" Moonbase Traffic Control repeated with weary patience, "*subject to priority override.*"

"What the fuck does that mean?" Marty demanded angrily.

"*It means we have a lot of traffic booked, and it's building up all the time, and what can I tell you?"*

"You can tell me," Marty snapped, "that we're not going to get bumped to make way for some flashy corporate flag carrier. Time is fuel, and at these prices, indies can't afford to waste it." He glared at Lauter.

"You can't blame me, dear heart," she said looking hurt and innocent. "Not for this one."

"No?"

"It's hardly my fault if you let your impatience get the better of you, is it?"

Nathan stood, and stamped his feet. It was cold. He turned the collar of his coat up and stared out across the chilly park. In the pale shadows cast by the low sun there were patches of frost, and a thin fog hung in the trees. Somehow, he had lost touch with the changes of season. Winter had been a surprise. He hadn't expected one-G to be this oppressive, either.

It was an odd feeling being back. Odd and oddly disappointing. Perhaps his ties to Earth were more fragile than he imagined. Perhaps he hadn't missed home as much as he thought he should have done.

He stamped his feet a couple more times. It looked as though it ought to have been warmer. The sunshine was sharply bright and the sky was blue. Suddenly he found himself remembering how much Lee had loved this time of year, and he was instantly overwhelmed by the melancholy beauty of it all. He wiped tears away with the heel of his hand and sat back down on the park bench. As he hunched into his jacket, he told himself it was the cold making his eyes water.

Behind him, someone said, "I got your message. Have you been waiting long?"

He was irritated to realize how dangerously preoccupied he had been.

"Long enough," he said, without looking round. "I began to think you weren't coming."

"I considered it. But then I figured you might not leave it at that. How did you find me?"

Nathan said, "Friends in low places."

"I guess you ran a trace on my user codes, didn't you? That's not strictly legal, you know."

Nathan gave a small noncommittal shrug, and said nothing.

"Come now, Commander, I thought you wanted us to meet out here so we could be candid with each other."

"You can be candid first," Nathan said, still gazing at the frozen landscape.

"Winter sunlight is the saddest thing, it's the memory of childhood, and the colour of passing years, it's loneliness and loss and all the people who are gone. You should avoid it as far as is humanly possible. You should never dwell on winter sunlight for too long; and never dwell in it at all… Do you know who wrote that?"

Nathan said, "I assume it wasn't your brother?"

"I never had a brother, Commander," Odile Goodman said, sitting down beside him, "as I think you know."

The visits were becoming more frequent and more irritating by the day but Devis couldn't find a way to stop them. Wangley Ho wouldn't take a hint, and it began to look as though physical violence would be the only way to dissuade him from dropping in whenever the mood took him. Like now, for instance. Devis tried the reasonable approach one more time.

"Sir, you really haven't got any right of access to this office." The man's snooping was getting beyond a bloody joke. It was blatant. This time he wasn't content with peering over your shoulder or poring over anything that was lying around, this time the bastard actually seemed to be trying to power up the spare workstation.

Ho said, "Come now, Colin. I am the Base Co-ordinator."

"That means nothing here."

"That is an interesting point of protocol."

"It's a point of law," Devis said and was about to make the point by offering to arrest him and file charges when the Ajax Salvage Company sidled in to register a claim on what they said was a discarded module.

It was Devis's view that you could trust a shit-sifter about as far as you could spit in a spacesuit, and under normal circumstances he would have been more searching in his interrogation of the cocky little pilot and her gloomy companion. He would probably have questioned how a complete module came to be unaccounted for on any of the routine databases. He might have been more sceptical about the logged retrieval position and its maximum hazard-to-navigation premium. And he would certainly not have issued an immediate license to open anything that had wound up in that thieves' swap meet they called a workshop. But these were not normal circumstances.

"What does the module contain?" Ho asked eagerly.

"We won't know until we cut it open," the woman said, and her face brightened with excitement.

Devis wanted to tell her to for fuck's sake not encourage Wangley, but instead he asked her partner, "Is the premium going through the Guild, or do you want a Base Credit?"

"*Guild,*" the man said, without any sign of his companion's enthusiasm. "*Please.*"

"It is necessary to cut it open. Why is this?" Ho asked the woman.

"*It's been sealed,*" she said happily. "*Welded shut. It's like a security strong box.*"

"I hope the contents are appropriately valuable," Devis said punching out the coded hard copies which Ajax needed to proceed. "This is just routine, sir," he added, as Ho came over to look. "There's nothing here that could possibly interest you."

"On the contrary, Colin," Ho said. "Routines have always fascinated me."

Marty did all the routine tests, every non-destructive procedure he could think of, without coming up with any really good reason not to go ahead and open the module. The sonic scan had showed something in there which looked suspiciously like it could be a body. But Lauter had demanded, "So what? Open the damn thing up, and we'll know for sure." And there was no answer to that.

Still he hesitated. What was it about the thing? Incongruously, it seemed much bigger here in the relative roominess of the workshop than it had in the cramped hold of the cargo shuttle. It was looming and shadowy, as though it was sucking away all the light. He could barely see the remote cutting frame. Not that he needed to see it. It was set and ready to go. All he had to do was touch the start control. Still he hesitated. What was he afraid of?

"What are you afraid of?" Lauter asked, in her most accusing voice.

Stupid question. Death. He was afraid of death. Living might be shitty but it was better than the alternative, which was nothing. "Nothing," he said.

"Then let's go, let's go." She was almost dancing with frustration. "For God's sake, Marty, love of my life, hit the switch and put us out of your misery."

So, because he could think of no alternative, and no way to say no to her, Marty set the cutters going.

On the other side of the workshop, the lasers flashed and bit into the weld which sealed the module's hatch. Marty felt the darkness thicken. His throat constricted suddenly and breathing became difficult. His head began to spin.

And then the cutters stopped. The control panel was dead. And the Chinese Base Co-ordinator was apologizing for such direct interference.

"You can't just march in here and stop us working," Lauter protested.

"It has been necessary to cancel the licence to open," Ho said, and proffered a Central Secretariat printout.

Marty examined it. "I don't believe this."

"I found myself concerned," Ho said, "to understand why this module was welded closed."

"Fucking bureaucracy," Marty complained, bitterly enough to cover the immense surge of relief he felt.

"Any time you want a job as a detective, Jiang Li," Nathan said to the happily beaming Ho, shaking his hand warmly.

Ho seemed genuinely flattered. "You are very complimentary, Nathan," he said, "but I think I could not meet the professional standards you require." There was no trace of irony in his voice.

"I don't think you've seen us quite at our professional best," Nathan said, with more than a trace of it in his.

"We are alive," said Ho. "That is what is important." And, turning to include Devis in the conversation, added, "Is it not, Colin?"

"It is indeed, sir," Devis said coolly.

"I offer everyone my congratulations," Ho said, "on a job most well done." Then unexpectedly he clapped his hands in a formal gesture of applause. That done, he bowed to Nathan, and was gone.

As the doors slid closed, Devis snorted, "Detective, my arse. He knew what was in that thing. He knew all along."

"He asked all the right questions," Kenzy said.

"Meaning I didn't, I suppose?" Devis challenged.

"Don't have a go at me," she said. "I'm on your side."

On his communications console, the 'message incoming' icon was flashing, and Nathan crossed towards it. "We were none of us very sharp on this one."

"Because it was a game," Devis complained. "Chinese bloody checkers.

And he outplayed us. Us *and* the Americans."

Nathan sat down at his workstation. "I don't think so," he said, cueing the message.

On his screen, Odile Goodman said, *"Nathan, sorry I wasn't around when you called. I just got your message. Is there a problem, officer?"*

Kenzy ignored the call and demanded with a small rhetorical flourish, "Who was the woman, then? If the Coms didn't set her up to expose the Yanks who did?"

"Dilly," Nathan was saying, "my information is they're both on their way to Earth. For some reason they've chosen to use Temple Bay."

"We've been fucked over by everyone and his uncle," Devis said.

"Yeah, we even let those two creeps on the *Ronald Reagan* get away with more rule violations than I ever thought of," Kenzy said.

"I wouldn't go that far," said Devis. "Attila the Hun didn't get away with more than you thought of."

"Thanks for the tip," Odile smiled. *"If there's ever anything I can do for you…"*

Smiling back, Nathan said, "I'm sure I'll think of something."

It was only at this moment that Devis and Kenzy realized Nathan was paying them no attention at all, but was totally absorbed with someone on his screen. And when whoever it was giggled, said, *"You know where I'm at, lover,"* and broke the connection, they knew they had missed something significant.

Moriarty and Lennox strolled across the concourse of the Temple Bay Spaceport towards the intercontinental transit lounge.

"It's routine." Moriarty was clearly getting bored with trying to reassure the other man.

"It's a full commission hearing, M-M." Lennox was equally obviously frustrated with Moriarty's confident lack of concern.

"If the record showed anything less than a full commission hearing it would look like a cover-up, for Chrissakes," Moriarty said.

"An emergency hearing?"

"Speed, Pete. Like teenage fucking. Over before anyone notices." He sniggered.

"I still think –" Lennox persisted.

Moriarty paused to interrupt irritably. "It will not come out into the open," he grated at him. "They won't let it come out into the open. It is in no-one's interest for it to come out into the open."

"Yoo hoo! Gentlemen!" Odile Goodman called from the entrance to the transit lounge.

"Christ," Lennox muttered. "What the hell is she doing there?"

"Who is that bitch?!" Moriarty demanded to know. "And what the fuck is it she wants?"

Odile waited until they got closer, and then said loudly. "Rumour has it there's been some very secret, very nasty and very fatal experiments out on the *Ronald Reagan*. Would you care to comment at all?"

"Who exactly are you?" Lennox asked.

She smiled. "Odile Goodman. No relation, of course. You know what they say; only the name's been changed to trap the guilty. Did you know that you can change your name quite legally as often as you like?"

Moriarty tried to push past her, but she stood her ground. "Get out of my way, you crazy bitch," he said.

"You might find that a useful tip," she continued imperturbably, "when you're looking for a new career. Assuming you don't go to jail, that is."

Moriarty moved again, and this time she stepped aside to let him reach the door. It slid open and he strode into the transit area. The waiting reporters surged forward eagerly.

Lennox got a good look at the goat-fuck and decided, very quickly, not to follow his boss inside. As the door shut again, he said to Odile Goodman, "Which one are you?"

"World Press Association," she said, flashing her ID and a big smile.

"You get my exclusive," Lennox said, "in return for protection from that." He nodded at the closed door. "And legal representation."

"Done deal," she said, and hustled him away.

Little Green Men and Other Martians

Rumours of what had been discovered on Mars, during seismic mapping towards the eastern end of the Valles Marineris, seemed to have reached Earth itself almost before Tolly Jardine got back to the colony with his find. It was not clear how these stories had got started, but what soon did become clear was that there was no hard information to be had. Nothing was definitely known about the burrow at survey grid reference 77436152, or about its mysterious occupant.

There was resentment among the rest of the colonists that Jardine, Dearman and the other four members of the Ground Team Mars Geological Survey were so close-mouthed over something which was important to everyone who had made the arduous journey to that inhospitable planet. If what was being said was true, then it was important not just to them, but to the whole human race. Only there was no way of knowing if what was being said was true.

"That's all you're going to say?" The chairwoman of the colony council was scowling with disapproval, but she knew that Tolly was within his rights.

"Look," he said, almost apologetically, "none of us came to Mars for the climate and the ocean frontage, did we? I mean, there's a good chance I can parlay this up into fame and fortune and a first-class ticket home. I'm not about to risk that."

"And the others?"

"Get a share of what I make."

"They've agreed?"

From the back of the meeting room, Stella Dearman spoke for the rest of the Base One Team. "Damn right we have."

"It could be a breach of your employment contract," one of the council members suggested.

"No it couldn't," Tolly said.

"Anything found during the survey belongs to the colony."

"Anything found as a *result* of the survey," Tolly corrected him, "belongs to the colony. The wording was to do with limiting the insurance you people gave us, if you remember."

"It was the same for everyone working outside the dome."

"I'm not complaining," Tolly said. "We weren't covered for accidental suit failures, and you weren't covered for incidental finds." He shrugged. "Just don't try and change the rules now, okay?"

As the council meeting broke up and members were folding away the table and chairs, the possibility of forcing Jardine and his companions to surrender their find came up. To her credit, the chairwoman's angry response made it very clear that any action of that kind would be illegal and unacceptable. She was not to know that it would also have been impossible.

Devis yawned. He disliked working the Moonbase immigration desk and he especially disliked working it on the third shift. Groundsider clearance procedures were depressing at the best of times, and when you were as tired as he was now, it was not the best of times.

The late shuttle had brought in the usual motley collection of humanity. There were general technicians, engineering staff and maintenance workers returning from Earthside leave. There were a few replacements for injured and retiring personnel. And there was one visitor with a full sheaf of temporary access passes, all of which required the many and varied eye-crossing, tee-dotting bureaucratic formalities.

While he waited for the computer to confirm the ID and entry permissions, Devis stared at the man in the prescribed manner. Such cold-eyed appraisals were supposed to make the guilty look guilty, but Devis knew from years of experience what bullshit that was. The only people who didn't look guilty under the hard gaze of a copper were the ones with something serious to hide. No point telling the little smart arses in the Central Secretariat that, of course, and more than his balls were worth to ignore their stupid training briefs. Nathan would castrate him with a low-powered laser if he did anything to jeopardize the drive to extend the power and influence of the ISPF. Everything was by the bloody book these days. Empire building depended on good PR, it seemed. And good PR depended on not offending anyone.

The man's name was Daniel Larwood and he appeared to be English, in his forties, average height, average build, brown hair, blue eyes, no distinguishing features. He was also quite unfazed by the scrutiny. If anything, he was mildly amused by it. So: Crook? Spook? The data began scrolling up on the screen. Devis snorted. He should have guessed. "A journalist," he said. "We're honoured."

Star Cops

Larwood said, "Is that an instruction, or merely a pious hope?" Then he smiled a rumpled grin, just in time to take the sting out of the words.

The mannerism reminded Devis of Nathan. "It's not our function to give people instructions, sir," he said flatly and without returning the smile.

"I must have misread your shoulder flashes," Larwood said. "I thought you were a policeman." He produced a battered hip flask, took a long pull from it and gave a small shudder.

"If that's booze, Mr. Larwood," Devis said, "it's a big mistake out here."

Larwood shrugged. "It's probably a big mistake anywhere, but then…" His voice trailed off abruptly as he saw David Theroux coming to the desk from one of the inner corridor links. Quickly recovering from his surprise, he said, "But then, mistakes are what make us human, no?"

"Out here, mistakes are what make you dead," Theroux said.

Larwood offered his hand. "Hullo, David. They told me you were a top cop now, but I stuck up for you anyway."

Theroux ignored the outstretched hand. "Still polishing your Pat O'Brien impression, Daniel?"

"Had to give it up," Larwood said. "Couldn't get the accent. Couldn't write like Ben Hecht either, unfortunately."

"So you settled for the more general image?"

Larwood nodded. "Drunken hack."

Theroux gestured at the hip flask. "If you please?"

Larwood hesitated for a moment and then handed it over with a repeat performance of the shrug and the rumpled smile.

Theroux took a swig from the flask. Showing no surprise, he said, "Water."

Devis let his surprise show. "Water?"

Larwood said, "I love a good miracle don't you?"

"You were always a phony," said Theroux, and he tossed the flask back at Larwood who, despite the deliberately straight and slow trajectory which one-sixth G allowed, did not catch it cleanly.

"What brings you to Moonbase, Mr. Larwood?" Devis asked. "Working on a particular story are we?"

"We hope so," Larwood said. "Though we are, in fact, not that particular these days."

"No change there, then," Theroux said coldly.

Devis frowned as he keyed in the acknowledgement codes and arrival confirmations. He was puzzled. There was obviously bad blood between these two but he had never known David Theroux to be so unsubtle about his hostilities. He hadn't known him that long, of course. "Your clearances are all in order, sir," he said to Larwood. "Have a nice stay."

Before Larwood could move, Theroux reached down and scooped up his flight bag. He opened it without a word and made a cursory search. Two bottles of brandy were wrapped in a spare jacket. He checked the labels carefully then put the bottles back and sealed the bag again. "Use it sparingly, Daniel," he said quietly. "You won't find another source out here."

Larwood looked rattled for a moment. "I liked you better as a student, David," he said.

"Why not? I believed what you told me in those days."

"I told you I was a journalist."

"Even that."

"Low blow. You were a disappointment to me, too. I was quite put down when I realized you and your friends weren't as radical as your reputations suggested."

"Pity the story you sold didn't say that."

"Actually it did. But the merest mention of the word 'radical', and your countrymen have always seen red. Comes of being the land of the brave and the home of the free, I suppose."

"Keep in touch," Theroux said.

"Depend on it," Larwood said, trying for 'casual' as he walked away, but looking clumsily uncontrolled in the odd gravity.

"Water in a hip flask and brandy in his bag?" Devis asked.

"A subtle double bluff, in his book," explained Theroux.

"I hate to seem picky, but in our book, the brandy was a violation."

"He was a friend, once," Theroux said. "I don't want to see him go blind on drive fuel."

"You serious? The Scotch they make out in shuttle repair is better than the real thing."

"Does it seem like a good idea to have a thirsty journo find that out?"

"Is that the sort of story he'll be looking for?" Devis frowned, though in fact he was almost amused. "Our leader *will* be chuffed."

Theroux shook his head. "Daniel Larwood doesn't look for stories any more," he said. "He's got a big rep, and he acts strictly on information

Star Cops

received. Something's coming down, Colin. Something big and ugly."

Devis yawned again. "Sounds like my third wife's divorce settlement," he said.

It had taken the crew of the freighter *Pohl Star* most of the long haul back from Mars to persuade themselves that they could get away with it. The pilot had a reputation as something of a chancer and a bit of a crook, but it was the co-pilot and navigator who was the keener of the two. She badly wanted to see what a Martian looked like. And once they'd opened the case, they were already in the worst kind of trouble – so there wasn't much point in being coy about a picture of the thing…

Nathan was not in the mood for this. He was sorely tempted to use the control-hopping that he had at last mastered and shake off Jiang Li Ho. But that would have been rude – and courtesy, he knew, was extraordinarily important to the Moonbase Co-ordinator. He supposed it must be a Chinese cultural thing. "I'm sorry, Jiang Li," he said, lengthening his stride a little, but not to the full looping hop. "You of all people should know I haven't got the authority to expel this Larwood character."

Ho matched his pace. "A police charge of any kind," he suggested, "would… work the oracle." He spoke the last phrase with a slight flourish, as he always did when he felt he had mastered a colloquialism.

"He hasn't done anything to warrant a charge," Nathan said, deliberately misunderstanding.

"Why is he here?" Ho persisted.

"Ask him."

"We are not comfortable to have reporters nosing around at this time."

"Why not? We've got nothing to hide," Nathan said, thinking *except that you obviously have*.

Ho said, "I have an important guest." It was by way of an admission.

"I don't think we were notified of that," Nathan said, with a show of polite surprise.

"Dr. Philpot is here by diplomatic invitation," Ho said gravely.

Nathan nodded. "I see." He wondered whether Jiang Li Ho really thought that because his visitor had bypassed the normal entry procedures, he had slipped in unnoticed.

"I do not wish him to be harassed."

"What exactly *do* you wish, Jiang Li?"

Ho stopped, forcing Nathan to stop as well, and turn back to face him. He beamed the broad, cheerful smile which had eased so many difficult negotiations. "We are friends, is this not so, Nathan? You trust me? You trust my good purposes... my good intentions."

"The road to hell is paved with those," Nathan said.

"You will deal with this journalist for me?" Ho urged.

Nathan smiled. "Of course," he agreed. Adding, "If he breaks the law," as he finally gave in to the impulse, and strode off in long looping hops towards the Star Cop offices.

Everything about Dr. Andrew Philpot was smooth and tasteful: from his perfectly uniform tan to his expensively tailored clothes; from the streaks of grey hair at his temples to his carefully manicured fingernails. Even his annoyance was languidly elegant. "I took it for granted that the local constabulary would co-operate more readily," he said, managing to combine boredom with just a hint of menace.

"I fear no-one is ready to be taken for granted, Dr. Philpot," Ho said thoughtfully. "Least of all, perhaps, Commander Spring."

"Confidentiality is the *sine qua non*. Without it..." Philpot left a threat unspoken.

Ho said, "We have the cover story, if it is needed."

"And if the press believe it."

"Why should they not?" Ho beamed.

Philpot raised a sceptical eyebrow. "Why should your policeman not do as he was told?" he said.

Nathan got the coffees from the General Mess dispensing machine and brought them across to where Daniel Larwood sat waiting at a corner table. "Since you declined my invitation, I'm afraid you'll have to put up with this stuff."

"Nothing personal, Commander," Larwood said. "I prefer to meet policemen on neutral ground, whenever possible."

"I do my best not to take things personally, Mr. Larwood. I know some people find police offices uncomfortable."

Larwood smiled. "Oppressive, even."

Nathan sipped his coffee, thinking – as he knew he always did at this moment – that it tasted lousy, but at least it was in a cup and not in a sealed pack with integral straw. "Drinks machines never change, do they?"

he said with a grimace.

"Nice to have something to rely on," Larwood said and poured a generous slug of brandy into his own cup. "Sweetener?" He offered the hip flask.

Nathan took the flask and sniffed the contents. "Nice," he said. "But no thanks."

"Aren't you going to tell me how dangerous that is out here, not to mention illegal?"

Nathan closed the flask and handed it back. "You already know that and we don't want to waste each other's time. After all, you're a famous man and I'm a busy one."

"Everyone's famous in their head," Larwood said. "Don't you think?"

"I'm just a simple plod," Nathan said, with a perfectly straight face. "Tell me, what's your interest in Dr. Philpot?"

"Have I got one?"

Wrong answer, Nathan thought, *you should've said: 'Philpot, who he?'*. "There's been a suggestion that you might have."

Larwood sipped his coffee. "Paranoia. There's a lot of it about."

Nathan shrugged. "He *is* an important man, though. A man with serious clout."

Larwood looked amused and a bit smug. "If you say so."

Nathan thought, *okay, let's see how vain you are*, and said, "But obviously you *do* know who he is. Don't you?" It was too late to deny it now without looking foolish, and just admitting it without comment would be almost as bad. Silence would have been his best option.

Larwood said, "He works at the Holdy Museum in Southern California."

Well, well, Nathan thought, *so what else will you tell me?* "Is that the one that's got more money than God?" he prompted, smiling.

"Story is, their accounts system crashed trying to keep up. Just before it went down, the computer suggested they give up counting and try weighing the money from time to time instead"

Nathan chuckled appropriately, and then put on a more or less earnest expression. "No wonder they can afford to hire people like Dr. Philpot."

"He's not exactly a major talent," Larwood said, unable to keep the scorn out of his voice.

"No?"

"They've got a hundred curators just like him. They're known as 'the bumbling herd'. Philpot's distinguished himself from the rest of them in no way whatsoever." And that, Larwood's expression finally said, was as far as he was going on the subject.

"Not just paranoia, then," Nathan suggested.

Larwood shrugged. "Routine information. Readily available."

"The sort of background you'd have on anybody and everybody you're not in any way interested in."

"I have a good memory. And, as it happens, I've been doing some stuff on the Holdy."

"Well," Nathan said, "what are the odds? Small world. Unless you've got the contract to paint it, of course."

Larwood drank some of his coffee. For a moment, he seemed tempted to top up the space he had made in the cup with more brandy, but then he smiled the rumpled smile and put the flask back in his pocket. "A joke," he said. "It's been my experience that a sense of humour is not that common among policemen." Across the mess, the wallzac began to change. The white beach, palm trees and clear blue ocean which was playing on the picture wall slowly dissolved, and reformed into an avenue of magnificent beech trees, bright with the first flush of spring leaves.

"I was under the impression you found most coppers funny," Nathan said. "What was that series you did for Global News?"

"*Cops and Robbers: A Plain Man's Guide To The Difference?*" Larwood smiled warmly. "I was at the top of my game then. Didn't you think so?"

"I'm not really qualified to judge," Nathan said.

Larwood's smile became more studied. "Quite a number of your colleagues felt qualified to judge. Several of them volunteered to be jury and executioner too. I took to carrying a gun."

Nathan shook his head. "Never an answer," he said.

"Depends on the question," Larwood said.

Nathan shrugged. "People get carried away."

"In body bags. That was a thought that kept bothering me."

"Not something you need worry about out here."

"You'll protect me. You being just a simple plod."

"You, and everyone else who stays within the law."

"That sounds like it might be a warning."

"Paranoia," Nathan said, and smiled his best smile. "There's a lot of it about."

* * *

Theroux could see that his enthusiasm had carried him away and he was being boring, but he couldn't resist the urge to finish the argument he was making. "And he looks at her and he says something like: You can ask me this one thing. And she asks him did he kill them, and he tells her a flat lie. Right there, the ground shifts and you know there is no such thing as truth."

Devis, who had not made much of an effort to look like he was listening, said, "It's just an old movie, for God's sake." The freight elevator stopped at the main cargo level and he thumbed the access request. As they waited for the computer to check the atmosphere balance, Theroux said, "Yeah, well, *Crime and Punishment*'s just an old book."

With no pressure differences registering in its control zone, the computer arrived at a low probability of environmental failure and opened the airtight doors. "Exactly," said Devis, as the two men stepped out into the vast warehouse.

For some reason of his own, Larwood now wanted to talk. It seemed to Nathan as if the man was deliberately trying to keep him at the table.

"Not just journalists like me," he was saying, "that's a cop-out, you should pardon the expression. Everyone has that responsibility."

But why does he want me here? Nathan wondered. "You're not suggesting everyone should tell the truth?"

"I'm suggesting that whatever you *say* starts to be true. Not truth, but *true*."

"The difference being?"

"Truth is an objective thing, true is just what people believe. And if you say it, you open the possibility of it being true. Say it often enough, and the possibility becomes a probability. Get enough people to say it often enough..."

Nathan smiled. "I take it you don't like politicians much."

"Love them," Larwood said. "Couldn't eat a whole one, mind. When do you leave for Mars, by the way?"

Nathan smiled more broadly. He hadn't expected to have one of his own tricks used against him. Was that why Larwood had kept him there, to interrogate him? "More routine information?" he suggested.

Before Larwood could press the question, a young woman approached the table and interrupted him. "Excuse me," she said. "You're Daniel Larwood, aren't you?"

"I was the last time I looked," Larwood said pleasantly.

Less irritated than I would have been myself, Nathan thought, *if a moment I had worked for had been stepped on like this.* The woman had the close-cropped hair and pale complexion of regular space crew, and she was clutching a paper book-pad and ink stylus. "I'm a great admirer of your work," she said.

"Thank you," Larwood said, going into what looked and sounded like a standard routine, "And you don't even look like my mother."

"I do a little writing myself," the woman said.

"Really?"

"I don't suppose you'd read some of my stuff?"

Larwood smiled his rumpled smile, and shrugged his tired shrug. "You seem very friendly," he said, "and I never read a friend's work."

"Why not?" Nathan asked, to cover the woman's embarrassment.

"Suppose I didn't like it?"

"Suppose you did?" the woman said.

"That would be worse. *Much* worse."

The woman laughed, and to Nathan's surprise she proffered the book-pad and stylus to Larwood and said, "Can I have your autograph, or is that too silly?"

"It's not silly at all," Larwood said taking them. "Who shall I make it to?"

"Jane," she said.

Larwood examined the book-pad carefully, and when he had found a suitable page he began to inscribe a message on it. "Actually," he said as he was writing, "I know why we collect autographs. If you think about it, someone's signature seems such an arbitrary and odd thing to want and yet... When my father died, the only real thing which remained of him to me, the most direct link, the thing which proved he had existed, was his handwriting." He finished and returned book-pad and stylus to the woman. "Thank you," she said, and – talking to Nathan for the first time – added, "I'm sorry to have intruded."

"No problem," Nathan said, and wondered, as he admired the skill with which she moved back across the mess, why she hadn't looked at the autograph.

"What happens here," Larwood asked, "while you're away bringing civilization to the Martian colony?"

"Nobody," Nathan said, and then remembered that he hadn't

admitted he was going, and thought he was definitely getting careless, "is indispensable."

"That's usually a good reason for staying put," Larwood said wryly.

Nathan swallowed the last of his coffee. "That's something you're not going to be doing if we should get any complaints. Harassing people, anything like that."

"I never harass anyone," Larwood protested mildly. "People come to me. I'm a lot like a policeman."

Nathan shook his head. "Mostly, we have to go looking. You're more like a journalist."

Larwood raised an eyebrow. "More like?"

"You get things wrong," Nathan said without smiling.

Main Cargo was the biggest structure on Moonbase. All the Earth-Moon freight, and most of the goods for the other colonies and bases, came there to be unpacked and distributed, or sorted and reloaded for onward consignment. Whatever the eventual destination, Customs and Contraband officers were required to check all incoming shipments for illegal products and controlled substances. Various scanners and detectors were operating, but the accepted wisdom was that nothing worked as effectively as experienced officers making random searches – especially if the searches were not completely random.

"It's not exactly the major drugs haul you lot came to the Moon to intercept, is it?" Devis commented. "Or am I missing something here?"

Bod Kitson, one of the Customs Service's most experienced field men, had recognized Devis as an old sweat like himself, and was not offended by the other man's amused scorn. "Don't be like that," he said. "You know we can't ignore a tip-off any more than you can."

Theroux looked sceptical. "A major CCS task force shipped out on the strength of one Earthside tip-off?" he said. "Must have been a hell of a good source."

"Ours not to reason why," Kitson said casually, and returned to his painstaking search of the cargo to which he had been assigned.

"What the fuck is this?" Devis demanded, as he examined the small stone carving of a squat bird – or maybe a man in a bird mask.

"Beats the shit out of me," Kitson said. "But it wasn't on the cargo manifest, so it shouldn't have been there."

"So it's contraband?" Theroux asked.

"Yes indeedy." Kitson did not even bother to look up from his scanner. "That's what it is all right." Devis's superior officer was too young and too obviously wet-behind-the-ears to be anything other than a minor irritation to him, and he made no effort to hide the fact.

"Where did you find it?" Theroux asked.

Devis shook the statuette vigorously, then scratched it with a fingernail. Kitson concentrated on adjusting the power on the handset a little, and said, "In one of the boxes."

"Yeah, well, I'm glad you lads are holding the line against ugly statues," Devis said. "It's my view, that they are the principle threat to civilization as we know and love it."

"Suit yourself," said Kitson. "Your guv'nor told my guv'nor he wanted to be kept in touch with developments."

Devis brandished the statuette. "And this is a development?"

It was Kitson's turn for amused scorn. "It didn't warrant sending your own little task force, I'll allow." He still did not look up from the scanner screen.

Theroux had finally had enough. Colin Devis could behave as though this guy was some kind of kindred spirit, but he had no intention of being treated like an asshole any longer.

"Mr. Kitson, show me exactly where you found it, if you please," he said brusquely.

Kitson hesitated. It was clear he didn't much care for the tone of voice, and they both knew that Theroux had no direct authority. He stopped what he was doing and looked at Theroux. Theroux stared back at him and waited in expressionless silence. After a long pause, Kitson pointed to a stack of cartons marked: EXPLOSIVES/WITH CARE. "Second one down," he said. "Under the top layer." But he pointedly made no move to show him exactly where.

"None of this stuff is actually for Moonbase, is it?" Devis asked as Theroux lifted out the carton.

"It's a Mars shipment," Kitson said.

Below the top layer of seismic test charges, several had been removed to make room for the statuette.

"Why all the attention, then?" Devis asked.

"Random search. You know how these things are."

Devis drew Kitson to one side and lowered his voice so that Theroux could not overhear. "You randomly targeted a Martian cargo? Come on

Bod, give me a break here. You people have always fucking ignored them."

"The policy must have changed. Don't ask me, I'm just PBI."

"Poor bloody infantry? Yeah, right." Devis juggled with the statuette, flipping it from hand to hand. "So, what, you just stumbled across this?"

"Live a good life and you can expect a little luck sometimes," Kitson said.

"Not in my experience."

Kitson glanced towards Theroux, who was still examining the hiding place, and murmured, "Seems we need to justify our existence and soon, Colin. Bollocks are on the block."

"You reckon this thing'll do it?"

"I haven't lived *that* good a life," said Kitson, setting the detector for a full spectrum drugs scan.

As they walked back towards the freight elevator, Theroux asked, "Did you get anything out of him?"

"Nothing we didn't already know," Devis said.

Theroux nodded. "I told you it wouldn't work."

Devis said, "Next time, try and be a bit more of a prat, will you? The officer we love to hate, remember?"

"I find it difficult to be a bastard," Theroux said. "It's casting against type."

"I'll believe you," Devis said. "Thousands wouldn't."

The shuttle was bucking and shaking. Visuals flashed through the screens too fast to be of much help. The instruments would not balance enough to give her an accurate reading of how close she was to the lunar surface. That much was normal, anyhow. She was considering boosting out into orbit for the rest of the run back, but it would cost her time and fuel. She might miss the freighter, and she would certainly lose most of her bonus. Still not a clear call, though.

"*Supply shuttle four, this is outpost seventeen, do you copy?*" The voice of that officious little outpost controller, the one she had disliked so much, cut across her thoughts. "Outpost seventeen, this is supply shuttle four, I thought we said our goodbyes already, I am a little busy right now."

"*That lift-off was rocky. Is everything okay?*" He sounded fussy rather than concerned.

"Lifting off in these things is always rocky. That's why they pay me the big money. Conserving fuel comes at a price." She decided not to bother playing safe after all, but to carry on rock-hugging. She was high enough not to run into anything sudden.

"*We put a lot of work into what you're carrying. It's fragile, you realize.*"

The obnoxious little prick was really beginning to irritate her. "No shit?" she said. "Well if you want it past main cargo in time for the next Earth freighter, you'll just have to cross your fingers and toes."

"*Not at these prices.*"

She was almost pleased that the shuttle was still heaving and juddering. "Wanna bet?" she demanded, as she overrode the flight computer and fought for control.

"*What--you say--are breaking up, repeat please.*" The transmission from Outpost Seventeen was difficult to hear now and not before time.

"Can we stop wasting time?" she shouted. "I'm too old, too cold and too fucking tired for this shit!"

Suddenly the outpost controller's voice came through loud and undistorted. "*You're dropping off our radar. Should you be doing that?*"

Dropping off the radar?

"*Do you copy?*"

Christ, no. No, she shouldn't be doing that. "Oh, Christ," she said. "No."

It was the last sound she made, as she was overwhelmed by the howl of the impact and the decompression scream to silence. Noiselessly, the shuttle shattered against a crater wall and tore itself to pieces among the tumbled rocks.

"She's dead?" Philpot looked astounded.

"She was killed instantly," Ho said.

"What was she doing there?"

"She was... moonlighting." Satisfied that he had the right word, Ho showed no awareness of the pun. "You must understand." He got up from behind his desk and tried to pace. "No international funds have been available for Moonbase Technology Section to construct a specifically designed lunar flight vehicle. People skilled in the handling of the modified shuttle are therefore at a premium." The gravity defeated him, and he sat down again. "It is a very erratic machine. Most difficult to fly."

"So it would seem," Philpot said, making no move to get up from his own chair despite some uncharacteristic signs of real anger. "Well, quite frankly, Dr. Ho, I'm appalled."

"Something should be done about the MTS," Ho agreed, misunderstanding. "It has been in my mind to try and –"

Philpot ignored him. "This could ruin everything," he said.

Ho nodded vigorously, then said with a sudden beaming optimism, "I am leaving for Earth immediately. Perhaps I shall manage to expedite matters."

Philpot's response was not warm. "I hope so. I assume you realize who will be blamed for failure." This time, the threat was quite clear.

"So you think she'll be blamed?" Dana Cogill said from the back of the Moonrover, where she was sorting through debris from the wreck of supply shuttle four.

Kenzy raised her voice above the whine of the motors. "No worries," she said, pushing the MoRo towards its maximum speed. She was more than a little relieved to be driving rather than making preliminary forensic lists. Cogill was welcome to that job. The tall Irishwoman was one of the more recent recruits, so Kenzy knew little or nothing about her. Apparently she had been a paramedic in a previous life, which probably explained her lack of squeamishness. True, there was only a very remote chance that pieces of the pilot were left among the stuff they were hauling, but just the thought made Kenzy's flesh creep.

"But then again, if you didn't blame the pilot," Cogill asked, "who would you blame?"

"If I was the betting type…" Kenzy began.

Cogill laughed. It was a musical sound, unexpectedly deep and bell-like for such a slim woman. "Which, of course, you're not."

"Which, of course, I'm not," Kenzy agreed, laughing. "But if I was, I'd say the boys in shuttle maintenance had been smashing back that home brew of theirs. Missed a few clogged pipes, forgot to service the flight computer. It's minor oversights like that make the difference between flying and bouncing. Especially in an engineering lash-up like a modified lander."

The MoRo heaved itself up and over a boulder, lurching ponderously. "On the subject of bouncing," Cogill said, clutching at a handrail as she made her stumbling way forward.

"Sorry." Kenzy eased off on the throttle.

"She was young to die," Cogill said, taking the pilot's ID from its wallet and running the three hundred and sixty degree visual in the image window. She held it out for Kenzy to see.

"No-one's ever old enough to die," Kenzy said, and glanced at the pilot's face and profile. "Don't think I ever saw her around, did you?"

"No. But then, I haven't been around that long myself." Cogill pulled a second identical ID from the wallet. "Now, what would be the point of that, do you suppose? If she lost the one, she'd lose the duplicate as well."

"Typical shuttle jockey," Kenzy said. "If they'd got any brains, they wouldn't be flying those things."

Cogill went back to the cargo space and returned to her forensic work.

After a while, Kenzy said, "Do we know when Nathan's actually leaving, Dana? I mean, is he booked on the next freighter, or what?"

"How would I know?" Cogill said. "I'm not his social secretary."

"I wondered if you'd heard anything is all."

"You're more likely to be in the know than I am."

Kenzy switched in the automatics and turned round in her seat. "Only somebody's got to take over the second spot to David Theroux's number one," she said. "You've got the qualifications. I thought you might have got the nod."

Cogill's bell-like laugh rang out again. "Chief assistant to the assistant chief? I don't think so."

"Got a private income, is that it?" Kenzy asked, slightly irritated by her manner.

Cogill was too absorbed to notice. "Oh, the money would be handy all right," she said, pulling the packing brace from a broken equipment carton. "But management isn't really my thing." From inside the brace, a thin trickle of powder was drifting into her cupped hand. "What do you suppose this is?" she asked.

Kenzy reached for her suit helmet. "Better go onto self-contained air," she said. "Inhaling it might not be the brightest way to find out."

"Drugs? Are you sure?" Devis adjusted the communications screen, but he still couldn't see her clearly.

"*No, but it's a lot of trouble to go to for beef casserole,*" Kenzy said – her voice, like her face, partially obscured because she was suited-up.

"Might be a vacuum effect," he suggested.

"*It might be fucking fairy dust, but does that seem likely to you?*"

"Better bring it on in then."

"*That's a good idea.*" Her sarcasm was clear, even if her voice was muffled. "*We were planning to stop and dump it over the side.*"

"I meant," he said, with more patience than he would have shown if there had been anyone with him in the main office, "there's nothing we can do till you get back here. But then, you've always felt that, haven't you, Pal?" He smiled sourly and killed the connection.

After a brief pause, Kenzy came back on screen using her override. "*I hadn't finished.*"

He sighed heavily. "Don't tell me, let me guess. You want me to arrange chemical analysis and, put a hold on all travel clearances in the pipeline for any personnel from outpost seventeen. Anything else?"

"*No.*" She sounded disappointed.

Devis said, "I'm not as stupid as I look."

"*Well, duh,*" Kenzy said. "*How could you be?*" And this time *she* killed the connection.

He had keyed the mess table he was sitting at to WNS, and was staring down at Susan Caxton, who was staring up at him and saying, "*But questions remain to be answered, and clearly there is a reluctance –*"

"Sound off," Devis said and the superstar newsreader, anchorperson and universal sex fantasy continued the bulletin in dumb-show.

"I was listening to that," Kitson said, without raising his eyes.

"No, you weren't," Devis said, "you were waiting to look down her cleavage."

Kitson looked up at him. "Something wrong with nostalgia?"

Devis shook his head and sat down. "You'll go deaf, though."

"Quarter to four," Kitson said in a loud voice, looking at his wrist. "What *do* you do for sex out here?"

"Quarter to four," Devis said, in an equally loud voice.

Kitson looked back down at the black Australian journalist on the screen. "She does make me homesick, I have to say."

"You've got someone like that at home?" Devis asked.

"No," Kitson said, "that's why I'm sick of it."

"Listen," Devis said, "I didn't come here to do tired comedy routines."

"Where do you usually go?"

"That tip-off you're working on…"

"We don't burn our sources, Colin. You know the score as well as I do. There is no point in asking me –"

Devis held up his hands. "You've been looking for contraband coming into Moonbase from Earth, right? Do you check stuff going the other way?"

Kitson looked suspicious. "Back to Earth? No. Why would we do that?"

Devis favoured him with a shrug and a smug grin. "You're the experts."

Kitson snorted. "Somebody been growing opium poppies in the hydroponics plant?

"Close," Devis said.

"Are you winding me up?"

Devis glanced down, and noticed the visuals now backing Susan Caxton appeared to be stock shots of Mars. "Sound on," he instructed.

"*Meantime, rumours persist,*" she was saying, "*that something astounding has been discovered there, and is now on its way to Moonbase for eventual transhipment to Earth. No-one seems to know what this discovery might be; only that it could be something that will change forever the way Man sees himself. Is this just another of those instant myths which are suddenly on everyone's lips, and which are just as suddenly forgotten? Or is there really a secret being kept from us by an over-cautious authority? Stay tuned; only time will tell. This is Worldwide News. My name is Susan Caxton.*"

Larwood was late for the rendezvous, but he was no longer trying to hurry because his lack of co-ordination in one-sixth G made him conspicuous. The time and place had been written on a page of the autograph-hunter's book-pad, and unless he had misread it, he should have been pretty close by now. He looked for the junction number. Down here in the service tunnels, there seemed to be better signs than in the public corridors. He supposed that was deliberate. It would be more important for maintenance and repair people to find their way about than anyone else. Except, perhaps, for journalists who were following up on fairly dubious leads.

Then he saw him. Level three, junction four just as promised. Slim, late twenties, he was leaning heavily against the sloping side of the tunnel. Ridiculous the lengths to which some people would go to look nonchalant. Larwood glanced around. Satisfied that there was no-one else about, he approached, and keeping it casual just in case, said, "I'm Daniel Larwood. I think you have something for me." The young man turned his head and stared at him. There was no recognition in his face at all. The look was totally blank. He seemed almost asleep. Watching the eyes blink slowly and grope for focus, Larwood realized that he was on something. Given his age and his profession it was unlikely to be alcohol, but whatever it was, he was long gone and out there. "Can you hear me?" The man's expression struggled with vagueness, but the effort was brief and unsuccessful. Larwood spoke more slowly and articulated very distinctly. "My name is Daniel Larwood? You have something for me?"

Acknowledgement flickered in the eyes, and for a moment the man was fully conscious. "I... I..." he whispered.

Conscious or not, the stupid bastard still couldn't speak apparently. "For Christ's sake," Larwood said, "snap out of it, man."

"I... I..."

"What have you taken, you stupid bastard?"

The man sucked in a breath. It made a slimy, bubbling sound. "I de..." he managed to choke out, and then he gurgled a little.

"What's the matter with you?" Larwood said. He was tempted to shake the man, but he had some experience of these things and was not eager to be vomited over by a complete stranger – especially not in reduced gravity.

There was another desperately determined breath and the man tried again. "I de..." he burbled, "I de..." And then the attention went out of his eyes and the tension went out of his thin frame and his legs buckled and he sagged forward and he flopped down. Instinctively, Larwood had stepped back as this was happening. Now he looked at the abandoned slump of the body, and wondered whether his assumption had been correct after all. He moved closer, and for the first time he saw the man's back. There was a small dark stain on the coverall just below the left shoulder blade. Larwood reached down and felt his neck. There was no pulse. He looked around again but there was still no-one else about. He squatted down and began to search the dead man's pockets.

He looked bored, but Nathan could see the small movements of feet and hands that suggested it was an act. He continued to watch surreptitiously, while slowly preparing coffee for the three of them.

"Did you know him?" Theroux asked. He was sitting facing Larwood across the workstation in the small office they had set aside for interrogations.

"No," Larwood said.

Nathan finished pouring the coffees and brought them to the workstation. "But you were there to meet him?" he suggested mildly.

"No."

Theroux smiled coldly. "You just happened to be in one of the more deserted areas at one of the quieter times when there just happened to be a murder."

"It's called a coincidence," Larwood said. "That's how I came to be in a position to report it to you people. It's called an act of folly."

"Not at all, we're very grateful for your help, Mr. Larwood," Nathan said, and smiled his warmest smile. "Tell me, did you touch the body at all?"

"No, of course not."

"Not to see if he was dead?"

"Well, yes, I did that."

"So, you did touch the body." Theroux made it sound as though they had just proved the case against him. "Did you take anything?"

It struck Nathan that Theroux was enjoying the role of hard cop a little too much. If he let it get personal then this wasn't going to work.

"Like what?" Larwood demanded.

"The pockets were empty," Theroux challenged. "You tell us."

"I gave up robbing the dead when I took up journalism."

"No you didn't."

Time to call a halt, Nathan thought, we're not going to get at what he knows like this. "Right, Mr. Larwood. Drink your coffee and tell me what you think of it, and you can go."

Larwood looked surprised. "That's it?" he asked.

"Thank you for your patience," Nathan said, catching Theroux's eye and adding pointedly, "If we think of anything else, we know where to find you."

"Don't leave town?" Larwood said grinning.

"You can't, I'm afraid," Nathan said. "Out here, there's nowhere much to go to."

"There is no record of the shuttle pilot's arrival on Moonbase," Box confirmed.

"Thank you, Box," Nathan said, "that's all I wanted." Lately, the name had not been infallible as a command override, and he found himself waiting to see if Box would leave it at that.

"They're smuggling drugs out, I guess they could be smuggling people *in*," Theroux said. "Ever get the feeling things are out of control?"

Nathan stared round the empty main office. "They'd better not be." It only took a minor crisis to leave them drastically undermanned. He wasn't sure that he should be leaving under the circumstances. Only Devis had any real experience of coppering. "When I leave for Mars, I don't expect to see this place fall apart."

"No chance of that." Theroux grinned. "We don't have a real-time link between here and there. And, hell, we don't have enough people to make falling apart work effectively anyhow."

"Push Central Registry for an ID on the dead man," Nathan said. "I'm going to find out about the shuttle jockey."

"You sound like you think there might be a connection."

"Not that I can see."

"I can see two straight off," Theroux said. "They were both in the wrong place at the wrong time; and they're both dead."

Nathan shook his head. "Those are coincidences, not connections."

The woman was in her forties, and tired. The cubicle she occupied was walled with gibbering screens. Her eyes darted unceasingly between the images of freight being loaded, cargo manifests updating, lift and orbit schedules adjusting. Restlessly, her hands flicked across the control board in front of her, transferring screen inputs to the interactive main monitor so that she could scrutinize them more closely and issue orders directly over her throat-mic or via the keyboard. Watching her work, Nathan assumed that the problems were too haphazard for decisions to be handled by anything but a top-of-the-line machine. People were cheaper. "I don't know where she came from," the woman said irritably. "I'm just the operations manager. How the hell would I know where she came from?" She had been studying pictures of a cargo pod which the loading crew were having trouble lining up. Now she said, "Bump freight seven to twenty-one hundred."

"*It's gonna knock on,*" a voice said over the speaker.

"It's already knocked on," she snapped. "Don't waste my time arguing about it, just fucking do it!"

"*You're the boss.*"

"She was flying one of your modified shuttles," Nathan said.

"She was qualified," the woman said. "There aren't too many of them around, you know."

"There's one less now," Nathan commented sharply, hoping to get her full attention.

But she was already onto her next crisis. "Would you look at that?" she muttered, and punched a loading schedule up on her monitor. "Blake?" she demanded – and when there was no reply, almost yelled, "Blake! Where is bloody Blake when I need him?" Switching channels she bellowed, "Svenson?"

"*Yah?*"

"That Martian stuff on three-four should be loading now. Who transferred the work order? Never mind, just get them back on it, do you read me?"

"*Yah, yah!*"

"We're maximizing Mars traffic, and they're wasting time on Earth freight. You know what a window of opportunity is?"

It was a second or two before Nathan realized she was talking to him again. "I know Mars is closer at the moment," he said. "I'm going there myself soon."

"Go now," she said. "Please? Chaos is coming." She gestured at the screens.

Nathan said, "The planetary conjunction can't have taken you by surprise, surely."

"People take me by surprise," she said. "Look at this." She transferred a scrolling list onto her main screen. It was a steady stream of requests for the priority clearance of chartered Earth-Moon and inter-station shuttles. "Bloody press are driving me crazy. Some stupid rumour about little green men, and suddenly I'm up to my arse in morons." She punched up *Request Denied* and left it to repeat down the list.

"The dead pilot," Nathan said. "Where did you get her?"

"Why are you wasting what little time and sanity I've got left asking stupid questions about some unlucky shuttle jockey?"

"Because it looks like she was some unlucky drugs runner as well," Nathan said, grabbing her wrist and pulling her hand away from the board. "And you might have a lot less time left than you think."

She stared into his face. "Drugs runner? What drugs? What are you talking about?"

"Where did you get her?" Nathan repeated, keeping his expression cold, his voice flat and hard.

"She was just a freelance looking to pick up some extra cash. There would be nothing out of the ordinary about it."

"Except that there's no record of her arrival on Moonbase," Nathan said, and watched for the telltale eye movement, the evasive glance down or away.

"Isn't there?" she said, her puzzled gaze unflinching.

"You didn't check." Nathan made it both statement and accusation.

"Why should I? It's not my job." She tugged her wrist from his grasp. "She was here. She was a registered pilot. She was in temporary guest quarters." She turned her attention back to her screens. "What more did I need to know?"

Nathan stood on the threshold of what the Moonbase International Commissariat's Bureau de Concierge called a 'twin berth guest cabin'. What this meant was that the accommodation people didn't have the budget to provide sleep cells for transients. Small rooms, each with two bunks and a couple of storage lockers, were provided instead. This one had been completely ransacked.

As far as Nathan could see, the job had been done thoroughly but probably not professionally. Linings and pockets had been ripped from clothing when it would have been quicker and less obvious simply to feel for whatever they were looking for. Which was small and deliberately hidden, or at least that's what the searcher must have thought. Nathan picked his way carefully across the room. Personal odds-and-ends had been broken and thrown around; another waste of time and energy. It was definitely something particular and small, and chances were they hadn't found it, which might explain the violence.

It was when he saw the book-pad that he realized he had missed a move somewhere. He picked it up and flipped through it. Pages had been torn out, but the autograph was still there: *To Jane, who is anything but plain, best wishes for your future success, from your friend Daniel Larwood.* So, the dead pilot was the autograph-hunter. If he'd taken the trouble to look at the ID he would have recognized her sooner, of course. She had been sharing with someone. Some of the stuff clearly belonged to him. There didn't seem to be as much of it, but what there was had been trashed as thoroughly as hers. That could be to cover himself. He had disappeared, but then if he was part of the drugs ring, he would.

He considered running a full forensic, but as he stared round, he knew it would be a waste of time and resources. His old regional crime computer would have ruled it out and he would have protested. Only now there was nobody to protest to. And besides, the bloody thing would have been right.

Dr. Jiang Li Ho was in his element. He should have been shuttle-lagged after the journey, but he was having too much fun. He liked press conferences, and the bigger they were, the more he liked them. This one was huge, and he was enjoying it hugely.

"Dr? Dr. Ho?"
"Dr? Sir?"
"Sir? Dr? Dr. Ho?"

The clamour was incessant and insistent, remotes buzzed about, lights glowed.

"Yes?" Ho pointed at one of the reporters. "Yes, your question?"

"Why have you given orders that the Earth's media are to be denied access to Moonbase?"

"Yeah, what's that all about?"
"It's unconstitutional, you realize?"
"Undemocratic, wouldn't you say?"
"Is it because you're still a red, sir?"
"Is this orders from Peking, sir?"
"Or Hong Kong?"
"Is it Hong Kong, sir?"
"Sir?"

"One at a time, please, ladies and gentlemen." Ho held up his hands for quiet. "I have given no such order. Indeed, I am not in a position to give such an order."

"Whose order is it then, sir?" the same reporter pressed.
"Is it coming from the top?"
"Are you saying you're not in charge out there?"
"Why are we being kept out?"

"There has been no such order, no such order that I am aware of, and you are not being kept out."

"You mean when you go back to the Moon we can all go with you, is that what you're saying?!" someone at the back shouted above the hubbub.

Ho beamed. "Much as I enjoy your company gentlemen, and ladies – especially ladies – I regret we have no facilities to accommodate –"

"That's a crock–"
"–how come some people are–"

Star Cops

"-yeah, that's right-"

"-would you care to comment on the fact that Global and Worldwide have been chosen to represent us all?" someone else demanded.

"Global News already had a reporter on Moonbase, and it is my understanding that the other reporter has been chosen by lot."

"Yeah, and we all know what it's a *lot of*," Kenzy commented as she sat alone in the main office, and watched the news conference on one of the big screens.

"Even if a full media turnout might be difficult don't you think a limit of two is a bit extreme?" a voice from the scuffling goatfuck of reporters demanded.

"The bastards have carved it up between them," Kenzy muttered.

"The line must be drawn somewhere," Ho said, smiling regretfully in big close-up, *"however unwelcome I for one may find it."*

"Bull*sh*it," Kenzy snorted. "Tell 'em what you got out of the deal, Wangly."

Coming into the office, Nathan said, "I don't want to hear you calling him that, okay?" He was about to add *keep doing it and eventually it'll be said to the wrong person in the wrong place and be misunderstood* but Kenzy wasn't putting up a fight.

"Okay," she was saying, "I still don't understand why you trust him, though."

Nathan was finding this newly reasonable Kenzy disconcerting. He couldn't quite believe that she was eager enough for the promotion to behave so blatantly out of character. "Did David get that ID?" he asked.

"It's on your recall."

From the screen, a voice focused out of the hubbub and asked, *"When does the Martian actually arrive on Moonbase, Dr. Ho?"*

Nathan and Kenzy both turned to the screen for Ho's reply.

"As I understand it, the freighter will be out of contact for some time yet." Ho beamed again. *"I think we can be sure that your two colleagues will not allow its arrival to go unheralded. You must excuse me now, ladies and gentleman."* He began to leave the makeshift podium, but the reporters were not finished with him.

"Sir?"

"Sir, Dr. Ho, Sir?"

"What's the Martian like?"

Smiling benignly, Ho pushed his way through the mêlée.

"Is it a little green man, sir?"

"Does he know?" Kenzy asked.

"Nobody's confided in me," Nathan said, and found that although he knew it was irrational, he did rather resent being kept in ignorance.

"Why are they playing it so cagey?"

"Why's usually the key," Nathan said irritably.

Kenzy turned off the screen and went to the properties locker to retrieve the statuette that had been found in the Mars shipment. "It occurred to me," she said, "that you might not know what this is. Do you?"

"Contraband on its way to Mars. Another why."

She looked pleased. "You don't know what it is, do you?"

"You obviously do, so tell me."

She ran a hand over the sculpture. It was almost a caress. "There's some collector in the Martian colony doesn't want to pay punitive freight rates for something that's already cost him an arm and a leg. *If* it's genuine." She stroked it again. "I'd say it was genuine," she went on, "but I'm not an authority on the pre-Columbian. My guess is, it's Mayan – which would make it maybe two thousand years old."

Nathan couldn't help smiling. Kenzy was full of surprises – most of them interesting, as it turned out. "You're an art expert?" he asked.

She said, "It was my first specialty before I switched to engineering." And then, misinterpreting his smile, she added angrily, "Don't let it throw you. The course was mostly given over to creative spitting and spray-can for colour-blind beginners."

Kitson opened the packing-case and pulled out the carton. "I thought Colin and your two-I-C were handling this," he said. "What, are you short of crimes, sir?" He was speaking to Nathan, but he grinned at Kenzy.

"Short of manpower," Nathan said amiably.

"Well, this is the one." Kitson lifted the lid and gestured at the neat rows of seismic test charge cartridges. "I found it underneath this layer."

"Anything to distinguish this carton from all the others?" Nathan asked.

Kitson grinned again at Kenzy, and said, "Apart from the serial number, you mean?"

Apart from the serial number, Nathan thought, *yes, it's definitely time I moved on or back or some damn thing to wake myself up.* "So long as they know which one they're coming to, and I know which one to watch," he said and began shifting cartridges, making a space for the statuette.

Kenzy had not responded to the customs man's tentative overtures and now – as much to avoid his eye as anything – she picked up one of the cartridges and examined its priming mechanism saying, "It's fairly expensive bait, you realize."

"Christ!" Kitson exclaimed, trying to snatch the charge away from her. "Don't do that!"

"It's quite safe," Kenzy said.

"It's fucking explosive, you silly bitch!"

Kenzy twisted the primer wheel, and when the indicator was flashing tossed the cartridge back into the box. "Only when it's primed," she said.

Kitson grabbed it out of the box and tried to reset it. "What is the matter with you?" he demanded.

"She's very touchy," Nathan said.

"I'm not touchy," she said. "I just don't like to be laughed at and I don't like to be called names."

"Oh death before dishonour, abso-fucking-lutely," Kitson raged, still fiddling desperately with the priming wheel. "Dear God almighty."

Kenzy took the cartridge from him and neutralized it. "I'm an engineer," she said, "and, as it happens, I do know what I'm doing. This thing can't be set off, except with a microwave trigger, which has to be specially tuned."

"I know that and you know that," Kitson said. "Does *it* know that?"

"The triggers will be stored separately. Do you want me to dig one out and show you?" she offered.

"I don't need a lecture, thanks all the same. Have you finished, sir?"

"All set," Nathan said, and put the carton back in the packing-case.

"Right then." Kitson was all bustling efficiency. "I'll notify your office of any change to the loading schedule, shall I?"

"I appreciate it, Bod," Nathan said.

Kitson renewed the customs seals on the freight cage. "No problem. We're all on the same side, aren't we?"

"You'll have to forgive my colleague. Sometimes she forgets which side that is."

"Not me," Kenzy said. "I'm on the side that found the drugs, in case you'd fucking forgotten."

* * *

The MoRo jolted and bounced heavily. Devis cackled. He had aimed for the rock and he was pleased that he had hit it just right. The chuckle – he thought of it as a chuckle, rather than a cackle – was largely for effect. Though, actually, he did love driving these monsters. "Having a good time, lads?" he asked his two increasingly nervous passengers. He glanced back into their pale faces. "Relax. No-one's managed to turn one of these over, let alone break one. I am right about that, aren't I David?"

On the communications screen Theroux shrugged. "*You've come closer than anybody yet. The book has you as front runner, and your odds are shortening as we speak. So, listen, how much had they destroyed when you got to them?*"

"Who knows? But there was enough left for us to fry their geeky arses. Dana's got all the evidence we need in the other MoRo."

"*But squat about the pilot, huh?*"

Devis gunned the motors harder. "I've asked them several times, but they're very reluctant to talk about anything other than their rights. They've made a lot of pompous noise about their rights."

"*They do have them, Colin.*"

Ahead, Devis caught sight of a crater that looked to be the sort of size, if he hit it square on, to stand the MoRo on its nose. That should convince them that he was reckless enough for what was coming. He wound up the speed still more, and said, "Yes in-fucking-deedy they do. Even scumbags that make designer drugs and sell them to groundsiders who are too thick to think: 'I'm killing myself to make some fucker rich'…"

The front of the MoRo dropped away sickeningly, and for a moment Devis thought he had gone too far. He was frightened and exhilarated by the way everything tipped and the cabin juddered, wheels individually grinding and digging hard for traction. Then the machine bounced, rocked, lurched and righted itself. "Even scumbags like that have their rights."

"*Could be they'll talk if you get them back here,*" Theroux said and then corrected himself with elaborate speed, "*when, I mean when you get them back here.*"

Devis cackled again. "I think they'll talk before then. I have a definite feeling that they're going to open their hearts to me very soon. Isn't that right, lads?"

Theroux leaned forward so that his face filled the screen, and he lowered his voice a little. "*Okay, Colin. But try and make it look like an accident, will you? Paperwork's a bitch if there's a hitch.*"

The smaller of the two men, the self-important little prat of an outpost controller whom Devis disliked on sight, said, "An accident? What do you mean, an accident?" He held up his hands so that the wrist-clamps he was wearing were in vision. "We're helpless here."

Devis ignored him. "What do you suggest?" he asked the screen cheerfully.

"*The faulty backpack thing always plays well,*" Theroux suggested.

"*How about two faulty backpacks?*" Devis's fat smirk made it impossible to see his eyes on the screen.

He might not be scaring them, but he's scaring the shit out of me, Theroux thought and said, "They do say troubles come in twos."

"Threes," an almost familiar voice said behind him. He turned round in his seat. Susan Caxton was possibly more gorgeous in the flesh than she was on WNS. "Trouble comes in threes, is what they say," she said. Absurdly, Theroux was tongue-tied. He had no idea what to say to her. He almost blurted out some inanity about being a big fan and the word 'autograph' popped briefly into his mind. Luckily, Devis chose that moment to say, "*I'll call in when the shock's worn off and I feel able to talk about it.*"

"Later, Colin," he said. He cancelled the link, and with his thoughts now collected, managed a really impressive, "Can I help you?" A coolly casual smile was still beyond him, though.

"My name is Susan Caxton," she said, as if there was likely to be anybody who didn't know that. "I assume that what I just heard was meant to be humorous?" The expression on her face suggested that there was something stinking up the place, and since she was looking directly at him, there wasn't much doubt what she thought that was.

"Assume away, Ms. Caxton," Theroux heard himself saying. "Isn't that what you press people normally do?"

"You *weren't* threatening the lives of two prisoners? That is that what they were?"

Theroux said, "We arrested two research chemists who have a sideline in drugs manufacture. They've been making a whole range of synthetics which have been smuggled back to Earth for sale." He badly wanted to say *and it's none of your goddam business, you and Daniel and all the rest of your backstabbing breed.* But he didn't.

"And this is a justification for making them frightened for their lives?" she said, jutting her chin and squaring her shoulders slightly.

He tried not to notice how her breasts lifted and pushed against the unfastened top of her coveralls. *Christ*, he thought, *it's like a dime video-novel; Gee, Ms. Caxton, without your clothes on – why, you're beautiful.* He said, "Personally, I'd make them frightened for valued parts of their anatomy." What? Say *what*? He could not believe that macho-fascist bullshit had just come out of his mouth. "Their lives would be the least of their problems," he went on. *Un-fucking-believable.*

She said, "You clearly don't subscribe to the idea that if you deny one man his rights, no man is safe."

I don't subscribe to crap aphorisms straight out of civics class is what he should have said, he realized. But instead, he said, "I have subscribed to one or two drug rehab centres, if that's any help. What can I do for you, Ms. Caxton?"

"Directions?" she said. "I was looking for directions."

"I'm good at those," Theroux said. "And the time. If you want to know the time, I'm your man." *Hell, where did that come from?* He was turning into a limey cop, with lame limey cop jokes. He considered smiling but decided it was too late.

Susan Caxton did not smile either. "There's a Dr. Andrew Philpot somewhere on the base. Can you tell me where he is?"

"*About an hour behind you, I would estimate*," Dana Cogill responded over the voice-only link from the following MoRo.

Devis switched all the motive systems to stop, and the MoRo settled down on its suspension. "Fine. Listen, love," he said, hoping she was sharp enough to understand what was needed here, "if you should see any hitchhikers when you get to this position –"

"*Sorry, didn't copy that, say again, Colin; sounded like 'hitchhikers'?*"

"Hitchhikers, that's correct. My passengers have decided to go for a bit of a walk. Think things over."

"*You're miles from anywhere.*"

"Okay, so it's quite a lot of a walk. They're slow thinkers."

Behind Devis the two men stirred uneasily. "You're bluffing," the larger man said. "They're bluffing," he repeated to the little controller, who suddenly looked close to tears.

Star Cops

"The thing is," Devis went on, "I don't want you picking them up."

There was a long pause, then Dana said, "*Well now, I'm a properly educated Irish girl. I was taught never to accept or to give lifts.*"

Devis's smile was genuine, but no less chilling for that. "Right. These two are not the sort you'd want to travel with, anyway. Very poor conversationalists. They don't seem to want to talk about any of the things I want to talk about. Very boring people." He yawned expansively. "So you'll leave them, then?"

"*No problem, Colin. Even if they're dying for a lift.*"

Devis made a mental note to buy her a shuttle-repair Scotch for that one. He fished out the laser pistol from his equipment pouch. "Right lads," he said, turning round and waving it at them, "let's get you out of those incriminating restraints and into your hiking boots."

"They couldn't wait to tell him all about it," Theroux said, grinning. "Refrain and two full choruses." He was relishing the story and dragging out what he obviously thought were the highlights.

Nathan stayed silent and kept his face deliberately expressionless. If David Theroux really didn't know that the line had been crossed with this, then all the present plans were looking shaky.

Theroux went on, "They swore the dead girl was just a freelance pilot who knew nothing about the drugs. And they never heard of Daniel Larwood's dead man either. It's sort of a major coincidence, but I guess they do happen. That's why we've got a name for them, right?"

They reached the guest quarters and paused, looking for the allocation number. Nathan still said nothing.

"I realize," Theroux said, "that I let things go a bit far. Cut some corners."

"It could have cost us the case," Nathan said flatly. "Still could. For Christ's sake, David, confessions under duress?"

"Yeah I know," Theroux said. "I know. But we can stand it up without the confessions. And we needed that information. *You* needed that information."

"Not at any price."

"It was a judgement call."

"Yes."

Theroux shrugged. "Okay, so I wasn't brilliant. You've never made a mistake?"

"Not with a journalist standing directly behind me, I haven't," Nathan said, and allowed himself to smile. He was always relieved when his assessment of people was there or thereabouts, especially when he thought they were bright, and it turned out that they probably were. He pointed. "That's his room there."

Daniel Larwood opened the door to them and said, "Psychic policing, I'm impressed gentlemen." He stood aside to let them in.

The 'twin berth guest cabin' was standard size, but Larwood was not sharing with anyone. Whoever had searched it had been just as destructive as the last time, but there was less debris than in the dead pilot's room and it was spread out more.

"I'm the methodical type," Larwood said, as he gestured round. "If I haven't got anywhere to put something, I put it anywhere."

"Why didn't you report this?" Nathan asked.

Larwood said, "Petty thieving isn't much of a story." He began picking things up and throwing them towards the bunk.

"He meant to us," Theroux said.

"You arrived before I had the chance."

"And before you'd finished tidying up?" Nathan suggested.

Larwood offered no reaction. "To what do I owe the pleasure of this visit, Commander?" he asked.

Nathan said, "A couple more questions about the corpse you discovered."

"I've told you all I know."

"That'd be a first," Theroux said.

"Did you know that there was no record of his arrival on Moonbase?" Nathan asked.

"How would I know that?" Larwood said.

Nathan picked up a coverall tunic from which the pockets had been ripped. He handed it to Larwood, and said conversationally, "In a manner of speaking, you found someone who wasn't actually there."

Larwood did not glance away but looked him directly in the eye, and smiling his rumpled smile, said, "Yesterday upon the stair; I met a man who wasn't there; He wasn't there again today; I wish that man would go away."

"You *met* a man?" Theroux challenged.

Larwood said, "In a manner of speaking."

"Anything missing?" Nathan asked.

"Nothing."

"And you've no idea what they were after?"

"None."

Nathan nodded. "The other two people to whom this has happened are being pretty close-mouthed about it as well. But then the dead tend to be." Again Larwood was unperturbed. He was well in control of himself this time. This time, as far as Nathan could see, there were no signs of stress, and that in itself was suspicious; most people whose belongings had been turned over were unsettled at least by the arbitrary threat of it. "Death isn't all they had in common," he went on. "They shared one of these rooms, though neither of them was officially on Moonbase. They were even in the same line of work." He caught Theroux's eye and nodded a small nod, at the same time saying, "If you should think of anything you feel you want to tell us, Mr. Larwood, you know where the office is."

"I do indeed," Larwood said.

At the door, Theroux said, "Daniel and I have some unfinished business, Nathan. I'll catch you later."

As Nathan hopped with easy looping strides along the corridor, there was no doubt in his mind that Theroux had noticed Larwood's failure to ask what line of work it was that the two dead visitors were in.

"Okay Daniel," Theroux said, closing the door, "you just changed your mind."

Larwood said, "I think it's more likely that you just lost yours," and continued to retrieve his belongings.

"With the Martian due at any time, you don't want to leave the field completely clear for the delicious Ms. Caxton – or do you?"

"You haven't got that kind of power, David."

"I think I can make a strong enough case to get you sent Earthside before the story breaks."

"Charge?"

Theroux went to the locker where Larwood was re-stowing his belongings, and pulled out one of the bottles of brandy. "Illegal possession of alcohol," he said.

"You bastard." Larwood seemed genuinely shocked.

Theroux thought, *It was my fault, I gave you Gary Benson and the others because I was more impressed by you than by them and I wanted your friendship more than theirs, I risked them, you betrayed them, and what goes around comes around*; and he said, "It finally gets to be my turn. Maybe there is a God."

Larwood had recovered. "Still angry after all these years," he said mockingly.

So not all-knowing then – because Theroux wasn't angry, he was ashamed. "We deserved better, Daniel."

"Get a grip, David, and grow up for Christ's sake. You don't get what you deserve in this life, you deserve what you get."

Theroux thought: *Fuck you, smartass*, and said, "Good to know you'll be philosophical about it. Getting kicked out of Moonbase I mean."

Larwood said, "That boy's suicide –"

"His name," Theroux interrupted angrily, "was Gary Benson." How long had he taken to remember that himself?

"His suicide was not your fault," Larwood said.

My fault? It wasn't my fault? "You sold us for a by-line," he said, "and a start in your lousy career."

Again the shrug and the rumpled grin. "I was a stranger in a strange land. I had to try harder."

"You were more at home in my country than I was."

Larwood opened the bottle and took a long swallow of brandy. He sighed. "David," he said, "the world is what you think it is, how can it be anything else? Better make sure you think it's something you can live with."

Theroux took a small sudden hop and landed directly in front of Larwood. He was close enough to smell the brandy on Larwood's breath, but leaned closer still and glared into his eyes. "Try living with this," he said, harshly. "I want to know what you know about the dead man, and I want to know it *now*, you hypocritical piece of shit."

An image? Killing each other over images? Could that really be all it was about? "He was peddling a picture of the Martian," Nathan said. "And Larwood believed that?" It sounded unlikely, but Theroux's judgement of Larwood was the best he had to hand.

Theroux said, "He couldn't pass up the chance that it might not be a hoax."

Nathan added the information to the model he was playing with, and let his workstation run crime scenarios. None of them made any sense. "Is he capable of killing, do you think?" he asked.

Star Cops

"Not face to face," Theroux said sourly.

"Not if he'd been lured somewhere quiet to be robbed?"

"Daniel would fight for a good story, but he wouldn't lift a finger over property, his own or anyone else's." He watched Nathan's obvious dissatisfaction with what he was getting from the computer, and said, "Why don't you give it to Box?"

"I'm just doodling."

"So doodle with something that might come up with the answer."

"Answers are easy. Asking the right questions is the tricky part, and there isn't a computer made that's any damn good for that. What else did you get from Larwood?"

"How do you know I got anything else?"

Nathan shrugged. "Because you've been waiting to tell me. Get on with it, will you?"

Theroux shook his head and sighed. "You can be a bit spooky, you know that."

"Trust me, David, that's one of my least threatening traits."

"Turns out the guy was still alive."

"He was still alive when Larwood got to him? Did he say anything?"

"Nothing that made any sense. All Daniel heard was just '*I de-*'... something."

"And Larwood didn't know what this something was?"

"Could have been any fucking thing. I desire, demand, denounce, declare. I de was as far as he got."

"Is that it? All the evidence your friend was withholding?"

Theroux snorted. "He's no friend of mine."

Nathan said, "Hold that thought." Though, on reflection, it was clearly an unnecessary comment.

Susan Caxton did not hide her surprise. "This is the Base Co-ordinator's private suite," she said glancing around the unusually spacious quarters. The personal items were few, but looked carefully chosen and precisely placed.

Dr. Andrew Philpot settled himself comfortably into Ho's chair. "I have the use of it." He rested his elbows on the desk and steepled his fingers, waiting for the young black woman to finish checking light and backgrounds. "You do appreciate," he said finally, bored with the silence and irritated at being ignored, "that I am not expecting any surprises in this interview, Susan." The use of her first name was meant to be friendly and informal, but sounded merely clumsy and patronizing.

She continued to set up her equipment. "Is it possible to expect a surprise, Dr. Philpot?" She had only the faintest trace of an Australian accent; like most things about her, it was distinctive without being extravagant, attractive without being intrusive.

"Don't chop logic with me," he snapped, abandoning the friendly approach for something more appropriate to his superior status. "You know exactly what I mean."

Susan Caxton was good at her job, part of which was to avoid outright hostility in the people she interviewed, at least until the recording was running. "This is ideal for our purposes," she said sitting down opposite Philpot, crossing her legs demurely and smiling. "And I'm ready if you are, so let's just clarify, shall we? I'm going to ask you about the deal which the Holdy Museum has made to buy the Martian."

"You will not mention figures, of course," Philpot put in. "That is commercially sensitive. *Extremely* sensitive, in fact."

"An undisclosed sum," she agreed. "I shall express surprise, however, at the whole idea. 'Can you really buy a Martian?' That sort of thing. And I may ask why a museum should be regarded as an appropriate custodian."

Philpot said, "And you will then give me the opportunity to explain that the Holdy intends to make it available to the scientific community, without delay or condition."

She smiled a warm, friendly smile. "Not quite without condition. I mean, nobody else is allowed to see it, are they?"

"Once the world's research scientists have completed their work, it will go on display at the Museum."

"But until then, Doctor, it remains firmly under wraps. In fact, the whole deal depends on that – or have I misunderstood?" She smiled her beautiful, emotionless smile.

He smiled back. "No, you've understood perfectly."

"Not perfectly. Your museum doesn't exactly have a cash-flow problem, does it?"

"It's hardly *my* museum, Susan."

"Why are you insisting on the exclusive rights to display and publication? The Holdy doesn't need the money."

"It's for precisely that reason," he said smoothly, "that the Holdy is the ideal guardian. We can ensure that the Martian is not the subject of tawdry exploitation. That it is treated with proper dignity."

As an answer it was obviously well-rehearsed, but this was not the time to challenge it – and so, equally smoothly, Susan Caxton said, "I think that will probably be an appropriate note to end on. Any problems with that, Andrew?"

"None that I can see," said Dr. Philpot.

The action in the operations module had maintained its frantic pace, but actually the manager seemed no more tired than before. It occurred to Nathan that 'exhausted and on the edge' could be her preferred working condition, but he waited more patiently this time anyway. "Svenson, for fuck's sake," she was shouting, "is that load complete or not?"

"*How should I know?*" an irritable voice responded from the control board speaker.

"By checking," she said, dropping her voice almost to a whisper, and then bellowing at the top of her lungs, "*Now*, you idle moose-fiddler! I want you to check it *now!*"

She turned and shrugged tiredly at Nathan. "It's obviously a computer foul-up either at the Martian end, or," and she made a wry face, "just possibly, here. Unlikely as that may seem."

"You're sure about it?" Nathan prompted.

"Do I look sure about anything? Listen, Mars base says those two were pilot and co-pilot of a freighter which is still en route. A physical impossibility. Ergo they must have been flying a *different* freighter which left some time *before* the one the computer says they're flying."

"Accidental or deliberate?"

She shrugged again. "Could be either. But trust me, we've made bigger cock-ups than that when things were quiet."

"I trust you," Nathan said. "Last question. Have the traffic offices been broken into recently?"

"They're never locked. It's a twenty-four hour service, in case you hadn't noticed."

"Constantly manned?"

"Give or take a shift change and the odd meal break."

"Easy to search, then. Would a search have been noticed?"

"How?" She gestured round the impersonally untidy cubicle.

"*I have checked,*" a voice, presumably Svenson, reported over the speaker. "*The load is complete.*"

"Well, bravo," she said, "and about time."

"*But it is being off-loaded again for customs spot check inspection.*"

"You are fucking joking."

"*We moose-fiddlers have no sense of humour.*"

"Thanks," Nathan said and started to go.

"Why should it have been searched?" she asked suddenly.

"Someone's running through a logical list," he said, and left before she asked the question he wasn't ready to answer.

Why the hell was she here? Kenzy eased herself into a less cramped position and yawned. It wasn't her function in life to follow up on Nathan's hunches, especially not when he was so unforthcoming about what exactly they were. Around her, the remains of the crashed shuttle were piled up in the darkness. She yawned again. *If Nathan Spring wanted someone to stand guard... well to sit guard... in this bloody storage bay then at least he...*

Why me? Everyone else is busy or on rest breaks which is what I could do with...

Would you rather process the extradition papers on our drugs barons? Or on rest breaks which is what I could do with...

Kenzy jerked awake. She had no idea how long she had been dozing, but it was not dark now, not totally dark anyway. Was it dawn? Wake up stupid, this is the Moon and you're underground. The safety lights. The safety lights had been switched on and were glowing dimly.

As her mind began to make sense of things, she started to get to her feet slowly. Somewhere close by, there was noise. It was a stealthy sort of noise. Pieces of the wreckage were being moved. She groped for the gun she had shoved into her equipment pouch and, crouching slightly, moved towards the sound.

She pulled the gun and said in her best hard-case voice, "Okay, you mongrel. Get your arse out here; you're nicked."

A storm of debris flew at Kenzy. She tried to fend it away. Abruptly, everything was back to black.

She was bruised. Her face was cut, but that looked worse than it was, according to the diagnostic examination. The concussion was mild. There should be no lasting effects, no scars. Her pride was hurting but Nathan was in no mood to sympathize with that. "You weren't expecting anyone to show? Why the hell do you suppose I wanted it staked out?"

She got off the scanner couch and began to dress quickly and angrily. "I have no idea. You didn't exactly confide in me. You didn't go into what might be called detail. Or did I miss a meeting?"

"How much detail do you need, Kenzy?" Nathan demanded, trying not to notice her body. "Anyone touches that shuttle wreckage, you arrest them. It was a simple enough order, for the love of Christ!" He knew he was overreacting, and he had a pretty good idea why, and there still didn't seem to be anything he could do to stop himself.

"Yeah, well," she was saying, as she keyed her acceptance of the medical data update, "I've never been very keen on simple orders. Next time –"

"Next time," Nathan interrupted her, "they won't be so careless. Thanks to your incompetence, they'll know for sure we're onto them."

"They'll know a bloody sight more than I do then," Kenzy snapped.

Nathan said angrily, "Try concentrating on the job in hand instead of a promotion you don't deserve and aren't likely to get."

"Fuck you and the horse you rode in on," she said, and left the treatment suite without a backward glance.

In theory, once the customs seals had been put on a freight cage no-one could touch the contents again. Loading and off-loading were handled by remote control. Direct access was forbidden to any and all personnel. That was the theory. In practice, there was little surveillance and no physical barriers of any significance to protect such cargo from interference. Which was how six of the seismic cartridges in the carton containing the statuette came to be primed, and the microwave triggers stolen. The number and location of these explosives was confirmed by the detailed reconstruction of what happened, as it was modelled by the best forensic computer available. Of course, the cargo security systems were tightened up after the disaster – but that would be too late for Nathan.

He found Kenzy sitting alone in the executive mess. Her table screen and all the wallzacs were showing the live interview which Susan Caxton of WNS was conducting for the news pool with Dr. Andrew Philpot, billed as "a senior curator" at the Holdy Museum. Interest in the Martian was now so intense that a rather dull interview was getting a lot more attention than it deserved. As Nathan crossed the small, almost luxurious turn-of-the-millennium style space, an out of vision Caxton was saying: *"As I understand it, there are at least six universities that have a legitimate right to examine the Martian?"*

"May I sit down?" he asked.

Without taking her eyes off the screen, Kenzy gestured to the seat opposite her.

Philpot smiled graciously into camera. *"There are a number of separate scientific communities who will have to be given access, it's true, yes,"* he said with a modest politeness that was almost humble.

"So it may be years before the public gets to see it?"

"That's possible."

"Anything's possible, if you're wealthy enough," Kenzy said.

Nathan said, "Even the rich have to die."

"Why isn't that any consolation?"

"Tell me, Doctor. why is the Holdy Museum insisting on the exclusive rights to display and publication? They don't really need the money that will generate, do they?"

"I'm sorry," Nathan said. Kenzy looked directly at him for the first time, but said nothing. "I was worried about you," he went on. "I think I resent being worried about you."

"It's precisely for that reason that the Holdy is the ideal guardian. We can ensure that the Martian is not the subject of tawdry exploitation."

"A good officer worries about his people," she said. "Isn't that how it's supposed to be?"

"That it is treated with proper dignity."

"That's not what I mean," Nathan said. "You know that's not what I mean."

"With a proper respect."

A reverse shot showed Caxton looking quizzical, amused, not quite sceptical. *"Respect? Dignity?"*

"Concepts not entirely alien in this day and age, even to your profession surely," Philpot said, momentarily allowing his normal arrogance to show.

"You've never forgiven me for that lapse, have you?" Kenzy asked.

"I have trouble seeing corruption as a lapse," Nathan said, uncomfortable with how pompous that sounded.

"People change," Kenzy said.

"But surely Doctor, we are not talking about a sentient creature, are we? Or are we?"

"I came to say goodbye," Nathan said. "The freighter's almost finished loading. It's my embarkation time."

"*That's not a question I'm in any position to answer, Susan.*"

"Already? Jesus, that's a bit quick."

"*Can you say whether it's alive at this time?*"

"No. I can't."

It sounded to Nathan as though she was genuinely upset. "I can't postpone it. Not if I want to stay with that statuette."

"*Though let me offer you this thought.*"

Nathan stood up and offered his hand. "I think you probably do deserve that promotion," he said, "but I've left it to David to decide. It seemed the best way under the circumstances."

"*It is not only the living that deserve to be treated with respect and dignity.*"

She stood too and shook his hand. "Take care of yourself, Nathan," she said.

"*As an expert on ancient cultures, I can understand how you might feel like that.*"

"You too, Pal." There was something in what he had just heard that meant more than what he had just heard. He did not let go of her hand and she made no attempt to free it. He wondered whether to pull her into his arms. He badly wanted her in his arms.

"*Thank you for talking to me, Dr. Philpot.*"

Then he heard his own voice saying, "You have very little time left Nathan. Lucifer Seven lifts to its fuelling orbit in seventeen minutes."

"*This is Susan Caxton for Worldwide and newspool affiliates on Moonbase.*"

"Thank you, Box," he said and released Kenzy's hand. As he turned away, he said, "I'll miss you," – and then left quickly, before she had time to say anything. He seemed to have done a lot of that recently.

With cargo pods secured and a full load of fuel, the Mars freighter *Lucifer Seven* disengaged from the bunkering shuttle at 22.28LST and was given clearance for minimum thrust on vector one six. Among the usual last minute communications traffic was a farewell from Star Cop headquarters to Commander Nathan Spring which read: "*Tell the little green men that where there's living, there's policemen.*" It has been suggested that, by some cruel irony, it was during the transmission of this message that the ship vanished from the navigation radars. This is not true. Nor is it true that there were any eyewitnesses to the huge flare in which the ship was destroyed. No-one was working on the lunar surface at the time, and though the silent burst of chemical brightness would have been visible from the Earth's surface, the *Lucifer Seven* was hidden by the Moon when it died; lost on the darkside.

"*...which is why it took so long to confirm the loss. Even now no-one understands exactly what happened,*" Daniel Larwood, said to camera, "*still less can they really believe it.*"

Watching the broadcast in the Star Cop office, Kenzy said flatly, "They can believe it. It's dangerous out here, you moron. Why are we listening to this shit?"

"Because it's better than silence," Devis said, and poured himself another Scotch from the soft-drink carton which shuttle repair provided.

Larwood's story cut to an interview with the duty operations manager. She looked tired and close to the edge. "*Operations is over stretched, underfunded, undermanned,*" she was saying. "*Something had to go, sooner or later.*"

Holding her cup out for more of Devis's Scotch, Dana Cogill said, "He should not have gone on that flight. It was an unnecessary risk."

"*Were corners being cut?*" Larwood asked.

"*And all this little green men crap that you people stirred up hasn't helped!*"

"*Would you say that corners had been cut?*" Larwood persisted. "*In safety, for example?*"

"*Corners? I'd say whole fucking streets had been eliminated,*" the woman raged.

"'Least she's honest," Devis commented, to no-one in particular.

"What's that supposed to mean?" Kenzy demanded.

"*Cheap costs,*" the manager went on furiously, "*and sooner or later, someone has to pay for it.*"

"Christ, Kenzy, will you shut the fuck up?" Devis said.

"*But it's never the greedy bastards who are actually responsible!*"

"He wasn't getting at you, Pal," Cogill offered.

"And you shut the fuck up too," Devis said, taking another drink.

Kenzy said, "Where the hell does honesty get us? The man's dead."

As if on cue, the screen was suddenly showing pictures of Nathan and Larwood was saying, "*Among the dead was Commander Nathan Spring...*", beginning what was obviously going to be an obituary.

Kenzy left the office hurriedly before it got under way.

Theroux was waiting for Jiang Li Ho at the sub-surface disembarkation airlock. The Co-ordinator was at his most inscrutable and showed no sign of surprise when, after the routine courtesies were over, Theroux said, "Tell me about the Martian."

"The Martian?" Ho repeated.

"The one that's coming to Moonbase," Theroux elaborated patiently, though obviously they both knew what he was talking about.

"You must forgive me," Ho said. "Perhaps it is my shuttle-lag, but is it not your first concern to examine the sad death of your Commander?"

Theroux frowned. "It's a question of when a coincidence becomes a connection. Nathan's death and his last investigation both involved Mars and Mars traffic. He wanted to know how come two pilots turned up on Moonbase when they should still have been en route from Mars. Now *I* want to know."

Ho tried to move on past him, saying, "That surely is something which you must ask them."

Theroux stood in his way. "I would if I could," he said, "but I can't. Because they're both dead, too."

Just for a moment, Ho's inscrutability deserted him. "Both are dead?" he said.

Once they were clear of the base, Theroux fed the destination co-ordinates into the MoRo's computer and waited for the beacon-grid navigation system to kick in. Meantime, he calibrated the ground radar to identify the target. Beside him, Ho remained deep in thought. As yet Theroux had not pushed him for the full explanation. One of the things he had learned from Nathan was that, when you had the time, silence could be an effective interrogation technique. Listening intelligently was important if you wanted the truth.

"It was agreed," Ho said suddenly, but in a tone that suggested they had been in a lengthy conversation, "that scientists in China should be first to examine the find."

"No problem keeping it under wraps while your people had it," Theroux commented. "Convenient, when you think about it." On the screen the drive compass flashed up, and he turned the MoRo in the direction indicated and wound up the acceleration.

"It was coming to the Moon first," Ho said, "and it was I who was to act as liaison. It seemed a natural arrangement." He sounded very slightly defensive. "I have never seen the Martian," he added, as if this exonerated him in some way.

"Even though it's been on the Moon all this time. Weren't you a little curious?"

"The responsibilities of my position far outweighed such questions."

They rode on in silence for a while. When Theroux felt that there was nothing to be gained from that, he said, "So, the plan was to make the Earthside move in total secrecy."

Ho nodded. "While the press still waited for its arrival here."

"Not just the press," Theroux said.

Ho said, "It was judged that if they knew it had already come from Mars it would not be possible to keep them at bay. To keep it from the press, it was necessary to keep it from everyone else."

Theroux snorted. "And vice versa," and then regretted it when he thought he saw a look of guilty stubbornness cross Ho's face. Anxious to avoid a bout of silent inscrutability, he said quickly, "Was it your idea to use the grounded freighter?"

"What could be more secure?" Ho asked.

Theroux smiled. "Seems like you should have paid the pilots better," he said. The ground radar found a promising trace at the extreme edge of its range, and began to narrow the search arc.

"There is an old Chinese proverb," Ho said. "The greedy, like the honest, can never be bought."

As the computer ran probabilities to define, redefine and identify the steadily clearing radar pulses, Theroux wondered who had taken money not to notice a freighter putting down way outside any authorized landing zone, and what they thought it might have been doing there. He was reminded of Butler and how nothing in this shitty life ever really changed.

"Is that it?" Ho asked. He was looking at the screen on which the computer was now displaying the results of its estimations. "That must be it, must it not?"

Theroux called up a full graphic of the radar's findings. According to the computer image the fragile cargo-hauler had landed in a very rough patch of low-lying and heavily-cratered terrain. Theroux whistled softly. "Like I said, you should have paid those pilots more. You realize the risk they took putting that thing down there?"

"It was expected they would write off the freighter," Ho said. "It was allowed for."

Theroux thought it was a fairly casual attitude to the safety of the crew – and what did it say about the Martian? *Allowed for*? One thing to be allowed for was that Wangley was still not telling what he knew. He decided not to challenge him on it immediately. He'd wait until they reached the grounded ship, or maybe he'd use the first physical sighting of it as a cue for some more aggressive questioning. There was high ground ahead. The chart suggested that the freighter could be visible from there. He gunned the drives, and the MoRo lunged towards the slope.

The flash was shocking, glaringly bright even from below the crest they were still climbing towards.

"What was that?" Ho wanted to know.

The ground radar showed a spreading mist of debris. "It blew up," Theroux said.

"An explosion?"

"Your freighter blew up. Strike one Martian."

Ho looked stricken. "No. Oh no. Why? What can have happened?"

This had not been allowed for, then, Theroux thought. What happened? And more importantly: why? As the MoRo reached the top of the slope and he braked so that they could peer into the empty distance, Theroux made up his mind. "As I remember it, Dr. Ho," he said, "the idea of being a detective appealed to you once upon a time. Well, now you can play for real. Can you think of a reason why someone should be systematically destroying evidence?"

Ho did not look at him but continued to peer out of the forward screen. "Evidence? What evidence? Evidence of what?"

"Evidence of the Martian's existence," Theroux said quietly.

Now Ho looked at him.

The Star Cop main office was in darkness, apart from the pale splash of light coming from the corridor. In the time-honoured way, the intruder had jammed both the doors partially open as an escape route.

From her hiding place, Kenzy could see dimly the figure of the man – she was sure it *was* a man – searching the area, slowly and methodically. He was using a micro-flash on soft beam, so even in the deepest shadows she was sure enough of his position to be able to pick her moment. She did not intend to make any sort of move until she could step between him and the door. The bastard was not about to get away from her, not this time.

She held her breath as he passed close by. For a dizzying moment it seemed as though his light must find her and she tensed, ready to jump at him. He missed her, and she allowed herself to breathe again.

Then the light stopped moving. He was standing at a workstation. She sucked in a deep breath and stood up. "Freeze!" she yelled and rushed at him.

She had expected him to turn towards her, and he did. She had a good idea how tall he was, so she knew – even in the pitch darkness – where his face and his balls would be. She punched at the centre of the face, and then kicked hard at the balls.

He lay at her feet groaning. "Lights," she commanded, pulling restraints from her equipment pouch and reaching down to grab his arms. The lights did not come on. "Lights!" The man started to struggle half-heartedly. She kicked him a couple of times and he subsided gasping, "Alright, alright, f'Christ's sake."

Clamping his wrists behind him, she said, "Still haven't found it, huh? Whatever it is? Well you've lost the chance now. *Lights*, for fuck's sake!"

"Box, lights please," a voice from the inner office said.

"Very well, Nathan," the same voice said, and the command override was immediately cancelled.

The lights came on. Blinking and still adrenaline driven, Kenzy had dragged Daniel Larwood to his feet and shoved him against the workstation before she realized that Nathan was standing in the doorway to the commander's office.

"He's looking for evidence, aren't you Mr. Larwood?" Nathan said.

Kenzy stared at him for a long frozen moment. Death, the implacable; death, the unchangeable; death, the ultimate fact – it was just imagination, after all. "You're alive," she said. She was waking from a dream of grief to find that everything was normal, no-one was dead. "You're alive." Two looping strides took her to him, and she threw her arms round him with desperate glee. "Nathan, you're alive. You're not dead."

Her embrace was fierce. He held her tightly for a moment, and then feigning breathlessness said, "Not yet."

She clung to him and babbled, "We thought you were dead, how come you're not dead? How come? Why didn't you tell us? Why didn't you tell us you weren't dead?"

Larwood was recovering. "A lucky escape, Commander," he said. "I'm impressed."

Kenzy let go of Nathan and stepped back. "How come you didn't tell us you weren't dead?" She was angry suddenly. "We wasted a lot of time working out how to replace you."

"More psychic policing?" Larwood said. "Did you expect something of the sort to happen?"

Nathan had wondered that himself. Had he known? Did he have an instinct about it? Even more guiltily, *should* he have known? "It never occurred to me that anyone would go as far as to blow that ship up," he said.

"It was deliberate, then," Kenzy said.

Nathan looked at Larwood and said, "Yes. Okay. Game's up."

"You think it was me?" Larwood exclaimed.

Nathan did not smile. Larwood made no secret of his mistrust of policemen, and he was clearly nervous about finding himself in custody and a suspect in a major crime. Let him sweat. "Read him his rights."

Larwood was now thoroughly alarmed. "Wait a minute, wait a minute. I'm a reporter. I'm looking for a story. I wouldn't sabotage a ship. Shit, it was me that had customs tipped off. The task force is out here because of me."

"Why would you do that?" Kenzy demanded.

"To shake the tree," he said, "to see what fell out."

"You did," Nathan said flatly.

"No, no, you don't understand," Larwood protested. "The reason I broke in here was to look for the girl's personal effects. The girl who crashed the shuttle."

"These," Nathan said and took the evidence bag from his pocket. "Or more precisely," he went on, extracting an ID plate from the bag, "this." He held it up, feeling mildly triumphant and slightly foolish; *I've summoned you all to the library because one of you is a murderer.* "She was carrying two IDs. That's what your dying friend was saying. Not I demand, or I declare or I denounce but simply: *ID.*"

"I don't know why I didn't see it straight away," Larwood said. "It wasn't until I said it out loud to David Theroux, when he was threatening me; it wasn't until then that I saw the possibility."

Nathan broke the plate in two and carefully pulled the sections apart to expose the tiny holographic plate which Box had detected was sandwiched inside.

Larwood said, "I hate being right when it does me no good." He twisted round to gesture with the restraints at Kenzy. "Any chance of letting me out of these?"

Kenzy ignored him and watched in silence as Nathan put Box on the workstation, slotted the plate into one of its access ports, and said, "Box, projection."

The hologram which Box immediately displayed above itself was a foot high and perfect in every apparently solid detail. It was another man-bird statuette, similar in style to the one which had been destroyed when the *Lucifer Seven* had been lost.

"What is it?" Kenzy asked, puzzled.

"It's a picture of the Martian," Nathan said.

Her disappointment was plain. "That's what all the fuss has been about?"

"It's evidence," said Larwood, "that there was once intelligent life on another planet."

Kenzy walked round, it looking for the clue. "It's just another Mayan sculpture," she said finally.

"That's the clever touch," Larwood said. "There've been all sorts of theories about the Mayans being contacted by space travellers. You must've come across them. '*Were the ancient Gods really astronauts?*' All that sort of rubbish? Well, here's the proof that what the Mayans made were representations of the Gods, and that the Gods took some with them as souvenirs."

"I'm missing something," Kenzy said to Nathan. "This is the same as the one Bod Kitson found in the customs sweep."

Nathan nodded. "You take a genuinely old and valuable artifact. You smuggle it to Mars and have an accomplice discover it. Then you both clean up on a genuinely old and priceless artifact."

"Of course, you need a sculpture which has never been catalogued by any museum," Larwood said. "It mustn't be identifiable. Preferably, it should have been excavated by someone involved."

Kenzy said, "The whole thing's a fucking con?"

"A scheme to swindle the Holdy Museum," Larwood said. "Take them for a lot of money, even by their standards."

"And that was the story you were working on," Nathan said.

"If you know that, why am I still trussed up like a Chinese democrat?"

Nathan said, "Why didn't you tell us?"

"With that much money involved? Word is, you haven't always trusted your people – why should I?"

Star Cops

"Sounds reasonable," Kenzy said, with a wry smile at Nathan. "Do I still read him his rights?"

"Let him go," Nathan said, and as she worked on it, he asked Larwood, "What started you on this?"

"I heard about the decision to purchase from a Museum trustee. I did some background on the curators, and found that one of them had a personal connection with the Martian colony. A cousin married to a surveyor."

Kenzy released the restraints. "You can think yourself lucky," she said.

Misunderstanding her, he reacted peevishly, "Major scandals have broken on less."

Nathan, looking towards the jammed doors, said pointedly, "No prizes for guessing which of the experts on pre-Columbian civilization is your prime suspect." And, feeling more than a little theatrical, went on after a brief pause, "Come on in, Dr. Philpot. We've been expecting you."

It was something of a relief when the furtive movement he thought he had seen did turn out to be Andrew Philpot lurking on the threshold. It would have been a bit embarrassing otherwise. The relief was fleeting. He wasn't sure why he assumed the man would be unarmed, but he did, and he was wrong.

"Don't do anything ill-judged," Philpot said, brandishing the bomb he had made by strapping together seven seismic charges. Then he added, as though concerned that someone might doubt the evidence of the brightly flashing indicators, "These are primed." He pointed at Box with the microwave fuse he held in his other hand. "Switch that off, and give me the picture plate."

"The last piece of evidence of an abortive con," Nathan said, not moving. "How did you find out about the picture?"

Philpot was dangerously calm. "Don't play for time, Commander. There's none left."

"I'm interested," Nathan said, "that's all." He went to Box.

"The pilot offered it to me, too," Philpot said. "I think the idea was that Mr. Larwood and I should outbid each other."

"Instead of which, you killed him," Larwood said.

"I have nothing to lose," Philpot murmured. "I should try to remember that."

Nathan fiddled with Box and the hologram vanished. He fiddled some more, and then said apologetically, "I can't seem to get it out. You must be making me nervous."

"Never mind. Just hand over the whole thing," Philpot ordered.

Nathan picked Box up, but before he could move Philpot changed his mind. "No. Put it down, and step away from it."

Nathan did as he was told and stood waiting for a chance. It took him by surprise when Philpot bent and tossed the seismic charges across the floor. He watched the lethal bundle bounce and slide under a workstation, and while he and the others were distracted, Philpot reached for Box with his free hand.

As the charges hit the floor, Nathan knew for certain that the plan was to kill them all. Apparently Larwood worked it out too, because he lunged furiously at Philpot who dodged back with unexpected speed and struck him a chopping blow on the side of the head. Larwood's skull cracked down onto the workstation, knocking him cold.

"Don't try anything stupid like that," Philpot said, stepping back empty-handed.

Nathan picked up Box. "It's all right," he said, "here, take... Box." The emphasis on the command word which primed the machine for an instruction was hardly perceptible. He tossed Box to Philpot who caught it warily, alert for any sign of an attack. As the moment passed and Philpot relaxed slightly, Nathan said, "Maximum alarm, please."

Box set off its deafening klaxon with stunning suddenness. Philpot was paralyzed with shock. Nathan leapt at him, and instinctively Philpot clutched more tightly onto the howling Box. Nathan grasped at his other arm and slapped the microwave fuse from his hand. As it skittered across the floor, both men scrabbled after it.

With no immediate chance at the fuse, Kenzy opted for the bomb and plunged under the workstation where the seismic charges lay blinking. Snatching the bundle up, she began to twist the priming wheel on the first of the cartridges. Her frantic fingers were stiff and clumsy.

Philpot was stronger than he looked. Nathan clung on as Philpot dragged himself towards the fuse and reached an arm out for it. Desperately, Nathan pulled him back. He could feel himself tiring.

Kenzy had neutralized three of the charges and was working on the fourth. This time, the wheel would not line up. It was jammed or something. She tried not to think how long it was taking. The tight bundle was making it difficult to get a purchase on the priming wheel. The indicator finally went off. Four down, three to go. And it was taking

Star Cops

too long.

Philpot was writhing and pushing with his knees and kicking wildly. Nathan wrapped his arms tighter round the man's legs and hauled back away from the fuse. A tearing agony shot though Nathan's side. The pain enraged him, and he lashed a punch at Philpot. It was a mistake. He had released part of his hold, and now the struggling and kicking was harder than ever. He was losing him. Philpot's fingertips stretched out to touch the fuse.

The fifth charge stopped blinking and Kenzy began to twist the priming wheel on the sixth charge. It was achingly slow.

Nathan couldn't get his grip back. He was slipping free. The only hope was to let go completely and make another grab for a stronger hold. Do that, and Philpot was bound to get to the fuse. Go directly for the fuse himself. Philpot was bound to beat him to it. His side ached like a bastard. Decide. Decide now. He let go, and launched himself at the fuse. Before he could touch it Philpot had it in his hand. The man's face was not calm now. He was wild with anger now, wild with failure now, and he pressed the switch now and Nathan closed his eyes now and Kenzy turned the last priming wheel now on the last charge now. The indicator went off, and Box screeched and howled deafeningly on.

Conclusions

Before he left the Moon, Daniel Larwood did try to apologize to Theroux. "I'm constantly amazed," he said, "at the way people take a change in their hormone balance to be an intellectual or even a religious insight. I don't believe in the road to Damascus; but for what it's worth, David, I'm sorry."

"Was it worth Gary Benson's life?" Theroux asked.

Larwood shrugged his weary shrug. "Nothing's ever worth a life," he said. "But then again," and he smiled the rumpled smile, "life's untidy, and it doesn't last. I prefer stories myself."

For the Star Cops, the story had some loose ends. Devis, Cogill and Kenzy – especially Kenzy – were angry and offended. When Nathan told no-one but Theroux that he was staying on Moonbase because of what he heard in Philpot's interview with Caxton; that was a betrayal. He obviously didn't trust them. They were not happy either with his explanation that after the destruction of the *Lucifer Seven* he stayed dead because it was the best way to bring the suspect out into the open. For fuck's sake, Kenzy managed to apprehend a suspect all by herself. Of course, she had been spoiling for a fight, and it was the wrong suspect, but she hadn't found it necessary to lie to them all. Because the feeling of the meeting was, that's what Nathan had done; he had lied to them.

"My grandmother always said, you can lock up against a thief, but there's no protection from a liar," Devis observed.

"Your grandmother never said that," Theroux said.

"Okay, so I lied," Devis agreed. "But we have been treated badly here. I think I speak for my colleagues when I say we deserve a drink, at the very least." And, with a flourish, he produced the brandy confiscated from Larwood just before he had been deported.

Nathan took it from him and, smiling his most charming smile, said, "Sounds reasonable." He opened the bottle and poured generous measures for all of them. By the time he poured his own the others had drunk theirs but he raised his beaker anyway. "If you make mistakes, make them with people you trust." It was about as far as he felt he could go with an apology. About as far as he wanted to go. He was tired, and a bit depressed. Reaction, he supposed.

Devis poured himself another drink and passed the bottle on. "Present friends; absent enemies," he said, sipping this one more slowly.

"This is it, is it?" Kenzy asked. "This is our apology?"

Nathan looked serious. "As Colin's grandmother always said, being in charge means never having to say you're sorry." He drained his brandy and watched them all as they waited for him to smile.

When he didn't, it was quite deliberate.

Also available from What Noise Productions

What Noise: audiobooks on CD and download from **www.whatnoise.co.uk:-**

When Harry Met Sheila: The Autobiography of Sheila Steafel
The Devil Take Your Stereo by Anthony Keetch
Blue Box Boy: A Memoir of Doctor Who by Matthew Waterhouse

Fates, Flowers: A Comedy of New York by Matthew Waterhouse
Vanitas: A Comedy of New York by Matthew Waterhouse
Wishhobbler by Francis O'Dowd
Jaggy Splinters by Christopher Brookmyre

Head Music: books and e-books from **www.whatnoise.co.uk:-**

Blue Box Boy: A Memoir of Doctor Who by Matthew Waterhouse
Fates, Flowers: A Comedy of New York by Matthew Waterhouse
Vanitas: A Comedy of New York by Matthew Waterhouse
Wishhobbler by Francis O'Dowd
The Devil Talk The Hindmost by Anthony Keetch